Angel Wings

The latest in the Chief Inspector Samson series

a novel by

Bill Dughaille

Dedicated to all Covid confreres

Translations from the West Country

buhy: boy
cakey: stupid
dreckly: (corrupted 'directly') the day after mañana
grockle: tourist (derogatory)
gurt: very
Lunnun: London
lush: nice
luvver: lover, platonic term of endearment, can be sarcastic
maid: girl, young woman
maized: daft
maized as a besom: daft as a brush
piskie: pixie
teddies: potatoes (from "tats")
that's the badger: that's the right one/the one I was looking for
trunkie want a bun: said of someone being overly nosey

Cockney rhyming slang

Adam: believe (Adam and Eve)
apples: stairs (apples and pears)
Brahms: drunk (Brahms and Liszt = pissed)
dog: phone (dog and bone)
half-inch: pinch (i.e. steal)
porkies: lies (pork pies)
Sweeney: Flying Squad (Sweeney Todd)
take a butcher's: take a look (butcher's hook)
tea-leaf: thief
trouble: wife (trouble and strife)

Other

flannel: face cloth (also to waffle misleadingly)
jim-jams: pyjamas
spiv: flashy, cheap con-artist (UK, twentieth century)
wazzocks: idiot (Yorkshire)

Arr be a grockle up our patch
cruel of heart and brain of ox
ee be fair grim sight to watch
whatter proper wazzocks

ee'z zet heself a piskie catch
iz wold ain't what it zeems
ee'm got teddies in iz thatch
eez living in iz dreams

piskies fill an empty space
ee'z piskie-maized
ee az a piskie face
little grocke's piskie crazed

wakey, wakey, cakey, cakey
who the piskied fule, he or me?

Sunday morning

'Well, looking on the bright side of things, it will mean a little more custom over the festive season. We'll be getting the tourist noir set in I would imagine. Ghouls galore. Bats and vampires and vampires and bats. Thrill seekers, or what they call them. Ambulance chasers. Oh, yes. To be sure.'

The top of a head rose slowly above the bar counter beneath which its owner had been packing away boxes of pork scratchings and prawn flavoured crisps. It was followed shortly by two green eyes. The auburn hair and pale face belonged to a woman of about twenty-six. She looked at the speaker for a few seconds, a reddish-cheeked, plump man wearing a red and green Christmas jumper decorated with reindeer, and a tea-towel over his shoulder. He was standing in front of a log fire, his hands together almost as if in prayer, having just finished rubbing them together and not quite sure what to do with them afterwards.

'Patsy,' the young woman said, standing up fully to reveal a baggy roll-necked seaman's jumper two sizes too large, 'a man was murdered upstairs last night in your pub and all you can think of is that it will bring more customers in.'

Patsy shook his head and raised a finger. The shake sent wobbles through his jowls, and the finger was quickly smothered by the tea towel in case it got ideas above its station.

'Hostelry, my sweet Mavourneen, it's a hostelry, not a pub. How many times do I have to tell you? It's much more than just a pub. After all, if it were only a pub we wouldn't be having rooms upstairs for guests to be murdered in, now would we?'

Another pause.

'Well?'

'Well what?'

'Is that seriously all you can think of? About – selling more pints?'

'Well, me dear little angel, it does rather save a poor overworked and conscientious landlord of having to think of other things. That is, apart from expecting the police, and apart, of course, from the poor

1

dear man who will never again be able to raise a glass of the finest. Believe me, there are worse things than thinking about keeping your customers happy with a few pints. '

'Worse things. What worse things?'

'Ah, sure, little one, you're an intelligent young woman. You know as well as I do.'

The little one, birth name Clarissa, known better as Carry, gave Patsy another emotionless look.

'Pretend I don't, Patsy. Or that I'm about to throw a glass at you if you don't stop your irritating, all-knowing Irish infallibility. A heavy glass. A Stein if I can find one.'

Patsy ignored the contradiction, lifted the hatch and came behind the bar. He opened the till.

'Patsy, you've already checked the till five times this morning. Nothing has changed. The leprechauns haven't raided it. The pixies haven't been in. The hobgoblins are on holiday. Nobody's been near it for the past half an hour. And if you don't leave it alone and tell me what you mean you might find your fingers trapped in it. With your hands detached. Or something.'

He closed it quickly and turned his attention elsewhere.

'I'm sure you're right, my little one, it's just that I like to –'

'And that's the tenth time you've checked those glasses and they're still clean and shining and dust free. So long as you stop touching them and stop leaving your fingerprints all over them. So leave them and leave the till alone and explain to me what these worse things are.'

'Well, if you think about it – we don't have a leak, do we?'

'No, Patsy, and stop polishing the counter.'

Patsy sighed and leaned on the bar counter he had been drying of a non-existent puddle.

'I think those windows might need a little wipe.'

'Patsy, you can't see a brick wall at two paces without your glasses. The windows do not need a little wipe. Unless you're planning on removing the snow outside and the fake Christmas frosting and snow angels inside that I spent ages doing. And if you even think of that I will kill you.'

'Do you think that painting goes there? I was after thinking that maybe –'

'There are at least five paintings where you're looking and you can't see one of them among the Christmas decorations and the lights. Enough, Patsy, now give.'

'They twinkle quite nicely, the lights. And that Christmas tree, well, it's a grand job you've done. I could never get the angel right –'

'Patsy.'

'I do hope the police get here soon. You would have thought they might be a little more prompt for a murder. And we can't expect Doctor Hamilton to look after the scene the whole day. Not after he's been up there already for ten hours.'

'Patsy. Glass. Throw. Head. Contact. Pain.'

He sighed.

'My dear little innocent, do you not realise that it means that the poor soul was murdered by someone who was in here last night? One of us, as you might say.'

'That's just silly. It was only regulars last night, and he's a total stranger. You can't imagine ...'

She stopped and looked at him. He appeared to be looking into a vague blurred nowhere of the future.

'I had a look out of all the windows. After Joe the Rescue mistook his bedroom for the loo and found him. There were no footprints in the snow around the side, no footprints in the snow at the back, nothing apart from the front doors.' He stood up straight and flicked the tea towel at the beer pumps and missed. 'Whoever it was had to be in here.'

'You were wearing your glasses when you had a look? Only –'

'Sure and of course I was wearing me glasses, you don't think I'm that daft? I'd trip over everything taller than an elf, for starters.'

'They could have slipped inside unnoticed. Whoever it was who – did it.'

He raised his eyebrows as if wishing it could be true.

'Slipped inside unnoticed? You reckon? Without being seen? By anyone?'

'Well, not here in the public bar, but maybe the ladies' bar ...'

'My dear Carry, now I know you're of the female persuasion, and I don't want to cast aspersions of anything on the feminine sex, but have you ever known a group of women not notice a new arrival? In detail? Down to the little buttons on her little shoes?'

'Well, it isn't just women who go into the ladies' bar.'

'True. If it were a man they would have measured the size of his cheque-book in seconds.'

'Maybe he climbed up the outside.'

'What, like up the drainpipes?'

'Could be.'

'The drainpipes don't go anywhere near a window or anything. Otherwise we'd have burglars in every other weekend. Might as well build them some steps. Or a lift or escalator or something. What they'd call a highwayman's way to heaven.'

'Did you check the roof? They might have got in that way.'

'The roof. Like parachuted in, you mean. Or one of those hanging gliders.'

'I don't know. Somehow.'

'Doesn't make a difference, really. I checked the roof at first light. Before first light, actually. While it was still dark. In the moonlight. As virgin a snow have I never seen. Not a lot. But enough. Quite pretty it was.'

'I thought I heard someone creeping around in the early hours.'

'I was not creeping around. I was trying not to wake anyone. There's a difference.'

'But it did snow during the night. Or early morning. After he was found. About three o'clock.'

He raised an eye.

'You were up at three in the morning? Creeping around?'

'I was not creeping around. I couldn't sleep and I needed the loo.'

'You have an en suite.'

'I thought I'd have a wander around and check things. Like I normally do. You know I get nervous.'

4

'Ah.'

'Patsy, don't give me your Ah like that. You make it sound as if you suspect me of doing it.'

'Of course not, my little turtle dove, of course not.'

He paused.

'No, definitely not,' he murmured to himself. He sighed and slumped again.

'Sure and he must have come over with the wings of an angel.'

'Who?'

'The murderer, of course.'

'Wings of an angel? Patsy, what are you on about?'

'It's the only answer. He floated in on the wings of an angel, did – did the thing, and then floated out again. That's it. It was the Angel of Doom.'

'Patsy, I don't know a lot about religion, but I've never heard of angels floating in to murder people in their beds.'

'In their cupboards.'

'Well, then, in their cupboards. Do angels murder people in cupboards? Or is that Narnia?'

'It's a very complicated thing, religion. You have good angels and bad angels, so I believe. Satan was a fallen angel. I remember Father Murphy telling us that in RI when I was at school.'

'RI?'

'Religious Instruction. Though I recall we called it something else. Now what was it?'

'You don't still believe that sort of thing, do you?'

'Well, belief is a great thing, you know. I like to believe that a fallen angel could have floated in and did the thing. Because, my little turtle dove, because otherwise we come back to the inescapable conclusion: whoever it was was in this very room last night. Someone we know.'

'Or the snug,' suggested Carry.

'Or the snug,' agreed Patsy.

'Or the private bar. Who was in the private bar?'

'Or the lounge. Could have been in the lounge.'

'Or the ladies' bar. You never know.'

'And they'll all be back this morning. It's crowded we'll be, within five minutes of opening time.'

'Most of them wanting to know more.'

'And one – or more – of them wanting to know exactly what everyone else knows. Perhaps. Just in case they know a little too much. To be sure. Just to be sure.'

'Let's hope they don't feel the need for a repeat performance. With someone else. To make them know less. It'll be like that story, Ten Little N–'

'Angels, my little one. Ten Little Angels. They changed it. To make it more modern, like.'

'And then there were none.'

'And then there were none what?'

'What?'

'What were there none of? They haven't been stealing the salt cellars again, have they?'

'No, that was the title they changed it to.'

'What?'

'Ten Little Angels. And then there were none.'

'Did they now? Change it again? Now why on earth would they want to do that?'

'Never mind, Patsy, that's just the way it happened.'

'So we haven't run out of salt cellars again.'

'No, Patsy.'

'Ah.'

Patsy drew something invisible on the bar top with his index finger, and then used the cloth to wipe it off.

'Probably just as well. It's bad for you, you know.'

'What is, Patsy, being murdered?'

'No. Salt. Me doctor says I should cut down.'

'He does?'

'You know, it was terrible what happened to him.'

'Your doctor?'

'No, no.'

'The man upstairs?'

'No. Father Murphy.'

'Oh.'

'Terrible, it was.'

'Patsy. If you don't –'

'They sent him to Canada.'

'Patsy – Why?'

'He was caught embezzling the altar boys' fund.'

'Embezzling the altar boys' fund?'

'Yes. And for that he got sent to Canada. I mean, Canada.'

'He was lucky.'

'Well, it wasn't really a bad thing to do. It wasn't as if the altar boys weren't going to spend the money on whiskey themselves.'

'What?'

'Sure, they were a terrible lot, those altar boys. Apart from little Eamon. He was a saint, to be sure. He would have bought the whiskey for his mother. She was a poorly thing, you know. Drank a little too much. Now, he sang in the choir.'

'Patsy. I am going to –'

'He had a lovely voice. And a face like an angel. Pale, with lovely blond hair. In curls. And light blue shining eyes. And during the nativity play he wore lipstick. Bright red lipstick. Sure and he was a sight to behold.'

'Patsy. Murder you if you don't –'

'And then there was Father Riley, Father Murphy's replacement. He was defrocked.'

'Patsy – Defrocked. What did he do, steal the whiskey?'

'Sure, no. There were some who said what he did was downright deviant. He ran away with a fifteen-year-old.'

'He what?'

'I didn't say so at the time, well, you wouldn't, but I didn't think he was entirely to blame.'

'For running away with a fifteen-year-old? He wasn't to blame?'

'Ah, but she was older than her years, you see. A right little tease. She wore short little skirts that showed all the way to her –'

'Oh, you mean a she. I thought –'

'You thought – what?'

'Doesn't matter. It was a she, you said.'

'Yes. But they were all the same from that convent. I used to think the nuns encouraged them.'

'Some girls are like that.'

'I had nightmares about those nuns. Especially after they started the sex education classes.'

'Patsy, you're waffling again. It's very irritating. Very. Irritating.'

'Ah, yes. Sorry, to be sure. Just trying to keep my mind off certain things and concentrate on the little things.' He paused. 'Just one little note of caution, though, my little turtle dove.'

'What's that?'

He gave her a wry, almost bitter, smile, the smile of a man for whom Fate has promised too few cocktails and delivered too many custard pies.

'Try not to show any of them you suspect.'

'Suspect?'

'That the person you're serving might be a cold-blooded murderer. It's bad for business. Kills the ambivalence.'

'Ambience.'.

'That too, my little angel, that too.'

'So that's why we have mirrors behind bars.'

'Why's that?'

'So when we turn our backs we can see if the customer we're serving has taken out a six-inch knife and is about to plunge it into –'

'Don't say it!'

'Sorry.'

'It's just – you know what they say.'

'What?'

'What?'

'What do they say?'

'Oh. Oh, the saying is father to the deed. Something like that.'

'Father to the deed.'

'Aye.'

He added, in an attempt to reassure someone else and to complete the point he had tried to start:

'There is one thing we can be completely sure about.'

'What's that?'

'It's the way these things work. There is always one indisputable fact. Something that cannot be denied.'

'What's that?'

'Well, it's like an undeniable truth sort of thing. Surely you know the sort of thing. You know, Descartes. Cogito ergo sum.'

'Yes, Patsy, I know Cogito, but what is this undeniable bloody fact?'

'Well, you see, of course, when I say "one of us", I wasn't including myself nor yourself in that. After all, we were here hard at work the whole time, were we not? If anyone of us did the thing, it couldn't have been you or me. Because we were both here all night. Were we not? That at least we can definitely, surely be sure about. We don't have to worry about turning our backs to each other, do we? No sir.'

He gave her a quick sideways glance. She raised her eyebrows at him, turned, closed her eyes and shook her head.

'Ah, well, the police will be here shortly. Sure, and they'll have it all sown up before you know it. Before the parcel arrives. Long before.'

'I never heard that. I do not want to know anything about any parcel.'

'Sorry, my angel, I forget.' He made a face. 'Can you remember now, is it Tuesday or Wednesday the parcel arrives?'

'I told you, I don't want to know anything about any parcel. Monday.'

'Ah, of course, Monday. Sure and I don't know why I keep thinking it's Tuesday or Wednesday, you've told me often enough. Honestly, if I didn't have my head screwed on to my shoulders I think I'd lose it. Maybe it's because the last time they delivered it was on a Friday.'

'I wasn't here then. I was off that day. Far, far away.'

'Sure, of course you were.'

The telephone behind the counter rang. Patsy hesitated before picking it up.

'Hello, Angel and Duck public bar and hostelry?'

Two men sat on a bench on the beach. It lay half-way between the parking lot and the sea as if someone had once decided that this was the ideal place for a wooden bench and had spent a great deal of time and effort underpinning it with a deep concrete base to prevent it being stolen or washed away.

'Don't suppose there's anywhere around here we could get a coffee,' said the young man. He blew into his cupped hands.

'It's winter, son. Shops around here only open for the tourist season.'

'Should have bought a thermos of something.'

'I did. It's in the boot.'

Detective Constable Sean Morton risked a sidelong glance at his new and very temporary boss. The old fool was staring out to the grey sea, hat jammed on his head, chin tucked into his scarf, his gloved hands rammed into his overcoat pockets as if he couldn't decide which he hated more.

'Well, don't just sit there, lad, get it out.' He took one hand out of its pocket and tossed over some keys which the other man fumbled and dropped. 'I could do with a hot coffee myself. Before we have a few words with them down this little pub of theirs.'

Morton picked up the keys, stood up and tramped up the crunching sand to the parking lot. He passed a solid-looking rowing boat, resisting the temptation to give it a swift kick. It was tied fast to a stake driven into the beach sand, its paint faded and peeling. It was twice as big as any rowing boat he had seen and looked ten times as malevolent. He swore at it under his breath in lieu of something else. He had been doing a weekend night shift, partly for the overtime but mainly to get away from Shirley's complaining. A call had come through from London telling them that a detective inspector – a chief inspector – was coming down to take charge and nothing must be done until he got there. The Home Secretary was personally following events. Another call would come through in half an hour with more information. Sensing a career opportunity he had immediately volunteered himself as the local contact and had rushed home during the available half hour to smarten himself up. He had slipped silently into the darkened bedroom to avoid waking Shirley, retrieved his camel-hair overcoat, his most expensive three-piece suit, browny-blue with thin red stripes, a fresh white shirt, and a pair of Italian shoes he had recently bought. He had taken them quietly into the lounge to get changed, which was when he had noticed the empty wine bottle and two wine glasses on the coffee table. That had irritated him. Shirley must have had a girlfriend over. Between them they had finished an entire bottle of the more expensive wine they had been keeping for a special occasion. She must have thought she'd have time to clear them away before he got back, and he wouldn't notice the missing bottle from the special stash. Or maybe she hadn't thought. A whole bottle between two girls? He hoped the friend hadn't been driving.

Then he noticed that the shirt he had taken out of the cupboard was the flashy cowboy style one he had once used for line dancing, black with white chest and shoulders, and gold embroidery across the upper half, including the collars. He undoubtedly looked good in it on the dance floor, but wasn't convinced it was the best thing to wear when meeting and greeting a chief inspector from London.

He hesitated. He'd already taken a massive risk of waking Shirley, who was not known for being the most cheerful person first thing in the morning, let alone halfway through the night. In the end he decided it wasn't worth the risk, he was running out of his allotted half-hour, and that the glaring loudness of the gold embroidery on a black and white shirt would be almost unnoticeable under a three-piece suit and overcoat. He changed and left his other clothes neatly folded on a chair. That gave him just enough time to race back to the station to take the second call. It turned out to be a different person, a breezy detective constable in London.

'Your name really Moron?'

'It's Morton. Detective Constable Morton.'

'Yeah, thought they'd got that wrong. I mean, having a surname Moron. That would really suck.'

'Well, it's not. Like I say, it's Morton.'

'Okay, Moron, keep your shirt on. Listen, you're a lucky lad, you are. You have one Chief Inspector Samson winging his way toward you, a man hated and feared by every London copper everywhere.'

'What?'

'And I'm a luckier lad because in one hour my shift ends and I can go home.'

'What did you say about this – this bloke, Samson?'

'We all love him to bits. Which is what we'd like to see him in. Bits.'

'What?'

'Put it this way, mate, if they found him murdered the suspects would be numbered in their thousands and most of them would be wearing blue uniforms.'

'You're winding me up.'

'Now why would I do that?'

'Because you think we're a bunch of hayseed rustics.'

'Well, you are, aren't you? How are the sheep? Nervous?'

'Very funny.'

'Okay, there I was winding you up. But seriously, Samson has absolutely no redeeming characteristics. None. Zero.'

'You're joking.'

'Listen, mate, you've got a notepad, right? For taking notes. like.'

'We have smartphones down here.'

'We have a lot of tea-leaves up here. They like nicking smartphones. Which is why we use tatty old notebooks. Not such a market for those. Anyway, suit yourself. Listen, what you do, right, when you feel your fingers tightening, turning into talons like –'

'Talons?'

'And you're looking at his throat and trying to decide whether to strangle him or rip his Adam's apple out –'

'Rip his Adam's apple out?'

'Or you start looking around for something handy, something short, heavy and solid –'

'What?'

'To hit him over the head with. Or maybe something nice and sharp.

Or even blunt, Sometimes blunt is good. Better. It's better, blunt. Get it?'

'Blunt?'

'What you do is you write down a word, or a phrase, to describe him, like obnoxious git. Can't be a swearword like motherlover, that's cheating. And unoriginal. Oh, and every time it's got to be a new word. Or phrase. Shit, write a fucking paragraph if you need to. Sometimes I feel can do an entire chapter. Like that song about the restaurant. Kill. Kill. Kill. Kill.'

'Why?'

'Why kill? Wait till you meet him, sonny, you'll find out.'

'No, I meant, why write something down?'

'Oh, that. It's a game we play.'

'Why?'

'It's to increase your word power. Nah, be serious, it's to stay sane, mate, to stay sane. Otherwise we'd probably end up punching him. And you know what, you can get fired for doing that sort of thing up here.'

'But – he is good at the job, isn't he?'

'Nah, couldn't find his own elbow with a SatNav on a sunny day. But don't worry, lad, much as he might piss you off, wait until he gets hold of any witnesses. They're going to hate him a lot more than you do.'

'You're joking. I know you're joking. I heard that the Home Secretary was interested in this one.'

'Dunno why you keep saying I'm joking, mate. Some things you don't joke about. Tell you one thing, though, don't bother telling Samson any jokes, he won't get them. When they were handing out a sense of humour he was in the line for pre-frontal lobotomies. And post-frontal and all. Probably thought he was getting a very short haircut.'

'But what about the Home Secretary. The other bloke said she was taking a personal interest in this one.'

'She always does when it's foreigners. Got a thing for them, she has. We was talking about that only the other day. Wondering whether she didn't have a fling with one of them years ago and is still looking for him. Poor bugger.'

'Foreigners?'

'Your vic. I heard he was Polish. Isn't he Polish? Or something like that? East Lithuanian with one eye named Fred. Other one's called Mary. Okay, I made the last bit up.'

'The dead bloke?'

'That's the one. You're sharp, you are. Catch on right away. You'd make a good copper, you would.'

'But surely that's even more reason to send someone who knows what they're doing. I mean, if he is a foreigner. Surely that's international.'

'Come on, get real. You don't think we send our best coppers out to the sticks, do you? No matter what the Home Secretary wants. Don't get promotion when you're out of sight. But look on the bright side.'

'Oh? What's the bright side?'

'So long as he's down there with you lot he isn't up here being a pain in the arse with us. Which makes us very happy. Cheers, mate. And now I'm off shift in fifty minutes. Aren't I lucky. And it's almost Christmas. And there's a boozer down the road that never closes. You don't have that sort of thing down there, do you?'

Now as he walked toward the car Morton was rapidly coming to regret his initial enthusiasm. Samson was proving to be exactly what the London bloke had said.

And apart from Samson, his shoes were too tight. They were Italian and the last the shop had had in stock, so he had bought them instead of waiting for his size to become available. His three-piece suit also appeared to have shrunk since he had last worn it, to a mate's wedding six months before, when Shirley had got drunk. Again. The camel-hair overcoat looked ridiculously fancy compared to Samson's more down to earth and rumpled trench coat. And Samson's warm and thick and solid scarf seemed about as common and sensible as you could get. Morton didn't like wearing scarves, they looked like something granddad might have put on before going down the rain-soaked mine to chew on a piece of coal for breakfast in preparation for a twelve-hour shift. But the first greeting he had received on returning to the station, after several open-mouthed stares, had been, "Yee-hah!" Which a thick and solid common and sensible scarf would have prevented. And he wouldn't now be feeling a cold breeze around his chops.

And what had begun as a minute suspicion as he drove back from the flat had blossomed into a close certainty: Shirley hadn't been in the bedroom as he tip-toed around silently in order not to disturb her. And the two wine glasses had now formed a big question mark in his mind.

He got to the parking lot and looked at the Chief Inspector's car. It was a brightly coloured 1965 Studebaker with the biggest flared wings he had seen inside and outside of movies. It belonged on the open range of Route 66 in a summer breeze with its hood down, not on a grey and miserable pebble-dashed winter's beach on the West coast of England. Driven by a grey and miserable-faced twat.

Precisely what bright colour it was he had yet to decide. It was definitely in the pink or red range. Mauve, under a certain light. Not quite purple. Probably not quite purple. Considering its owner, it ought to be puce. Samson wasn't puce. But it was a colour that would have suited him. That or the colour miserable. Whatever colour miserable was. White, probably. The white of wedding dresses a year after the wedding.

He remembered the first time he had clapped eyes on the car, earlier that morning in the darkness.

'My wife ran away with a used-car salesman,' the Chief Inspector had said. 'I got it in part exchange.'

It was the kind of silly statement designed to elucidate a response which Morton had no intention of giving. He had guessed that it was what passed as a sense of humour for the old fool. Instead he had responded with what he thought was a non-committal and supposedly appreciative, 'Gurt lush.' To which the London man had replied, 'If that's yokel talk I don't speak it, never have and never will. You want to talk haystack, save it for your fellow hayseeds down the pub. Or the sheep. Stick to English while I'm around, sonny.'

The only thing Samson hadn't made a sarcastic comment about was his embroidered shirt. He couldn't decide whether that was because his overcoat and suit hid it, which he knew it didn't, or whether Samson had presumed that that was the sort of thing the locals liked wearing. He couldn't help but feel that the latter was correct. Which made it even worse.

That hayseed comment had really got to him. The memory made his fingers curl. He vaguely considered punching the Studebaker. But that was made of solid iron.

That was another thing about Samson's scarf. It hid his Adam's apple. Morton had never seriously considered any man's Adam's apple before.

'Orl rite me luvver,' he muttered, 'here goes, you cakey Lunnun buhy.'

He took out his smartphone and typed in the words,

"Arr be a grockle up our patch".

To his surprise it made him feel a lot better. The London copper had been right about that. He put the phone back in his pocket. Then he pointed the key fob at the boot and pressed the button with force.

'Ooh, isn't it exciting, Philly?'

Phillipa Mountjohn looked at her breakfast companion over her half-moon reading glasses.

'Exciting is not quite the word that I would choose, Bertie,' she replied before returning to a perusal of the Parish weekly. 'Not in polite company, anyway. A complete bloody nuisance sounds like a better description.'

'Ooh, come on, Philly, it's the most exciting thing that's ever happened around here.'

'Do calm down, Bertie, it's bad for your heart. Anyway, I'm sure that the police will have worked everything out by lunchtime, and it will turn out to be quite boring. Petty robbery gone wrong, I expect.'

Bertie's wrinkles danced excitedly.

'But we were there! Just think, it could have been one of us.'

Miss Mountjohn sighed and turned a page to the Mothers and Infants section. She picked up a pen and drew a little red circle between the eyes of one of the infants pictured. She filled it in. Then she added a couple of outer circles until it became a target.

'One of us being murdered, or the other?' she asked as she was setting the infant up.

'The other?'

'Doing the murdering bit, my dear.'

'Ooh, really, Philly! That's just silly!' She giggled. 'Oh, I say, that rhymed.'

'Your boiled egg is going blue.'

Bertie looked at her boiled egg and began an apologetic, circuitous and clinical operation on it with a very sharp knife.

'Can't go for a sherry on an empty stomach,' she said. 'I'd be quite tiddly after only one sip.'

'Bertie, you're quite tiddly after just a sniff of the damned stuff. Never mind an empty stomach. Anyway, we will not be rushing out for a sherry. I will not have any of – them – thinking that I am a common voyeur.' She paused. 'An uncommon voyeur will be quite acceptable.'

She drew a series of red arrows flying towards the infant's head.

'In fact, I think I could make a very good uncommon voyeur. If there was anything worth voyeuring in this place.'

'But Philly we always go for a drinky at lunchtime down the Duck after our little walk. Why should today be any different?'

'I said rushing out, Bertie. Twelve o'clock will do nicely. We'll pick some berries on our walk. Make some jam for that WI bunch this week. Sugar free. It should taste sufficiently revolting. But good for the figure. Or is it the soul?'

Bertie grinned.

'We can put our special ingredient in. If the parcel arrives on time.'

'You always say that. You know it doesn't work in jam. More's the pity.'

'So, who do you think did it? I think it must have been a love affair gone wrong.'

'Bertie, the only thing that worries me more about your confident assertions is the fear of the explanations you devise afterwards to justify them. So please don't tell me the thinking behind that one. I have this horrible feeling that it will involve Patsy, his wheelchair-bound wife, and a tempestuous summer twenty years ago in Rome. Or Venice. Or the Ploesti oil fields.'

'Oh, no, Philly – Patsy? Patsy wouldn't harm a fly.'

'In which case he's bound to be the guilty one.'

'Actually, I was thinking of Carry.'

'Carry? I thought you liked Carry?'

'Oh, I do, I do. But isn't that what always happens? The murderer turns out to be someone everyone likes and never suspects? After all, we haven't really known her for long. She's a sort of mystery-figure, don't you think? A femme fatale. She is pretty. Isn't it always the pretty one who done it?'

'Yes, that's why Miss Universe is always a carnage. Blood all over the place.'

'Yes, but Carry's intelligent, too.'

'Bertie, my dear, that is one other thing that I never understood. How you were able to be so good at philosophy at university all those years ago, and yet never learnt the rudiments of logic.'

'Ooh, I don't think it was philosophical, murders never are. They're normally a crime of passion. A cream caramel, as they used to say. You see –'

'A crime passionnel. Bertie, you haven't a clue what I'm talking about, do you?'

'Well, no, Philly, but that usually works itself out in the end. Now –'

'Bertie. According to your logic, Carry is the guilty party because you like her and don't suspect her. Except that that's precisely why you do suspect her. But she can't be guilty if you do suspect her. Which would mean that she's innocent. Which would instantly make her guilty as sin.'

Bertie thought about that for a couple of seconds before nodding.

'You know, Philly, you always put these things so much better than I can. It has to be Carry. Pity. I quite like her.' She sucked on her egg spoon. 'You don't think it might be dangerous, do you?'

'Dangerous?'

'Going to the Duck after someone has been slaughtered there.'

'Possibly. But not to us. Little old ladies very rarely get murdered. And stop using words like slaughter. It's only one so far. You can start calling it a slaughter when it hits double digits. I'm pretty sure that's the rule.'

'That's a thought. Do you suppose everybody else will be at the Duck?'

'That's yet another thing I've never understood about you, Bertie.'

'What's that?'

'The way you insist on asking questions when you know perfectly well what the answers are.'

'Such as?'

'Such as, of course everybody will be at the bloody Duck. Might as well try to keep bees from a honey pot.'

'Do bees like honey? I thought they made honey. Isn't it wasps you get at a picnic?'

'Only if you have some honey there. Have some toast, Bertie.'

'I might take my grandfather's bayonet just in case. The one with the serrated edge. I oiled it last week. It's only slightly rusty.'

'Have some Marmite on your toast. And some Rice Crispies on top of that.'

'I've never had Rice Crispies on Marmite.'

'Well, today's your lucky day, isn't it.'

'Where are the Ploesti oil fields?'

'To the right of Turkey and up a bit.'

'I like turkey.'

'There you go then, Turkey's guilty. Guaranteed.'

'With cranberry sauce.'

Nigel Stokes groaned at the sound of the vacuum cleaner, rolled over and fell out of bed. He groaned again, pulled the duvet down over himself and tried to close his eyes against the slow opening of his bedroom door. An eye peeked through the gap.

'Ah, you're awake Mr Stokes, I'm ever so glad, I wouldn't want to have woken you up with the cleaning.'

Nigel kept his eyes firmly closed.

'Mrs Potts,' he croaked, 'what time is it?'

'Oh, my goodness, it's almost ten. Well, gone half nine at least, almost. Anyway, it's after nine, I'm sure. I think.'

'Half nine, dear sweet Jesus,' whispered the young man. He raised his voice a demi decibel. 'And tell me, Mrs Potts, what day is it?'

'Well, Sunday, of course. Now you remember I said as how I'd be in on Sunday on account of missing last Thursday because of my aunt's bunions. And my goodness, you are an untidy man, Mr Stokes. If I'd left it until next Tuesday I'd never have been able to catch up. Now I know that you artists are of an untidy temperament as they call it –'

Nigel raised a hand out from under the bedclothes surrounding him.

'Mrs Potts, remind me of something. Perhaps my memory is playing up, so help me on this one. Did you or did you not say that you'd pop in on Sunday afternoon. That is to say, after midday. In the noon time of the sun's graceful orbit across the heavens? Or, to put it rather more selfishly, after I'd had my desperately needed and well deserved sleep? And while I was down the pub re-energising?'

'Oh, yes, Mr Stokes, of course, I would never have done else, after all, my late husband was exactly the same after a night out at the pub. Not human before lunchtime, he wasn't, just like you, though he wasn't an artist, seeing as he was a bricklayer. Though he was just as untidy, dropping clothes all over the place, well, I never could match his socks up, there was always one missing, though –'

'Mrs Potts?'

'I'll just carry on, Mr Stokes, you won't know I'm here –'

He poked out half his head and one eye.

'I already know you're here, Mrs Potts, the evidence is incontrovertible. Like God, you are omni-whelming.'

'Well, you know what I mean, Mr Stokes.'

'Mrs Potts?'

'Yes, dearie? You don't look too well, Mr Stokes –'

'Mrs Potts, help me with another thing. Just why are you here at such an uncivilised time?

'Haven't you heard? Oh, I suppose – but I thought – well, she was probably mistaken, she often is, it's her eyes, you see, she's getting on, though she won't admit it –'

His hand came up again.

'Mrs Potts, let's try the one-two-three again. One ... who is "she"?'

'Well, Mrs Pleat, of course, She who does for –'

'Two, what was she mistaken about?'

'Well, she thought she saw that young Miss Carry coming in here earlier, while it was still dark. Miss Carry from the –'

'Three, what is it that I haven't heard about?'

'Well, about the man who got himself murdered at the Angel. The one who was bludgeoned to death. With a heavy ... bludgeoning thing. I think it must have been a crowbar. Or an iron or something. A golf club. One of those foreign ones. Japanese, they are. So they say. That's why I coughed when I came in. In case you had company.'

'Company.'

'You, know, that Miss Carry. She's very pretty, you know.'

'Thank you for telling me, Mrs Stokes, I hadn't noticed.'

'So is she?'

'Is she what? Very pretty? If you go for that sort of look, yes, I suppose she is.'

'No, here.'

'Here?'

'Is she here? Only I wouldn't want to, you know.'

He sighed.

'Chance would be a fine thing.'

'Sorry, Mr Stokes?'

'Nothing.' He sneezed. 'Well, there you go, that all makes sense now. And no, Carry isn't here.'

He rose slowly, untangling himself from the duvet to reveal a mop of thick brown hair, a paisley-patterned pair of pyjamas with the trouser fly open and the top misbuttoned, and made his way carefully and delicately through the lounge towards the little kitchen.

'So she really wasn't here earlier, Mr Stokes? Miss Carry, I mean? Just asking, like,' Mrs Potts asked from the lounge. 'I'll just carry on.'

'Wouldn't mind doing that myself.'

'Sorry?'

'Someone,' Nigel said as he switched on the kettle and watched it with blood-shot eyes, 'someone had the temerity to knock at my door at some stage in what seemed like the early hours of the morning. The very early hours. I debated briefly about some possible retaliatory action and decided that the only being which I might interrupt my dreams with would be the Angel of Doom or the four horsemen of the Apocalypse. And since the Angel of Doom and the four horsemen of the Apocalypse are not known for banging on one's door – being able, I understand, to effect ingress and egress without such humdrum means – I resolved to continue my perambulations in the bosom of Morpheus.'

'Eh?'

'I thought, stuff that for a bunch of monkeys, and went back to sleep.'

'Ah. Er, Mr Stokes?'

'Yes?'

'You sure it wasn't a nightmare you had? The banging. That's what my late husband used to have. Only he thought it was me banging the pots, which I would never do.' She switched the vacuum cleaner on.

'I dare say you might be right, Mrs Potts.'

'Sorry? I can't hear you over the cleaner.'

'I dare say you might be right, Mrs Potts,' he shouted as far as his head could stand it. 'I'm sure all will be revealed in due course, as they say.'

The kettle having boiled, Nigel made himself a cup of coffee and took a sip.

'Murdered?' he asked.

'What's that, Mr Stokes?'

He poked his head around the kitchen doorway.

'You said that someone had been murdered.'

'The foreign gentleman staying at the Angel. The one you were having an argument with over young Miss Carry. Bludgeoned to death in his sleep, they say. While we was all downstairs. Blood all over the room, they say. Right up to the ceiling. I'm glad I won't have to clean it up. I'd have to charge extra for that.'

'Oh, flaming Norah,' muttered Nigel, closing his eyes. 'As they say.'

'Are you going to paint it?'

'Paint it?'

'The gruesome corpse. You like painting that sort of thing, don't you?'

'Ancient Greek and Roman mythology. As allegories.'

'Yes, that's what I meant.'

'What?'

'Well, they's all full of gruesome corpses and bloody allegories, ain't they? Orgies, and so on. I mean what about that raping of the saving women?'

'I certainly hope they aren't going to start doing that sort of thing down the Duck.'

Nothing happened. Morton pressed the button again. And then harder. Still nothing happened.

Old fool must have handed over the wrong keys.

'You have to put the key in the lock and turn it,' the old fool called without turning around. 'It's one of the pre-war generation.'

'Which one, the Boer one or the Chinese fucking Opium one?' Morton asked under his breath. He inserted the key in the lock. He turned it and the boot rose slowly and silently. It was almost full with random objects tossed in. A box of folders containing papers which might once have been important. An old car jack with associated long-handled iron lever alongside, suggesting recent use – hopefully a flat tyre, or even two. One dark green Wellington boot; an old tartan blanket; a coil of cheap, thin, plastic cord of the sort that was always on sale somewhere but was useless because it was too thick for string, too thin for rope, and impossible to tie knots in; a boxed doll with a plastic cover which looked at him with wide open psychopathic eyes and looked as if it were about to suddenly cry, "Mummy! Mummy!" before pulling a knife out and running amok.

And a lidless hamper containing two vacuum flasks labelled 'Thermos', one dark blue, one dark red; two insulated plastic mugs with lids, one a luminous yellow with a picture of a laughing Mickey Mouse, the other luminous pink with a laughing Minnie Mouse. The red Thermos looked as if it had already been used. There were stains running down the sides.

The doll watched him looking at the hamper and its contents. It was waiting for his hand to come in touching distance.

'The dark blue one,' the old fool called. Morton jumped and almost hit his head on the lid of the boot.

He picked up the dark blue Thermos and the two insulated mugs with lids, closed the boot on the doll and locked it. He trudged back to the bench, the sand damp and heavy.

'Well, don't just stand there, man, pour the bloody stuff. Or do you need instructions?'

He sat down and poured the coffees.

'It's a special blend of Kenyan and Ethiopian roast beans. I make it myself.'

Morton handed a mug to the old fool and took a sip of his own. It was hot and wet and strong and rather quite good. He couldn't quite put his finger on it. Whether it was more smooth than sweet. Or more sweet than smooth. More honey-sweet than sugar-sweet. But it was definitely something. Better than anything he had bought from a coffee shop.

The phrase "nutty-caramel" came into his mind and he thought of Belgian chocolates. The nice ones.

Nobody was completely useless at everything. Everyone had some little hidden talent, whether it was running marathons, performing brain surgery, keeping children amused, solving crosswords, playing Dixie on a whistle, cooking baklava or being able to remember all the Wimbledon winners since 1932.

Samson's saving grace was now clear.

He could make the coffee.

'My goodness,' said Margaret Coombes-Neeston as she put the receiver down. 'Richard? Richard! Where are you?'

'In the conservatory,' came a muffled voice. 'Like every bloody Sunday morning,' it added almost inaudibly.

Mrs Coombes-Neeston frowned and found her way through the drawing room to the self build conservatory where her husband sat in an armchair reading a Sunday newspaper. She made sure to close the door immediately behind her. The room was like a greenhouse, and the cat sleeping on her husband's lap and the dog at his feet were apt to object loudly to any incoming draft.

'Oh, Richard, Nelson will refuse to go for walkies today, you know that. He hates the cold after he's been in here. I should have taken him out earlier.'

Nelson cocked a worried eye up at his master.

'Don't worry, love, I'll run him round the nursery a few times later.'

'It's not the same.'

'Yes, dear.'

'Richard, you know –' She paused. They had been happily married for over thirty years, thirty years in which she had gone from the belief that his "Yes, dear" was a sign of agreement to realising that it meant that he was about to totally ignore whatever she might feel on a subject. They had now reached a stage where she mostly said "Richard, you know –" and he mostly replied "Yes, dear", saving both a lot of bother.

'Richard, you remember my saying that we shouldn't go to the pub last night?'

He paused almost imperceptibly, as if briefly tempted to correct that statement or just deny all memory.

'Yes, dear.'

'Well, it turns out that I was right all along.'

'Yes, dear.'

'Richard, are you listening?'

'Yes, dear.'

'A man was murdered while we were there! While we sat drinking! Garrotted! Honestly, his blood could have seeped through the floorboards and into our glasses!'

Her husband folded his newspaper slowly and deliberately, put it down next to him, took a sip of tea, and stared out of the condensation-smeared window.

'You know what I mean, Richard! I didn't mean his blood, of course not, not if he was garrotted, but, well – you know what I mean.'

'You mean it's not the garrotting so much, but rather that those old biddies at the Women's Institute will all be gossiping on behind your back, saying how awful it is that one of their members should be found in a common pub where the locals garrotte each other on a regular basis.'

'Well, precisely.'

'And who, exactly, passed on this wonderful news? That Fernely-Shaw creature, by any chance?'

'Well, yes it was as it happens. But –'

'And how did she come to hear of it?'

'Well, I didn't ask her –'

'Precisely. One of them heard it from their maid or au pair or cleaning lady, who heard it from their husband or boyfriend, who heard it from the usual gossiping grapevine in this place.'

'You think it's – not true?'

'Oh, I suppose it's true. Or some of it will be true. Might be a she rather than a he. And guillotining rather than garrotting. Or maybe someone just stubbed their toe. Who knows? Point is, Margaret, if you'd asked Fat Fucking Fernely-Shaw where she had got the news from she would have clammed up immediately. Very common to pass on tittle-tattle from below stairs. Would have put the stupid woman in her place.'

'Richard, dear I do wish you wouldn't use that word.'

'Fat?'

'No, dear, the other one.'

'There's a reason she got that nickname.'

'I know, dear, but that was from other men. But, Richard, if it's true

_,'

'It is true. It's bloody obvious. She's fat. And we all know she –'
'No, dear, I meant the thing at the Angel. Richard, if it is true –'
'Yes, dear?'
'Well, what are we going to do?'
'Margaret, if his, the victim, if there is one, if his name turns out to be Lazarus you could go looking for someone called Jesus and have him raise the poor chap from the dead. Apart from that I rather suspect that, if he is dead, he'll continue being dead for the foreseeable future. Not much we can do about that.'
'Darling, I wish you wouldn't be profane.'
'Yes, dear. I'll start tomorrow, dear.'
'But Richard, we can't do nothing, now can we?'
'Of course not, my dear.'
'So what are we going to do?'
Her husband smiled.
'Have to go down the pub at lunchtime to find out what all the fuss is about, I suppose,' he said. 'It's terrible, but there you go. One must protect one's interests.'
'Richard! We can't do that! It wouldn't be seemly.'
He picked up his newspaper and flipped through to the society section where there was an article and photographs of a teenage film starlet who had had a wardrobe malfunction in the middle of an ill-advised jeté in a mini-skirt.
'Yes, dear.'

DC Morton looked at the waves. He had finished the coffee and the brief lifting effect was receding to leave him feeling a deeper gloom. The sea was very lightly choppy, but no more than that. On a bright summer's day it would probably have appeared enticing. It was only the overcast sky with its pendulous storm-laden clouds that made him think of waves crashing down, bearing helpless sailors to watery graves.
Or perhaps it was Chief Inspector Samson alongside. If ever a man could carry the shades of a soul-destroying, wet and windy

Apocalypse with him, that was the man. It was like sitting alongside a Scottish Death with a brightly covered insulated plastic mug of coffee in his leather-clad hands. With Mickey Mouse's wide eyes peeking out from between his fingers.

A seagull had come to investigate them. It was one-eyed and limped along the beach until it was side-on to them, about ten feet away. It was huge and scrawny at the same time. It was white and grey and looked dirty. It had cast its single yellow eye on Samson for a good thirty seconds. Then it had given out a squawk of derision before limping away towards the sea, faster and faster until it managed to get its wings out, get airborne, and fly away. Morton had felt lonely after it had gone.

While he had been sipping the coffee he had almost forgot about the old fool, he had even felt a smidgeon positive. But you couldn't forget about Samson for long when he was right next to you. It reminded him of his father-in-law at the wedding reception. Sitting there, saying nothing. He had the hollowed-out appearance of a man who was dying and looking forward to it. That had been a portent. He should have rushed from the church screaming. Though of course by the time of the reception it had been too late. He'd already bought the package. Happily ever after. Like fuck.

He pushed that thought away and tried to concentrate on something more pleasant. But nothing came. He was dying to ask when exactly, if ever, they were going to make their way to this pub where a murder had been, allegedly, committed. He also knew that Samson was waiting for precisely that question. He was that sort of man. So he wasn't going to give him any pleasure by asking him it. He looked back at the choppy grey water and wondered what drowning must be like.

'Just sitting there. Doing nothing.'

Morton started. It was almost as if someone had spoken his thoughts out loud. He looked around. There wasn't another soul in sight.

There wasn't another human in sight.

He looked back out to sea. There was some sort of freighter out there, not moving, hove to. The distance made it look tiny. He hadn't given it a thought. But now it seemed to be watching them. Sitting there. Doing nothing. Watching them. Maybe someone on board had spoken. Maybe the breeze had brought the ghostly voice to his ears.

This was wreckers' country. Wreckers and smugglers. Wreckers lured unwary ships onto the rocks, waiting until they were being smashed to pieces before going out to rescue what goods they had been carrying, ignoring the bodies of the drowned sailors and innocent passengers. Smugglers carried on a lethal game of cat and mouse with the excise men. No quarter given on either side. Cudden Point. Prussia Cove. Piskies Cove. All not far away. Names to inspire fear. Places to keep well away from. Ghosts still haunted them, they say. The rocks were slick and treacherous and an unwary walker could be found mysteriously drowned if they ventured where no man should.

He wondered what nationality the freighter was.

'Ten fifty-five, son.'

'Sir?' He instinctively hated himself for using that word.

'Ten fifty-five. That's when we turn up. Pub opens at eleven. They know we're here. The local jungle drums will have been beating overtime. Owner's going to be wound up like an alarm clock then, wondering when we're coming. And worrying about opening time. He'll be nicely done by then. The psychological moment.'

Morton nodded as if he understood and agreed. He hadn't found a pub in the region that opened before midday on a Sunday. He presumed that the old fool was still living in London-land where pubs opened at any time of the day. Beer for breakfast and the football world cup on the telly. If he'd been in charge the pub wouldn't be opening at all.

'Oh, yes, nothing like a couple of ducks doing nothing to wind a watcher up. A guilty watcher.'

Ducks?

He wasn't going to ask.

'Ducks?' he asked.

'Ducks and geese. Police. Don't tell me you didn't know that.'

'Right.'

At one time he had dreamed of being posted to London and living the high life. Not any more.

'And by then, my son, everybody else will know about it. They'll be wetting themselves trying to be there when the doors open, and pretending it's a pure coincidence they've turned up. And before they can take themselves a sip we'll have them into a room for a quiet chat.'

Samson's mouth curled.

'All part of my plan.'

Plan?

'That's if they don't come to us first, of course.'

'First, sir?'

'Oh, yes, my son, first. Right now they'll all be peeking out from behind their net curtains, looking at these two blokes sitting here on a bench through their binoculars. And they'll think, "Ah, coppers." Know what will happen then, son?'

They'll think that, if we are coppers, we're barking mad coppers.

"Arr, be two cakey coppers onna beach bench."

"Arr."

"Arr."

"Baint one frum Lunnun?"

"Arr."

"Arr."

'No, sir. What will happen then?'

'Probably nothing. But if one of them accidentally bumps into us to get their porkies out first, well, that'll be our man.'

That image did not rest well in Morton's mind.

'Get their porkies out?'

'Porkies. Porky pies. Lies, man, lies.'

'Ah.'

'Or woman,' Samson added. 'Sometimes it is a case of cherchez le femme.'

Morton nodded slowly, deciding against correcting his superior officer. And he really didn't want to think of a woman getting her porkies out first.

'The psychological moment, son. Get them when they're weakest.'

Morton covertly slipped open the special camouflage cover on his watch. One hour left.

If Samson wanted to interview everyone before they had a chance to get a drink down themselves the probability was that they'd have to split up and interview people separately. Which suited him fine. The less he had to do with the old fool the better.

Why the hell did London always send down their rejects?

Because they weren't stupid.

They were probably throwing a party in Scotland Yard. On a Sunday morning. Down the local. Just before Christmas.

As a kid he had dreamed of joining the Sweeney. They were the main men. Now they were having a right knees up and he was stuck with their Inspector Grim.

Sorry, Chief Inspector Grim.

Sir Anthony Freechin squared his shoulders. He flexed his knees slightly, turned his hips to the right and then to the left, wincing slightly. He looked down at the luminous-green sphere on the tee in front of him.

'Now then, Mr Ball, straight into Mr Hole this time, eh?'

He lifted his head and squinted along the snow-speckled fairway to see the limp flag some hundred yards away.

'Not a sound, Huckleberry, not a sound, now, I'm in the groove. This is going to be a zinger.'

His caddy, who had been apparently quietly falling asleep over the golf trolley, squeezed one eye open, and then shut it.

Sir Anthony looked down once more, again squared his shoulders, raised his driver, paused to the count of three and a half, and brought it down in the swift but gliding motion the double-glazing-selling chap had told him about the week before.

Just milliseconds before the club connected with the ball the golf bag suddenly erupted into a rendition of Queen's "I Want To Break Free".

'Oh for hell in a hand basket and the King's Fusiliers!' shouted Sir

Anthony, whirling around to find Huckleberry and the golf trolley lying on the frosted grass in expressions of surprise. He twisted his head left and right, threw down the golf club, danced from one foot to another and then stomped over to the bag. After delving into every single pocket and ten seconds of Queen he finally retrieved a mobile phone from one of the pockets and jabbed at the answer button several times until he managed to hit it.

'Codswallop? You were watching me, weren't you? Did that deliberately, didn't you? All I can say is that you'd better have a bloody good excuse this time, or you're fired. Again.'

'Of course I wasn't watching you, Sir Anthony,' came the urbane and assured voice of his secretary, Phillip Codwallader. 'I'm on my way to the mansion now, I have no idea where you are. I presumed that you might be in your study looking though those papers I gave you on Friday.'

Sir Anthony harrumphed a few times.

'Well, what is it, Codswallop? It had better be something good for you to use this number.'

'I believe it could be somewhat of an emergency, Sir Anthony. About last night.'

'Last night? Last night? Don't tell me that her Ladyship has found out? Don't tell me that.'

'Not as far as I know, Sir Anthony. However I'm afraid I have some bad news.'

Sir Anthony nodded at the phone. As the silence continued he took a deep breath.

'Codswallop, if you don't get on with it I will not only fire you I shall do it with a blunderbuss! Get on with it, you drivelling fool!'

'There appears to have been a murder at the public house last night, sir.'

'A what?'

'A murder, sir.'

'A murder? At the Duck? Don't be ridiculous. Who on earth would murder someone at the Duck? That would be downright ... bad manners. Besides which, I was there. You think I'd miss something like that?'

'Quite so, sir. A foreign gentleman, I believe. Eastern European.'

'Well, that makes sense. Typical of them. But what's that got to do with us? Not more bloody EU legislation, is it? I thought we were out of that. Or are we still in? Have we joined again? Or left again?'

'No more than normal, Sir Anthony. However it means that the police will probably want to ask you some questions.'

'What for? I didn't murder whoever it was, did I? Did I? I didn't have that much to drink. Did I? I haven't murdered anyone since – I don't think I've ever murdered someone.'

There was almost a sigh from the other end.

'It's part of their routine, Sir Anthony. They interview everyone who was there around the time.'

'Nothing to do with me, Codswallop. I wasn't there, remember? Hah! I was at the Fenchincham British Legion memorial dinner, wasn't I, Codswallop? Nowhere near the Duck, was I? Everyone at the pub knows that.'

This time there was a distinct sigh from the other end. The kind of sigh that translates as "They might be willing to keep the truth from her Ladyship, perhaps even tell her the odd fib, but their loyalty doesn't extend to telling outright untruths to policemen. Not when the prize for doing so is a stay in one of Her Majesty's less comfortable housing projects."

'I believe the common phrase is, "Pals don't ask pals to commit perjury", Sir Anthony.'

'Perjury? Nonsense. Just asking them not to tell the truth too much. Too much of it floating around as it is. Anyway, how come you know all about this?'

'All about what?'

'This European person at the Duck.'

'It's my job to know these sort of things, Sir Anthony. To maintain sources. To protect your interests. That's what I'm paid for.'

'Complete codswallop, Codswallop. Yes, that's what they pay you for, but you never do it. You heard it on the news or something. Found it on that Internet thing. You've been reading Wicked Paedia again, haven't you? I've warned you about that sort of thing. It's not good for you.'

'I don't believe it has been on the news yet, Sir Anthony.'

Sir Anthony harrumphed again for want of anything better to do.

'Okay, Codswallop, okay. Have to take the bull by the horns on this one. Make sure the police understand the situation properly, and don't go asking her Ladyship the wrong sort of questions. And definitely not giving her the right type of answers. Where are they now?'

'Who, Sir Anthony?'

'The police, you fool, the police. Crawling all over the pub, I presume. Taking it apart piece by piece. Grilling Patsy and the girls. Poor things.'

'It appears not, Sir Anthony. The latest information I have is that what appear to be two police officers are sitting on a bench on the beach.'

'Sitting on a bench on the beach? In this weather? Eating ice cream cones, I suppose? Bobbies in uniform, no doubt. Singing something from the Mikado. Codswallop, have you been drinking?'

'No, sir, I –'

'Well, whoever told you that must be either barking mad or having the DTs. What sort of police officer would sit out on a bench in this weather while he could be inside a warm pub? Those buggers know all the moves, believe me. If there's a warm hole they know where it is. Listen, Codswallop, I'm off down there right now. If her Ladyship asks, I've had to go into the City on urgent business. Trouble with the tootsies.'

'The Footsie, Sir Anthony.'

'That's the one. Stock market's taken a tumble, that sort of thing. Bulls and bears all over the place. Okay? Meerkats, too. Little buggers.'

'Well, that was another thing, Sir Anthony –'

'Not now, Codswallop, not now.'

He switched the mobile phone off and tossed it to the caddy.

'Huckleberry, back to the Jag double quick time, I'm on a mission.'

Just beyond the boundary of the golf course a figure stood half-hidden by a tree. He had a pair of binoculars to his eyes.

'Silly fool didn't even realise he'd got a hole in one,' Phillip Codwallader muttered to himself.

He paused before adding:

'One of these days he'll get really clever and remember that the stock market doesn't open on a Sunday.'

DC Morton covertly undid the camouflage cover on his watch and took another surreptitious glance at the time. Three more minutes and they could be in a nice, warm pub.

'Don't look now, son, but I think we've got a bite.'

'A bite?'

'Female, on the skinny side, about five ten, long blonde hair, probably late sixties, but walks well. Black dress. Looks a bit of a dyke. Coming towards us from the car-park. Don't look!'

'Um, excuse me?' called a voice from behind them. 'I say? Er, hello there?'

The two men turned slowly.

'Sorry to intrude, but are you police officers?'

'Ah, yes, as it happens we are,' the Chief Inspector said as both men stood up. Morton suppressed a smile. They were looking at a youngish man with broad shoulders wearing a winter jacket, cassock, dog collar and large straw hat.

'I'm Vicar Brayley, how do you do? Are you here about the business at the Angel and Duck? Only I couldn't help noticing you here after I'd finished morning service, and I thought, well, perhaps you'd like a cup of tea or coffee indoors while you're waiting, it gets a bit chilly on the beach. It's the wind, you see. It's quite cold at this time of year. Winter, you know.'

'Er, yes, Vicar, we're here about the alleged murder. Only we weren't waiting, we were discussing – our approach to the issue, as it were.'

'Oh, I see, tactics. Now that's interesting. I hadn't thought about that. Yes, I suppose in your job that could be quite important, tactics.

Not so much in mine. Don't need tactics much for heaven and hell. Or a strategy, really. Things tend to be rather fixed. For eternity, really, come to think of it.'

'Well, not exactly tactics, Vicar, more like – well, it's not important. We've finished now, so we'll be off to the scene of the incident immediately. But thank you for your kind offer.'

'My pleasure, er – is it Inspector? Chief Inspector? Commissioner? Captain? I'm not very good at titles, I'm afraid. I keep getting the bishop wrong. And I do like to be precise about these things. It's very important. People get upset when you get it wrong. And it's only Christian politeness to try.'

'Chief Inspector Samson. Without a P. And this is Detective Constable Morton. Also without a P. But with a T.'

'I say, that's wonderful. Tell me, is that your rhubarb Studebaker parked up there? The one with the huge flared wings?'

'Yes. My wife ran away with a used-car salesman. I got it in part exchange.'

'Only, it's a controlled parking zone. You have to buy a ticket from the machine between ten and three.'

'Ten and three?'

'GMT.'

'GMT?'

'And the machine's broken. It's been broken since November. There's a number you can phone But they tell me it's wrong.'

'Make a note of that, constable, it will probably be an important clue.'

Morton took out his smartphone and typed in
"cruel of heart and brain of ox".

'It was when I dialled it, you see.'

'Dialled it?'

'The number that's wrong. I dialled it and the person who answered said they weren't the parking people.'

'Not the parking people?'

'No, they were a retired butcher called Cooper. Mr Cooper. And his wife. They've gone vegan.'

'Vegan.'

'You do know where the pub is, I take it?'

'Just along the coast and back up the hill a bit.'

'That's it. Precisely. Just along the coast and back up the hill a bit. It's a bit of a windy road. I keep having to explain that to tourists in the summer. God knows why they come to a vicarage to ask for directions, but they do.'

'Very kind of you, vicar.'

'Yes, well, it's not much of a hill, there's a bigger one behind it, of course, if you like that sort of thing. You've probably noticed. Hard to miss, really. Well, lovely to meet you. I'll leave you to things, then. I need to change into something a little warmer. I only popped down quickly once the parishioners had left, you see. The church is freezing. There's a heater under the altar. It's quite well hidden. There's nothing under the altar, really, apart from the heater. Not like one of the old ones. All marble, I mean. You can't see it from the front. The altar cloth hides it. It's one of the fan ones. Surprisingly powerful on the ankles. I'll no doubt see you later for interrogation.'

'Interrogation, Father?' asked Morton.

'Vicar. I was in the Angel and Duck pretty much most of the evening, I'm afraid. I go because of my flock. I presume that means that I'll be on the list of suspects.'

'Of course, Father. I'm sure that the Inspector will put you at the top of the list if you'd like.'

'Vicar. Top of the list? Oh, I see, you're joking. Most funny. Well, must fly before I freeze. I'll see you both later then.'

'Morton,' said the Detective Inspector once Vicar Brayley was out of earshot, 'your job is to keep your mouth shut and look intelligent, not to open it and prove what a moron you are, understand?'

Morton nodded. And decided to keep his mouth shut. Forever. He should have paid more heed to the London DC. No wonder the bastard had sounded so happy with himself.

"He's very reliable."

"Is he?"

"Yes. Very reliably obtuse, irascible and any other word you can think of for it. And unpredictable."

"He's reliably unpredictable?"

"Yeah. Keeps suspects off balance. Good fun to watch. Not such good fun when he uses it on you."

"Sort of Jekyll and Hyde?"

"More like a chameleon which changes colour every few seconds just to piss people off. One other thing, though."

"There's another thing?"

"If he ever smiles, run like fuck."

'Right let's be off to this pub. That bloody vicar's messed up my plan.'

When they got back to the car there was a note under the windscreen wiper. Samson pulled it off and read it while Morton put the coffee things back in the boot. They got back in the car and Samson handed the paper wordlessly to Morton. Morton read it while Samson started up and drove off slowly. It was a speeding ticket with the word "speeding" crossed out and "Parking" written in blue biro above it. Apparently they had been caught parking illegally between the hours of ten and three GMT while doing n/a miles an hour.

The pub doors had officially opened at 11h00 precisely as they did every Sunday. At that time there wasn't a soul to be seen. Gradually, it might seem to a hidden onlooker, wraiths began to float and flit hither and thither, innocent passers-by suddenly noticed the pub was open and entered on a whim, and by 12h00 the various bars were beginning to be well stocked with guests, everyone with their favourite Sunday lunchtime tipple in front of them, nonchalantly looking around as if surprised to find themselves there, and merely curious to see who else might have popped in.

The internal entrance door opened and a keen wind blew snow in, indicating that the external door was also being held open.

'Who the hell's keeping the door open?' demanded Sir Anthony, sitting at the bar.

'He's got his eye on you,' declared a quavering voice from the still-open door.

'Oh, god,' said Richard Coombes-Neeston, 'it's Mad Molly with her broom.'

A lined old face pushed itself just into the pub, arms held behind it.

'The angel of death is here,' the face quavered.

'Molly, could you come in while you're sending us to the devil,' said Sir Anthony. 'You're letting all the warmth out.'

'I'll not enter the hotel of sin.'

'Oh, be a dear and do,' said Sir Anthony, 'there's a good girl.'

'Mine eyes have seen the glory of the coming of the Lord.'

'Been watching pornography again, Molly?'

'He is pounding out the grapes of wrath.'

'I know, we're trying to enjoy the end product.'

'Jest ye not that ye might not be jested. His truth is marching on and his chariot is in train for righteousness.'

'Sounds like the entire public transport system there, Molly old girl. Do be a sweetie and close one of those bloody doors. Preferably both.'

'Whoosh, oh bugger,' said the head and then disappeared.

'That's a new one,' said Sir Anthony.

'Sorry, Molly, didn't realise that was your broomstick keeping the door open,' Vicar Brayley said, stepping inside while looking back. 'Shall I pick it up for you?'

'Evil! Evil! Black dress and dollar! The wings are coming. The winds are coming. His trumpet shall sound ye out.' Vicar Brayley let the door go and both internal and external doors closed. A face appeared briefly at a window, fist waving, and then was gone.

'The wings are coming? Chicken wings by any chance? I could do with some of the Southern fried ones. Hello Vicar. Any chance, Patsy?'

'Roast spuds and drumsticks,' said Patsy. 'It's Sunday.'

'Is it? Yes, of course it is. Good service, Vicar?'

'Not bad. Small congregation, though. Mostly widows giving thanks.'

'Oh, bad luck, Vicar. Probably the weather or something.'

'Those two police officers are on their way. You can probably see them through the window now.'

'Let's have a squint,' said Sir Anthony.

He went to the window and peered out through the net curtain and frosted angels.

'God on earth, what is the man driving?'

'It's a purple Studebaker.'

'Pink, I would say.'

'Purple.'

'Port. Definitely Port. One of the lighter ones.'

'Better send Thuthan out to play. She could do with the practice.'

'That would be ironic.'

'What would be ironic?'

'If the coppers get nicked.'

There was a slight pause before a burst of hilarious laughter.

'I say, I didn't catch that,' said Vicar Brayley.

Samson and Morton climbed out of the Studebaker. A little girl wearing a white shirt, tartan waistcoat and skirt, knee-length white socks, black shoes and a tam-o-shanter came out of the pub. She put a long rectangular case on a snow-topped pub table, took off a box slung over her shoulder and placed it alongside the case. Then she stood blocking their way, arms folded.

'You can't go in until you danthe,' she said.

'Danthe?' asked Morton.

'Yeth.'

'Oh, dance. With you?'

'No.'

'No?'

'No.'

'What's your name, little girl?'

'Thuthan. And I'm not a little girl.'

'Aren't you? My goodness. Well, Susan, we're –'

'It'th not Thuthan, it'th Thuthan.'

'Sorry?'

'Apolothy acthepted.'

'Look, Susan –'

'I told you. It'th Thuthan.'

'Ah. I thee. I mean, I see. Your name is Thuthan.'

'Yeth. That'th what I thaid. Are you deaf?'

'Er, well, Thuthan, the thing is, we're police officers, and we need to go into the pub to ask some questions. And it is winter, and you shouldn't be standing outside dressed like that. So, if you don't mind ...'

'You have to danthe firtht.'

'We'd love to dance, Susan, Thuthan, but we're very busy and –'

'Oh, for god's sake Morton, just bloody danthe so we can get in and get started.'

'What?'

'When you were a kid with a football, didn't you ever want a passing adult to play with you, have a kick-around for a few minutes?'

'No.'

'God, you miserable Boxer generation.'

'Don't you mean X-Box?'

'Dance, you idiot.'

Morton looked at Thuthan.

'Wait,' she said. She opened the long case on the table and took out a sword. She placed it carefully on the ground. Then she took out another sword and placed that crossways on the first. She pressed a button on the box, which turned out to be a cassette player.

'It'th the Ghillie Callum,' she said.

'The gilly what?'

'The thord danthe.'

Morton looked at Samson, eyes wide.

'Get on with it man, you just have to dance about and not get your feet chopped off. Five or six steps should be enough. Ten to be on the safe side. Do a knees up Mother Brown.'

Morton stepped reluctantly forward, placing his feet across the squares left by the swords. He began to hop hesitantly from one leg to another.

'Farthter, farthter,' cried Thuthan. Morton hopped faster until one of his shoes clipped a sword and it bounced up, nipping his ankle.

'Fugging hell!' he exclaimed. He bent down and picked it up. He gingerly tested the blade against his thumb.

'These things are bloody real! And they're bloody sharp!'

'Of courth. It wouldn't be the thord danthe otherwithe. And you're bloody utheleth.'

Thuthan stopped the music and rewound the tape. She took the sword from Morton and put it back in place.

'I thee you,' she said to Samson. 'Your turn.' She switched the music on. Samson unbuttoned his coat, stepped into position, raised one arm over his head, placed the other hand on his hip, and began executing a reel between the blades. Thuthan clapped her hands.

'Yeth! Yeth! Farthter! Farthter!'

To Morton's amazement it seemed as if the old fool was going farthter, faster, his coat flapping as he danced. The music came to an end and Thuthan switched the tape recorder off. Samson picked up the swords and handed them to her, handles forward. She took them one by one and returned them to their case. He bowed to her formally, and she executed a perfect curtsey to him. She hefted the strap of the cassette player over her shoulder, picked up her sword-case, and wandered back into the pub.

'Quite amazing,' said Samson.

'You can say that again. What the hell was that all about?'

'Oh, just a bored child wanting someone to play with. But, yes, quite amazing.'

'You can say that again. Those swords were bloody sharp.'

'I'm surprised they allow her to use that.'

'You can say that again. A bloke could get seriously hurt.'

'That tape recorder. It's a 1970s Nakamichi 550. You could sell it for a small fortune these days.'

'What?'

'In good nick, considering.'

'What?'

'Nothing beats a Nak.'

'What?'

'You do know what a tape recorder is, don't you, son? Before your time, I suppose. You youngsters, don't know you were born. All CD players and digital music these days.'

'What?'

'Come on, man, stop gabbling. Let's get this investigation started.' He checked his watch. 'Bloody midday already.'

'Aaargh,' he cried.

'Aaargh,' cried Morton.

They turned around to find two mature woman standing there, one with a dainty, sharp-pointed umbrella in her hands, the other carrying a solid walking stick and holding it at the port. Nothing in their faces suggested they had just poked the two policemen in the back with the weapons.

'Excuse me,' said Phillipa Mountjohn.

'Are you going in or staying out?' asked Bertie. 'Or just shaking it all about?' she added, giggling.

The two men stepped aside and the ladies sailed past. Just as they entered the pub Bertie turned around.

'A word of advice, gentlemen, never have Rice Crispies on Marmite on your toast, it tastes foul.'

They watched as the doors closed.

'Rice Crispies on fucking what?'

'Marmite.'

'What the hell is that all about?'

'Breakfast, I suppose.'

'Are all these people mad?'

'Trust me, son, they're all perfectly sane. And they know exactly what they're doing. Every last one of the buggers.' He looked around. 'Better get in, Morton, we're getting killed out here. We may as well get killed inside. It's warmer.'

There was a hubbub of recovering hangovers as they entered the pub. For a brief few seconds some customers glanced idly in the direction of the strangers. One or two jaws dropped before quickly turning away. Artificial conversation nervously sprang up as they walked past.

'They say it might snow for Christmas.'

'It snowed last night you twat.'

'Yes, but it does look rather grim, doesn't it?'

'That face reminds me of a bulldog the neighbours had when I was a child. Growled at everything. Though it has to be said that it was the stupidest dog in the county. Won prizes for it.'

'I remember that. They called it Cecil, didn't they?'

'And a purple alpaca, but only on Tuesday afternoons for the parrot.'

'What the fuck is that bloke wearing?'

'Looks like a cowboy rodeo.'

'Thuthan, that's enough, put those away now. I'll give you a Bowie knife to play with later. We can play darts again, would you like that? Like they did in that James Bond film.'

'Had him right up the arse. That's the only way you could get a Tiger, you know.'

Samson looked neither left nor right, his eyes locked on Patsy behind the bar with the little group comprising Vicar Brayley, Sir Anthony and Richard Coombes-Neeston in front of him, apparently chatting away, oblivious to the new entrants. Morton initially glanced around with curiosity before noticing a couple of looks and trying to fold his coat lapels over what little could be seen of his shirt.

'Are you the landlord?' Samson asked Patsy. Vicar Brayley, Sir Anthony and Richard Coombes-Neeston turned to look as if only just noticing him. They blinked in unison at Morton's shirt. Then they turned back to Patsy as if shocked but still mildly curious to find out what Patsy's answer would be.

'Indeed I am sor. And what can I get you? A large brandy to clear the sea air, sor?'

Vicar Brayley, Sir Anthony and Richard Coombes-Neeston turned back to look at Samson.

'Police,' Samson said, showing his warrant card. 'I'm Chief Inspector Samson, without a P. This is Detective Constable Morton with a T. I hear you had a murder here last night.'

'Well tank heavens you're here, Major Chief Inspector Commissioner. Sure I was beginning to wonder if anyone was coming. Now I know that the police are busy, and when I had the pub in London it wasn't uncommon to wait days for them to investigate a burglary, but I did rather think a murder might be treated with some urgency, even out here in the countryside. After all, there's the body to think of. It can't be comfortable for the poor soul.'

'Comfortable?'

'Well, it must be nerve-wracking knowing your murderer is still walking free.'

'Nerve-wracking?'

'Well, precisely, Major Chief Inspector. His ghost will be roaming the battlements.'

'Is that where he was murdered?'

'Where?'

'On the battlements.'

'To be sure, general inspector we don't have battlements, we're a pub. I mean, a hostelry. It's just a figure of speech.'

'Hostelry?'

'Sorry?'

'Hostelry is a figure of speech?'

'No, battlements are a figure of speech. Or were.'

'Were?'

'When I said them.'

'When did you say them?'

'Just now. When you asked me about his ghost.'

'I did not ask you about a ghost. Do I look like someone who believes in ghosts?'

'Well, now you come to mention it –'

'I don't. Definitely not. Where is the victim?'

'Upstairs, your honour.'

'Where the battlements aren't?'

'Exactly there, sor.'

'I see. Are the forensic team still there?'

Patsy glanced sideways at Carry who was concentrating on pulling a pint as far away as possible.

'Forensic team, sor?'

'Yes, forensics. The ones in the white overalls with clipboards.'

Patsy gave Carry another sideways look.

'You haven't seen a forensics team, have you?' he called in an audible whisper. 'The ones in the white overalls with clipboards. They aren't wandering about upstairs witout me knowing? The wife will kill me.'

Carry pursed her lips as she pulled the pint, looking down at it. She had that look on her face of someone about to commit serious sarcasm. Then she glanced up and caught Morton's eyes.

'No, Patsy,' she said, looking down again, 'no forensic team. Or any other porcine elements.'

'Pretty sure I haven't seen a forensic team,' offered Sir Antony. 'I'd recognise a man with a clipboard. Dangerous buggers.'

'Could be tricky, white overalls,' put in Richard Coombes-Neeston. 'Someone might mistake them for ghosts. On the battlements.'

'They don't exist, you know,' said Vicar Brayley.

'Yes, Vicar, I thought we'd established that.'

'Had we?'

'Yes, there are no battlements.'

'Oh, I didn't mean battlements, I meant ghosts. Church teaching. They don't exist. No such thing.'

'No ghosts. No battlements. No forensic police officers. I'm beginning to wonder if I shouldn't ask for my money back.'

'What about exorcism?'

'Oh, not my field, I'm afraid. It's a bit of a speciality, that one. We normally get a Roman Catholic priest in for that sort of thing. We can't do it because we don't believe in ghosts. Tricky, really.'

Patsy nodded and turned back to the two officers, smiling broadly.

'Well, that settles it. I'm afraid yours is the first police presence we've encountered today, Inspector General. Actually, we haven't even seen Constable Clueless since Thursday, either. Unless that was Wednesday. We did call, but there was no answer.'

'Constable Clueless?'

'The local police constable, sir. He's normally in just shy of ten o'clock in the evening for a discounted pint and to make sure we aren't breaking the licensing laws. Maybe he's taking his annual holiday. Though to be honest he retired twenty years ago, he just keeps it up as a hobby.'

Samson's lips moved as if he were trying to say something. He turned to Morton.

'Morton, get on the dog, call the station and ask them where in hell forensics are.'

'Sorry?'

'I said, get on the dog to the station and ask them where in hell forensics are. Are you deaf?'

'Er, no, sir.'

'Well?'

'Um, I don't quite understand.'

'Morton, it's quite straightforward. What exactly do you not understand?'

'The dog, sir. What dog is it?'

'The dog. Dog and bone. Phone. Don't you speak English, man? Give the station a call and tell them to find out where in hell forensics are.'

'Yes, sir. The dog, sir. Right you are.'

'If it's any help, Inspector, Doctor Hillman had a look at the body. He said at the time that death had occurred –'

'Doctor Hillman?'

'Our local doctor, Inspector. Though he is getting on a bit and –'

'Quite so, Mr ...'

'Sorry, Chief Inspector?'

'Mr ... ?'

Patsy leaned forward and raised his eyebrows, his lips moving as if trying to help Samson get the words out.

'What – is – your – name?'

'Oh, my name? Ah, well, everyone just calls me Patsy. We're all very informal around here, you know.'

'Well I'm a police officer and we tend to be very formal. Now, your name, Mr ...?'

'Constantine,' admitted Patsy.

'Sorry?'

'Patrick Constantine, Inspector. It's a long story. It goes back to when the Spanish came over to the old country. Only it was actually a Greek –'

'Is this a black spot?' asked Morton, looking at his phone.

'Sure and it's a wonderful area. Nothing black about it at all. It might look a bit grey in the day at the moment, but it is winter after all, and the sun rises later and sets earlier and –'

'I meant, can you get a phone signal here?'

'Ah, sure, no you can't. You have to go up the Saxon Way, the road that takes you up the hill behind this hill, you can get quite a good signal there on a sunny day.'

'The Saxon Way.'

'Aye, sor.'

'But the Saxons never got this far west.'

'Morton, we aren't here for a history lesson. Come on, don't just stand there, lad, I want to know where the forensic boys are. Get a move on.'

'Sir?'

'Go up the hill and see if you can get a signal there. Chop-chop. Up bloody Anglo-Saxon Way.'

'Saxon Way, sor. There's no angle to it.'

'Whatever, just bloody get up it.'

'Well, sor, if it wouldn't be too forward of me –'

'Yes?'

'There is another way.'

'Yes?'

'Your man could row out to sea .'

'Out to sea.'

'I don't think I can do that, sir.'

'For half a mile.'

'Half a mile.'

'I get seasick you see.'

'And then you can get a signal.'

'You can get a signal. Half a mile out to sea.'

'Even on a boating pond.'

'Sure and I've never understood why. But they tell me it's a very good signal.'

'A very good signal.'

'One of the best signals in these parts. If it were a colour it would be green.'

'Green.'

'It's a fine colour, green, sor. One of the best. In fact, where I come from, the best.'

'Morton?'

'Sir?'

'Remember that rowing boat on the beach.'

'It's tied up, sir.'

'Have you got a pen knife on you?'

'No sir'

'No. God help us. A copper who doesn't carry a pen knife. Well, you'll just have to untie it then. Chop-chop, Morton.'

'Well, sor, if it wouldn't be too forward of me –'

'Yes?'

'There is another way.'

'Yes?'

'Well, your man could use our landline here, just behind the bar.'

'Landline.'

'Yes, sor. It works with wires. There's a pole in the road. The wires go up to the pole. And then on to the exchange.'

'Wires.'

'Yes, sor, indeed. It's old-fashioned I know, but it works very well so long as the wires aren't blown down in a storm. Show them, Carry, my angel.'

Carry came over and brought up an old, black, Bakelite phone with trailing cord. She put it on the counter and turned it so that Morton was looking at its face. He blinked.

'You put your finger in the hole of the number you want,' she said, leaning forward and demonstrating. 'Press firmly, then gently revolve the dial around until the pressure from this little silver bit stops your finger, like this. Then you let it go and watch it return all the way to its original position. See? Like that. Just like the wheels on the bus. It goes round and round and round. Do try to be soft and gentle.'

'Yes, thank you, I do know how to operate one of those.'

He stood away from them and began dialling clumsily.

'Sure and it takes me back to Dial M for Murder,' said Patsy. 'Those were the days.'

Samson looked at him.

'Dial em for murder.'

'The film. You know, the movie. With – with – now who was in that film now?'

'James Stewart,' suggested Coombes-Neeston.

'No, you're thinking of The Lodger. Dial M For Murder was Nureyev.'

'Didn't he play Grace Kelly?'

'We could ask Bertie. She knows all the old film stars. Their names, anyway, don't think she's actually met them. But then you never know, maybe she has. Some of the things she comes up with, she must have been a wild child at one stage.'

'That's enough. We aren't here to discuss the golden age of Hollywood.'

'Ah, now surely, Inspector, they were times worthy of –'

'Morton.'

'Er, Inspector,' said Morton, putting down the receiver, 'it appears there might have been a little confusion.'

'A little confusion, Morton? What little confusion?'

Carry's right hand appeared, wearing a washing-up glove. She picked up the receiver with the tips of her thumb and forefinger and wiped it and the base thoroughly with a damp cloth before putting the telephone away beneath the counter.

'Well, apparently, Doctor Shepstone, the pathologist, he's on call you see, anyway, apparently he claims that someone told him that a murder had been reported at the Angel Undertakers in Three Oaks.'

'Three Oaks?' asked Patsy. 'My goodness, that's well over three villages away. But lovely people at the Angel Undertakers, very friendly, service with a smile and very reasonable rates. I think they have a discount on cremations at the moment, on account of the ground being frozen. And if they don't get it right the first time they use dynamite for no extra charge. And there's not a bad little pub next door for the wake.'

'Morton, I did not tell them to tell Shepstone that it was the Angel Undertakers. I told them to tell him that it had the word Angel in it. And we'd be needing undertakers. I gave them explicit – Oh, the hell with it. Did you tell the station to get him down here right away?'

'He's on his way, sir.'

'Well, thank god for that. Seems to me that if you want anything doing you have to do it yourself. Now, Mr ... Constantine, where is the body?'

'Ah, well, Inspector, the easy answer to that is that you go through that door over there, up the stairs, and it's the fourth on your left. Room number fourteen. Only, about Doctor Hillman –'

'We'll have a word with him later. Come on, Morton.'

'And please don't go through to the right up the stairs, Inspector, only that's our living quarters, you see, and the wife really doesn't like, and I mean she really doesn't like –'

'We'll do our best to keep any disturbance to a minimum, Mr ... Constantine.'

'And she's got a revolver,' Patsy ended lamely and so softly it was unheard by any but the closest. 'A big one.'

Every single eye in the public bar, plus a few peeking from the saloon and ladies bars, watched the two men exit toward the stairs.

'Jesus, Mary and the Saints,' whispered Patsy.

'Reminds me of a chap I knew in the army,' commented Sir Anthony Freechin. 'Became a bit of a saying, really. "Nobody could be that stupid." But he was. Not that we were a bunch of rocket scientists, mind you. He just made us feel that we could be.'

'What happened to him?' asked Patsy.

'Emigrated to South Africa in the Seventies. They made him a General. Last I heard he'd had a sex change and was calling himself Matilda in Des Moines. Strange chap.'

'I think we could have a little fun with that one. Samson, I mean.'

'Can't take the pee, he doesn't have one.'

'I say, do you think that's wise?'

'Probably not, Vicar. But it'll lessen the tedium. And put him off the scent. Sir Anthony, if he asks what you do, tell him you're a rocket scientist. See if he's silly enough to believe you.'

'You know, I could tell him I'm a general.'

'We could all tell him we're generals.'

'Which regiment?'

'Someone could be Matilda from Des Moines.'

'Sure, I don't think I could tell him I'm a general, not from where I'm from. Wrong army for this side of the sea.'

'What on earth would Matilda be doing here?'

'I think I might be a deaf general. From all the shouting. On the parade ground.'

'Generals don't shout. Corporals shout. Sergeants shout. Sergeant-Majors bellow, you know. But not officers. Not the done thing.'

'I know that, Sir Anthony. But he doesn't.'

'A strip show?'

'I wish I could be a general with a stutter. Never did learn how to stutter, you know.'

'No, I suppose we can't all be generals.'

'Don't be ridiculous, he might want to see the next performance.'

'Oh, I don't think I could tell him I'm a general. Partly because it would be a lie. We're not supposed to do that. Partly because they already know I'm a vicar. I met them on the beach, you see.'

'You met the generals on the beach?'

'You aren't allowed to lie? My goodness, vicar, I thought you chaps did that all the time. All those fairy tales.'

'They are not fairy tales. Really. They are parables.'

'Sure and if he's in charge we'll be selling pints by the barrel load. It will be like Jack the Ripper.'

'Jack the Ripper?'

'I see what you mean, Patsy. They never worked out who done it – Jack the Ripper, I mean. People have been writing books and making films ever since. You could advertise this place as the pub where nothing was solved.'

'Hostelry. And Inspector Chuckles up there certainly isn't going to solve anything. He'll be lucky if he manages to fall over the body.'

'Chief Inspector.'

'You think, Patsy?'

'Ah, Carry my angel, after a lifetime in running pubs you can judge a book by its cover.'

'If you say so.'

'Just so long as he doesn't fall over anything else.'

'You could give tours. Patsy.'

'Well, my little turtle dove, now there's a thought. Sure and you're a ray of sunshine in the gloom.'

Nigel Stokes sat at a corner table with a half-full pint and looked on at the little turtle dove with the face of a woebegone Cocker Spaniel trying to attract his mistress's attention by twitching his ears.

'Did you notice that shifty-looking person down there?' whispered Samson as they got to the top of the stairs.

Morton ran through his memory of the faces. All of them had looked shifty. People did normally look shifty when they were obviously trying not to look as if they were gawking. Normal people looked even more shifty when trying to look as if they weren't gawking at coppers. Had anyone not looked shifty he would have been suspicious. But if the old fool thought he had spotted something he was not about to contradict him.

'The one with the, you know ...?' he suggested, making an unidentifiable hand gesture which could have suggested height, width, a moustache, the number seventeen, or pregnancy.

'That's the one. Keep an eye on them. They had something to do with this business, I'm sure.'

'Yes, sir.'

'There's something going on here, Morton. Mark my words.'

'Yes, sir.'

'It's not going to be a simple case of murder. I can feel it in my water.'

'No, sir.'

'Be alert at all times.'

'Yes, sir.'

'And keep your eyes open. Especially on that person.'

'Yes, sir.'

'So long as we follow my plan we've got them.'

'Yes, sir.'

Morton took out his smartphone.

'What the hell are you doing, Morton? I thought those things didn't work down here?'

'Making a note, sir. I can make notes without a signal.'

'Can you? You must show me sometime.'

'It depends on the model.'

'Does it? I'll have to get one like that sometime then. Good lad. Carry on.'

Morton typed in

"ee'zum fair grim sight to watch".

'Right. According to Constantine their living quarters are on the right, that'll be that door blocking the passage. Then there's the laundry room, one, another room, two, third room, keep up, Morton, another room, and then this one, number fifteen.'

'Er, didn't the landlord say it was the fourth door, sir? Number fourteen.'

'Quite right, Morton, just testing. Let's first see where the exits are around here. Because where there's an exit there's an entry.'

They carried on to the end of the corridor. There was a window covered with a net curtain.

'Have a look out there, Morton. See if you can see anything.'

Morton pulled the net curtain aside and tried the window catch. It didn't move.

'Locked.'

'Are you sure? Not just stuck?'

Morton put more effort in. The window still didn't move.

'Whatever it is, it won't budge. There's a catch with a key hole, but no key.'

'Can you see out?'

Morton put his eye to the window and looked out.

'Side garden,' he said. 'Covered in snow. Not deep, but virgin.'

'Good to know there's something virginal around here. So, what does that tell you?'

'No-one's been in from that side overnight?'

'You know, I think you might just be right. Well done. We might make a real copper out of you yet. Given enough time. Let's have a look at this room number fourteen then.'

They turned to walk back. Samson suddenly stopped and held up a hand, looking down.

'Notice that?' he whispered.

Morton listened. He couldn't hear a thing. Not even a sound from the rooms downstairs.

'Well, come on, Moron, don't you notice anything?'

'Er, it's very quiet, sir?'

'The carpet.' He went down on one knee and massaged the deep and thick carpet between finger and thumb. 'Askminster, that. Quality. Extra pile. Must have cost a fortune.'

Morton looked at the carpet and blinked. He was about to say, "Don't you mean –" but caught himself in time. Samson stood up.

'And the wallpaper, son, that's really good quality thick wallpaper. And you know what that and the carpet does?'

Lines the walls and floors? thought Morton.

'Kills noise. That's why you can't hear anything. It's a real assassin's treat, this is. You could be padding along in your bare feet soundlessly while downstairs in the pub it sounds like a teenager's rave party. Last time I saw this sort of quality was in a hotel in London, one of the really, really expensive ones. They don't like hearing maids and butlers walking along the corridors. Course, it means they don't hear the executioner coming either. That's what happened in London. Nobody heard a thing. Including the victim. Come on, son.'

Samson walked back to number fourteen and ran his eye over the door. He put a finger to his lips and a hand on the doorknob. He opened the door slowly and peeked in. Then he nodded and stepped in.

'Regardez the victim, Morton. Fully clothed. Means he hadn't gone to bed.'

They looked at a white-haired man sprawled across the bed, arms dangling either side, worn boots hanging over the end.

'Er, sir, he doesn't look very dead.'

'You suddenly an expert on dead bodies, Morton? I think I might have seen one or two more than you. In so far as London being the murder capital of the world. In so far as I didn't become a Chief Inspector through passing exams at some hick university, son. In so far as I've been a copper a lot longer than you've had hot dinners. In so far, son, to put it briefly and succinctly, that I think I might have a little more experience than you in such things. Unless, Detective Constable, you wish to disagree and illuminate me?'

'Er, no, sir.'

'Thought not. Now, let's start by finding out who our vic is. Go on, son, see if he's got any identity on him.'

Samson stood back as Morton leaned over the figure on the bed, lifted his suit jacket, and slipped his hand into an inside pocket.

'Ha! Got ye, ye thieving little basket!' shouted the old man, sitting up abruptly, gripping Morton's arm as Morton yelped and tried to fall back into a corner. 'Thought ye could have me wallet while I was sleeping, eh? I'll learn ye!'

'Police!' cried Morton as the old man pushed him to the floor and raised a gnarled fist.

'Excuse me, sir,' said Samson, showing his warrant card, 'police.'

'Police?' asked the old man, looking up in surprise. 'Ye got here quickly. This little bastard was trying to rob me.'

'He's also a police officer. Detective Constable Morton. With a T.'

'Wha? A police officer trying to rub me in broad daylight?'

'I think he thought that you were dead. He hasn't had much experience with bodies.'

'Daid? Ye mean he was planning on rubbing the daid? Ah, weel, that's different.'

'I was not robbing you,' Morton said, standing up. 'I was checking for a pulse, that's all. We were told that you were dead.'

'Checking for a pulse in ma wallet, ye were. And ye canna tell the difference between the living and the daid. Tis some poor police officer ye are. You youngsters of today, you know nothing. Nothing, I tell ye, absolutely nothing.'

'We were told that a man had been murdered here,' said Samson. 'There's obviously been some sort of mistake. We'll be on our way.'

'Now hang on a wee minute, laddie. There's been a modder right enough. here. Let me show you.'

He stepped across the room to a cupboard and opened the door. A body tumbled out. It was wearing a white shirt and cream-coloured trousers.

'Ye see? No use robbing that one, mind. I've already checked. Not even a sixpence. Just this letter.'

'Well, I intend to tell the truth, the whole truth and nothing but the truth,' decided Sir Anthony Freechin, banging his pint pot on the counter both as an expression of his determination and an indication that it needed refilling.

'Mostly,' he added.

'That might not be the best of ideas,' said Richard Coombes-Neeston.

'A dangerous thing, the truth,' agreed Vicar Brayley. 'Especially in the wrong hands.'

'It's a two-edged sword.'

'I never did understand that saying. Aren't most swords two-edged?'

'Have to ask Thuthan about that.'

'Let's ask young Carry,' Sir Anthony said, smiling at the girl behind the bar as she refilled his tankard. 'What say, Carry, tell the truth or not?'

Her expressionless eyes hovered over his for a moment.

'It's a question of percentages.'

'Is it? Like betting, you mean?'

'No, Sir Anthony, what percentage. How much.'

'How much?'

'How much of the truth do you intend to tell?'

'How much? Well, all of it, of course.'

'All of it? Do you think people are ready to cope with all of it? Excuse me, someone's waiting at the end of the bar.'

'What a strange child.'

'Very perspicacious,' said Vicar Brayley. 'There are some things you don't want to know about. Did you know, according to Otto von Bismarck, one should never inquire how either sausages or laws are made. I read that somewhere.'

'Not sure about Bismarck. He was German, you know.'

'Indeed, Vicar,' said Richard Coombes-Neeston. 'Reminds me of the time I was taken around a plum jam factory.'

'Funny you should say that, but I had very much the same experience,' said the Vicar. 'Only in my case it was Christmas puddings.'

Sir Anthony looked from one to the other.

'You know,' he said, 'one of the reasons I enjoy coming here for a quiet pint is the strange intellectual conversations you two have. However, part of the enjoyment is not having to contribute, as I can never tell what the hell you two are talking about.'

Coombes-Neeston smiled.

'Sir Anthony, I'm sure that you would understand when I tell you that I have never touched plum jam since seeing how they made it.'

'And Christmas puddings were quite destroyed for me. All the – things – that drop in during the process.'

'Well, yes, I can see that, but I still don't follow.'

'Sir Anthony, that chap you knew in the army. Suppose that you had tried to explain the plum jam factory to him.'

Sir Anthony sucked on his lip.

'See what you mean. See what you mean indeed. Explain the plum jam factory to that Inspector Samson. Would take a long time and he still wouldn't get the point. Probably have to sign a statement about it all, every single detail.' He paused. 'What plum jam factory?'

'The one we were just talking about.'

'Were we talking about a plum jam factory? I don't remember that. You sure you don't mean the Angel Cake factory?'

'No, Sir Anthony, plum factories in general.'

'Nothing drops into the Angel Cakes, trust me.'

'Now we're back to the generals again. Are we?'

'I quite like Angel Cake. Especially the special edition.'

'I'm not surprised.'

'Sir Anthony probably is.'

'I still haven't a clue what you two are talking about. Never mind, I'm used to that.'

'Pretend you do, Sir Anthony.'

'Used to that as well.'

He shook his head and looked at Carry as she returned from serving at the end of the bar.

'No, you're quite right, my girl. Keep stum about plum jam factories and that sort of thing. No need to go overboard. Be like dad and keep mum. As we used to say back in the day.'

The edge of her lips gave the slightest indication of a smile.

'I do like working here,' she said. 'You never know what to expect.'

'Ah, that's youth for you, always want something new. We do try our best, my dear, but you know, you can't expect a murder every day of the night.'

'I'd better get back', Coombes-Neeston said, finishing his pint after a quick look in the mirror behind the bar. 'The ladies have just finished their bridge hand.'

'Speaking of such things, fancy a few hands of poker after lunch?' asked Sir Anthony. 'Along with a couple of snifters, of course.'

'Not sure if we'll be able to.'

'No,' put in the Vicar, 'I would imagine it might not be the best of ideas while there are police officers around. I suspect it might be illegal.'

'Wouldn't surprise me. Anything enjoyable is illegal. Bloody Cromwell. Did you know he banned mince pies?'

'Oh, I wish he'd banned Christmas puddings. I used to enjoy Christmas puddings.'

'I love a good slice of Christmas pud. Swimming in hot custard. But then, I haven't seen your plum factory.'

'Let me have a look at that envelope.'

'Er, sir, what about fingerprints?'

'Too late for that now, Morton, this doctor has already covered it in his.'

'I only held it by the corner with the wee tips of me fingers.'

'Never mind, wouldn't have anything useful on, paper never does. Let's see.'

He took a piece of paper out of the envelope.

'It's blank.'

He turned it over.

'Completely blank.'

He handed it and the envelope to Morton.

'Look after that, son, I think it might be a clue. He might have written on it in secret ink. Lemon and urine. Old trick, but it works.'

Morton almost dropped the envelope and paper as he tried to take it from Samson without touching it.'

'So, you searched the body?'

'Aye. I was doing nothing and thought I might find something that might tell me about the state of his health.'

'But he was dead.'

'And there was nothing. Not a thing.'

'Wallet?'

'Not a thing.'

'He must have had something on him. How was he going to pay the bill?'

'Mebbe he'd already paid it. I wouldna do that myself, but some people are strange. What if ye dee before ye check out?'

'He did.'

'I rest me case.'

'Speaking of cases, what about luggage? Spare clothes?'

'Not even a hankie.'

'You checked for a handkerchief?'

'I had a wee sniffle. And he wasn't going to be needing it.'

'So if you didn't find a handkerchief, then –'

'Don't ask that, Morton. You don't want to know the answer.'

'Weel, ye've had ye look, I'll put it away then. Always leave a crime scene as you found it, that's what I've been told.'

Samson and Morton looked on as the old man pushed the body back into the cupboard and shut the door with a couple of grunts.

'Just who are you?' Samson asked.

'Me? Who am I? Is that a philosophical question?'

'Your name, please,' Samson asked.

'Mai name? Och, I'm Doctor Hillman, the local GP. Everyone around here knows who I am. I retired but got bored. Now then, I've been looking after this body of yours all evening, and I reckon it's time for me to be off home now.'

He pulled a fob watch from his jacket pocket, frowned, and shook it a few times.

'Damn thing has stopped. Must have forgot to wind it up. Would either of you have the time?'

'It's just gone twenty-five past twelve,' offered Morton, as the Inspector seemed incapable of taking his eyes off the Doctor.

'Twenty-five past twelve? Ye're daft, young man, I've been here since ... Would that be in the morning or in the evening?'

'The morning, sir. Well, technically the afternoon, of course.'

'Saturday or Sunday?'

'Sunday, sir.'

'Aye, well.' He beamed. 'It's been a long cold night, ye ken. And since I'm still on the premises I might just have a wee dram to wake me up. If ye want me I'll be downstairs in the public bar. I think they owe me one or three.'

The two officers watched him as he almost skipped out of the room in his boots, closing the door behind him. There was silence for a few seconds, until Samson groaned and sat down on the bed.

'Wonderful,' he muttered. 'Absolutely bloody wonderful.'

'Sir?'

'We've got a dead body in the cupboard – that's presuming that it is dead – a doctor supposedly looking after it who was asleep all night, a pub full of people most of whom were probably here last night, anyone of whom could have walked in and done it, the body's been flip-flopping in and out of a cupboard, no forensics, his luggage has disappeared ...'

Morton composed his face into a look of sympathy. He studiously avoided looking at the cupboard or making any suggestions. Samson sighed and lay down.

'Get it back out, Morton. The body, I mean. From the cupboard. I suppose taking a look can't do any more damage.'

Morton stepped forward. He opened the cupboard door and the body rolled out once more.

'Cause of death?' asked Samson.

'Shot in the temple, sir. Just between the eyes. Single bullet, probably small calibre. Can't see any powder marks.'

'Not strangled as well, by any chance?'

'Now you come to mention it, there does seem to be some discolouration around the neck.'

'His tie was probably too tight. Next thing you'll tell me he was poisoned too.'

'Well, I can't say for certain, but there's a white residue around his lips.'

'Oh, give it a break, Morton. What else? Hit over the back of the head? Stabbed between the ribs?'

'Um, could be, sir, there's definitely some sort of wound just below his ribs, and ... yes, a suggestion of blood and bruising at the base of the neck.'

'Not electrocuted as well? Someone chuck a toaster in while he was having a bath?'

'Well, no, sir, he wasn't–'

'Chopsticks up his nostrils? The Chinese method?'

'Chopsticks? No, sir.'

'Plastic bag over his head?'

Morton decided not to answer that.

'Well, a plastic bag in the cupboard, then. After he'd been asphyxiated.'

Morton checked.

'No plastic or other bag in the cupboard.'

'And the clothes are dry so presumably not drowned at the same time. Well, thank god for that, that does simplify things for us, doesn't it.'

'Well, actually his clothes are a bit damp.'

Samson sat up.

'Morton, stop inventing nonsense. What we have is one victim, shot. Pretty straightforward stuff. Once we've interviewed everyone who was here last night I'll be well on my way to feeling someone's collar.'

He lay back again and closed his eyes.

'As soon as forensics turn up. There's been enough messing around with this crime scene. We aren't going to let anyone else wander in to rifle through the poor bastard's pockets.'

He opened one eye and cocked it at Morton.

'Don't just stand there, son, start going through his clothes and find out who he was. Check the labels. Just in case that Scottish idiot missed something. Which I doubt. We should have searched him.'

'I thought you said –'

'I said anyone else, Morton, I didn't say us. We aren't anyone else.'

He closed the eye again.

'If he's Scottish I'm the queen of Timbuctoo.. And Patsy Constantine is as Irish as a tea cosy. This is going to be a real bastard of a case.'

'One down,' Phillipa Mountjohn noted as she scored the bridge pad. 'Pretty close run there. Richard was right to put you back into spades. If he had had one more spade you would have made it and that would have made rubber.'

'Bidding is one of Richard's specialities. He used to say that that's what made a good businessman. Knowing when to take a chance. Before he retired, you know. Of course in the days he was in the Forces he said the sign of a good soldier was getting someone else to take the chances.'

'I think that's called delegation.'

'Very unusual in a man,' Bertie commented, genteelly licking her lips after a sip of sherry to make sure none of it had escaped. 'My late husband insisted on bidding to play every hand, no matter what his partner did. It was most upsetting, I could have killed him at times. I was so relieved when he passed on to better things. Or at least different things. I do hope they don't play Bridge where he's gone.'

'Know what you mean, Bertie. Met plenty of those. I have to say, Margaret, you've got that man well trained. You must tell me how you did it some time, I could never manage it.'

'Richard says the worst kind of manager is the one who tries to do everything themselves and then walks away when it fails. A bit like the Prime Minister.'

'Which one?'

'All of them.'

'Reminds me of hockey, you know. Girl at school always used to hog the ball to herself, never passed to anyone with a clear shot. Course, soon as the opposition realised, they were all over her, a right tangle.'

'Ooh, that was Jane – what was her name? Jane something or other. I thought she'd never get out of that habit. But she did, if I recall correctly. Sadly men don't.'

'Jane the Vac, wasn't it? Her eyes were like a vacuum, suck in everything, understand nothing. And I remember when she gave up that habit. It was after I got into the tangle and gave her a whack on the ankle and told her never to do it again. She couldn't walk properly for a week. Made sure the ref didn't see, of course. But it worked.'

'I remember. You told her her tits would be next.'

'You have an inventive memory, Bertie. From what I recall I told her I'd do her properly the next time.'

'Yes, but didn't that mean –'

'Don't think it meant anything. It was a phrase we got off some film or other.'

'Didn't she marry a millionaire in the end? He was twenty years older than her, wasn't he?'

'Yes. It was the only intelligent thing she ever did. Banged him to death from what I heard.'

'Richard!' cried Margaret Coombes-Neeston. 'You're just in time for the next hand, I've just dealt. You are a clever darling!'

'I try my best,' her husband said, taking his seat. 'Did we make it, partner?'

'One down, I'm afraid. Still, worth a go, one more spade in your hand and we would have had the rubber.'

'I was a little worried about that. Still, thought it worth a punt. Sorry about that.'

'Nothing to be sorry about. Now, my go. Yes, a heart.'

'I'll have to pass, I'm afraid,' said Bertie. 'They say that the police have arrived, Mr Coombes-Neeston. Through the public bar.'

'Yes, they came in while I was chatting to the vicar and Sir Anthony. An inspector and a detective constable. Sorry, a chief inspector and a detective constable, I do beg his pardon. Let's go for spades again. One spade.'

'I hope you're not playing one of those strange conventions again, Richard. Two clubs.'

'Have you ever known me play a strange convention, Philly?'

'No comment.'

'I do hope they sort this business out quickly, it is rather distressing. Two hearts.'

'Nonsense, Margaret, you're enjoying it as much as the rest of us. The victim has nothing to do with us, we're all agog to find out who dunnit. No sense pretending we aren't interested in all the blood and gore.'

'That's presuming he does have nothing to do with us.'

'What do you mean, Richard?'

'I'll pass again. What's he like, Mr Coombes-Neeston, this chief inspector? Glint-eyed and razor-jawed? Is he wearing a trilby and smoking a pipe?'

'Honestly, Bertie, you do live in the past.'

Richard Coombes-Neeston stroked his jaw.

'Three hearts. You know he reminds me of a gardener chap called Briarley.'

'Oh, dear,' whispered Margaret Coombes-Neeston. 'He can't be that bad, surely.'

'Briarley? Who is this Briarley person?'

'He was a gardener we hired when we lived in Hampshire,' said Margaret Coombes-Neeston. 'The only thing he knew about was Japanese knotweed. It was a fixation. He thought it exotic. And apparently it had medicinal qualities. He'd listen to what you told him, that it was illegal to grow it, that it was an invasive species, he'd say he understood, yes, ma'am, of course, ma'am, and he'd then plant Japanese knotweed anyway. Richard had to fire him when he planted the things in the herb patch. We couldn't get rid of it. It grew under the patio and then through it. Everywhere. In the end it was easier just to pour every single chemical we could find on the stuff, set it on fire, sell the property and not mention the fact.'

'It's your bid, Margaret.'

'Oh. No bid.'

'Three hearts it is. In with a shot of rubber again, excellent bidding, Richard.'

'Well, that makes me dummy again. I'll just pop over to the bar, there's something I forgot to ask Sir Anthony.'

'Mr Coombes-Neeston, are you seriously saying that this chief inspector is – well –'

'He's a complete idiot,' Richard Coombes-Neeston replied, standing up. 'I know the police generally are completely useless, but this one is the village idiot with a badge stuck on him for a bit of a laugh.'

'A bit like Constable Clueless then.'

'I must say, in an intellectual race of two they'd both manage to come last. I doubt if either could find the finish line even if they started from it.'

'What about the detective constable? Is he a dashing young man with good calves who will solve the case and show his superior how it's done?'

'He's wearing a three piece suit.'

'Oh, I say.'

'And a cowboy shirt.'

'A cowboy shirt?'

'And brown Italian shoes. Pointy brown Italian shoes.'

'Well, Italian shoes – they make rather nice shoes, the Italians.'

'These are the faux shiny leather Italian shoes that have Made In A Sweatshop In Bangladesh stamped on them. You can always tell.'

'Oh, dear, a bit of a spiv, then?'

'Let's put it this way, if he went to an art museum his favourite picture would be the mirror in the ladies.'

'You mean the gents?'

'The ladies. So they could admire him admiring himself.'

'Now who does that remind me of?'

'I only hope they replace them with someone who has half a brain cell soon. I really do not fancy having to navigate my local pub while trying to avoid policemen all over the place for the next few months. They might discover something we don't want them to.'

'Do you think he might let us see the body? You know, in situ?'

'I'm sure you're going to ask him, Bertie. The young one. Narcissus.'

'They aren't out yet, are they? I haven't seen any. Isn't it too early?'

'What?'

'For narcissuses.'

'Narcissi. For them, it's never too early. Pond life.'

Morton stood half-leaning against a wall trying to think of several things not to say. Out of the corner of his eye he could see Samson sitting in a chair glaring a the corpse which had been propped in another chair. There almost seemed to be a personal animus between the two, though probably unrequited on one side. All Morton could do was to presume that Samson was not a man who liked having his weekends disturbed, far less to have to come down to this godforsaken part of the world on a winter's day.

There was a booming of knuckles at the door, the door burst open, and a man in plus-fours carrying a medical bag burst in.

'Samson, you old bugger, after all these years. I might have known it was you. I was just having a round of golf when I got a call to go to some undertakers. They were closed so I had to find a pub to make a call. Now here you are in another pub. Just like the old days. What's this about a murder?'

Samson nodded his head at the other chair.'

'My goodness, yes,' said the other man, 'it's a body alright.' He bent over and peered at the face.

'Well, Shepstone?' asked Samson after about five seconds.

'Well, what, Samson?'

'Well, when did he die, what of, that sort of thing. The sort of thing you're paid to work out.'

'Samson, I'm paid to prescribe pretty pills to elderly women who may or may not have a slight fever. Pink concoctions for little baby girls, and light blue concoctions for little baby boys. Anything serious I refer to a specialist. Being called out to bodies, now – well, I tend to divide those into those who are dead and those who aren't. I can charge a little extra for real dead bodies. The ones that turn out to be still alive are just more bother than they're worth. They complain, you know.'

'Shepstone, I thought that you were supposed to be a pathologist.'

'Don't be silly, Samson, when did you ever hear of my becoming a pathologist? I'm a GP. Always been a GP. Maximum pay for minimum effort. I'm only deputising for them. You've been watching too many of those American television shows. Do you know how much it would cost to call out a proper pathologist? Much cheaper to get someone like me to decide on the basics and send the body in for further investigation if necessary. Cheaper to transport a corpse than a pathologist, if you see what I mean. Though, having said that, someone in London asked especially for me.'

'Someone in London asked for you.'

'Said they wanted someone who knew how to keep his mouth shut. Must have remembered me coming down to these parts a few years back. It was a close thing, mind, I made the mistake of leaving my mobile on while I was on call. Even bigger mistake, I answered it while I was playing golf. The others don't like that sort of thing, you know.'

'I thought you said you had to go to a pub to make a call?'

'Well, these so-called smartphones don't serve drinks, you know. Don't know why they call them smartphones.'

'Okay, Shepstone, I'll settle for the basics then. What are they?'

'Well, he's definitely dead.'

Samson closed his eyes and rubbed his face with both hands.

'And the probability is that he was shot. That hole in his forehead definitely looks like a bullet-hole.'

Samson waited. He opened his eyes again when Shepstone made the kind of cough that indicates the person making it is being polite for the last time before abruptly leaving.

'So, what you're saying is that he died of a gunshot wound?'

'Don't be silly Samson, you know me. I said he was shot. It looks bad to the layman, but he might have survived. Who knows. He could have died from something else.'

'Such as?'

'Heart attack? He doesn't look very healthy to me. Probably didn't get enough exercise. Looks a bit pale, too. I'd prescribe a holiday in the sunshine. You know what you want?'

'What?'

'A pathologist.'

Samson sighed.

'Time of death?'

'At a guess, last twenty-four hours. Providing there hasn't been any funny business. You know, like reheating the corpse, that sort of thing. Was he draped over the radiator when you found him?'

'No. Could it have been suicide?'

'Not my field, Samson. It looks unlikely, but he could have set up some contraption which allowed him to shoot himself between the eyes. Maybe when he fell it collapsed and folded away into the ceiling. You'd be surprised at how inventive some of these buggers can be.'

Samson looked at the ceiling.

'Make a note of that, Morton. We'll have the check what's above the ceiling.'

'Dreckly, sir.'

Morton took out his smartphone and tapped in "In your dreams, Lunnun lummox". He knew who would be expected to go into the ceiling and he wasn't going to have any of that if he could avoid it.

Then he deleted that and typed in

"whatter proper wazzocks".

'I don't suppose you know where the rest of the forensic team are by any chance, Shepstone?'

'Rest of the – there is no rest of the anything, I'm all you're getting today. And I'm about to be out of here. I still have an appointment with the nineteenth hole.'

'How the hell am I supposed to conduct an investigation without a forensics team?'

'Don't ask me, Samson. Ask the government. You know, cut backs and all that. And it is Sunday, after all. That's time and a half for the forensics boys if they were called out. At least. Comes of having a decent union. Me, I just charge them whatever I feel like. They never question it. Ironic that. It's what comes of trying to save money when you don't know where you're spending it.'

'I suppose we'll have to do as best we can under the circumstances. I've seen worse.'

'That's the spirit, Samson. I'll be off then. Oh, and just because it's you, I'll tell them to send an ambulance to take that chap away. Isn't that nice of me?'

Samson said nothing as the doctor slammed the door closed behind him. Then he stood up.

'Come on, Morton, time to turn this place inside out. We'll start by making a list of everyone who could have done it. Won't be hard, they'll all be downstairs as we speak. We'll interview them separately, you take one half and I'll take the other. Then we swap suspects around and see if they still tell the same story the second time around.'

'Sir, wouldn't it be better to –'

'No. I'm going to run this one by the book. My book. My rules. My plan.'

As he came down the stairs Shepstone poked his head into the public bar, rubbing his jaw in a fashion that suggested that he was wondering whether having a quick one for the road was a good idea and finding the startling answer, yes.

'Coomsy!' he exclaimed as he saw Richard Coombes-Neeston at the bar. 'My goodness, long time no see. Glad to see you're still propping up the same bar after all these years.' He strode up to the bar. 'Double whisky without the rocks,' he called to Carry. 'Can't stay long, I've got to get home for lunch. Mother's coming. Say, I've just been looking at your – thank you, young lady – for want of a better word – deceased chap.'

'The murder victim? How did he die?'

'Ah, no, no, you won't catch me admitting anything, maybe murder, maybe not, maybe he's dead, maybe not. Well, yes, dead I'll grant you, but that's it. Cause of death I leave to those paid for that sort of thing.'

'Was that inspector up there still?'

'Chief Inspector.'

'Samson? Oh yes. Haven't seen him for ages either. Did you know, London asked for me especially. Shows I'm not forgotten in those parts.'

'You know him?'

'Know him? Knew him years ago when I was still working in London. Know his reputation well. He's a man of ... hidden talents. Very well hidden.' He laughed uproariously and tipped the rest of his drink down his throat before banging the glass on the bar.

'Must go. Listen, Richard, I'll give you a call. We'll do lunch sometime when you can afford it. I'll show you my current drinking hole. Reassuringly expensive.'

He turned to leave and saw Samson and Morton standing just inside the doors watching him.

'Hidden talents,' he exclaimed and walked past them, bellowing with laughter. Samson watched him go with a look on his face. He turned and came up to the bar.

'How many different bars do you have here?'

'Ah, sure, now's that's a good question, sor. There's this one, the public bar, of course. It's for the general public. Then there's the saloon bar, of course, that used to be for the gentry you could say, though we hire it out for private parties if anyone wants, very popular with wedding groups, small wedding groups –'

'Was there one last night?'

'A wedding?'

'A private party in the saloon.'

'Ah, no, sir, it was open to the general public.'

'The same as the public bar.'

'That's the one, sor. Though there wasn't anyone in the saloon bar, seeing as how it was empty. Then there's the ladies' bar, of course. Not that it's only for the ladies, of course, not these days, but the ladies normally prefer it. What you might call more mature women. The younger set prefer the public bar when they're in town, it's normally livelier. And cheaper. And there's the snug for shy or private parties.'

'More parties?'

'Ah, no, sor, not parties in that sense, parties in the sense of people.'

'Parties in the sense of people. People having parties?'

'Ah, no, sor, more as in you might say a party of one, or a party of two. Discreet parties being discrete. Or do I mean discrete parties being discreet? Sure and I can never remember which one it is.'

'You'd call a single person a party? Sounds like a very small party.'

'Thank you for that contribution, Morton. Was there anyone in the snug, Mr Constantine?'

'No, sor, not last night. Not most nights in the winter, not without the tourists.'

'Tourists like the snug?'

'It gives them a kind of thrill when I explain it.'

'Any other rooms?'

'There's the pool room.'

'The pool room. You have pools in there?'

'No, sor, we have pool tables. You know, like snooker. Only smaller and different.'

'Any players?'

'Cigarettes? They're in the cabinet. It's the law these days. Do you want some? I had you down more as a pipe man.'

'No. Pool players.'

'No, sor, not without the tourists. It's a young person's game, is pool.'

'Any others?'

'No, sor, I think that's the lot.'

'What about cellars?'

'Sure, we have cellars. To keep supplies in and such stuff. We don't have customers in them. Though now you come to mention it we could turn them into a restaurant. Now there's a thought. Italian, with candles and such. We'd just have to do something about the rats.'

'You must need a lot of bar staff.'

'Ah, sure, no, sor, There's only the one bar.'

'Come again?'

'It's circular. If I walk that way I walk into the saloon counter. Then the next bit becomes the ladies' counter. If you're standing in front of the bar it looks like I'm leaving, but I'm only stepping into the next bar.'

'And after the ladies'?'

'That's the gents.'

'Sorry?'

'After the ladies. You get the gents.'

'I meant after the ladies' bar'

'Sure and that's the door to the kitchen.'

'What about the snug?'

'It's over there.'

'Yes I know it's over there. How do you get from this bar to there?'

'We walk, sor.'

'I meant, if the bar is circular, how can it stretch around to the snug?|'

'Oh, no, sor, there's no bar in the snug. The snug's just for customers who wish to be private. If we had a bar in there it wouldn't be private.'

'So, anybody working behind the bar could move between the bars without anyone else realising. Apart from the snug.'

'Ah, well, the customers would see them.'

'Not if they were crouched down.'

'Ah, no, sor, but then I'd see them.'

'But what if it was you crouched down. Then nobody would see you.'

'Ah, sure, your honour, maybe thirty years ago, but now, my poor knees, they haven't crouched in many a year.'

'That's what you say. However we shall see. Right. We'll need an interview room. Two, in fact.'

'Sure and I'm afraid we don't have one of those, Inspector. We have bedrooms. I can let you have a single for forty-nine ninety-nine, or a double for just under a hundred. It's a special offer for the boys in blue, and the festive season, while it's cold.'

Samson looked at him.

'Are you trying to be funny, sir?'

'Sure, not at all, Inspector, those are our winter rates. Very reasonable they are too. This time of the year can be quite busy, what with people wanting to get away from the family like. You'd be surprised.'

'Mr Constantine, let me be quite plain about this. I am here to investigate a murder. I need a room for interviews.'

'Oh, you mean for, like interviewing – suspects?'

'Precisely. Suspects. And witnesses. And witnesses. And suspects.'
'And witnesses. Ah, now why didn't you say so, Captain. Sure, you can use me office. Just be careful if you would, I always like to keep it tidy.'
'That'll do for me. Do you have a single room for Constable Morton here?'
'Room number 1. It's on the ground floor. It's a single bed.'
'Good enough. First I want to see the person who discovered the body.'
'Ah, that will be Joe the Rescue.'
'Joe the Rescue?'
'He manages the lifeboat. There's another Joe we call Joe the Drunk. So we call Joe the Rescue Joe the Rescue so we know we don't mean Joe the Drunk.'
'Joe the Drunk.'
'He's teetotal.'
'He's teetotal.'
'He used to drink a lot, you see, sor.'
'He used to drink a lot.'
'But then so does Joe the Rescue.'
'Is he here?'
'Joe the Drunk?'
'No, Joe the Rescue.'
'Ah, no, he'll be drinking at the harbour office now. He's on duty, you see.'
'He's on duty.'
'Yes, but he should be in this evening. If he's not too drunk.'
'I'll speak to him later then. Does anyone know how he discovered the body.'
'Ah, yes, sor, he was after going to the gents.'
'Going to the gents.'
'Only he was a little drunk.'
'A little drunk.'
'A lot drunk, really.'
'Where is the gents?'

'Ah, just down the passage, sor, first on your left, just past the ladies', be careful of the urinals, they can flush unexpectedly.'

'I don't want to go to the gents, I want to know where it is. What was this Joe the Drunk doing on the first floor if he was going to the gents?'

'Joe the Rescue, sor. It's easy to get confused, they look very similar.'

'What was this Joe the Rescue doing on the first floor if he was going to the gents?'

'Ah, well, he wasn't going to the gents, sor, he was after going to the gents.'

'What?'

'Only he was a little drunk.'

'A little drunk.'

'A lot drunk, really. He thought he was at home.'

'He thought he was at home.'

'Yes, sor. You see, at his place the toilet is on the first floor, just next to the stairs.'

'So he went up the stairs to use the toilet and found the body.'

'Well, not quite, sor.'

'Not quite.'

'You see, sor, he thought the cupboard was where the toilet was. He didn't realise it was a body until he'd relieved himself. Which is when the body fell out. It was stuck before. So he said excuse me, put the man back in, and came downstairs again.'

'He relieved himself.'

'It was quite wet. His aim isn't very good when he's had a few.'

'Which is why the man's clothes are damp.'

'Could be, your honour, could be.'

'And then what happened.'

'He came down, sat on a stool, said there's a body in the loo upstairs, leaned on the bar counter and fell asleep.'

'And you went to check.'

'Aye, sor. We're used to his little ways. When he says something like that he's always got one part right. You just have to work out which part.'

'So what happened then?'

'I went upstairs, checked the room, opened the cupboard, and there he was. Dead. And wet.'

'And then you called the police.'

'Right away sor.'

'What time was this?'

'Closing time.'

'Which is?'

'Oh, sometime between eleven and twelve depending on whether there's anyone in.'

'Eleven and twelve.'

'Maybe a bit later.'

'A bit later.'

'Possibly half-twelve. Or one o'clock. Two at the latest.'

'You don't check the time?'

'Ah, well, time was always what you could call flexible in a pub. And when they relaxed opening hours, well, it became even more flexible.'

'What happened to Joe?'

'Which Joe?'

'The Joe who – who found the body.'

'Joe the Rescue.'

'Yes, that Joe.'

'Oh, he went home, sor. Like clockwork. He falls asleep for ten minutes, wakes up, and finds his way home. Like a homing pigeon he is. Sometimes he crawls out. We normally don't even notice him go.'

'And he's on duty now.'

'Yes, sor.'

'In charge of sea rescue.'

'Yes, sor. No-one else wanted the job. Poor lad.'

'Poor lad?'

'He gets seasick.'

'He gets seasick.'

'And carsick. I think that's why he drinks so much.'

'So he doesn't get seasick?'

'So he doesn't notice he's been seasick.'

'We'll need to interview him at the earliest.'

Samson turned to the assembled drinkers to find he was the sole focus of their fascinated attention.

'Right, listen up you lot. I want to see you one by one, alphabetically, in the office. Everyone who was in here last night at any time. The first one is to come through in five minutes time. Starting from the other end of the alphabet you go to room number one where Detective Constable Morton will be waiting for you. Spread the word to anyone in the other bars. And don't anyone try to slip away uninterviewed. Got that? Good, five minutes then.'

He strode down the passage towards the office. Morton looked after him. Then he looked at Patsy and Carry. Then at the customers looking back at him.

'Where's room number one?' he asked Patsy softly.

'After your Captain, end of the corridor. It's an add-on.'

'Right.' He looked at the expectant customers. 'Five minutes,' he said, and strode off.

How the hell did the old fool expect that lot to know what their alphabetical order was?

He opened the door to room number one. It was probably the smallest bedroom he had ever seen. There was a door marked 'Bathroom'. He opened it and walked in. It only opened a quarter of the way before stopping suddenly as it hit something, and he almost barked his shins against a toilet bowl while simultaneously catching a sink in his stomach. He stared at the unbelievably small room for a few seconds while nursing his midriff.

Then he squeezed in and very thoroughly washed his hands.

Sunday afternoon

'Okay,' said Sir Anthony Freechin, standing up, 'alphabetical order it is. A is first. That's me first.'

'Surely I'm before you,' said the vicar, 'Brayley comes before Freechin.'

'Anthony comes before Brayley, though, vicar.'

'But my first name is Allan.'

'As in an Allen key?'

'No, with an a.'

'Yes. I know, Allen starts with an A, what else could it start with?'

'An H.'

'What? How can Allen start with an H?'

'It could if it were Helen.'

'I don't want to complicate things unnecessarily,' interrupted Richard Coombes-Neeston, 'but Sir comes after Brayley.'

'Sir?'

'Sir Anthony Freechin.'

'Point. Never thought about that. Complicated things, titles. Did you know, there was this chap by the name of Dudley back in the time of the Tudors. John Dudley. Became Viscount Lisle, so they called him Lisle. Then they made him Earl of Warwick so he was called Warwick. Few years later he became Duke of Northumberland, so they executed him as Northumberland. Sort of thing a chap remembers. Never understood why.'

'Vicar comes after Sir.'

'Executed him.'

'Oh, yes, Bloody Mary, you know. Loads of people getting executed then. Protestants.'

'Bloody Mary? Would you like one? I think we've got the tomato juice around here somewhere.'

'This is ridiculous,' said Carry. 'Look, it doesn't matter what order you go in, just so long as everyone has a turn. He's not going to send you back because you're not in order, will he? How does he know who's supposed to be next, he hasn't got a list of our names, has he?'

'Actually, come to think of it, it's Xavier,' said Sir Anthony.

'Xavier?'

'My first name. Could never abide it. Called myself Anthony instead. That's my middle name. Well, my middle name is really Trevor. Xavier Anthony Trevor Cuthbert Henry. That's what they called me. Named after me uncles.'

'What if an A goes in after a B?'

'How do you mean?'

'Well, he interviews the B, not knowing there's an A waiting, then A comes in and he wants to know why B came before A.'

'See what you mean. Could be tricky, with that one. He'll definitely demand an explanation. He's that sort.'

'Oh, for God's sake, just tell him bloody B was in the loo and you didn't want to keep him waiting.'

'That's a good one.'

'I say, that's not right, it would be A in the loo.'

'Look, one of you go in to see the idiot. I'm going in to see the Detective Constable.'

'But you're not last, Carry. You're a C.'

'Okay, think of it this way: once I'm finished in there I'll be free to concentrate on serving you lot drinks without worrying about that nonsense. Which would you prefer?'

'Good point my girl. Got your head screwed on the right way. Priorities. Right, Carry in to the DC first, then Patsy, then whoever. I'll go in and see the DI.'

'More like i-d-i-o-t than DI.'

'Detective Idiot? It has a ring to it.'

'He's a CI, not a DI.'

'CI?'

'Chief Inspector.'

'I say, How will we know everyone has been?'

Carry looked around.

'Every time someone has finished I'll give them a straw. Blue for the idiot, red for the DC. Wear it in your button-hole and we'll know at a glance.'

'God, that girl's efficient.'
'Very pretty, too.'
'She is that.'
'Pity about the clothes.'

Morton sat on the end of the bed with his notebook in hand. He looked around, put down his notebook, stood up, and looked around again.
'Can't sit on a bed and do an interview,' he told himself. He looked around for a chair.
None.
He went to the top of the bed.
The central heating was on. The room was warm. Warmer than the public bar. He took his camel-hair overcoat off, folded it and lay it on the pillow. He sensed rather than saw the black part of the shirt with its gold embroidery. He went back to the bathroom. Holding the door half-open he looked behind it. There was a mirror. He studied his reflection looking back at him leaning around the bathroom door. Not too bad looking. Maybe a bit more solid than when he had been a constable on the beat. Only to be expected.
But.
The shirt.
He tried pulling his jacket collar across it.
No. It was still there.
There was no getting away from it. The only place to wear that shirt without seeming out of place was either in a fancy dress party or Texas or a fancy dress party in Texas.
Or Cape Town. He had seen someone dressed in full cowboy regalia in Cape Town once. Unfortunately he had been shot dead at the time. There was a knock on the door. He went back to the head of the bed.
'Come in,' he said, leaning against the wall nonchalantly. The door opened and Carry entered.
'Take a seat,' he said.
'Where?' she asked. He waved vaguely at the bed.
'You're asking me to sit on a bed while being interviewed? What's

next, you take down my particulars?'

'Ark at ee making jokes like.'

'Ah, that explains it. You're a local yokel.'

He sighed. He took his jacket off and threw it on top of the coat.

'Look, just sit down, okay?' He did so himself, next to the pillow. She sat down at the end of the bed.

'Could you pass me my notebook? Thanks. Now, first things first, what's your name?'

'What happened to your smartphone?'

'Eh?'

'You've been making notes in your smartphone. Now you're using a notebook.'

'Clever girl, well spotted. Well, some notes go in the notebook, and some go in the smartphone.'

'Because anyone can read the notebook, but your inspector doesn't know how to read the smartphone.'

'Very perceptive. I'm amazed.'

'I thought that when I first saw you. He's maized. Maized as a besom.'

'You know the talk. Very clever. Not bad for a Lunnun maid.'

'What makes you think I'm London made?'

'To get back to the matter in hand. If you could answer the question.'

'What question?'

'What is your name?'

'I'm not a name, I'm a number.'

'A number?'

'Number Five.'

'Number Five, eh? I hope you haven't been taking drugs or smoking anything strange.'

'What if I have?'

'Well, that would make you High Five.'

She paused.

'So now you're the one making jokes. Well, well. A pig with a sense of humour. How strange.'

'Oh, it's how I get most of my confessions. Five or six jokes like that and most people crack.'

'I'm not surprised.'

'So what is your name?'

'Fifi Trixibelle.'

'And where did you study sociology then, Fifi Trixibelle?'

'What makes you think I studied sociology?'

'Oh, a chip on both shoulders, calling the police pigs, generally thinking it's the 1960s, flower power versus Vietnam. Trying to take the piss out of me. A bit obvious, really.'

'For your information, Detective Constable Moron, I did not study sociology. It was Fine Arts. With law as a minor.'

Morton laughed.

'That's what the Inspector calls me when he's angry. Moron.'

'Has anyone told you what a shit you are?'

'Oh, yes, all my girlfriends have.'

'You have a girlfriend?'

'Well, sort of. She's available if I'm home and fancy some company. Nothing long-term. Tell the truth I'm looking for someone with a bit more commitment.'

'I don't believe you. You really are a loathsome shit of a chauvinist pig.'

'Terrible, isn't it? And you're such an attractive young woman. Right, let's get on with this. Your real name, if you don't mind, unless you want to be here all night. Not that I'd object, mind you. I'd love to spend more time with you. Serious time. Night time sounds even better.'

'Clarissa.'

'People call you Carry.'

'Sometimes.'

'Surname?'

She paused.

'Hope,' she admitted.

'Clarissa Hope. Telephone number?'

'What?'

'Your telephone number.'

'Are you seriously asking me for my telephone number?'

'A chap can but try.'

'Are you trying to chat me up?'

'Course not. Okay, a little. Anyway, I'm afraid I have a job to do so we'll have to be serious for a few minutes. Where were you last night between the hours of six and midnight?'

'Is that when he was murdered?'

'We don't know yet. It's a bit of a guess. We have to start somewhere.'

'I was doing bar work.'

'In the bar?'

'In the bars.'

'You didn't go down to the cellar at any time?'

'Quite a few times. The entrance is a hatch behind the public bar.'

'Can you get to the rest of the hotel from there?'

'Hostelry. No.'

'What about the ladies'?'

'Which ladies?'

'The ladies' loo? You did go at some time, I presume.'

'What do you think?'

'And can you get to the guest rooms from there? Up the stairs?'

'Yes. But I didn't.'

'How much did you know about the dead man?'

'Not a lot. He arrived before I started my shift. He stayed in his bedroom mostly. Patsy said he didn't want to be disturbed.'

'So you didn't see him?'

'He came down to take a telephone call. About eight. The phone behind the bar. The same one you used. He finished the call and stayed for a drink. I got the impression it was a bit of a celebratory drink.'

'Someone called the pub?'

'Yes.'

'There aren't any phones in the rooms?'

'They've been taken out. They never got used, just made the rooms look untidy. People normally have their own mobiles these days.'

'But there's no signal here.'

'They go up the hill.'

'They go up the hill.'

'They go up the hill.'

'Up the road called the Saxon Way?'

'Up the road called the Saxon Way.

'The Saxons never made it this far west.'

'I'm told it's an insult. Like the Welsh archers showing two fingers to the French. I think they might have made that up.'

'You really aren't from around these parts, are you?'

'Not originally.'

'What if it's raining?'

'What if it's raining when?'

'When they go up the hill.'

'They get wet.'

'They get wet.'

'Okay, so sometimes we give them an umbrella. At no extra cost. So long as they bring them back. Sometimes it doesn't rain and they forget.'

'But they could have a telephone in their rooms? Instead of going out in the rain and snow, up the hill?'

'They could. They could have an internet connection. But people are strange. They have this weird kind of a relationship with their mobile phones. In the summer they get up early and walk up the hill to check their emails before coming back down for breakfast. Same thing in the evening after dinner. During the day I guess they're out anyway.'

'But not locals, I guess?'

'No.'

'They don't walk up the hill?'

'They drive.'

'Do you know if the dead man had a mobile?'

'No.'

'No he didn't or no you don't know?'

'No I don't know.'

'Do people often phone the pub to talk to guests?'

'It's the first time I've heard of someone calling a guest on the bar phone.'

'Any other phones?'

'One in the office. Mrs Patsy has one upstairs.'

'The first time. How long have you worked here?'

'Just over six months.'

'Before here?'

'Does it matter?'

'I was wondering why an attractive young woman would choose to work in such a small place far from the madding crowd.'

'I have my reasons.'

'Which are?'

'Noyb.'

'Noyb?'

'None of your business. In fact I think they might be noyfb.'

'I can guess. Right. Going back to this caller. Male or female?'

'Male.'

'English?'

'Polish.'

'Polish? How do you know?'

'He said so. Apologised for his English, said he'd only arrived from Poland a week ago.'

'So, he didn't say he was Polish, just that he'd arrived from there a week ago?'

'If you want to be pedantic, yes.'

'I do, thanks. Did he speak to anyone else in the pub? The man upstairs.'

She hesitated.

'Nigel bumped against him the one time when he came for a refill.'

'The man upstairs came for a refill.'

'Nigel came for a refill.'

'Nigel?'

'Nigel Stokes. He's an artist.'

'An artist? My goodness.'

'Now who's being sarcastic?'

'What sort of artist?'

'He paints. Pictures, not walls. Oil on canvas mainly.'

'What sort of picture? Stripes? Circles? Nudes? Boiled eggs? What's that bloke, Dolly? Painted floppy watches?'

'He says he's Modern British Structural.'

'Ah, stripes and boxes with a hint of circles.'

'More Munch but darker.'

'Munch?'

'Edvard Munch. He painted The Scream.'

'He painted a scream?'

'The Scream.'

'How do you paint a scream?'

'Are you serious?'

'I'm not into art.'

'Obviously.'

'Has he ever asked to paint you in the nude?'

'What's that got to do with the murder?'

'Oh, nothing, I'm just interested.'

'Trunkie want a bun.'

'No, seriously. I'm genuinely interested.'

'Trying to get your rocks off, more like.'

'So what's the answer?'

'To what?'

'Has he ever painted you in the nude?'

'He says so. It's an interpretative work.'

'I wouldn't mind seeing that sometime.'

'It's hanging on a wall in this building.'

'Is it? Where?'

'I'll leave that up to you to find out.'

'I shall keep my eyes out for it. Getting back to the reason we're here. The chap upstairs. Did he have any kind of accent?'

'Everybody has a kind of accent.'

'Now who's a pedant. What accent did he have?'

'I couldn't say. He didn't say much.'

'Not even on the phone?'

'He took that at the end of the bar. I wasn't listening.'

'Nigel Stokes, artist. You say he collided with the man on the phone. Do you think that was deliberate?'

'He wasn't on the phone. He'd finished the call by then. I think Nigel saw him smiling at me when he handed the phone back. That sort of thing always gets him.'

'He gets upset because a man smiles at you? He's going to have a very busy life picking fights, then.'

'That's just Nigel, he's always doing that. Has a drink too many, thinks some bloke is trying to chat me up and tries to pick a fight with them. Fortunately nobody has taken him up on the offer yet. They'd probably thump him senseless.'

'You two are going out? You and this Nigel person.'

'Stokes. Not really. He can't afford me. Neither can I if it comes to that.'

'This chap didn't react when Nigel tried to pick a fight?'

'He apologised for being in the way. Sincerely. Difficult to carry on trying to pick a fight with someone who just apologises all the time.'

'Oh, I don't know. I've known people who can manage that quite easily.'

'You must have some strange friends.'

'I do. They weren't friends. He didn't speak to anyone else? Our friend upstairs?'

'No. Just sat there looking – happy with himself, I suppose. A bit like the cat that had stolen the cream.'

'Stolen the cream?'

'Yes. There's a cat-look after you give it cream, and there's a cat-look after it's stolen the cream you wouldn't give it. And there's the cat-look when it knows you'll never work out how it did it.'

'You think we'll never work out who did it?'

'I didn't say that, did I?'

Morton opened his mouth to ask another question, then closed it as they heard a shout coming from a room nearby:

'Every single one of us is concealing a terrible secret. What's
yours?'

'What the hell was that?'

'Sounded like your boss. Putting the thumb screws on someone.'

'He's not –' Morton paused, then shook his head to clear it. 'Never
mind. Where was I? Ah, yes. Tell me, do you have a mobile phone?'

'Of course.'

'How often do you check it?'

'Once a day, if I remember.'

'You're not that attached to it?'

'Not really.'

'Not desperately waiting a message from someone.'

'What do you reckon?'

'I reckon that sounds like a challenge.'

'Let me know when you find that picture. The nude one.'

'I might need to ask you some more questions later. In fact I'm
pretty sure of it.'

'I can give you the answers right now. The first word is fuck and the
second is off.'

'I like a challenge.'

'Was that shirt the result of a bet which you lost, or do you just
naturally have bad taste?'

Richard Coombes-Neeston reached out automatically to open the
door marked 'Office'. Underneath someone had once squeezed in
another sign: 'Staff Only'. He paused and knocked first.

'Enter.'

He entered to find Samson sitting behind a desk. It was bare of
anything apart from a computer which had been moved to one side,
and Samson's notebook in front of him. Behind him was a door
marked 'Kitchen'. It had exactly the same 'Staff Only' sign
squeezed beneath it as if there had once been a sale of them.

Samson gestured to the chair without looking up. Coombes-Neeston
sat down.

'Name?'

'Thank you.'

Samson waited. Coombes-Neeston waited.

'Your name. If you don't mind.'

'Oh, sorry, General.'

'General?'

'General, retired.'

'That's a rank.'

'Yes. General. Retired.'

Samson looked up.

'Are you deaf at all, sir?'

'No thanks.'

'I beg your pardon?'

'A pudding?'

Samson took a breath.

'Are – you – deaf – at – all – sir?'

'Oh. Yes. Just a little. Not much. More in the evenings, really. It's the cold weather.'

'I see. Let me speak a little louder then. What – is – your – name – General – Retired?'

'Oh. Neeston. Coombes-Neeston. It's double barrelled.'

'Coombes-Neeston. Double barrelled.' Samson wrote down, saying it out loud.

'Richard Coombes-Neeston. My friends call me Richard.'

'Friends call him Richard Coombes-Neeston, General, retired, double barrelled,' Samson wrote down, bawling the words. He looked up at Coombes-Neeston. Coombes-Neeston looked back with mild disinterest.

'So, Mr Coombes-Neeston General-retired,' Samson said slowly and loudly, 'at what time did you arrive here last night?'

'Six p.m. on the dot.'

'You drove here?'

'No, I walked. I have a limp.'

'I see. And that's why you normally walk, is it?'

'No, that's why I normally limp.'

'How did you come by the limp?'

'Old war wound.'

'Which war?'

'I can't tell you that, I'm afraid.'

'You can't tell me?'

'Classified information. We don't want the enemy to know.'

'I see. Did you know the victim?'

'I don't know.'

'You don't know?'

'I didn't see him. So I don't know if I know him. I can have a look if you want.'

'I'll arrange a viewing once the interviews are concluded.' Samson made a note. 'Did you at any time last night have occasion to go upstairs?'

'No.'

'Did you notice any foreign strangers come in at any time?'

'I didn't notice any strangers, local or foreign.'

'And what time did you leave?'

'Eleven twenty. I promised the memshahib I'd leave at eleven, but Penelope grabbed me to discuss the peonies for the spring parade.'

'The spring parade.'

'You can never start too early. Not if you want to get top prize. Not with peonies. Poppies, maybe, peonies, never.'

'And who is Penelope?'

'She's the person who does the peonies. For the spring parade. She's very particular.'

'I see. She was here last night?'

'Only in passing. She popped in and prattled on ten minutes or so. It was about eleven-ten we parted.'

'She didn't stop for a drink?'

'Oh, no, she doesn't partake. Practically never.'

'Peonie Penelope doesn't partake. Practically never,' Samson said as he wrote it down. He scanned his notes slowly, and then looked up.

'One last thing for the moment, General retired. Every single one of us is concealing a terrible secret. What's yours?'

'Sorry?'

Samson took a deep breath.

'Every single one of us is concealing a terrible secret,' he yelled. 'What's yours?'

'No need to shout, old boy, I'm not deaf you know.'

'You said you were.'

'Sorry?'

'So what's your answer?'

'My answer?'

'To the question.'

'What question?'

Samson took another deep breath.

'Every single one of us is concealing a terrible secret,' he yelled. 'What's yours?'

Coombes-Neeston stroked his chin and gazed into the distance.

'I once put the recycling bins out on the wrong day,' he said finally.

'You put the recycling bins out on the wrong day?'

'Deliberately.'

'Deliberately.'

'Indeed. I wanted to block off a parking space for a delivery van. The driveway was already chocca, you see.'

'The driveway was chocker?'

'Absolutely chocca.'

'That's a style of driveway? Chocker?'

'No. It was full. Stuffed to the rafters.'

'Your driveway has rafters?'

'What?'

'You said your driveway has rafters.'

'What? Rafters? I said – Yes, our driveway has rafters. Doesn't everyone's?'

'And what was it filled to the rafters with?'

'Eh? Cars, of course. Mother in law was visiting with her car. Son was back from Uni with his car. Daughter had left hers with us while she went on holiday to Australia. Mine was in the garage. So was the wife's. So I put the bins out to block off part of the road and pretended I'd got the date wrong. I was expecting a delivery of compost. For the peonies.'

Samson tapped his pen.

'I'll make a note of that,' he said, and made a note of it.

Once finished he read through the notes silently, his lips moving.

'That will be all for the moment, General, retired.'

Coombes-Neeston stood up with a limp.

'Just one more thing, General. We have reason to believe the victim wasn't from this part of the world.'

'Not from around here?'

'Not from anywhere near around here. From somewhere they don't have English as a native language.'

'Aaah. France.'

'Mmmm.' Samson made a gesture to suggest 'Further East.'

'Germany?'

'Mmmm.'

'Poland?'

'I couldn't say, General, retired. But keep it under your hat, we don't want everyone knowing. But if you hear of any Polish or other strangers in the area, keep it quiet and let us know. It could be significant.'

'I'll do that.'

Coombes-Neeston turned around towards the door.

'One more thing, General Neeston.'

'Coombes-Neeston.'

'You spoke of a memshahib. Who or what is this memshahib?'

'Oh. It's Indian. It means the little woman,' Coombes-Neeston told the door.

'Little Indian woman' Samson said, writing it down in his notebook. He tapped the notebook with his pen. 'Little Indian woman, eh. Interesting. I wonder where she comes in.'

Coombes-Neeston turned back to face Samson.

'You said something?'

'Okay, General that's enough for now. Tell the next person to come in. And don't forget, alphabetical order. I don't want to see any Yankees before Zulus.'

'Yankees before Zulus?'

'It's the phonetic alphabet.'

'I know, but don't Yankees always come before Zulus?'

'Not in my book, General Retired. And I intend to run this one by the book. My book. The whole way. My book. My rules. My plan.'

Richard Coombes-Neeston closed the door behind him. He rubbed his right ear to get the noise out, then the left. Carry came down the corridor from her interview with Morton.

'That man is a prize ass,' he said softly as they walked. 'But bloody hard work. I told him I was a retired general, and deaf. So he started yelling into my ear, and I had to pretend I could only just hear him.'

'I know. We heard.'

'Next thing I knew for some weird reason I was inventing things with the letter P in. Because his name doesn't have a P, I suppose. If anyone asks, there's someone called Penelope who looks after the peonies. For the spring parade.'

'What?'

'My feelings exactly. Trouble is the man is such an idiot you can't help but invent nonsense to see how far he'll fall for it.'

'No, you mean you can't help it.'

'We'll see what happens if you get a turn with him.'

Carry didn't reply.

'What's the DC like? Morton?'

'I'm not sure.'

'You're not sure?'

'Either he didn't know who painted The Scream or what it is, or he's deliberately pretending to be artistically illiterate.'

'Who did paint the scream?'

'Edvard Munch.'

'Isn't that a breakfast cereal?'

'And he thinks he's a smooth talker. And he has very clean hands.'

'Ah, one of those.'

'If he interviews you be careful of one thing.'

'What's that?'

'It's a very small room and a very loud shirt. My eyeballs are still hurting.'

'A bit like Nigel's paintings then.'

'Worse. Much, much worse.'

They came back into the public bar. The others looked up with question marks.

'We thought we heard someone shouting.'

'That was the chief idiot. I told him I was deaf. I think I am now.'

'We won't try that again, will we? said Carry. 'Who is next? Patsy, I think you'd better go and get it over with.'

'Good thinking my angel turtle dove. I'll go see the constable.'

'Be careful of him, he thinks he knows what he's doing. Whether he does or not I haven't worked out.'

'He does? I think I'll go see the other one then, the impresario.'

'You sure, Patsy? He's a bit of an obnoxious know-it-all. And stupid with it. I should know, I've just had him first hand.'

'Sure and when you've been pulling pints as long as I have, that's normal human behaviour. A man like that, all you have to do is humour him and call him Sir every so often. Like the Americans do.'

'I'd better go too,' said Vicar Brayley. 'I've got confessions at five. I suppose I'll have to risk the constable. I shall protect myself with the shield of truth.'

'A girdle of lies might be better, Vicar.'

'Good thing I've got confessions at five, then, I might need one myself.'

'Can you give yourself absolution?'

'I always have. I've never bothered to ask whether it's allowed. After all, chefs can cook their own food.'

Richard Coombes-Neeston resumed his seat on the stool at the bar as the other two left.

'Apparently the murdered chap is Polish,' he said. That idiot inspector told me not to tell anyone.'

'Have a blue straw.'

'What am I supposed to do with that?'

'Put it behind your ear.'

'Why?'

'So we know you've been.'

'I haven't been yet. I've only had one pint.'

'I meant your interview.'

'Oh.' He tapped the straw on the counter. 'You know, initially I thought it best to keep out of this. But I'm beginning to wonder if we shouldn't do something about it.'

'Do something about it?'

'Work out who done it. So we can get rid of that idiot and go back to normal.'

'There are two questions.'

'Two questions?'

'How do you know I didn't do it?'

'That's absurd, Carry.'

'And how do I know you didn't do it?'

'What absolute … you can't be serious.'

'Of course, it could have been Patsy. You have considered that, haven't you?'

'Patsy? You must be – Of course!'

'Of course? You think it was Patsy?'

'Of course not. But Patsy's wife, now that's a different story. If ever a woman could kill without a second thought it's Elvira.'

'You know her that well?'

'It was a long time ago.'

'Didn't Patsy once try to kill her?'

'That was an accident.'

'You sure? Or is that just what you heard?'

'Of course I'm – What do you mean?'

'Well, this is one of those times you really don't want to be dead right. Do you?'

'Take a seat,' Samson said to Patsy.

'That's very kind of you, Commissioner, thank-you.'

'Right, this guest of yours.'

'Yes.'

'He was foreign?'

'He was?'

'That's what I was asking you. I thought I heard someone say he was Polish.'

'He was Polish?'

'That's what I'm asking you.'

'If you say so, your eminence. I thought he had a bit of an accent. Not from these parts. Then again, neither am I.'

'If we could get back to your guest.'

'The Polish gentleman.'

'So he was Polish, then. When did he turn up?'

'Oh, ah, roughly around exactly seven minutes past four o'clock yesterday.'

'And he booked a room.'

'Oh, no. No, sir.

'He didn't book a room.'

'Oh, no, he'd already booked it.'

'He'd already booked it. I see. And when did he do that?'

'Ah, my goodness, I couldn't tell you.'

'You can't?'

'I'd have to look it up. It'll be on the records.'

'I see. Someone else took the booking?'

'The computer took the booking.'

'The computer took the booking?'

'Over the interweb. It's very good that way. Doesn't sleep, night or day. It's a most marvellous invention, your honour. I don't know how we'd manage without it.'

'Oh, I see, over the Internet, of course. I didn't expect you'd have such an up to date system.'

'Oh, to be sure, we refurbished top to bottom when we took over, top to bottom. All mod cons, no expense spared. Well, hardly any. We had to take the phones out in the end. Nobody used them and they got dusty. And one or two got stolen. You wouldn't believe what some people will steal from a hostelry, sir, you wouldn't believe it.'

'And when was that?'

'When was what? When was the phones stolen? Well, it was different times. Not on the same day, like.'

'When did you take over the pub?'

'Hostelry. It was, my goodness, it was, my goodness, to think of it, it must have been, well, now I come to think of it, nearly, no, it was, it was five years ago. Five years, one month and three days. You know, come to think of it, you know what?'

'No, what?'

'We haven't had a Polish gentleman murdered in here before.'

'You haven't?'

'Not in all the five years we've been here, and that's the honest god's truth.'

'What about other gentlemen? Or ladies?'

'Sorry, sir?'

'Have you had anyone else murdered here before, non-Polish people for example. A Turk or two? The occasional Australian?'

'Ah, sure, you're jesting now, your eminence, you had me going there, to be sure. It's a wonderful sense of humour you have there. Had anyone else murdered! What a suggestion. Of course not. You know what?'

'No, what?'

'We have never even had a fight in here, sir. Never. Not even Christmas when the married couples and families come out for a drink. Sure and the things I've seen in my time, uncles against nephews, brothers against brothers, mothers-in-laws and daughters-in-laws, fists flying, hair pulling, you wouldn't believe it. Wigs too. But not here.'

'No?'

'Well, not downstairs. The wife throws a frying pan at me every so often upstairs, but that doesn't count, I think. it's just her way.'

'No, I suppose it wouldn't. Back to this Polish gentleman. Presumably someone was on duty when he arrived?'

'Oh, yes, of course. Now let me see. I was in the public bar with Mary Anny.'

'Mary Anny?'

'She's French you see.'

'French.'

'But very nice. A very good girl, sir. She doesn't smile a lot, though. Reminds me of the wife, come to think of it.'

'Is she in at the moment?'

'The wife?'

'Mary Anny.'

'She'll be in later. When everybody's had a drink or two.'

'She only comes in when everyone's had a drink or two?'

'No, sir, she's on the late shift.'

'Okay. So what happened when the Polish gentleman arrived? What's his name, by the way?'

'Name?'

'The Polish gentleman. I presume you took down his name.'

'Oh, no, we never do that.'

'You don't?'

'No, dear me, that would be a waste of time.'

'It would? You don't bother taking people's details? Why is that? Because they're likely to give you a false name?'

'Sure and I wouldn't know about that. I don't know if they could. You see, their details is already on the computer. Along with their credit card details. The computer checks those. It's very clever that way. Sometimes I think it's almost human. But German human, you know. You wouldn't get an Irish computer acting like that, dear me, no. It would want a chat first, you know.'

'Right. Of course. Yes. Now, Mr Constantine, can you tell me what the Polish gentleman's name is? Or was?'

'Ah, sure, no.'

'No?'

'I don't remember it. It's always been that way. Ever since we got the computer. I can never remember these things. I don't have to. It's on the computer, you see. If I need to find out, I ask Mary Anny to look it up.'

'So when you greeted him, when he walked in, you didn't know his name?'

'Ah, sure, I knew his name then, to be sure. I knew his name when I took him upstairs. I knew his name when I showed him around the room and told him about the fire escape and such. But I'd forgotten it by the time I came downstairs again. Sure and it's terrible. You know, sir, once upon a time I'd remember a guest's name for ages. If I met them after years I'd immediately say, Ah, sure, Mr Smith, now how are you, haven't seen you for donkey's years. Ah, Mrs Jones, how's the husband, does he still have the wooden leg? Now I have that Internet memory. But, don't worry, it'll be there on the computer still. So long as it hasn't got a virus and lost its memory. Or being chopped up.'

'Chopped up?'

'You know, when they attack it with an axe. Chop chop chop. That sort of thing.'

'You mean hacked?'

'That's the one. Hacked. It's terrible what these youngsters get up to these days. Hack it to pieces.'

'Has it been hacked before?'

'Oh, no, never. We paid for anti-chopping software. I insisted.'

'I see. So we can get all the details from the computer.'

'Sure we can, sure we can.'

'Good.'

'When Mary Anny gets here.'

'Let me guess. Mary Anny is the only one who knows how to work the computer?'

'She's the only one who knows how the computer works.'

'And when she isn't here?'

'What?'

'When she isn't here?'

'Well, then she isn't here.'

'What happens when she isn't here?'

'She's somewhere else?'

'Yes, but how do you manage guests and so forth. With their details on the computer.'

'Oh, I see. Well, your honour, it's like this, you see. Thuthan also knows how the computer works.'

'Thuthan.'

'Yeth. I mean, yes. So if she's around she gives a hand. She's very good that way. Wonderful little girl. Very talented. She dances the Ghillie Callum, you know.'

'And if she isn't?'

'If she isn't dancing?'

'Around. To work the computer.'

'Ah. Well, Mary Anny's very good. She leaves me print-outs.'

'Print-outs.'

'Print-outs. On paper, like.'

'I'll need a look at those for the last week or so. Now, going back to yesterday. Did your Polish guest have any luggage?'

'Luggage? But of course. How could you stay overnight without any luggage? But sure and it was only a little thing, a day-bag or whatever they call them these days. But then they hold an awful lot, don't they. They expand like. And it was quite a large small bag.'

'And he took it up with him?'

'But of course. What else would he do with it? He had it with him as I showed him the way up the stairs.'

'So you showed the Polish gentleman to his room. Then what?'

'Then what ... what?'

'What happened after you showed the Polish gentleman to his room?'

'I came downstairs.'

'Yes?'

'Yes.'

'And?'

'And ...'

'And .... I stayed downstairs?'

'Yes, but what did you do? What did he do?'

'Well, I carried on with me work, to be sure. I don't know what he did in his room. We don't have cameras in the rooms, you know. Someone did suggest it once, but as a joke, what the butler saw, they said. My goodness, no, we'd never be doing that.'

'Why not?'

'Why not what?'

'Why wouldn't you have cameras in the rooms?'

'Would you?'

'Yes. We have cameras in our cells. Saves a lot of time when prisoners claim they've been beaten up.'

'You beat prisoners up?'

'Not in the cells. We have cameras there.'

'Ah. I've never had a guest complain that they've been beaten up.'

'You might want to try it.'

'Beat guests up?'

'No, put cameras in the bedrooms. If you'd have had one in the Polish man's room this case would have been closed by now.'

'Sure and I'd never thought of it that way.'

'And you'd know who stole the telephones.'

'Sure and we would now, wouldn't we. Now there's a thought. But we'd have to put cameras in the rooms and then put the telephones back. And they're awful for collecting dust they are. Sir.'

'You don't have cameras in the passageways?'

'We don't have cameras anywhere but the front. That's to deter burglars.'

'Burglars come through the front?'

'No, we have cameras there.'

'We'll need to see the tapes.'

'I shall tell Mary Anny as soon as she gets in.'

'Back to last night: did you see the vic after you'd come downstairs?'

'Vic?'

'The Polish man.'

'His name was Vic?'

'It's short for victim. Did you see him after you'd come downstairs?'

'Now, who would name their child Victim, however short he was? Sure and that's asking for trouble. But then it probably means something different in Polish.'

'Did you see him again after you came downstairs?'

No, I didn't see him again before he was ... before he ... whatever happened.'

'You're absolutely certain?'

'Absolutely. Not a word of a lie. I'd swear on the grave of my late, beloved –'

'Every single one of us is concealing a terrible secret. Tell me, Mr Constantine, what's yours?'

'Sorry?'

'I said, every single one of us is concealing a terrible secret. Tell me, Mr Constantine, what's yours?'

'I thought that was what you said.'

'Well?'

'To be sure, I don't think –'

'I don't think Mr Constantine. I know. What's yours?'

'What's my what?'

'The terrible secret you're concealing.'

'Well ...'

'Yes?'

'You see, it happened a long time ago ...'

'Yes?'

'My wife accused me of sleeping with one of the barmaids.'

'And?'

'I didn't do it.'

'You didn't do what?'

'Sleep with one of the barmaids.'

'You slept with all of them?'

'No, sure, I didn't sleep with any of them. That's God's honest truth.'

'And? That's it?'

'Well ... she came at me with a frying pan, you see. She likes frying pans. She collects them. I think most of them have a dent or two these days, so we couldn't resell them.'

'And?'

'And I was standing in front of the bannister, you see, next to the stairs. We had a bannister at that pub. And some stairs. To the second floor.'

'And?'

'And I stepped aside, out of the way, like.'

'And?'

'She went flying over the bannister.'

'Oh, god.'

'Indeed, sor. She's been in a wheel-chair ever since.'

'You tried to kill your wife.'

'No, sor, she tried to kill me.'

'A likely story. Very well, Mr Constantine, that will be all for the moment. We'll probably need to speak to you again, later.'

Patsy stood up and turned towards the door.

'Just one more thing, Mr Constantine.'

Patsy turned back towards Samson.

'Sor?'

'Tell me, was the pub always known as the Angel and Duck?'

'Sure and it wasn't. Before we took over it was the King's Arms. But what with me being Irish, well, I couldn't run a pub called the King's Arms, now could I?'

'You couldn't?'

'Not unless it was King James, and that would be silly. And anyway, we wanted a pub that people could say, sure and why don't we go down to the Lion for a pint, or wherever, which they never did.'

'Well, they wouldn't. Not if it was called the King's Arms.'

'Sorry, sor?'

'If it was called the King's Arms they would say why don't we go down to the King's Arms for a pint. They wouldn't say why don't we go down to the Lion.'

'Well, exactly, your honour. They weren't saying that. It doesn't trip off the tongue. So we decided to call it the Angel. Because of the factory that makes Angel cakes. And then people would say, why don't we pop into the Angel for a pint after work, or on a Saturday or Sunday, when the weather's good or the football's on.'

'But you called it the Angel and Duck.'

'Ah, yes, your honour, well, you see, that was the wife, you see.'

'The wife?'

'Yes, sor. She did the paperwork. I didn't notice until the sign went up.'

'And she called it the Angel and Duck.'

'Yes, sor.'

'Why?'

'She likes ducks.'

'She likes ducks?'

'She likes ducks.'

'So why didn't she call it the Ducks and Angel? Or the Ducks and Angels? Or just Ducks? Or The Duck?'

Patsy stood for a few seconds.

'Sure, and I'd never thought of it like that before. I suppose most of the paperwork was already done.'

'Very well Mr Constantine. You can go now. Send in the next person. In alphabetical order. I don't want to see any Romeos before Charlies.'

'I don't think we have any Romeos. Sir.'

'Just send the next person in please Mr Constantine.'

'No Charlies either.'

'The next person, Mr Constantine, whatever their name is.'

'It wouldn't work, you know.'

'What?'

'Calling it the Ducks. I just can't see people saying, Why don't we go to the Ducks for a pint.'

'Well of course you wouldn't.'

'Precisely, sor.'

'I meant you wouldn't see people saying Let's go to the Ducks for a pint. You'd hear them.'

'Ah, no, your honour, that's the whole point. I wouldn't hear them.'

'The next person, Mr Constantine. Now.'

'Take a seat,' Morton said to Vicar Brayley. 'Anywhere on the bed will do.'

'On the bed?'

'Yes, on the bed.'

'I don't think I should. I mean, the church is very open on such things these days, well, some of the church, but I think the Bible is reasonably clear on that point.'

'What point is that?'

'Two men sharing a bed.'

'Well, we aren't sharing a bed in that sense.'

'Ah, but you can't be too careful. It's like shellfish.'

'Shellfish?'

'You can get seriously ill eating them. That's why the Bible forbids it.'

'The Bible forbids it?'

'Leviticus. Anything in the seas and rivers not having scales shall be an abomination. I mean, the language is a little strong, but the point does come through.'

'What about swimmers?'

'Sorry?'

'Swimmers. People swimming in the sea or a river. In swimming costumes, that sort of thing. They don't have scales.'

'My goodness. You're right. I hadn't thought about that. But I'm pretty sure you aren't supposed to eat them either.'

'Not even the ones in bikinis?'

'Sorry?'

'Never mind. If you could just take a seat. Pretend I'm a WPC. Is that allowed?'

'WPC?'

'Woman Police Constable.'

'Just a minute, there's a stool in the bathroom.'

'There is? How did you know?'

Vicar Brayley opened the door marked Bathroom. He bent around the door and fished out a low, three-legged stool.

'Ah. That sort of a stool.'

'Patsy always has a stool in every bathroom,' he said, putting it down. 'People always need to sit down in a bathroom for some or other reason. I've never quite understood why. I think it might have something to do with women and makeup.' He sat down on it and beamed up at Morton.

'You call that a bathroom.'

'It says Bathroom on the door.'

'So it does. I must remember that. Right, Father, a couple of questions about last night.'

'Vicar.'

'Sorry?'

'I prefer the term Vicar. Father sounds too – Catholic. There's so few differences between us, I like to keep the ones we do have.'

'Okay, Vicar, then, Vicar. Tell me, do you know the victim's religion?'

'Well, no, not definitely, but Polish – they're all Catholic, aren't they?'

'You think the victim is Polish? Did you speak to him?'

'I thought he was Polish? No, I didn't speak to him.'

'What makes you think he was Polish?'

'Someone else said he was Polish. Didn't they?'

'Ah, interesting. I haven't interviewed everyone. No doubt it will come out in due course. So, you didn't speak to him. Did you see him?'

'No, I got here about eight o'clock, I understand he'd retired to his room by then.'

'Did you see anyone acting suspiciously?'

'Suspiciously? In what way?'

'In a suspicious manner.'

'Such as?'

'Trying not to be seen. Acting in a furtive manner. Concealing something. Not meeting your eyes. Shifty. That sort of thing.'

'No, not that I recall. In fact I often find people quite the opposite in a pub. Especially after a few drinks. They tend to look deep into your eyes and tell you their life story. Especially if you're wearing a dog collar, as I am.'

'Do you always look people directly in the eyes? All the time?'

'Of course. I am a man of the cloth. Caesar's wife and all that.'

'Caesar's wife?'

'It's an allusion.'

'I suppose most religion is.'

'What?'

'An illusion.'

'Exactly. Allusions and parables and that sort of thing. Religion by its nature will always use metaphor.'

'Right. Did you see anyone going up the stairs?'

'Not that I recall. But then I never do notice such things. Oh, forgive me, I think I've just lied.'

'Lied?'

'I did see someone going up the stairs.'

'Who?'

'Joe the Rescue. I remember now, I thought it was odd that he should be going up the stairs.'

'Yes, well, I think we know why he was going up the stairs.'

'You do? Why?'

'He was going to – it doesn't matter.'

'Doesn't it? What a pity. It's the only thing I remember. Well, out of the ordinary, anyway. I mean, obviously I hadn't drunk so much I couldn't remember anything, that would never do. I do have certain standards I –'

'Don't people find it disconcerting?'

'My drinking too much?'

'Staring into peoples' eyes like that.'

'Oh, no, they expect it.'

'I see. Very well, Father, that will be all. Send the next person in.'

'Vicar.'

'Yes, send the next vicar in. I mean, the next witness, Vicar.'

'You sure that's all?'

'Quite sure, Father.'

'Vicar. Do you mind if I ask you a question?'

'Go ahead.'

'Were you going to a fancy dress party when you got the call to come here?'

'Fancy dress?'

'Your shirt. Or is that the way you normally dress?'

'Ah, fancy dress. Yes, fancy dress. Now you come to mention it, yes, yes I was. Yes, I should be off duty, but, you know, they needed someone with the relevant seniority and experience. At short notice.'

'Such a pity, such a pity. I'm sure you would have won. Was your partner dressed as a squaw?'

'Won?'

'The fancy dress competition.'

'Oh, yes. No. I mean, I was going alone. I mean my partner couldn't make it. Shift work. At the hospital.'

'Of course. I'm always amazed at how dedicated you all are, the extra time and devotion you're all willing to put into what is really a sense of public duty. I'll let you get on now.'

'Thank you, Father, very kind.'

'Vicar.'

Vicar Brayley had just got back to the others in the public bar when Patsy returned, mopping his brow.

'I think I'll have a little Scotch,' Patsy said. 'For medicinal purposes.'

'That bad, eh?' asked Sir Anthony.

'One of God's special children, as we say,' agreed Patsy, taking a large Scotch from Carry. 'But God's special children don't normally become police inspectors.'

'Chief Inspector. I'm sure he's very proud of being a chief.'

'The constable seemed a nice enough fellow,' remarked Vicar Brayley. 'Quite well educated, I thought. But I think he might be Catholic. Kept calling me Father.'

'Kept asking me what terrible secret I'm hiding,' Patsy said. 'The high commissioner, that is.'

'He tried that with me,' Richard Coombes-Neeston said. 'I told him I once blocked off the pavement for a delivery of manure, something like that.'

'Any good?'

'What?'

'The manure?'

'Oh, it wasn't a true story, I just made it up on the fly.'

'Shouldn't have flies, good manure. Is my name up? Are we on the S's yet? Or the X's.'

'Do you feel up to Inspector Idiot, Sir Anthony?'

'Chief Inspector Idiot.'

'What are the options?'

'Well, we'll have to start sending the girls through soon, and I'd rather not have them inflicted with his interview methods.'

'Good point, good point, don't want the little ladies to have to put up with that sort of nonsense. I'll go through and see him now. Give him a part of my mind.' He stood up. 'Right, full speed ahead. Er, what do I tell him?'

'You were in here last night, you saw nothing, heard nothing.'

'Course I heard things and saw things. Not deaf and blind you know.'

'I am. Officially. Deaf, that is. Now, anyway.'

'What I mean is ... if he asks, just tell him exactly what you saw and heard. Don't invent anything. Just the plain, unvarnished truth.'

'Oh, and he'll suddenly ask you another question just as you think it's over and you're about to leave. Just when you're least expecting it.'

'Gotcha. Remind me, where is he, now?'

'Straight down the corridor, in the office.'

'And here's a red straw for you, Vicar. And a blue one for you, Patsy.'

'I'll go and see which of the little ladies wants to go face the Moron chap.'

'Hasn't he got a P in his name?'

'No, a T. It's the Chief who hasn't a P.'

'I've just realised. The constable is a cowboy and his boss is a chief.'

'Right, ladies, the constable's waiting. Who wants to be first?'

'I'll go,' said Bertie, 'he looks like a sweet boy and I don't think I

really want to be questioned by the inspector. I hear he's quite rude.'
'In that case I think I'll wait for the inspector,' Phillipa Mountjohn said, 'I could do with being rude to someone. And I can out-rude any person on this planet.'
'As I know from experience.'
'What was that, Richard?'
'Nothing, Philly, just thinking out loud.'
'And I know exactly how you think, Richard. Like a corkscrew, only more twisted.'
'I never thought I'd ever feel sympathy for the idiot.'
'What was that, Richard?'
'Oh, nothing. Where's Margaret?'
'In the ladies.'
'Ah, I'd better go too. To the gents, I mean. I mean, see you later.'

'Name?'
'Anthony Freechin. Sir Anthony.'
'I see.'
'Look, I promised I'd tell you the truth, so here it is. Xavier Anthony Trevor Cuthbert Henry.'
'Xavier Anthony Trevor Cuthbert Henry.'
'Yes. Couldn't stand Xavier, so I use Anthony instead.'
'You couldn't stand Xavier?'
'What I just said.'
'Why couldn't you stand Xavier?'
'Sounds poncy. Like I should be wearing silk shirts with ruffles and quoting poetry. Like that chap who died in Greece.'
'Someone died in Greece?'
'Eh? I would imagine loads of people have died in Greece. Same as any country. Can't live forever, you know. Take the Ancient Greeks. Pretty sure they're all dead. Didn't a lot of them die fighting the Persians? Sure I read that somewhere. At school. We did ancient Greek stuff, you know. And Latin. Can't remember any of it, mind. Wasn't there something about Amos?'
'But this Xavier, specifically, died in Greece.'

'What? No, I was talking about that poet. Keats or Yeats or Freaks or whatever.'

'So who is Xavier?'

'I'm Xavier. I told you. Xavier Anthony Trevor Cuthbert Henry'

'Xavier is actually your real first name. Not someone you dislike.'

'Exactly. Given name. I didn't want it. So I took Anthony.'

'And your full names are Xavier Anthony Trevor Cuthbert Henry.'

Samson wrote down Xavier Anthony Trevor Cuthbert Henry.

'As it happens I prefer Anthony anyway.'

'Of course. Well, thank you for giving me the time, Sir Anthony. I realise this must be quite stressful for someone in your position.'

'Must do one's duty. Ask me anything, I'll be as honest as I can.'

'Very helpful, Sir Anthony, very helpful. Obviously nothing we say in here will go any further unless absolutely necessary.'

'That's just it. Wife mustn't find out.'

'Your wife mustn't find out?'

'She thinks I was at a Legion dinner last night. Ghastly things. People keep talking about how much fun it was in uniform. Camping under the stars together. Marching everywhere. Parades through city centres. Complete nonsense, you know. It's mainly sleeping in the mud next to people you know too well who smell after a few days. Much rather be sitting in front of a warm fire with a glass of brandy. With friends. You know. Here. Lovely pub. Patsy's a fine landlord. And Carry is a lovely girl. And the others. Mustn't forget them. All lovely girls. Thuthan, too. Very bright little thing. Dances with swords, you know.'

'I fully agree, Sir Anthony. I'd much far rather be sitting in front of a blazing log fire in my own local at the moment. With a glass of Scotch, in my case.'

'You would?'

'Who wouldn't?'

'The wife, for a start.'

'Well, yes, of course, that is a little complication. Fortunately I don't have that problem, but I do sympathise, Sir Anthony, there's absolutely no need to get your wife involved. Tell me, were you in front of the fire the whole evening?'

'Went to the loo a couple of times. Does that count?'

'Of course not.'

'Happens as you get older.'

'It does?'

'Oh, yes. Very much so.'

'What does?'

'What?'

'What happens as you get older?'

'Oh. Oh, that. Yes. Going to the loo.'

'Yes, so I hear. Tell me, did you see the – the man involved?'

'Polish chap? Don't think so. Don't talk to strangers much. Ignore them. If they come a second time, or a third time, maybe, but strangers? No, never. Life's too short. I'm sure they're fine chaps, nothing against them, but, really, they are strangers after all. What the word means.'

'I couldn't agree more, Sir Anthony. Well, that's pretty much all I need to know. I'll let you get back to that log fire and brandy.'

'What?'

'I said you've been very helpful, and we'll try not to trouble you again, Sir Anthony.'

'What? You're not going to ask me what terrible secret I'm concealing?'

'My goodness, are you concealing a terrible secret, Sir Anthony? Worse than telling Lady Freechin little fibs?'

'Well, I don't know whether I should tell you this, Samson, but you seem like a man of the world.'

'Very kind of you to say sir, Sir Anthony. And if you're unsure as to whether or not to tell me something, have a think on it first, and then tell me later if you want to. But probably best not. I might have to write it down.'

'No, no, get it out now, out in the open, man to man, no mucking around. You see, truth is, truth is, we had a few games of poker last night.'

'Poker?'

'Yes. Poker. For money. Know it's illegal, but some things are. There you go.'

'I'm afraid I went deaf there for a while, Sir Anthony, I missed what you said. However, speaking in a purely theoretical sense, if a few friends happen to play poker for money in their local pub, well, as the Chief Constable told me, we have far more important things to worry about. So long as the game doesn't become shoot-out at Dry Gulch City, if you see what I mean. This other chap, he wasn't playing with you, was he?'

'The other chap? Oh, you mean – the Polish chap? Goodness, no, wouldn't ask a stranger to play, wouldn't even think of it. Specially not a foreigner. Card sharps, you know. Can't trust 'em. Don't understand good old English ways.'

'Well, there you go, no harm done. We don't need to mention it again. Call it Bridge in future, no one will know the difference.'

'Bridge? God, no, that's what the little women play. Could never stand it. I mean, love em to bits and all that, but they don't half go on. Apart from Carry. She's a lovely girl. Makes me wish I was thirty years younger. But then I wouldn't have met the wife.'

'Of course, Sir Anthony. You've been very helpful.'

'Just one thing, Inspector.'

'Yes?'

'Where is this Dry Gulch place?'

'Dry Gulch? Oh, it's from the movies. American ones. With cowboys. Where they end up in a shoot-out.'

'They always end up with a shoot-out in Dry Gulch?'

'I think it became something of a stereotype.'

'Ah, you mean a metaphor.'

'I'm sure I do, Sir Anthony.'

Sir Anthony stood up, turned to the door, put his hand on the handle and stopped. He stood there for a few seconds. Then he turned around again.

'Well?'

'Sorry, Sir Anthony?'

'Well, aren't you suddenly going to ask me another question just as I think it's all over?'

'You think I should?'

'I thought you did.'

'What sort of question?'

'Something penetrating. And unexpected.'

'I'm not sure I know something unexpected and penetrating to ask you, Sir Anthony.'

'Don't you? Are you sure? I'm sure you must. I know you police chappies, sharp as razors. Go on, then, ask me anything.'

'Anything? Okay. Um, do you know where your wife was last night?'

'Ha! Knew it. Knew you'd ask the killer question. No.'

'No?'

'I presumed she was at home. But maybe she wasn't. Clever. Very clever. That was a very clever question. I wonder where the old girl really was.'

'Thank you, Sir Anthony. Could you send the next person in, please.'

'Well, that wasn't that bad. Quite a decent chap that Samson. Sharp as they come, mind.'

'Sharp? You sure you went into the right room, Sir Anthony?'

'Of course I went into the right room. It said "Office" on the door.'

Patsy looked around before leaning forward confidentially.

'Apparently that Polish man's name is Vic. That chief commissioner let it slip.'

'Vic? I say, that doesn't sound Polish.'

'Probably Viktor.'

'No, I don't think it was that.'

'Viktor? You know, that sounds Russian. Can't be that, surely. The Poles hate the Russians.'

'Yes, but they must share some words, they're neighbours after all. Like us and the French. We say savoir faire and they say le weekend.'

'We do? Don't think I ever said savoir faire.'

'Viktor ... Viktor from Poland ... Has a certain sound to it, that.'
'William the Conqueror. He was French.'
'He was Norman.'
'Norman? I thought his name was William.'
'Norman the conqueror?'
'Very English, that.'
'What?'
'William.'
'It's actually Guillaume.'
'Isn't that next to silly mid on?'
'Where?'
'Gi-ong.'
'Mort.'
'Mort? That was on the television, wasn't it. Inspector Mort.'
'It's French for dead. Like the Polish bloke.'
'Oh, I say, poor chap. Victor Mort. No wonder he died young.'
'Apparently he was short. That's why they named him Vic. That's what the Inspector told me.'
'Well, if he was a baby when they named him – well, babies are hardly tall, are they?'
'Is that a Polish thing? Naming people because of their size?'
'I think that's more Red Indian.'
'You mean Native American.'
'Yes, what I just said. Red Indian.'
'Oh? I thought that was dogs. Two dogs fighting. That sort of thing.'
'True story. Back in the days of the Wild West. These twins were born, so they look out the tent flap when the first comes out, you know, they name it after the first thing they see, like blazing sun or swooping eagle or dark cloud, that sort of thing.'
'What if it's raining?'
'So anyway, this first twin, they look out and there's these two dogs, well, you know, doing what dogs do.'
'Going to the toilet?'
'No, Vicar, you know, being very friendly.'
'Sniffing?'

'No, no. A boy dog and a girl dog. You know. Doing you know what.'

'Oh.'

'So the first twin gets named after that. Then the second comes through and they look out the flap and name it after the first thing they see. Know what that was?'

'I couldn't guess.'

'Bucket of water being thrown. True story. Chap in the army told me. Years ago.'

'My goodness.'

'Know something else?'

'Well, Sir Anthony, I'm sure –'

'All this talk about water. I've just remembered. I need the loo. Be back shortly.'

'Ah, to be sure, Vicar, now there's one man who definitely could never have done it.'

'Done what, Patsy?'

'You know. The Polish chap.'

'Vic?'

'That's the man.'

'What about him?'

'I was saying Sir Anthony couldn't have done for him.'

'Done for him? Like a batman?'

'No. You know. Terminated him. Permanently.'

'Terminated?'

'Ended his sojourn in this vale of tears.'

'I'm sorry, you've lost me.'

'Killed the mother, Vicar. I mean the Pole. I was saying Sir Anthony would be the last one you'd think of who could have done the thing.'

'I'm sure none of us could have. Done the thing, as you call it.'

'Well, Vicar, you know –'

'It would be very un-Christian to think otherwise.'

'You mean it wasn't a Christian that did him? That's interesting. I think you may have a point there, Vicar.'

'Do you normally interview suspects in a bedroom, Detective Constable?'

'No, not normally, Miss Berenson.'

'Mrs. Call me Bertie, everyone calls me Bertie.'

'I'd love to, but I'm afraid it would be against the law.'

'Would it?'

'We're not allowed to become too friendly with witnesses. In case we influence them. It looks bad when it comes to trial.'

'Am I a witness?'

'Well, that depends on whether you saw anything –'

'You mean I'm not a suspect?'

'Would you like to be a suspect?'

'Ooh, yes, I've never been a suspect before. Go on, call me a suspect.'

'Very well, Miss Berenson, you're a suspect. Now –'

'Mrs. Call me Bertie, everyone calls me Bertie.'

'Right. Now –'

'And what do people call you?'

'Eh? Er, Detective Constable, or Constable Morton. Now –'

'Oh, go on, you must have a first name. What does your girlfriend call you?'

'Long distance.'

'Long – oh, I see, that was a joke. My goodness. that is a very old joke, do they have long distance calls any more? What is your first name? I think Reginald would suit you. I knew a Reginald once. He was such a nice boy. But he died in the war.'

'Did he? Which war was that?'

'Well, he didn't, of course. But people think because I look old I must have been in the war. World War Two, that is. And it sounds better than saying he went to South America and died in a bolas accident, doesn't it? Just under the ribs, it was. A few inches lower and he would have lost his –'

'I don't know. I've never thought about an accident with a bolas. Anyway, –'

'So what is your real name then? I can see Carry fancies you. She doesn't show it, but she never does. I think she's been through le grande amour tragique. She's pining.'

'You think so?'

'Ooh, yes, I can tell. So what is your name?'

'If you must know, it's Luke.'

'Luke? That's American. I remember that, Cool Hand Luke. Are you Cool Hand Luke? It's a man thing, I think. Cool Hand. I wouldn't like to go out with someone with cool hands. I'd shiver. Especially if he put his hands down my –'

'Well, not quite. Actually my mother named me Luke after the author of the Gospel. You know, Matthew, Mark, Luke, and John.'

'Ooh, of course, my goodness, I'd completely forgotten about them. My goodness, yes, and to think I could quote them off-hand when I was a girl. Salome and that other one who had what's-his-name's head chopped off. The one with the seventeen veils. Strange how some things lose their importance over the years. You know, I don't think I've been to church for years. Apart from Christmas Eve service. One likes to do one's bit. And it's such a cheerful occasion, not at all like Easter. And there's egg-nog. I do like egg-nog. And most other people don't, so I get seconds. And thirds. On a good night I can get quite tipsy.'

'Did you see the gentleman who was here last night?'

'The one that got – done?'

'Yes.'

'No.'

'Not at all?'

'No, I hear he was in the public bar. We always go to the ladies' bar. Though it isn't really the ladies' bar any more, is it? Not like it used to be. Back in the days when it was the Ladies.'

'Isn't it?'

'Oh, no, anyone can go in there. And ladies can go into any of the other bars. Though they aren't really Ladies, after all. I must say I find it difficult to get used to. Do you know, during the summer we get all sorts of tourists, Germans and Swedes and Swiss and Australians and so on. Quite a few young girls, mostly in pairs, but some on their own. And they sit anywhere. Without a qualm. In those very short shorts. I mean, they look very pretty, and I'm sure there's nothing wrong with it, but, my goodness, we would never have done anything like that in my day. Daisy dukes I think they call them. Why, I don't know.'

'Are you sure about that ... Bertie?

'About the gentleman?'

'About the shorts.'

'Oh, well, you know I must confess, I did have a pair of tennis shorts which were a little short, at least shorter than when they left the shop, we knew how to alter clothes ourselves in those days. My mother was very disapproving, but she let me get away with them, so long as I only wore them to tennis parties. We had a lot of tennis parties in those days. Especially at Christmas time. We didn't play much tennis, though. Other games with balls.'

'So you never saw him?'

'The foreign gentleman? No, not at all. And Americans, too, of course.'

'Americans?'

'Tourists. Quite a few Americans come over. They're a funny lot. I mean, I'm sure they mean well, but they're so terribly loud and full of energy.'

'What about Poles?'

'You know, that's strange. I don't think I've ever seen a Pole. What do they look like?'

'Foreign, Miss Berenson. Well, thank you for that, you've been a great help.'

'Have I?'

'Oh, yes. You've helped us in a process of elimination.'

'They have lovely legs, it has to be said.'

'The Poles?'

'The girls. Tourists. I was also quite proud of my legs when I was that age, you know. But we never showed it. Well, you wouldn't, would you?'

'I'm sure you were, Bertie. Could you ask the next legs to pop in. I mean the next person.'

'You're thinking of Carry, I can tell.'

'I assure you I'm not, Mrs Berenson.'

'Liar. I can tell. You become ever so pompous and try to hide it.'

'Pompous?'

'Where on earth did you get that shirt? Did you do the embroidery yourself?'

'If you could ask the next person to come in, that would be most helpful, Mrs Berenson.'

'Bertie. Tell me, Luke, that inspector of yours. Is he as stupid as they say he is?'

'I try not to speak ill of the afflicted, Bertie.'

'So he is?'

'Well, I would never say so myself, but a colleague did say recently, and if you'll excuse the language, he couldn't find his backside with a Satnav on a sunny day'

'Oooh. Oh, that's quite funny. Shouldn't it have an elbow in it?'

'An elbow?'

'Isn't there a saying about arses and elbows?'

'You may well be right, Mrs Berenson. Now, if you could ask the next person to step in, that would be most helpful.'

'Bertie.'

'Bertie.'

Bertie sat down opposite Philly, bright-eyed.

'Isn't it exciting! That nice detective constable told me I'm a suspect. I've never been a suspect before.'

'I can't imagine why. After all the times you've almost been caught shoplifting. Has Sir Anthony finished with that idiot yet?'

'I think I saw him hurrying to the gents. Why don't you speak to the young constable. His name's Luke, by the way.'

'Luke? Who the hell calls their son Luke in this day and age? Apart from the Americans. He's not American, is he?'

'No, I don't think so. It's after the bible, you know. Matthew, Mark, John and – who was the other one?'

'Luke.'

'That's the one.'

'Here comes Sir Anthony now. Right, I'm off to see the Detective Inspector.'

'Chief Inspector.'

'By the time I'm finished with him he'll be chief something. And he won't like it.'

'Can I come watch?'

'Don't be silly, Bertie. Tell you what, I'll give you a blow-by-blow description when I'm finished.'

'Pity.'

'I've brought you another sherry, Bertie,' Carry said. 'Oh, and a red straw.'

'A straw? I never drink sherry through a straw. Well, not very often, apart from Christmas.'

'It's to wear. So that we know who's been interviewed. And by whom.'

'Ooh, that is a clever idea.'

'And, Sir Anthony, here's a blue straw for you.'

'A blue straw? Ah, yes, of course. Have to wear the straw. Must say, though, that Samson chap isn't that bad. Very agreeable, in fact.'

'Agreeable? Sir Anthony, are you sure you went into the right room? I heard he was quite awful.'

'Absolutely. Told him we played poker last night and he said he'd gone deaf. Very decent of him. Right, must get on, my brandy is getting cold.'

'He told a policeman you'd been playing poker last night. I don't believe it.'

'Well, we don't play for very high stakes, Carry dear. And we only join in after we've finished our bridge rubbers.'

'I saw at least a thousand pounds on that table last night. That is, I didn't see at least a thousand pounds on a table last night.'

'That was after we joined in.'

'If the licensing lot hear about it Patsy could lose his.'

'Ooh, no dear, they wouldn't do that, Patsy's such a nice man.'

'You keep thinking the good thoughts, Bertie. The way things are going we're going to need them.'

'I've just realised, my dear. Philly's gone to see the Chief Inspector. What about the constable?'

'Time Nigel stepped up to the plate and did something for king, pub and country.'

'I think he fancies you.'

'Who? The detective constable?'

'And dear Nigel. Both of them. You're a lucky girl.'

'Is that what it's called these days.'

'You don't think Nigel did it, do you? You know, that never crossed my mind. But that's what Philly said. If I don't suspect someone then it must be them. She's very good at that sort of thinking.'

'Right, Bertie. Just one thing. Whatever you do, never suspect Philly.'

'Oh, I never would. Really, Carry, what an idea.'

'Your name, please.'

'Phillipa Mountjohn. Miss.'

'Miss Phillipa Mountjohn,' Samson wrote down carefully, his tongue sticking out. He looked up.

'You were in here last night?'

'If I wasn't I wouldn't be here talking to you, would I?'

'You'd be amazed at what some people will do. I've seen it all. I'm told there's a technical word for it. Wanting to be involved. Something to do with psychology. A lack of motherly attention when potty training or something. Did you see the man who was killed?'

'The one who was murdered?'

'Who else?'

'I don't know. Was anyone else killed last night?'

'We haven't found anyone else as yet.'

'You think there might be another one?'

'No.'

'But you don't know.'

'No.'

'You don't know who the murderer is.'

'No.'

'You don't know very much, do you?'

'No.'

'Aren't you going to ask me any questions?'

'Yes.'

'Well?'

'Did you see the man who was killed?'

'No.'

'Did you go upstairs at any time yesterday evening?'

'No.'

'Did you see anyone else go upstairs yesterday evening?'

'You can't see the stairs from where I was sitting.'

'Answer the question please, Mrs Mountjohn.'

'Miss. No, Inspector, I didn't see anyone go up the stairs which I couldn't see from where I was sitting.'

'Did you at any stage go to the ladies' during the evening?'

'I beg your pardon?'

'Did you go to the loo at any time while you were here last night?'

'Of course I went to the loo.'

'Could you see the stairs from anywhere on your way to the loo?'

'Okay, clever clogs, yes I could. And, no, I didn't see anyone going up the stairs carrying a knife or any other weapon.'

'Did you see anyone going up the stairs without a weapon?'

'No, I did not see anyone going up the stairs. Apart from Patsy the one time.'

'You saw Patsy go upstairs last night?'

'No, it was a week ago. He does live upstairs, you know. With his wife.'

'You're quite sure about that.'

'About Patsy living upstairs?'

'About not seeing anyone go up the stairs last night.'

'Quite sure.'

'Tell me, Mrs Mountjohn, every single one of us is concealing a terrible secret. What's yours?'

'I beg your pardon?'

'Every single one of us is concealing a terrible secret. What's yours?'

'I am most certainly not concealing a secret, terrible or otherwise.'

'Very well, Mrs Mountjohn. You're free to go.'

'Miss. I am most certainly free to go whatever you might think.'

'For the moment.'

'For the moment? For the moment? Inspector, you have an over-inflated opinion of your powers.'

'And you have an over-inflated opinion of yourself, Mrs Mountjohn. You despise people like me but you need people like me to deal with the gutter-life in society. We clean the sewers of rats so that you can lead your little miserable middle class lives in peace.'

'Miss. How dare you. I can have you fired you know.'

'You can't fire the rat-catcher. Not unless you want to live with the rats.'

'What?'

'Do you know the Chief Constable, Mrs Mountjohn?'

'No I do not. Miss.'

'Neither do I. Good day.'

'What?'

'I said good day, Mrs Mountjohn.'

'Well, precisely. Miss.'

'Close the door on your way out.'

'Well. Really.'

'Goodbye, Mrs Mountjohn.'

'Well. Miss.'

'There's a good little girl. Off you go.'

'Take a seat. On the stool, or the bed.'

'I think I prefer to stand.'

'As you wish. This won't take long. First, your name please.'

'Stokes. Nigel Stokes.'

'Ah, so you're Nigel Stokes.'

'And what's that supposed to mean?'

'Mean? Nothing. I asked someone who had painted the painting over the fireplace in the main pub, and they said Nigel Stokes. I take it you're the Nigel Stokes in question?'

'Was that Carry?'

'You mean Miss Hope? You know, I can't remember. It just came up in conversation, while I was asking some routine questions. Can you tell me what time you entered the pub last night?'

'Entered the pub? I don't know. About eight, I suppose. I'd been doing some work in my studio. I tend to lose track of time when I'm working. You can't create to a stopwatch.'

'About eight,' Morton wrote down. 'What is the title of that painting over the fireplace?'

'Sorry?'

'The painting over the fireplace. In the public bar. It has a title?'

'Which one?'

'The big one.'

'Oh, yes. It's called Diana in the Wild.'

'Diana?'

'Ancient Roman mythology. She was a huntress.'

'A huntress.'

'Amongst other things. She was also a symbol of the underworld, goddess of the moon, and childbirth. She was often represented by a Y.'

'Why?'

'Yes. A Y.'

'No, I mean why was she represented by a Y?'

'Oh. It's a fork in the road. Mainly in the forest. She looked after travellers on the road. The fork also represents the pathway to the underworld.'

'She stopped people from descending into the underworld?'

'No, I think she just made their final journey more pleasant.'

'Is she a good god?'

'What?'

'This Diana of yours. Is she a good god? Benevolent. Friendly to humans. That sort of thing.'

'I don't think any of the Roman gods were good in that sort of way. People used to worship them in the hope they'd leave them alone rather than anything else. They had quite fierce tempers, you know. The story goes that Actaeon was out hunting when he came across her bathing by mistake.'

'Who?'

'Diana.'

'Diana was bathing by mistake?'

'No, no, she was bathing and he came across her by accident.'

'Sorry. Was it a lucky accident?'

'Lucky? In revenge she turned him into a deer, and his own hunting dogs tore him to pieces.'

'What, just for getting a look at her in the nude?'

'Like I say, Roman gods are known for being touchy.'

'Is she naked?'

'What?'

'In your painting. Is it a nude representation of Diana?'

'Oh, no, no, there's that towel covering her. The semi-triangular representation.'

'Ah, of course, I was thinking of a different picture. I haven't had the time to give it the attention it needs. Hopefully later.'

'There are my other paintings. The one on the main staircase is Nude Ascending.'

'What time did you end up leaving last night?'

'What?'

'Last night. What time did you leave the pub?'

'Leave? Ah. Well, I'm not entirely sure. I'd been working really hard, and I don't normally keep track of time, you see. You can't, as an artist. It interferes with the creative spirit.'

'The stopwatch again.'

'Exactly.'

"Too pissed to remember," Morton wrote down.

'Nude ascending. Who is the nude?'

'Sorry?'

'You said the painting on the main staircase was nude ascending. I was wondering who the nude was. The sitter. Did you hire someone, or was it a friend?'

'Oh, it isn't a nude.'

'It's not a nude.'

'Oh, no, no, that isn't how art works these days.'

'It isn't?'

'My goodness, no. Hasn't been for years.'

'So what does Nude Ascending refer to?'

'It's a homage to Duchamp. He painted Nude Descending a Staircase. I took that and reversed it, so it's Nude Ascending.'

'We used to do those at school when we were kids.'

'What?'

'Homages. Where you stick loads of things together on a piece of paper. Then you take it home and your mum sticks it on the fridge.'

'I think you mean montages.'

'Nude Ascending a Staircase.'

'Sorry?'

'Your painting on the staircase.'

'Oh, no, no. Just Nude Ascending.'

'To heaven?'

Nigel Stoke blinked.

'Exactly. Yes. Could be to heaven. Why not. Could be up the staircase. Could be somewhere else. Maybe a pear tree. Why not? That's what liberates my work. There is no definitive is.'

"No definitive is" wrote Morton, and added, "Fruitcake."

'Did you come into contact with the murder victim at any stage in the evening?'

'I bumped into him accidentally when I was going to the loo once. I tripped on the carpet.'

"Really pissed!" wrote Morton.

'How did he react?'

'Oh, fine. I don't think he really noticed. He was quite drunk. He even apologised, even though it was really my fault.'

'He was drunk?'

'Oh, yes, quite sloshed. But happy sloshed, you know. As if all was well in his little world.'

'Interesting. Did anyone notice?'

'Notice?'

'You bumping into him?'

'No, no, I don't think so. Well, yes, Carry was behind the bar, she looked up. But I'm pretty sure no-one else noticed. They weren't paying him any attention. It's that sort of place. If you just want a quiet drink people leave you alone.'

"Blind drunk" wrote Morton.

'Any other pictures?'

'Sorry?'

'Are there any other paintings of yours hanging around?'

'Oh, yes, here and there.'

'I mean, in the pub.'

'Yes, yes, in the pub. In some of the guest rooms. You know.'

'What did he say to you?'

'What?'

'When he apologised for you bumping into him. What did he say?'

'Sorry.'

'What did he say when he apologised to you?'

'I told you. Sorry.'

'Sorry?'

'That's what he said – sorry. Sorry, my friend. Something like that.'

'Did he have an accent?'

'His voice was slurred. I can't really say. I thought he sounded Spanish.'

'I see. Apart from that, did you have any contact with him?'

'No. No, he'd gone up to bed when I came back. At least I presumed that was where he'd gone. He wasn't there, at any rate.'

'He wasn't where?'

'Sitting at the bar.'

'Was Carry still on the bar? She hadn't gone to bed?'

'No. No, Carry's a night owl. I don't think she goes to bed before two or three in the morning. I mean, I know she doesn't go to bed before two or three in the morning most nights. Sometimes I think she doesn't go to bed at all. I mean, some nights she doesn't go to sleep at all.'

'How do you know?'

'Well, you know.'

'No, I don't know.'

'Let's just say I know her very well.'

'I see. Are any of the other paintings of nudes? Or any paintings of other nudes?'

'Sorry?'

'The other paintings in the other rooms. Are any of them nudes?'

'There is one direct nude, and one or two indirect nudes.'

'Direct nude?'

'Made directly from a nude model or the imagination of a nude model. An indirect nude embodies the concept of nudeness but not the physicality.'

'Where is it?'

'What?'

'The nude you painted of a real nude.'

'You mean the direct nude?'

'That's the badger.'

'Well, it was in the public bar, but they moved it when I finished Diana in the Wild. I don't know where they moved it to.'

'Is it easy to recognise?'

'Oh, yes, I'd recognise it anywhere.'

'No, I meant, say a normal – I meant for the average member of the public.'

Nigel Stoke scratched his jaw.

'I think so. Well – it's difficult to say, really. Thing is, you have to know what you're looking at. An untrained observer might not realise a painting is of a nude. There are signs and symbols that you have to be aware of. You have to be able to experience the work in depth.'

'Like having aesthetic 3D glasses in your mind.'

'Aesthetic. Yes. Yes, that's one way of putting it. 3D glasses in the mind. That's rather good. I might paint that.'

'Right, well, thank you for your time, Mr Stokes, that will be all for the moment. I might need to clarify some points later, but probably not.'

'That's it?'

'Yes. No. One more thing. This Nude Descending a Staircase. By this bloke Doochump. Is that a nude?'

'Oh, yes, definitely.'

'I'll have to have a look at it sometime. Are you sure it's a nude?'

'Oh, yes. No-one in the art world disputes that.'

'Do people still worship her?'

'Who? Carry?'

'No, Diana.'

'Oh, oh yes, she has a cult following.'

'A cult following.'

'Yes. If you know the right people to talk to. And they trust you.'

'And they trust you.'

'Yes. They trust me. I'm an artist. I'm in touch with that side.'

'The feminine side.'

'No, no. The underworld side. The dark side. The rebellious side. The non-conformist side. For artists there are no rules.'

'Do you play football at all?'

'Certainly not.'

'Thought not.'

'What?'

'Nothing. Oh, just one more thing, have you ever painted a scream?'

'Ice cream? No, I haven't. I don't know anyone who has. Most still lives are apples and pears, that sort of thing.'

'So there isn't a famous painting of a scream?'

'I'm pretty sure there isn't. I studied Fine Art for three years and I've never heard of anything like that.'

'I see. I thought that might be the case. Thank you Mr Smokes, you've been a great help.'

'Stokes.'

'That's the one. Could you ask the next person in.'

'That Man,' said Phillipa Mountjohn as she came up to the group at the bar.

'Yes?'

'That Man.'

'Yes, Philly? What about that man?'

'That Man. Just, That Man.'

'Oh, I see. You mean, That Man.'

'Precisely. I need a drink.'

'Objectionable?'

'Good word, that.'

'Extremely objectionable. I need a stiff drink.'

'Rude.'

'Yes, not bad, rude.'

'Overbearing, stuffed windbag of a pompous, know-it-all, jumped-up little tradesman's boy. I need a stiff double followed by another stiff double.'

'Wow.'

'And probably a socialist. Definitely a socialist.'

'Oh, I say, Philly, isn't that pushing it a bit?'

'Socialist? I thought we'd got rid of that type when Blair got in. That's what he was there for.'

'He is certainly no gentleman.'

'Ooh, now that hurts.'

'Working class … working class … working class wanker.'

'Oh dear. That bad.'

'I didn't know you knew such words, Philly.'

'Have a blue straw, Philly. Nigel, you've survived. How was the little constable?'

'Not bad, actually. He was very interested in my paintings.'

'He was very interested in your paintings. Why do you suppose that is?'

'Well, I suppose some police officers do have an artistic side. I mean, I don't think he's an artist, but I think he could appreciate art if he worked at it. You can tell by the way he dresses. He's unconventional.'

'Oh, I wouldn't be surprised if he was an artist. Just not the sort of artist you're thinking about.'

'Sorry?'

'He didn't happen to show an interest in your directs and indirects, did he?'

'He did, as it happens.'

'More the directs than the indirects.'

'Sorry?'

'Beer?'

'Yes, please.'

'Nude Angel Rising?'

'We mentioned that. You know, I might do some work later. I was feeling really drained this morning. I had a really good stint of work yesterday, got quite a bit of work done. It takes it out of you, you know. But I think I've recovered. In fact I've got an idea about a still life. It's unique.'

'Have a red straw, Nigel. Wear it with pride.'

'Sorry?'

'Remind me, which colour is the idiot?'

'Someone had better go in to see the constable.'

'Thend Thuthan in. He deserves it.'

'That's a good one. Very funny.'

'Who's joking?'

'Carry, is there something about the constable you need to tell us?'

Morton looked up as the bedroom door opened. Then he looked down again to find Thuthan closing it behind her. She jumped on the bed and sat looking at him with her legs tucked underneath her. He looked at her hands and around her for any boxes.

'And what can I do for you, Thuthan?'

'Mummy thaid you had to interrogate me.'

'And why would we do that?'

'Becauthe I was here latht night. When the man wath done in.'

'You were? What time was that?'

'I got here at five. Mummy got here at theven. We left at clothing time.'

'You were here for two hours on your own? And you stayed until closing time?'

'I wathn't on my own, there were other people here. And we had to leave at clothing time becauthe they weren't having a lock-in.'

'They weren't having a lock-in. Do they often have a lock-in?'

'I'm not telling you.'

'Don't you have a bed time?'

'Yeth. Of courthe.'

'And when is that?'

'When I go to bed, thilly. Otherwithe it would be breakfatht time or bath time or thomething. Don't you go to bed at bedtime?'

'Okay, okay. Tell me then, what other people were here when you arrived?'

'Patthy and Anne-Marie and Claritha and Thir Anthony. And thome other cuthtomers.'

'Anyone you recognised?'

'Yeth.'

'Which ones?'

'All of them. They're all localth. We only have thtrangerth in the thummer. Or when thomeone getth killed.'

'I see. And what did you do until your mother arrived?'

'Thith and that. I'm whittling a rattle for my baby brother. Tho I did thome of that. And I did thome homework on the computer.'

'You have a computer?'

'It belongth to the Duck. But Anne-Marie letth me uthe it.'

'Right. And what homework did you do on it?'

'Thith and that. I altho looked up dretheth.'

'Dresses?'

'For danthing.'

'Ah, I see. Find any nice ones?'

'Yeth. And thordth. Tharp oneth.'

'Tharp thordth? I mean, sharp swords?'

'Yeth. Really, really tharp thordth.'

134

'Why?'

'Aren't you going to athk me about the murder?'

'Do you know anything about it?'

'No. But I'm not telling.'

'Eh?'

'I thaid, no. But I'm not telling. Are you deaf or thomething?'

'Shouldn't that be, yes, but I'm not telling?'

'No.'

'Okay. Well, if you don't know anything about it, I guess I don't have any more questions.'

'Okay.'

'Just one thing, though. What's with the fascination for swords?'

'It'th one of my hobbieth.'

'Dancing?'

'Scottith and Gaelic danthing.'

'With swords?'

'Thometimeth. It cutth down the competithon.'

'I suppose it would. Very well, thank you, Thuthan.'

'My pleathure. Thall I thend the nexth perthon in?'

'Not just yet, Thuthan. I need to have a word with the Inspector first.'

'Okay.'

Morton watched her close the door behind her. He couldn't help but wonder whether Thuthan had herself decided to come in, or whether someone had encouraged her. Either was likely. Whichever it was, there was decidedly something wrong with people who let a little girl wander around with razor-sharp swords to dance on. And comments like "it cuts down the competition" could only have come from an adult and been subtly dropped into the girl's subconscious. If Thuthan had thought that one up on her own … Then she was a lot weirder than weird. It was undoubtedly true that there was something seriously wrong with the people around this place.

Maybe it was inbreeding.

Except half the people seemed to have come from elsewhere.

He put his jacket on, put his notebook in the side pocket, picked up his coat, opened the door, and walked down to the office. Unfortunately, even if your superior officer is a complete idiot, sometimes you do have to speak to them.

'Name?'

'Coombes-Neeston, Margaret Coombes-Neeston. My friends call me Marge. Well, most of them. My real friends, that is. Some insist on Margaret, but I always think that's just putting on airs and graces don't you think? My mother and father always called me Marge. Some girls at school said it was after margarine, but it was that kind of school. Girls can be rather nasty to each other at times. Oh, dear, I'm waffling. Do you need to know that? I'm sorry, I've never been interviewed by a police officer before. I mean, Constable Clueless did ask me about my tyres once, in the High Street. But that isn't quite the same, is it? It's not a hanging offence, is it? Oh, I shouldn't have said that, they don't hang people any more, do they? Not these days.'

'Were they okay?'

'Sorry? Was who okay? The girls at school? Well, they were – girls. You know. Girls. Girls of that age always are.'

'Your tyres?'

'My tyres?'

'When Constable Clueless asked you about them. Were they okay?'

'Oh. Oh, yes, yes, of course. Richard arranges a service every year. He's very good like that.'

'Yes, I thought he sounded very efficient when I spoke to him. Ex-army, I understand.'

'Oh, my goodness, years ago, absolutely years ago, I mean he hasn't killed anyone since then. Not that he did then, of course, but, um, I mean – well, he never talked about it much, it's not the sort of thing a husband and wife would, would they? Killing people. After all, it wasn't really killing people, it was his job. Someone has to do it.'

'You mean he wasn't likely to have killed the vic last night?'

'Well, I'm sure he's never met Vic. Why would he want to kill the poor man? And even if he wanted to, he wouldn't do it. I mean, it's against the law, isn't it? And we've always been very law-abiding people.'

'Well, you know what they say, every single one of us is concealing a terrible secret.'

'Do they? A terrible secret? Everyone? What's yours?'

'I'm a police officer, Mrs Coombes-Neeston. We aren't allowed to have any terrible concealed secrets.'

'Well, then, surely the saying should be every single one of us is concealing a terrible secret apart from police officers who aren't allowed to have one.'

'It's a bit of a mouthful, don't you think?'

'Is it? I suppose you're right. I've never been into that sort of thing much. They did ask me whether I'd write a monthly article for the parish magazine once, but it's not as easy as you think. I mean, there's the grammar and all that. You can get someone in to do that, of course, but if you forget to mention certain people, they can get quite annoyed. And of course if the WI have a function and you don't include that, well, you never hear the end of it, they don't speak to you for months, sometimes.'

'So you don't think your husband is concealing a terrible secret.'

'Certainly not. My husband is a very upright man, Inspector. He doesn't conceal secrets, not even from me.'

'Well, that's what you'd expect in a General.'

'I suppose in an ideal world it's what you'd expect in general, but we don't live in an ideal world, do we? I think I'm getting flustered.'

'I don't know, Mrs Coombes-Neeston. What do you think?'

'About what? Getting flustered? I don't normally get flustered. Is it hot in here?'

'No, living in an ideal world. Do people still have principles, for example'

'Some of us do.'

'You do, of course.'

'I'll have you know that I come from a long line of staunch Anglicans, Inspector. We do have certain principles and we do not think. Oh, sorry, did that sound a bit offensive? Or do I mean aggressive? I don't mean to be. I'm not normally.'

'You were at the service this morning?'

'The service?'

'The church service. At the church.'

'No, why would I want to attend the service this morning?'

'No reason. Back to last night, Mrs Coombes-Neeston. Could you give me a brief summary of where you were and what you did?'

'We arrived at seven as we normally do. We played bridge until eleven. And then we went home to bed. That's all we did.'

'Your husband was with you the whole time?'

'The four of us were together the whole time.'

'Four?'

'Bertie, Philly, Richard and myself. The four of us. Together.'

'You always play with your husband?'

'Of course. Who else would I play with? He is my husband, after all.'

'Who normally wins?'

'Who normally wins what?'

'The bridge games.'

'Oh. Oh, it's luck of the draw, really. It pretty much evens out. Though Richard is a very good bidder. You have to bid for the game. Some people bid for themselves, you know.'

'Nobody else plays?'

'Plays?'

'Bridge. I mean anybody else in the pub. Any of the regulars.'

'Oh, very rarely. Occasionally in the summer there might be some tourists who also play and fit in, but not often, not often, no.'

'How long have the four of you played?'

'Not that long. We didn't realise Bertie and Philly played bridge until recently. Well, Richard knew Philly did, many years ago. They go back a long time. But you lose contact, don't you? I mean, I think back on all the girls I knew at school, and those who went to university together, Then there were the clubs, tennis and so on. Golf. And then, well, I don't know, we just kind of drifted apart, I suppose. We used to live in Hampshire, you know. Before my husband retired.'

'You don't play professionally? County level?'

'Play? I've never played golf. Well, apart from once, which I didn't enjoy. It's not really a woman's game, you know. You keep having to interrupt things to hit the ball.'

'Bridge.'

'Bridge? What bridge? Where?'

'The game. You don't play professionally?'

'Oh, no, we're very much social players.'

'I'm sure you could play competitively if you wanted, Mrs Coombes-Neeston. What is the saying? About hiding your light under a bushel?'

'Oh, no, I'm sure I couldn't. But it is very nice of you to say so, Chief Inspector.'

'Just one or two other things, Mrs Coombes-Neeston. You were playing in the ladies' bar?'

'Of course. We always play there. It's much quieter.'

'You couldn't see the stairs to upstairs?'

'No, I don't think so.'

'You never go upstairs?'

'I've never had occasion to.'

'Well, Mrs Coombes-Neeston, you've been very helpful. I might have to ask you some more questions later, but probably not.'

'That's it?'

'For the moment.'

'Oh.'

'Was there something else?'

'Well, I thought there'd be more of a – well, more of an interrogation.'

'There isn't much to interrogate about an evening of bridge. Is there?'

'Oh. But what if I were lying?'

'Were you?'

'Well, no, of course not. But don't you want to see the score sheets?'

'What would they tell me, Mrs Coombes-Neeston?'

'Well, I don't know. They could be a clue.'

'In what way?'

'Well – I don't know. I read a story about that. Something about the way people bid. How they played their cards. I can't remember how it went, but apparently it was tremendously important.'

'Do you still have them?'

'The cards?'

'The score sheets.'

'No, we leave them behind and they get thrown away. I would imagine they're probably in the rubbish now.'

'Well, I don't think it's worth getting my suit dirty in the vain hope that they'd provide a clue.'

'I suppose not.'

'That's a very attractive frock you're wearing, by the way.'

'Oh? Do you think so? It's Sunday. I do like to make an effort on a Sunday.'

'If only others would try as hard it would be a much better world. Now, if you wouldn't mind – don't ask the next person in, I need to have a word with the constable first.'

'Oh.'

'If you wouldn't mind, Mrs Coombes-Neeston.'

'Sorry? Oh, of course. It's from Selfridges, you know.'

'What is?'

'The frock.'

'Of course, I should have guessed that. There's a certain style to it you can't find anywhere else. Very feminine.'

'How very kind of you to say so.'

'My pleasure, Mrs Coombes-Neeston.'

'At least you noticed it. Most men don't. Richard is … Richard is better than most, but expect him to notice a new frock, well, I'm afraid you'd be waiting a long time.'

'It's a lovely frock, Mrs Coombes-Neeston. Now, I'm afraid I need to get on with the case.'

'Oh, of course, I am sorry, what am I thinking about? I'll let you get on.'

Morton blinked at Mrs Coombes-Neeston as she came out of the office, patting her hair, smiling, a faraway look in her eyes. He slipped in and closed the door behind him. Samson had his feet on the desk and was staring up at the ceiling.

'I thought maybe we should review things before going further, sir. It's getting late. It's already dark out there.'

'Does that in winter.'

Morton tried to adjust to that statement.

'None of the ones I've interviewed saw or heard anything. I think maybe we should –'

'None of mine either. Some time or other we're going to have to get hold of the person who found the body. Joe the Bottle.'

'Joe the Rescue. Well, yes, that was what I was thinking.'

'Until then ...'

'Yes, sir?'

Samson swung his feet of the desk and glared at Morton.

'Morton, we're going to have to stay here overnight to protect the evidence.'

'What evidence?'

'I don't know. I haven't found it. But I know it's here somewhere. I can feel it. Have you brought an over-night bag?'

'No, I wasn't expecting to need one.'

'Not?'

'Do you have an over-night bag, sir?'

'Of course. Always carry one. You never know how long the job's going to be. It's called dedication, Morton, if you haven't got it you shouldn't be in the job. You'll have to call your trouble and tell her you won't be back for a day or two.'

'Call my – what?'

'Your trouble. Your missus. Your wife. Trouble and strife, man, don't they teach you anything down here?'

'Ah.'

'Just a second.'

Samson picked up the telephone on the desk and dialled a number.

'Mr ... Constantine? This is Chief Inspector Samson. We'll be staying the night. I need a room for myself and one for Constable Morton.'

'Yes, Chief Inspector Samson. I'm in your office, remember?'

'No, not admiral. And we'll need dinner at some stage.'

'Yes, Mr ... Constantine, Samson without a P. Chief Inspector. In your office. I interviewed you less than an hour ago.'

'Yes, in your office.'

'Yes, one room for me, one room for Constable Morton.'

'No, as in bedroom. As in sleeping. Overnight. Not to interrogate suspects.'

'Yes.'

'Dinner, yes.'

'Book it via the Internet? And where would we find a computer to do that then?'

'In your office? Thank you, Mr ... Constantine, I'll leave that up to you to do.'

He replaced the receiver.

'Do you think he's as stupid as he sounds, or is it a big act?'

Morton tried not to think of the ramifications of the chief inspector being able to class someone else as stupid.

'Seemed genuine enough to me.'

Samson grunted. Then he stood up.

'Let's slip out so they don't see us. There's a town along the road, we'll take a drive down before the shops close. You can pick up some overnight things. Come on. You can tell me all about your susses as we drive.'

Susses, thought Morton as he followed the other man. Only Samson would call suspects susses and think it meant anything to anyone else. He probably caught it off some badly made movie shown only in the early hours of the morning to encourage viewers to go to bed.

And only Samson would drive the Studebaker as if he were a nineteen year-old in California, one elbow on the open window, gloved fingers nonchalantly resting on the top of the window, the other casually holding the white steering wheel. It was fucking freezing.

'Ye'll tek the high road
and I'll tek the low road
and I'll be in Scotland afore ye,' Samson sung, off-key.

'Recognise that?'

'Er, no sir.'

'Not? Thought you'd be full of Scottish living down here. What with you all being Celtish like. Don't you all wear kilts? Anyway, enough of that, come on, lad, spit it out. What did your lot say?'

Morton took out his notebook and smoothed it over. The he smoothed it over again. He cleared his throat. And smoothed the notebook over once more.

Kilts? Scottish? What the hell was the man on about? Had he ever been outside London before?

'The witnesses. Right. In a nutshell. Three monkeys, basically. Saw nothing, heard nothing, said nothing. I would say most of them had the opportunity, though they all deny it.'

'Opportunity? You mean they could have slipped upstairs without being noticed?'

'I think so. Someone says they're popping off to the loo, no-one notices.'

'Or maybe they're in it together, some or all of them, eh?'

'Could be.'

'Go on.'

'None of them seem to have a motive. They're all completely harmless as far as I can see. Nigel Stokes seems like the type to get himself into a pub fight, but he'd probably lose that, even if he was the only one having it. Clarissa Hope – I can't really figure her out. I think she knows a lot more than she's willing to tell. I'd like to have another go at her. The vicar – he lives in his own little world.'

'Personalities, Morton, personalities. When they aren't telling you anything, listen to the personalities. Take that pub owner, Constantine. Likes to make out he's a bit dim-witted. Very eager to please, so eager he keeps on tripping over himself. That's a very good way to disguise yourself.'

'You think he's hiding something?'

'They're all hiding something, Morton, haven't you realised? That's what makes the job almost impossible. Ninety-nine percent of it isn't relevant, but they'll hide it. Who's having an affair with whom? Who's nicking the petty cash from where? Who's the ex-con trying to lay low by pretending to be someone respectable? Who's the little old lady who wouldn't harm a fly but turns out to be a mass-poisoner?'

'You think it was definitely one of them, then?'

'Well, it wasn't the pixies, was it? Or do you people actually believe in such things out here?'

'Which one?'

'Which pixie? How many do you have? I thought they were all called John or something. Jacky Lantern. That's the one.'

'Which, er, suspect.'

'That's the question, isn't it. Just who is our Mr X?'

'Or Miss X.'

'Or Mrs X.'

'Or maybe X is trans. They do that these days, you know.'

Morton coughed.

'I wonder if that vicar was ever a fairy.'

'A fairy?'

'A pouffe. You know. Don't you have them down here in the sticks? Or are the sheep enough?'

Morton gave out a strangled noise which could have been "guess so". Nobody would ever have described him as politically correct. They wouldn't have described him as career-wise suicidal, either.

'Pixies … maybe it was the pixies … in a manner of speaking. You know, Morton, you may have something there.'

'I'll make a note.'

'Good lad.'

Morton took out his smartphone. He typed in "ee'z set himself a piskie catch". Then he spent another minute pretending to do something important with the phone that the old fool wouldn't understand in order to avoid having to continue the conversation.

Finally he had to give up and put the phone away. Fortunately Samson appeared to have lapsed back into a world of his own.

After twenty minutes of Samson humming some unidentifiable but suspiciously Christmassy tunes they pulled into a parking space alongside a row of brightly lit shops.

'Consider this, Morton: is the person we're looking for hiding behind one of those supercilious middle-class mugs, or is it someone who is in fact missing from our little line up? Is it in fact someone who wasn't there?'

They got out of the car.

'Let's get you kitted out while you're thinking about that.'

Their first stop was at a small chemist. The posters in the window were faded, and the goods on display looked like they needed a good dusting. There was a girl on a stool behind the till at the back who looked up from a magazine as they entered. Her face registered an initial interest, but then went blank and returned to her magazine. It was as if she had hoped it was her boyfriend, but then realised they were just two boring middle-aged old men, quite possibly shop-lifters, but it wasn't her shop and she didn't much care, and it was still an age before shutting up time.

Morton found a toothbrush enclosed in unbreakable plastic. It was a bilious-looking yellow colour, but the plastic cover offered proof that it was probably not previously used. It had a price sticker attached showing that it cost about ten times what it would in any normal shop.

'Electric,' said Samson, wandering behind Morton and inspecting the offerings. 'That's what all top dentists recommend these days, electronic toothbrushes. You can get ones these days that automatically stop when you've brushed enough, you know. And there's this light that goes on if you're brushing too hard. Clever little things. Amazing what they can do these days.'

Morton gritted his teeth and kept quiet. He'd had such toothbrushes ever since he could remember, the latest and most modern now sitting at home. He'd also noticed the faded boxes advertising electric toothbrushes hiding behind locked glass cabinets. They too were outdated and ridiculously overpriced. He wasn't going to waste that sort of money just to please Samson's belated discovery of the modern world, not just for one night.

And there were a couple of dead flies in the cabinets. They looked mummified but he certainly wasn't going to brush his teeth with anything that had been close to them.

He added a small, dusty box of toothpaste, the price of which suggested it was made with gold leaf and unicorn tears. Then a bar of soap in case the Duck didn't supply any. Or, as he suspected, supplied half-used bars. The choice in the chemist was either an aggressively male bar of industrial soap or a small selection of pastel-coloured plastic bottles containing ladies' bath salts. He chose the industrial offer with a grimace. He had always had very sensitive skin, ever since he was a child.

Samson dropped a toiletry bag on top of the soap.

'Need one of those,' he said.

It was red with white polka dots. And brittle plastic. It reminded him of bouffant hairdos and butterfly glasses from a television documentary of failed fashion of the Seventies, a blurry, washed-out reminder of a time before he had been born.

'And a flannel,' Samson said, adding a piece of cloth to the pile in Morton's hands. 'Can't not have a good bit of flannel.'

That was the colour of what someone had once told Morton was 'baby puke brown'. It felt like cardboard sandpaper.

'And a comb.' Samson dropped a huge pink comb with a large spatula-like handle on top of the flannel. 'Mind you get good use out of it, lad, you're getting to the age where soon you won't need it much. Still, means you won't have to worry much about dandruff after that.'

Morton headed for the single checkout before the idiot could add anything else to the pile. When he got there the girl had abandoned her magazine to check for important calls on her mobile. She remained fixated on it until Morton made some throat clearing noises. The girl reluctantly looked up with a slightly hopeful look that suggested she thought he might merely be lost and need directions and she wouldn't be required to do anything that resembled work. The look faded and she even more reluctantly put her mobile down and got off the stool. Morton put the items on the counter. She sighed, picked up the flannel, located the price tag and punched the value into the old till. Then she looked around for somewhere to put the flannel while entering the next item. There was none. The counter was largely occupied with bottles of watery perfume which appeared to be on sale.

'Wanna bag?'

'Please, yes. If you have one.'

She sighed and disappeared beneath the counter. There was a great deal of unenthusiastic rustling before she re-appeared with a large used plastic bag with a Woolworths logo on it. She handed it to Morton. He took it. She handed him the flannel. He put it in the bag. In this manner they processed the toothpaste, yellow toothbrush, pink comb, industrial soap and polka-dotted toiletries bag in silence.

'Do you take credit cards?'

'Machine's broken. Cash only.'

Morton felt an internal sigh as he took out his wallet and handed over sufficient notes to cover the amount showing on the till.

'Anywhere the lad here can buy some pyjamas?' asked Samson, popping up next to him.

The girl stopped counting out Morton's change and looked at Samson. Then she looked at Morton as if trying to imagine him in pyjamas.

'Ladies' shop has a onesie,' she said. 'It's black and white like a giraffe. Very modern. Someone bought it but didn't want it. So she took it back.'

'Giraffes aren't black and white. You're thinking of a zebra.'

'Well, this one is. I know what a zebra looks like. And this is a giraffe.'

'No, thank you, I do not want a used lady's onesie.'

'We don't have a blokes' shop. Not much call around here.'

'Not many men? Hear that, Morton, we might be in luck here.'

'Nah, they just don't change their clothes very often.'

'That's okay, I'm sure I'll be fine –'

'Don't be silly, Morton, you can't wander around in the altogether. You'll frighten the sheep.'

The girl's mouth twitched.

'There's the school outfitters. They do boys' uniforms. Because of the school. Might be a bit tight on you though. How big are you?'

'No, thank you, I –'

'Sports shop.'

'What?'

'Sports shop. They do shorts and stuff. And tracksuits. Because of the school.'

'Where –'

'About six doors down the road. On your left.'

'We'll have a look in there. Much obliged. Come on Morton.'

'They're closed on Sundays.'

'We'll have a look in the window, then.'

'Come again soon. Have a nice day.'

Morton followed Samson out, restraining an urge to hit him over the head with something heavy. All he had was the large Woolworths bag, and that wouldn't do much damage, not even with the large pink comb inside.

They got to the sports shop just as a lanky youth with a dropped chin was closing the door.

'Evening,' Samson said, opening the door and forcing the boy back.

'We're closed. It's Sunday.'

'Won't be long, son.'

'We're closed. It's Sunday.'

'We're police. For us every day is Monday.'

'Who is it, David?' called a voice from the back.

'It's the police, mum.'

'Tell them to go away.'

'I did, mum. They won't.'

'Bleeding hell, what you done now, Jason?' There was a shuffling and a prematurely middle-aged woman with rolls of fat and a cigarette hanging from her lip appeared.

'What you two want?'

'Lad here forgot his jim jams,' said Samson. 'You got a t-shirt and shorts in his size?'

'What, him? We only stock boys' sizes. Because of the school.'

'No adult sizes? At all?'

The woman contemplated Morton.

'Jim jams, you say.'

'Jim jams.'

'Well, now, I may have something. Just a tick.'

She went behind a cracked glass-topped display cabinet covered with cellotaped notices about pre-payments and non-payments and began opening and closing drawers.

'It's somewhere here,' she muttered. 'I saw it only last week. Mebbe the week before. Too large for the schoolkids. Only I didn't know that, did I. Bloke said it was the right size for beginners, so I thought he meant little ones. Here we go.'

She stood up and dumped a large, opaque plastic bag on the glass top. She took out the contents.

'Perfect,' declared Samson.

'Perfect?' asked Morton, staring down at a white Martial Arts outfit with black belt.

'You'll be able to wear it for your karate classes afterwards. Go on, lad, try it on.'

'It's not a karateji, it's a judogi.'

'A whattery?'

'A karategi is the uniform used by a karateka when performing karate. A judogi is what judo fighters wear. It's much stiffer and heavier and coarser than a karategi.'

'Well, there you go, lad, it'll last longer. Think of it as a Jimjammygi. Try it on.'

Morton reluctantly took his camel-hair overcoat and jacket off and tried the judogi on. He didn't really need to. It was exactly the same size as his other one back home, the one that spent almost all of its time hanging in the wardrobe with its white belt. He noticed the woman and the boy blink at his shirt.

'See, fits like a glove,' said Samson. 'Or it will do when you aren't wearing your waistcoat and all the rest of your kit. He'll take it.'

The woman put it back in its old plastic bag, picked it up and shuffled over to the till. She rang up a price that would probably have paid for two of them anywhere else. In pink.

'Do you take credit cards?'

'Course we do. Cause of the school.'

'The machine not broken, then, missus?'

'It's an old machine. They never break. We don't hold with this modern plastic nonsense.'

Morton handed over his credit card. The woman placed it and a payment slip into a machine which had been state-of-the art forty years before, swiped the lever across, took the payment slip out, wrote the amount in the box provided, and handed it to Morton to sign. He leant over the counter and signed it much in the manner he had seen ex-arrestees sign for their belongings after they had been released from the police cells and were looking forward to getting out before something worse happened to them.

'Thanks, love. Come on Morton. Cheerio, lad you can shut up shop now. Now, do we need to get you a towel or do you think the Duck will supply one?'

'I'm sure the Duck will have towels,' Morton said through gritted teeth as he followed Samson out of the shop, the woman and her son watching them, heads to one side as if trying to work out what these visitors were and where they were from. He knew without thinking exactly what sort of towel would be found around those sort of shops. Something designed for the beach about twenty years before, which would need three cycles in the washing machine before the dirt and dust was extracted, and even then would be too thin and rough to be of use.

'Better phone your missus now if you're going to do it. I'll wait in the car. Be rude to listen in.'

Samson got into the car while Morton took out his mobile and dialled a number.

'Shirley, it's me,' he told an answering machine. 'Listen, I'm going to be away for a day or two. I'm with this idiot from London called Samson, he's a chief inspector. He's decided we need to stay at this pub to protect some evidence or something. It's called the Duck and Angel. I'll give you another call as soon as I can. Oh, by the way, there's no signal at the Duck, so I don't know when that will be. See you soon.'

He switched the phone off and looked up into the dark sky. Late winter Sunday afternoon, he thought. Early evening, really. He had been on the go for over twenty-four hours. It was over twelve hours ago he had taken that terrible phone call and made the unwise decision to volunteer himself for hell. And now it looked like hell might go on for at least another night.

He tried to remember if they had anything planned for that evening. Anything was better than spending it with Samson in the middle of nowhere, even Shirley. He took a breath and got back into the car.

'Right, back to the Duck, said Samson, tossing an empty chocolate bar wrapper into the back and starting the engine. 'Time for a bit of dinner then an early night. Got a lot of work to get done tomorrow.'

Morton sat wordlessly in the car as Samson drove. Samson was trying to get a radio station on the car's old radio, pushing in buttons and twirling knobs while looking up occasionally to make sure they were still on the dark road. With anyone else Morton would have pointed out that they were likely to get killed very shortly unless he paid more attention to his driving. With Samson he could only wonder if that wouldn't be a blessing.

Samson picked up a radio station. It was playing Delilah.

'Tom Jones,' he said, 'one of yours.'

'What?'

'He's Welsh isn't he?'

'He's Welsh. I'm not.'

'Aren't you? Close isn't it? Even closer than Scotland.'

Morton decided not to respond.

'Why, why, why, Delilah?' sang Samson.

Morton shuddered.

'Just a second,' said Samson, looking up and braking. He switched the radio down. 'Up there, see them? Those lights.'

Morton looked up. There were some small lights low in the sky, red and green flashing and one constant white.

'Light aeroplane,' he muttered.

'I know it's a light aeroplane, Morton, I didn't think it was the little green men in a spaceship coming to take us for sexual experiments in the sky. I meant, what's that little light aeroplane doing?'

'I think it's coming in to land.'

'So, there must be an airfield around here. Interesting.'

'Why's that, sir?'

'Come on, Morton, make the connection. There's a Polish freighter lying out there pretending to be doing nothing. There's an aerodrome somewhere around here they've kept hidden. Obviously they're flying something in from that freighter, something they don't want us to know about.'

'Er, it's a freighter, sir.'

'And? So?'

'Well ... it isn't an aircraft carrier. They can't fly an aircraft off of it.'

'Morton, use your nous. They could have a helicopter platform. If they can have a helicopter platform they could have an aircraft platform. Or it's got those things planes use to land on water. Buoys or whatever. Those things on flying boats.'

'Floats.'

'Of course it bloody floats, Morton, that's the whole bloody point. God's sakes, lad, what did they teach you at school in these parts?'

'You think it's a seaplane, sir?'

'Why else would they keep it hidden?'

Morton decided to give up.

'If you say so, sir.'

'Question is, where does the Polish bloke come into it?'

Morton's lip curled.

'He could be the pilot. Maybe he hid his pilot's uniform somewhere. In the bushes, perhaps. He had civilian clothes stashed somewhere. Maybe he swam over during the night.'

'Don't be silly, Morton. More likely he escaped from that freighter somehow. Took one of those boats they have along the side. Life rafts. That's the one. Life rafts. Thought he'd be safe in the Duck for a night. But someone was waiting for him. Someone had been warned to be on the lookout. Or someone recognised him. Someone he didn't recognise. Someone we interviewed today who looks just like any other local. But someone who is concealing a terrible secret.'

'You think so, sir?'

'Oh, yes, Morton, these are cunning bastards we're up against.'

'These?'

'It could be one. But something in my gut tells me there's more than one of them involved.'

Morton resisted the urge to suggest the Chief Inspector might want some antacid.

'First thing tomorrow, Morton.'

'Sir?'

'We've got work to do. There's Mrs Constantine. I want a word with her. I don't buy this wheelchair business. Flying frying pans. It's too much of an act. If she hated her husband that much she'd have left him. And there's Lady Freechin. He's too much of a caricature. She sits home all meek and mild while he pretends he's out at a Foreign Legion dinner? Nah, that doesn't hold water. Plus there's that aerodrome. Need to pay that a visit.'

He put his elbow on the door windowsill with his hand tapping the roof.

'Something wrong with that Caroline girl too. I know her from somewhere.'

'Clarissa?'

'That's the one. Calls herself Carry. If her name's Clarissa she'd be Clarrie, wouldn't she?'

And, thought Morton, if you claim to suspect absolutely everyone you're absolutely bound to be right ninety-nine percent of the time. Even if you are a complete fucking idiot.

He took his smartphone out.

'Want to be careful playing with that thing too much, lad, you'll go blind.'

'Just making a note, sir.'

'Good lad.'

This time Morton's fingers did not even contract. It was almost zen-like. He had passed into the second zone. He was beginning to look at Samson as if through a telescope, from far, far away.

He typed in "iz wold ain't what it zeems".

His stomach rumbled, and he felt pleasantly light-headed.

Sunday evening

They returned to a brightly lit but almost empty Sunday evening Angel and Duck. Apart from an old couple in a far corner, the only occupant was Carry sitting on a stool behind the bar with her feet up on something behind the counter. She was inspecting a cloth in her hands with the attention one gives to the last item which might keep you from dying from boredom. She looked up as they walked in.

'Patsy asked me to tell you dinner will be ready when you are. It'll be served in the snug. There's no-one in there at the moment.'

'Patsy's making dinner?'

'Patsy's good at making roast drumsticks and tats en masse. Apart from that he couldn't boil an egg. In fact he couldn't roast one tat and a drumstick on their own. It would confuse him.'

'So who's making dinner? Mrs Patsy?'

'Anne-Marie is making dinner.'

She pushed a key across to Samson.

'You're in room 101. First floor, first on the left.'

She pushed another key across to Morton.

'You're in room number 2. Just beyond the room you used as an interview room.'

'Right,' said Samson. 'I'm going upstairs for a shower. Dinner in one hour. See you then.'

They watched him head for the stairs.

'Not joining him?'

'Very funny. I suppose I'd better have a quick shower too. But if I've got an hour then I've got time for a pint before a shower. What do you recommend?'

'Soap is normally a good bet.'

'I meant to drink.'

'Why didn't you say so.'

'You knew what I meant.'

'I know what you said.'

'Okay. I'll say this very slowly. What would you recommend to drink? Of an alcoholic nature, not water or Earl Grey tea or any New

Age nonsense.'

'There's a local bitter, Bishop's Drain. Some people like it.'

'Bishop's Drain? What sort of a name is that?'

'Post modern ironic.'

'Sounds like a piss-take. I'll pass. Give me a pint of Stella.'

Carry slipped off the stool, lifted a thick glass pint mug off a hook and poured the pint. She put it down in front of Morton.

'How much?'

'You want to pay now or put it on your room tab?'

'Good point. You know, I think I might put it on the room tab.'

'Thought you might.' She made a note on a pad and pushed it and a pen across. 'If you could initial that.'

He did so and pushed the pad back.

'Do we get itemised bills?'

'Only if you ask.'

'I'll make sure not to ask.'

'I didn't think you would. Can I get my pen back?'

He pushed the pen back.

'I'm surprised you don't have a tablet or some electronic gizmo to do that.'

'We tried that once. Patsy was very eager. He likes new technology. Only thing is, you should never leave stuff like that in range of someone who's had a few pints. Not when you're surrounded by liquid. It gives wiping your tab clean a whole new meaning. The customers weren't the only bright sparks around that night.'

'I never thought of that.'

'You would have. In about two seconds of getting your bar bill. Oh, dear, whoops, it slipped.'

'You are a suspicious one.'

Carry shrugged.

'Any idea what's for dinner? I'm starving. Haven't had anything since – hell, since midnight, last night, and that was a bag of crisps from the machine.'

'What flavour?'

'What?'

'The crisps. What flavour were they?'

'What? What does it matter what flavour they were. Salt and vinegar or something. I don't remember. Right now I'm too hungry to remember.'

'You poor thing. Doesn't your chief allow you a lunch break?'

'The work doesn't lend itself to office hours. And he's not my chief. It's only temporary.'

'And your girlfriend didn't make you any sandwiches.'

'She's not really my girlfriend. Not enough to make me sandwiches.'

'My heart bleeds.'

'Unsalted.'

'What?'

'That's what flavour the crisps were. Unsalted. There weren't any flavoured ones left.'

'Did you have difficulty choosing them?'

'I just told you. There wasn't any choice.'

'It makes for a simple life.'

'So? What's for dinner?'

'I don't know. But I do know that Anne-Marie's French. She loves French cuisine. She doesn't have a very high appreciation of British cooking.'

'Sounds typically French. What does she normally cook?'

'She doesn't normally cook anything. She isn't allowed. The locals aren't into French cuisine. But needs must when the devil flies.'

'Not garlic.'

'Oh, I think I can guarantee you garlic.'

'I hate garlic.'

'So did Dracula.'

'Has anyone told you that you have a lovely neck?'

'How can you tell?'

'I can tell. You can try hide it behind that thick polo neck, but I can tell.'

'Is that supposed to be a chat-up line?'

'You are hard work.'

'Beans too, I reckon.'

'Dracula hated beans?'

'No, Anne-Marie. She likes cooking beans.'

'Ah, well, I can live with that. I love beans. Give me beans on toast with a sprinkling of cheese any day. And they're good for you. Lots of fibre. Keeps you going.'

'Green beans.'

'Green beans?'

'They're good for you. Lots of fibre. Keep you going, too. Hopefully to somewhere far, far away.'

'Green beans? They taste bloody awful. That's the sort of thing you serve to five-year-olds.'

'No comment.'

Morton drained his pint.

'I'm going for a shower. Sounds like I'll need to order a take-away.'

'Good luck with that.'

'Oh. No take-aways around here.'

'Not this time of year. They close for the winter.'

'There's always Hungry House.'

'Out here? Good luck with that.'

'God, this is a miserable place.'

'Very kind of you to say so.'

'I didn't mean it like that.'

'Oh, by the way …'

'Yes?'

'Room number two has a shared bathroom with rooms three and five.'

'A shared bathroom.'

'You might like to practise your singing. Sometimes the latch doesn't hold.'

'A shared bathroom.'

'Mmm-hmm.'

'It doesn't have a lock on it?'

'It has a lock on it.'

'So?'

'Someone stole the key.'

'You don't have a spare?'

'Someone stole that too.'

'Jesus, aren't there any honest people around here?'

'People around here are very honest. It's the visitors who steal everything.'

'And who's occupying rooms three and five?'

'No-one.'

'No-one.'

'At the moment. But you never know what might turn up.'

'You mean who will turn up.'

'You haven't met some of the – guests – we get.'

'What about room number four?'

'What about it?'

'Does it have an en-suite?'

'Yes. And a double bed. And a real fireplace. With a log-fire.'

'So why can't I have room number four?'

'It's occupied.'

'It's occupied.'

'It's occupied.'

'By who?'

'Whom.'

'O-fucking-kay, Miss Pedantic. By whom.'

'By me. I get to use it in winter. Because we don't normally have guests in winter.'

Morton smiled.

'Why didn't you say so? I might knock on the door later to be sociable.'

'How about you don't.'

'I'll see you after my shower. Have a cold Stella waiting.'

As he left Samson walked in wearing the freshness of the newly showered. He had on a bright yellow polo shirt a size too large, loosely fitting light brown chinos held up by red braces and what appeared to be two-toned golf shoes.

'Hope I didn't take all the hot water,' he called after Morton's retreating back.

Carry looked at him deadpan as he popped himself onto a bar stool.
'It comes direct from the boilers in the bathrooms, there's no central boiler,' she said. 'You can't use all the hot water. It's instant.'
'I know, love. He doesn't. Probably never had the experience.'
'Probably.'
'You lot have it soft these days. You'll never experience the joy of turning up at a grey B&B in Great Yarmouth on a wet winter's day to find the other residents have taken all the hot water and you have to have a cold bath or stay grimy.'
'This happened when?'
'When I was a nipper.'
'But it made you the man you are.'
'Made me hate bloody cold water and second-hand baths, more like. What's on offer?'
'What?'
'What would you recommend to drink?'
'Oh. You can have Bishop's Drain. It's a local bitter. I'm told it's full of flavour. Or there's the usual.'
'The usual?'
'What you see's what you get.'
'Would you drink it?'
'Drink what?'
'Bishop's Piss.'
'Bishop's Drain.'
'That's what I said.'
'I don't like bitter.'
'Okay, I'll try a pint. Put it on the tab.'
She poured the beer, concentrating on the glass the whole time. She placed the pint in front of him and popped herself back on her stool. He took a deep pull.
'Mmmm. Not bad. A bit fruity for my taste, but I dare say you get used to that.'
'You can get used to anything.'
'Like living here.'
'I like living here.'

'Better than London.'

'Safer.'

'Cleaner. For some.'

'Cleaner. For me. What other people do is their business.'

'Wish that could be the motto of the world. Do you have a map of this place?'

She took a pamphlet from a stack behind the bar.

'It's a tourist one. Shows all the walks and scenery.'

He opened it up.

'This'll do. Roads and all.' He tapped a section of it. 'Local airport, yes?'

'Aerodrome. It's for hobbyists, mainly.'

'Ever been there?'

'No. I don't know anyone who owns a plane.'

'That's the nice thing about being a copper. You don't need a plane to walk into an airport.'

'Aerodrome.'

'That's the badger.'

'How long have you been here?'

'Since this morning. Why do you ask?'

'You seem to have picked up the lingo quite quickly.'

'I like that one. That's the badger. I think I'll use it quite often.'

'I'm surprised you didn't say that's the beaver.'

'I keep that sort of thing for the detective constable. He likes to think he has a filthy mind.'

'So why are you interested in the aerodrome?'

'I'm always interested in things that fly. Especially things that fly at night.'

'Like angels.'

'Angels fly at night?'

'Apparently bad angels fly at night.'

'Ah, bad angels. Wait a minute, didn't the angels appear over Bethlehem at night?'

'True. While shepherds watched their flocks.'

'And they were the good ones.'

'Good shepherds?'

'Don't try that on me, girl. You'll catch a cold.'

'Try what?'

'If you had wings where would you go?'

'What?'

'If you had wings and could fly where would you fly to?'

'Depends.'

'On?'

'What sort of wings.'

'Flappy type wings. Sort of things birds have.'

'Not the sort that would get you to New York then.'

'You want to go to New York?'

'I wouldn't mind. I wouldn't mind being a bat on top of the Empire State Building, or just one of those brownstone buildings of flats in New York. Just sitting on top watching everything below. People. People living. Loving. Dying.'

'And then flapping away.'

'And then flapping away.'

'Interesting.'

'So where would you fly to?'

'Around this building.'

'Around this building? Why? Oh, because of – you know.'

'Exactly. Because of you know. But, since I can't, and since I'm having a pint I must be off duty, I'll leave that thought for tomorrow. Who's making dinner?'

'Anne-Marie.'

'Damn, I need to interview her. I'll do that tomorrow. Remind me.'

'So who do you think did it?'

'Can't say. I'm not on duty.'

'One of us?'

'Had to be. Can you make me a list of everyone who was in last night?'

'Why?'

'So that I can be sure I've done everyone.'

'No, why did it have to be? One of us.'

'If there'd been a stranger in I would have twenty different descriptions of him by now. Or her. All of them wrong.'

'He could have slipped past. Got to the stairs. Crept up without anyone noticing.'

'You reckon.'

'I reckon I could do it.'

'A penny says you can't.'

'You're on.'

'What's that noise?'

'Sounds like someone singing.'

'Sounds like Morton singing. Or a cat being strangled. What on earth is he doing that for?'

'I think he's taking a shower.'

'He sings in the shower?'

'Don't you know?'

'No. And I don't want to. I'm not paid enough to know what Morton's ablution habits are. Why's he singing in the shower?'

'He thinks the latch doesn't work properly.'

'Let me guess. A little bat told him that.'

'You could say.'

'He thinks there's something odd about you.'

'He told you that?'

'Aye. Said he doesn't understand you.'

'Really.'

'Really. What's that freighter doing out to sea?'

'Not sinking.'

'What?'

'It's not sailing. The most important thing about a boat is that it doesn't sink. So it's doing what good little boats do when they aren't sailing, not sink.'

'Is it allowed to just sit there?'

'It's a free sea, it can do what it wants.'

'I'm glad I asked. Where's the nearest harbour?'

'Down the road.'

'Where's the nearest harbour large enough for something like that freighter?'

'About ten miles south. I think.'

'Mmm.'

'Or ten miles north. Roughly. I think.'

'As the crow flies.'

'As the crow flies.'

'Do freighters often park out there?'

'Often enough. It's something to do with the weather.'

'Handy stuff, the weather. Useful thing to blame if you need something to blame.'

'Probably riding out the storms.'

'Aren't any storms. I checked.'

'Could be in the Bay of Biscay.'

'It's not pointing that way.'

'I don't think boats always point where they're going when they're not going there.'

'Sounds like my job description. What's for dinner?'

'Who are you asking?'

'I don't know, who's here to ask?'

'Me. And the bat.'

'Ah. Of course. Silly me. I have a feeling I shouldn't forget the bat. So what's the bat say? What did the bat tell little Morton?'

'Garlic and green beans.'

'Sounds good to me, if a little sparse. Do the beans come in butter?'

'They would if they did.'

'Ah, those kind of beans. Bat beans. Now, what does Carry say is for dinner?'

'Steak, egg, chips and beans.'

'Green?'

'Baked.'

'Pity.'

'With white bread and butter.'

'Couple of nights of that and we'll end up in the morgue with the vic. Cholesterol overdose. Pour us another pint, love, this Bishop's Sewer's not bad.'

Carry hopped off the stool to pour the pint.

'Does the job make you want to be human for just a while every so often?'

'My job?'

'No, the plumber's.'

'There's a lot of love in my job. A lot of love.'

'A lot of love.'

'Yes. Thanks, love. Whenever I investigate a robbery it's been done for love. Love of money. Love of goods. Love of nicking stuff. Love of the girlfriend or missus who likes bright shiny things and loadsa money. And the last murder I did it was because this bloke loved his wife so much he killed her lover. Isn't that sweet? Every single crim I've known turns out to be a gentle soul with a heart of gold and a soul full of love.'

'There was a case once of a young girl who carried some drugs for her boyfriend. Because she loved him. Only she got caught. She had dreadlocks then.'

'Don't remember anything about that.'

'And this copper told her to sort herself out and fly right.'

'Don't remember anything about that either.'

'And he let her go.'

'Don't remember anything about that neither.'

'Are you here just because of me? Unfinished business?'

'Pure coincidence, love. I never knew you were here. And any unfinished business has nowt to do with you. Time-sheets, mainly.'

'Time-sheets?'

'Yeah, my boss is always nagging me for them. He thinks they're important.'

'You don't.'

'Waste of time.'

'You ever let anyone else go free?'

'I've never let anyone innocent go free. Nailed every single one of them. Up until now.'

'No heart of gold then.'

'Gold wouldn't make a very good heart. Can't pump blood, for a start.'

'There's something about you that doesn't add up. I've never understood you.'

'Do us a favour. Don't mention it to anyone else.'

'What? That I know you?'

'Precisely.'

'I wasn't going to. They might wonder why.'

'Good girl.'

'You're weird.'

'I'm like one of those submarines, I lurk in the depths, a hunter-killer.'

'You mean a killer-hunter. Something that hunts killers.'

'If you say so. Heard of Rupert Brooke?'

'Yes. One of the war poets.'

'One of the early war poets. He wrote a poem called Peace. There's these two lines,

To turn, as swimmers into cleanness leaping,

Glad from a world grown old and cold and weary.'

'Swimmers into cleanness leaping. I like that.'

'Good lines. Rest of it was crap. Celebrating the fact they were going to war. Talking of idiots, here's Morton. You're late, laddie, the garlic and green beans are going cold.'

'I'll ask Anne-Marie to bring your food to the snug.'

'Come on, Morton, grub time.'

'She forgot my Stella.'

'I doubt it, lad, that one doesn't miss a trick.'

They sat down in one of the seven booths in the snug, a low-ceilinged area of even thicker carpets and curtains to dampen down any voices.

'Know what's wrong with this little area, laddie?' Samson said, dropping his voice.

'Looks okay to me,' Morton replied, leaning forward so that he didn't have to speak loudly. 'Just right for private little conversations you don't want anyone overhearing.'

'Would you trust it?'

Morton looked around and up at the ceiling.

'You think it might be bugged?'

'If I was the devious type with a devious little mind and a devious little will I'd put more bugs in here than you'd find cockroaches in a kitchen in a student house. I certainly wouldn't trust it to have conversations I want kept secret. But there's something else a bit more obvious.'

'Which is?'

'You have to go through the main bar to get here or leave. A proper snug would have a nice quiet little door leading into the shadows of a dark side-street where a person so-wishing could swiftly walk away with a scarf wrapped around their faces to ward off the swirling fog on a cold winter's night. See what I mean?'

Morton nodded.

'Even if your conversation in here was private people would know you'd had a conversation. They can all see who comes in and goes out.'

'You've got it, lad. Whether it was with the local good-time girl or chief head of smugglers. I wonder if Patsy liked the idea of having a snug and this was the closest he could get to it. Or did he design this this way for a reason. Ah, grub time. Vous êtes Anne-Marie, n'est-ce pas?'

'Oui monsieur. I hope neither of you are the vegetarian.'

'He is the vegetarian. His mummy doesn't like him eating foreign meat.'

'I am not vegetarian.'

'Bon. Steak, egg and chips for you with the beans, and steak egg and chips for you with the beans. I'll bring some bread through now.'

'Merci buckets, Anne-Marie, that looks gorgeous.'

'Je t'en pries. Bon appetit.'

'Merci again mademoiselle. That's about my limit of French. Apart from the usual voulez vous coucher avec moi bit. Though I would avoid using that if I were you, lad, I once got punched in the Boulognes trying that on. Bloke didn't have a sense of humour.'

'Steak, egg and chips? Carry said –'

'Lad, I wouldn't trust anything Carry says, son. You might end up singing in the shower.'

'Sorry?'

'If you must be. Now tuck in like a good lad. I don't believe in letting good nosh go to waste, there's starving kids in India, you know.'

Morton looked at Samson, his mouth open. He closed it and looked at the plate of steaming food in front of him. His stomach fell in love with it. He tucked in.

When Carry came through with his Stella both men were absorbed in the methodical consumption of the meal. Carry received an absent-minded wave of a forked hand to convey thanks for the beer. They were almost finished when Anne-Marie brought their dessert twenty minutes later.

'Our special edition Angel Cake with the hot custard and the cold ice-cream.'

She looked at Morton who had paused, mouth full, to wrinkle his nose at the dessert. He began to chew faster. She looked at Samson. He waved a hand.

'I'll give it a miss, love, never could abide sweet things. Besides which, any more and my buttons will pop.'

She shrugged.

'I leave it here. Perhaps he want seconds.'

'Reckon he wants more than seconds and all.'

Samson finished his food and pushed his plate away. He glanced at Morton, picked up a tooth pick and began chewing it while looking nowhere special. Morton finished his by cleaning his plate with a thick slice of white bread, took a draught of lager, and then began on the dessert. He finished that and looked at the second plate.

'Sure you're not having any?'

'All yours, lad. Like I said, can't abide sweet things.'

Morton pulled it towards himself and took care of that. Once finished he took another gulp of lager and burped.

'Pretty, that, wasn't it?' said Samson.

'What's that?'

'The way they laid out that pudding in the shape of an angel.'

'Did they?'

'Didn't you notice it? Angel cake for the body and wings, bit of custard for the face, chocolate drops for the eyes. Very pretty. Artistic.'

'Didn't notice.'

'There's no pleasing some people.'

Morton burped again.

'I am pretty pleased. That really hit the spot. I was starving. Sunday's normally a pig-out day for me. When I'm off duty. Full English down the caff in the morning. Huge Sunday lunch down the pub. Roast beef, roast teddies, gravy, veggies, the works.'

'Roast teddies?'

'Teddies. Tats. Taters. Pertaters.'

'I wouldn't ask our Carry to do you roast teddies. You might find yourself eating roast teddy bears.'

'Reckon she knows what teddies is.'

'Reckon she knows what teddies is when it suits her. So what's for dinner chez yours on a Sunday evening? Some little nibbles to round off the Full English and teddies?'

'Sunday evening we take easy. We order a take-away, pizza usually. Or curry, I like a good curry. The hotter the better.'

'Blimey, son, I thought I was a big eater when I was your age.'

'I work it off. Gym three times a week. Most weeks. Football most weekends. Squash when I can get some games in. Oh, and karate classes. When I get a chance.'

'Sounds too much like exercise to me, son. I keep my energy for thinking. Never walk when I can drive. Never stand when I can sit. If you've got to chase after a crim he's already won. Better to make sure you're waiting in the right place for him when he comes running and puffing around the corner out of breath. Right, lad, bedtime. We'll have an early start. Breakfast at eight and then we'll be up and at em. See you here then. Oh, and watch your back. Don't forget there's a murderer around somewhere and he's maybe not finished his business.'

'Or she,' he added. 'Don't make the mistake of underestimating the female of the species.'

Morton watched him go. An early start with breakfast at eight? The old fool must be ready for retirement. For Morton an early start was three a.m. on a freezing cold winter's morning with just a hurried cup of coffee inside him, standing in darkness along with other heavies and a bloke with a door-breaker waiting for the order to go in and do some damage.

He sat contemplating the empty plates for some time, too full to think or even think of moving. Eventually he finished his beer and heaved himself to his feet before grabbing hold of the table, feeling strangely groggy. After a few seconds he felt better, and concluded that it must have been a result of the beers and food on top of an empty stomach. Not to mention the stress and strain of a day full of Samson. He walked back into the main bar, weaving a bit. Carry was in a far corner wiping a table, her back to him. He looked at her back for a few moments, then carried on to his room. He unlocked the door, opened it and switched the light on. He hadn't paid much notice when he had dropped his newly acquired overnight bag on the bed. There had been a low-light lamp on the bedside table, the room had been semi-dark and there had been little to attract his hunger-led attention. But now, with his satiated stomach and with the little room bathed in the white brightness of the main light, two things struck him. Firstly he was looking at a single bed. He hadn't slept in a single bed since leaving home. Secondly there was a painting on the wall above the headboard he hadn't noticed before. It looked like two golden wings on top of a knife blade in front of a red and blackened boiling sky. The wings and blade reminded him of the SAS logo and the banner, Who Dares Wins. It was signed NAR stokes.

Nigel, he thought, Nigel Stokes.

But beyond that there was nothing but a feeling of bloatedness. He recalled a vague memory of being slim and thinking of volunteering for the SAS once, many years before.

He managed to get out of his clothes, dumping them on the end of the bed.

He regarded the judogi for a few seconds.

It just felt like too, too much trouble, and he was really, really tired.

He grunted and climbed under the sheet and duvet, sinking into the deep bed unclothed, and fell asleep, any thought of perhaps knocking on number four with the double bed and en-suite having escaped his mind.

Monday morning

Morton was running. He'd been running forever. He didn't know what he was running from. He was running into darkness. There were buzzing red lights shooting around in front of him. Bright shop lights were chasing him. One came up alongside and asked, 'Wanna bag?' The others screamed with laughter. He jumped. He jumped into the clouds. He was flying. He was flying between huge clouds, diving and swooping. It was a beautiful sensation. There were things on the clouds with harps. He took no notice of them, revelling in plunging for miles before suddenly shooting up again. Up and up and up until he came to a huge balloon-like image of Carry, her cheeks puffed out. She blew. She blew a stream of angels and ducks towards him. One of them turned into Thuthan on a magic carpet juggling swords. She was circling his head her weird eyes locked on him. He fled tumbling down slipstreaming down falling down racing away. Vicar Brayley chased him shouting 'It's Vicar! It's Vicar!' He swung around and a shadow said 'Hello Luke it's Bertie, where do you want to put your cool hand?' before bursting open and emitting a shrieking cackle. He dived into the safety of a cloud and banged his head on a bright magenta 1965 Studebaker. Only it wasn't a Studebaker, it was a cupboard. It was a cupboard with a body in it. Only it wasn't a cupboard. It was a headboard. A solid wood headboard of a bed. Except his bed didn't have a solid wood headboard.

Morton sat up up in the darkness, suddenly fully awake, sweating, his heart pumping.

He knew he wasn't in his own flat. The bedroom door would have been slightly ajar, and there would have been a night light on in the passage. It was only Shirley who always closed the door when he wasn't there. He stretched out his left arm slowly and soon found the edge of the mattress. He always slept on the right, unless he was in someone else's bed and they had refused to give up that privilege.

He stretched his right arm out slowly, feeling for the warmth of another body. It quickly found the other edge of the mattress.

He was in a single bed. He hadn't slept in a single bed since leaving home.

Since leaving his parents' house.

He felt the sheets around him and remembered: he was in the Angel and Duck. In a single bed. With the sheets damp with sweat.

A memory made him suddenly hope it was just sweat.

He remembered that he had put his watch on the right hand bedside table and stretched out to pick it up. It was a heavy, chunky thing designed for the man on the go. It was waterproof and fireproof and shock-absorbent. He had bought a dull leather camouflage-coloured cover for the face to prevent accidental reflection in the dark of the night. It had eight almost-recessed buttons, four on each side. One was for a little light that would illuminate the face sufficiently to read the time, but not bright enough to attract the attention of the enemy sniper thirty yards away. Another was for setting an alarm. The last time he had tried to press the light button he had unwittingly pressed the button to set the alarm, along with several others. The alarm had gone off some hours later in the middle of a briefing by the Chief Constable, and he had stabbed desperately at every button he could find in order to shut the thing up. The alarm had been the tune Yellow Rose of Texas. Every time the Chief Constable saw him thereafter he had declared, "Ah, it's the Yellow Rose of Texas, play a song for us, son."

The Chief Constable didn't see him often. Not after the second time.

He sighed and got gingerly out of the bed. He knew the light switch was to his front and left. He took two paces and kicked a low stool with his shin.

'Fuck!' he said, and limped the last two paces. He groped for the light and switched it on. He turned around and noticed the lamp on the bedside table that his watch had been on.

'Fuck!' He looked at his watch.

'Fuck! Five o fucking clock.'

Too early to get up. Probably too late to go back to bed and try to sleep. The ideal time to go for an early-morning run before a shower and breakfast if (a) he had his running togs and (b) it wasn't freezing winter outside and (c) he was in his own flat with his own shower and his own kitchen with a coffee-maker and toaster and stove and tin of baked beans and eggs and bacon and (d) he felt like going for an early morning run. Which he didn't. In fact he felt bloated for some reason. And the room felt too hot, the sort of stuffy warmth you get in institutions that don't allow their inhabitants to open windows.

He pulled the curtains back on the single window. It was pitch black outside. He tried the handle. The window was locked. There was a keyhole, but no key.

Perhaps they had experience of what happened when guests were allowed to open ground-floor windows in the early hours of the morning.

He considered the option of having a shower and getting dressed. That would mean sitting around doing nothing in his already-crumpled suit until eight o'clock. He could possibly phone ... no-one. Not unless he went up the hill. Or risked using one of the land-lines. He had a feeling that any calls made through the land-lines would be overheard, however accidentally. If not deliberately recorded. There was something he didn't quite trust about the Angel and Duck's communications systems.

He noticed the painting above the bed. Golden wings against a red-blackened sky. Who dares wins.

Get a grip, he told himself.

He decided he would go up the hill. After a shower. But first, on a spur of the moment, he'd take a wander around the Angel and Duck during its sleeping hours.

He pulled on trousers of the judo suit, vaguely noting that they were a bit on the small side. Then he put on the top, wrapped the black belt around his waist a couple of times and tied it in a knot. He paused. He put his legs together, his arms by his side, and bowed. "Sensei!", he said.

Then he switched the light off and counted to ten thousand in thousands before slowly opening the door an inch. The passageway was lit by the dim light of a night light. Despite the patterned wallpaper and Samson's thick Askminster carpet there was a moody air of a pre-dawn hospital corridor about it. Not the pre-dawn of the sun about to rise, but the pre-dawn of the morning shift come to see how many patients had outlasted the night. Or rather, how many hadn't made it and needed disposing of before the others came to.

He slipped out, closed the door and padded along the carpet in his bare feet. Ahead was Patsy's office. There was a thin sliver of light coming out of the bottom. He paused to listen. There was a slow patter of clicking noises. Then silence. Then another slow patter. Then another silence.

He reached out a hand to try the handle. Something made him pause and the hairs on his neck stand up. He could feel someone watching him from the other end of the passage. He whipped round. For a split second Thuthan stood there, swords in her hands held across her chest. Then she was gone. She didn't move anywhere. She just vanished.

He blinked. Thuthan didn't live in the pub. Thuthan was at home, wherever that was. With her mother. And presumably father. And swords. He must be imagining things.

He turned back to the door. He tried the handle. It was unlocked. He opened it a crack and put his eye to it. Carry was sitting at the desk, looking directly into his eyes, her hands on the computer keyboard, the screen to one side, the back facing him.

'Well, constable, are you coming in, staying out, or just going to stand there like that?'

He opened the door and entered.

'I didn't want to disturb whoever it was.'

'You didn't want anyone to know you're a Peeping Tom.'

'I am here on official business.'

'I always did wonder what attracted men to become coppers. Apart from the joy of beating innocent people up.'

'It's not like that. I didn't know who was in here. I thought it would be Patsy.'

'Well, there is that. If it had been Patsy you could have come straight in and danced the fandango without him noticing.'

'Bad eyesight?'

'Pretty much.'

'So what are you doing up this early?'

'I was looking something up on DuckDuckGo.'

'Duck duck go? What the hell is that?'

'It's a search engine. Like Bing.'

'You mean like Google.'

'No. Like Ask.'

'Like ask what?'

'Ask. It's a search engine. Like DuckDuckGo.'

'You're trying to wind me up. Duck duck go. I'm not that stupid. Come on, what are you really doing?'

'Okay, then. I'm watching Youtube.'

'Youtube?'

'It's an Internet site. You can watch videos. Mainly about kittens.'

'I know what Youtube is. Why are you watching it at this hour?'

'Is there something illegal about watching it at this hour? When is it legal to watch Youtube?'

'It's unusual.'

'I don't sleep much. What's your excuse for wandering around at this hour dressed like a Ninja warrior?'

'I'm not dressed as a Ninja, it's just a standard martial arts suit. For judo. It's the closest they had to a set of pyjamas.'

'If you say so, Karate Kid. So, why up so early? Planning an early start?'

'I woke up early. I couldn't get back to sleep thinking of you so near.'

'I wish you had. The sight of you wearing that thing will stop me sleeping for weeks. Though I can't say your cowboy outfit does a lot for me either. Is that a real black belt?'

'Yes. So what are you watching on Youtube?'

'Famous funeral blunders.'

'I don't believe you.'

'Don't then.'

'Let me see what's on that screen.'

She stretched out an arm and pressed the power button with her finger, looking at him. She held it down until there was a sigh from the machine as it shut down and died.

'You can't do that. You'll … you'll have lost anything you were doing … you ….'

'I just have.'

'I could arrest you for interfering in the course of an official investigation.'

'Got a search warrant?'

'I don't need a search warrant.'

'You'll need something.'

'You know I haven't got anything.'

'Well, then, shove it.'

'You can be coarse sometimes.'

'Let me guess: I look like a sweet little girl at other times?'

'Well, yes. You could put it that way.'

'An angel, in fact.'

'Well, I don't know –'

'There was another copper once, said I'd look like a real angel if I got my hair cut and washed.'

'What other copper?'

'Oh, it was somewhere far away and long ago. Have you found the House of the Rising Sun?'

'What?'

'That's a no, then. How about, have you found the Nude Angel Rising?'

'What?'

'The Nude Angel Rising.'

'What's that?'

'It's the painting of me you were going to look for.'

'The Nude Angel Rising.'

'Yes.'

'What does it look like?'

'A naked duck.'

'What?'

'Quack quack. I'm going to the kitchen to prepare breakfast. It's off limits to non-staff.'

'I'm not non-staff.'

'You can say that again.'

'I'm a police officer. There's no such thing as off-limits to a police officer.'

'You reckon. Remember Thuthan's blades?'

'Thuthan's blades.'

'You remember Thuthan. Most people do. She doesn't like it when people forget her. She takes it personally. She's precocious.'

'I noticed.'

'What they call a child prodigy. An enfant terrible. Apparently they have a psychopathic streak. A psychopathic streak a mile long.'

'Where is she?'

'Tucked up in bed at home, probably. Unless she's also a night owl.'

'She's not here?'

'Why would she be here?'

'That's not what I asked you.'

'Okay, I swear that as far as I know, Thuthan is not here at the moment. But, who really knows? She might be hiding somewhere. Changelings often do. They lost her in the forest once. Found her talking to the wolves.'

'I thought I saw something, a flash of steel.'

'Trick of the light. It happens. Especially in the early hours before dawn. This place has ghosts. You'll see them if you stay still long enough.'

'How can they allow her to carry real swords around with her?'

She turned and moved to the door behind her.

'They're nothing compared to what's in the off-limits to non-staff kitchen. We have bendy butcher's knives.'

'Bendy butcher's knives.'

'Lovely and thin. And sharp. They slip in and out silently. Ideal for popping cloves of garlic into the flesh.'

'Right.'

'We tie the meat up first, of course. Before making it sizzle. Have you had your meat sizzle?'

'Why Angel? Why Rising?'

'Ask Nigel.'

'Carry –'

But she was gone.

He debated following her. And decided against. It was too early and she was too weird.

He padded through to the main pub and inspected the paintings. Diana in the Wild over the fireplace looked nothing like Diana in the Wild, whatever that looked like. There were two representations of what could be bared fangs, and possibly the blood of the man who had been accidentally ripped to pieces, but if there was any woman in there she was the ice maiden, hidden. He walked around, looking at the other paintings. They were all signed "stokes", the lower case "s" smaller than the other characters. None of them had titles. There was a common theme of bold, wide brush strokes, of bright slashes of violence against a dark background, like a massacre in an ice-cream parlour set against the bright orange dying light of the smoking battle of Waterloo. If any of them contained a nude it would have to be the body on an arc-lit dissection table distorted through same maniacal piece of software. He wondered what on earth possessed Patsy to allow them to be hung in his pub, and remembered that Patsy was so short-sighted as to be blind.

He glanced in the direction of the ladies' bar. Somehow he couldn't see any of the ladies accepting such explosive creations in their bar. Instead he went into the snug. The lights were off. He found the light switch and switched it on. He saw a body lying on the table in the cubicle directly in front. He turned the dimmer up as high as it would go. It was just light enough to see that the body was a pile of used tablecloths, presumably dumped there last thing at night with the intention of clearing them first thing in the morning.

He wondered who had dumped them there. Not Carry. She would always tidy up. Not Anne-Marie. Not Patsy.

Patsy, possibly. He'd probably left them there, forgotten them, and spent half an hour trying to find them again before giving up.

He wandered round, looking around the darknesses of the upper walls and ceiling. There were generic prints hanging about head-height in each of the cubicles, small overhead brass lamps showing black racing horses held at pose, most with manes done up in corn rows. They were exactly the sort of reproduction prints imitating paintings he would have expected in a rural pub, none of them nudes.

Or perhaps all of them were nude.

He thought of the word filly.

Then his imagination pictured them wearing frilly dresses and straw bonnets.

His gaze was drawn to the rear end of the horse in front.

He shook his head and walked out. His brain was playing tricks on him. Weird tricks.

He went back to his room and collected his shower things. He added an unopened tube of eco-sensitive shower gel from the complimentary basket on the light stand. He walked to the shared bathroom and pushed the bolt home behind him. The previous evening he had been tired and had accepted the story about singing to warn off others without question. Rather more awake now he realised that there was no way anyone could possibly get through that bolt. Carry had led him straight up the garden path to stupidity. Or perhaps just pointed him in the right direction and he had blindly gone there by himself. Well, that was the last time that little maid was going to do that. He was much better at that game than she would ever be.

The thought revived his libido.

The hot water in the shower revived him even more. He grinned and began to sing his own song.

'Hey Nude, don't be afraid,
I was made to
go out and get you
the minute
you let me under your skin
then you begin

to make it better
Nah nah nah nah nah nah nah nah nah …'
Outside the room someone paused at the sound. Samson blinked, cocked his head, and listened. Then he shook his head as if in disbelief, buttoned his overcoat, pulled on his gloves and padded silently away, torch in hand.

Morton finished his shower and washed his teeth with the yellow toothbrush and unicorn tears toothpaste. Then he picked up the large pink comb to comb his hair. He paused as he remembered Samson's comment about not needing it for much longer. He looked at his wet hair in the mirror, turning his head left and right to check the hairline. He continued doing so as he started to comb his hair. A little thinning, perhaps, but nothing like what Samson had been suggesting. It was hardly noticeable.

Then he reached out for his razor. There was nothing there. He had forgotten to buy a razor or anything to shave with. Samson had so irritated him with his additions of face cloth and toiletry bag and the rest that he hadn't been thinking straight.

He felt his jaw. He hadn't shaved for over twenty-four hours. By rights he should have a manly stubble, at least a pronounced five o'clock shadow. Instead there was just a slight hint of his cheeks being a bit fuzzy, not quite clean.

He shaved religiously every morning precisely because he had never been able to develop the dark stubble of the Hollywood hero.

He rubbed his jaw again. It would have to do, he knew, but he still felt uncomfortable. He'd buy a razor and some shaving gel as soon as he could, they were bound to pass some shops sometime. Even a corner shop would stock something basic.

He padded back to his room, dressed and slipped out of the front door. The lock clicked to as he closed it. He shrugged and headed towards the road up the hill. A crescent moon hung high in the sky, its spikes seeming to reach upwards. The street-lights and pavement soon ended but the moon spread a pale yellow-blue light across the landscape and the road and the pine trees lining it. Every thirty paces or so he checked his mobile to see whether it was receiving a signal. No vehicles passed him until the fourth time he stopped, when a huge artic came barrelling up the road before missing him by inches. A loud blast on the horn as it sped away was presumably the driver's comment on pedestrians whose frightened white faces suddenly materialised out of nowhere in the dark early hours of a winter morning.

He waited for twenty seconds until his heart had stopped palpitating and his eyes had re-acclimatised themselves to the sudden dark. And then trudged on, continuing to check the mobile screen regularly.

There was nothing until he reached the very top of the hill, a place barren of plants and trees, just snow-dusted rocks and an open space next to the road which looked like a well-used and muddy impromptu car park. Someone appeared to have buried a pet towards the back, with a small mound topped with a wooden cross with what looked like some text burnt onto it. He used the light of his mobile phone to read it. It had the word "Snuffles" written on it.

'Cemetery Ridge,' he whispered. 'And I'm the last man alive on it.'

He looked out on the valley below. The moon shone down on fields covered with snow and the occasional scattered clump of houses, the road from the hill snaking down before disappearing amongst them. Here and there a light shone in a window to show that the occupants were awake and moving. And warm. In the distance he could just make out what was probably an airfield with a small hangar and what looked like two or three toy planes covered with tarpaulins, one without. The runway was clear and black and strangely straight in a landscape of curves and camouflaged chiaroscuro. There was also a perceptible wind blowing, a biting cold breeze that made up for speed by driving straight through his clothes and ruffling his hair, turning his head cold, making him wonder whether his hair wasn't thinning a lot more than it looked. He made a mental note to check the top of his head in the mirror the next time he combed his hair.

Suddenly his phone showed 5 bars. There must be a transmitter down in the valley below. He cursed the stupidity of the person who could have sited it on the hilltop instead, and checked his watch. It was six-thirty, a time which, before the invention of the mobile phone, it would have been regarded as bad manners to disturb anyone so early on a Monday morning. He dialled a number.

'Shirley? Shirley, if you're there, pick up. It's me, Luke.'

He gave it three seconds.

'Shirley, pick up.'

Nothing.

'Okay, listen,' he told the answering machine, 'I'm still stuck in this little village, there still isn't any signal down there and I have to come up this hill to get one, so I don't know when I'll be able to call next. I'll try to convince that idiot Samson that we don't have to stay another night here, so hopefully I'll see you tonight, Shirl, love you, see you later, bye.'

He ended the connection.

Love you, he thought. Well, it was true once. Or at least he had once thought it was true.

He looked down at his mobile. A barely visible blinking light told him he had a message waiting. It must have downloaded when he was speaking to Shirley's answering machine. He pressed a button and listened.

'Moron? This is Doctor Shepstone. Listen, I can't get hold of that idiot Samson so I'm leaving this message with you. His voice mail's full or something. Tell him to clear it sometime. Anyway, pathologist's department had a quick look at your body for you yesterday. They were feeling generous. Anyway, turns out your victim was shot, knifed three times with different sharp objects, strangled, garrotted, and hit over the head. Oh, and he might have been poisoned too. Possibly suffocated. But they need to do further tests to confirm that, can't do it with just a visual, but his lips look dodgy. Anyway, from the sounds of it quite a few people had it in for him. So tell that idiot Samson before he suddenly decides to arrest someone. He needs to arrest all of them. Got it?' There was a raucous laugh. 'And tell him to clear that bloody email of his. Voicemail. What's it called. This stuff. Show him how if you have to. He'll need it.' The recording ended.

Morton looked at the phone. He continued looking at it for a few seconds. Then he shook himself and began checking every communication app on his phone. There were no other messages.

He dialled another number. It connected to another answering machine.

'Dick? It's Luke. Listen, I need a favour. I'm stuck out in the middle of nowhere with no signal apart from here, high on a mountain at the end of the world. I need you to run a check on someone for me. Name's Clarissa Hope. Age around mid twenties. Auburn hair, good bod, cold eyes. Sounds like she's from the South East, posh sort of voice, though she tries to hide it. Oh, and –'

He paused.

'No, that's it. I would have got more details if I'd thought about it before. Can't be many girls of that age called Clarissa. Keep it to yourself though, I don't want the boss finding out about it. Oh, and check any missing person reports from around the country, especially Eastern Europeans, Poles, that sort of thing. You can use that as an excuse to ask about Missy Clarissy. Okay, leave a message if you find anything. I'll pick it up later.'

He checked his watch: seven-fifteen. The sky was just beginning to lighten in the grey horizon. He began walking slowly back down the hill, checking his back regularly for any surprise artics. As he descended the breeze eased, but still left him wishing he'd brought a hat of some kind. The black balaclava in his bottom drawer back in the flat would have been ideal.

He got back to the Angel and Duck just before eight. The door was unlocked, most of the lights were on and there was a sense that the pub had woken up and was preparing breakfast. Breakfast for two today. He went into the snug and found Samson with a cup of coffee, his attention fixed on an old, much-thumbed paperback Western. The body made up of tablecloths was gone.

'Morton, you're a late riser. Have you ever read this? I've never read one of these before. Fascinating. It's a Western. Found it lying around. There's this gunslinger just rode into town. Well, just rode into a homestead near town. It's been run by this widow, her old man got shot by these cattle rustlers, and she's got her ten-year-old son with her.'

'I've been up for hours. I went up the hill to check for messages.'

'Only I don't reckon they were real cattle rustlers, she thinks they were sent from the boss of the K Ranch cause he wanted their land real bad, real bad.'

'There was a message from Dr Shepstone. He wants you to call him as soon as you get a chance.'

'Shepstone? He's an idiot. This gunslinger's name is Luke. He's normally a gun for hire but I reckon he's going to be the good guy in this one. You can tell with these Americans. He's got a lean jaw and pale blue eyes. That's what it says here.'

'Something about the pathology department.'

'Oh. What about the pathology department? He isn't wearing a white hat. I thought the good guys all wore white hats. They did in the movies when I was a kid.'

'I think they've an idea of how the vic was killed.'

'How?'

'I think that's why he wants you to call him.'

'Straight after breakfast. I'm starving. I was out well before the crack of dawn. Morning, Carry. What's for breakfast?'

'Continental or Full English.'

'I'll have the Full English, please love.'

'Me too. Without fried tomatoes. Can't stand fried tomatoes. Oh, no black pudding either. Eating dried blood gives me the heebie-jeebies.'

'I'll have his black pudding. Good protein.'

'Any chance of a coffee, Carry?'

'I'll bring some more through now.'

Her name's Louise.'

'Sorry?'

'The widow. He's renting a room from her. I'm not quite sure why. I think he's come to do a job, needs somewhere out of town to stay for a few days.'

'Who has?'

'Luke. The gunslinger. The son admires him, but the mother doesn't want him to have anything to do with Luke. She knows what sort of a man he is, she knows he's there to do a job and move on. I bet you she falls in love with him. You can tell.'

'How?'

'How does she fall in love with him? How the hell am I supposed to know that?'

'No, how can you tell she's going to fall in love with him?'

'They always do in books.'

'Do they?'

'Course. Name me a book where boy and girl don't get together.'

'Don't know a lot of books.'

'There's that one by, oh, what's her name? Got Mr Darcy in it. Never forget that, I nicked a bloke called Darcy just when the movie came out. They never let me forget that.'

'If you say so. So what's the plan for today?'

'Breakfast. Have to call Shepstone I suppose. Have a good look outside in the daylight. Carry was going to make a list of everyone who was here Saturday night. Check who we've interviewed and who we haven't. See if we can get hold of some of those we haven't. I want a word with this Joe the Drunk who found the body. Mrs Patsy. We'll need to drive out and see Lady Sir what's his name. It's going to be a busy day. Thank you, Carry. Now, breakfast, talk later.'

Morton addressed himself to the plate Carry had just put in front of him: bacon, eggs, mushrooms, sausages, chips, with a basket of fresh bread. He began by lacing his plate with tomato sauce and then heavily buttering some white bread. The two men sat in almost companionable silence as they hoovered the food up. Morton finished shortly before Samson and poured himself a leisurely cup of tea.

'It's one of the questions I've never found an answer for,' Samson said, putting his knife and fork down and dabbing his lips with a napkin. He poured himself a cup of tea as Morton waited for further explanation.

'What's that?' he asked in the end.

'Why do we not have pudding with breakfast?'

'Pudding?'

'You can have pudding at lunch and supper. Soup too. Entrée or starter or whatever they call it. But never breakfast.'

'Oh. I thought you meant black pudding.'

'Not black pudding you idiot, dessert. Bread and butter pudding. Jam roly-poly and cream, Ice-cream and bananas. Stewed prunes and custard.'

'Some people have something sweet. Waffles with Canadian Maple syrup. That sort of thing.'

'Some people are stupid. Anyway, it's not the same. They don't have it for lunch or supper, do they? Come on, let's go see what that idiot Shepstone has to say.'

Morton followed him to the main bar where he sat on a bar stool and waved vaguely at the counter.

'Phone, please, love, I need to make a call.'

Carry wordlessly placed the phone in front of him.

'Ta, love.'

He dialled a number.

'Shepstone? Samson here. I hear you've got some news.'

'Yes, it's just about nine here too. We've been up for hours. What's this news?'

'Oh.'

'Really.'

'Shot. We know that.'

'Strangled.'

'Stabbed.'

'Three times.'

'Hit over the head.'

'Something blunt.'

'Signs of poisoning, too.'

'Well, well. Seems like a lot of people didn't like him very much. They going to send anyone out to go through the room?'

'Thursday. Might as well not bother.'

'Backlog. I know that word. Never met a frontlog, mind.'

'Yes, yes, I know, preliminary findings etc, etc. Let me know when it's post preliminary.'

He put the receiver back down and pushed the telephone back towards Carry.

'Sir?'

'Well, well.'

'Don't you think –'

'Well, well. So that's their game.'

'– it would be a good idea to –'

'I might have known.'

'– tell Dr Shepstone the –'

'Know what they've found, Morton?'

'– number here so that he can –'

'It wasn't just one of them.'

'– can call here with updates.'

'We're looking at seven, maybe more suspects. This place is in the telephone book, Morton, that idiot Shepstone could look it up if he wanted, he just likes being contrary to show how important he is. Listen, you know the vic was shot, right. He was also stabbed.'

'He was? My goodness.'

'Three times.'

'Three times? My goodness.'

'You won't believe this, but someone strangled him, too.'

'Strangled as well, eh?'

'And someone else hit him over the head.'

'Hit him over the head?'

'With a blunt object. Several times.'

'My goodness.'

'And get this. He was poisoned as well.'

'Poisoned. Well I never.'

'So we're not looking for one person. We're looking for – one, four, five, six – seven.'

'You don't think maybe the same person – or two or three people – maybe did more than one?'

'Morton, do you ever listen to yourself before you speak? Why?'

'Why what?'

'Why would one person try to kill him more than one way?'

'It could be a bluff?'

'Yeah, it could be a double bluff, then a triple bluff, then a quadriffle bluff, before you know it you've chased your tail around so often you don't know whether you're Arthur or Satchkewan. No, my lad, we start off by treating the evidence as gospel until otherwise. I reckon they were queuing up to do him in. The question is, how?'

'How?'

'How did they queue? Was it an orderly queue at the door, leading out in the corridor, each waiting their go, or were they watching surreptitiously, from alcoves, or behind curtains, or from doors just ajar, waiting for the last person to finish before nipping in? Was someone hanging in the ceiling, waiting, waiting, waiting, with the patience of a zebra and the strength of an orangutan? Did they know about the others? Were they watching each other watching each other? Did one pop in and hit him over the bonce, another wait until bonce man had left so he could slip in and knife him a few times? Were the later ones in such a hurry they didn't realise he was already dead?'

Morton treated those as rhetorical questions. He was acutely aware of Carry just a couple of feet away. He knew that Samson was talking absolute nonsense, but he wasn't sure that Carry realised it. Above all he didn't want to get a bollocking from the idiot in front of Carry, though he wasn't quite sure why he should be worried about that.

'Ask yourself, what drives someone to murder, Morton? Answer that one, my son, and you're almost home and dry.'

Morton took out his smartphone.'

'What on earth are you doing now, Morton?'

'Just making another note, sir.'

'Good thinking. Wait here. I'm going to put my book back in my room, get my coat, and then we'll get started with the day's work.' He paused. 'Waffles with Canadian Maple syrup, eh? That sounds rather good. Right, I'll catch you back here in a few minutes.'

Morton typed in "ee'm got teddies in iz thatch".

He turned to find Carry inspecting him neutrally, a bit like a specimen.

'You knew all that, didn't you. About – the man who was killed.'

'What makes you think that?'

'How did you know? Unless you were the one who did it.'

'I didn't say I knew.'

'You don't have to. Your eyes give you away.'

'My eyes.'

'Don't ever take up poker.'

'Okay, so I did know. And if you're a good little girl I'll tell you one day. And if you're a naughty little girl I'll tell you even sooner.'

'And if you try anything on I'll send Thuthan after you.'

'That's not very funny.'

'Still haven't found the nude yet, have you.'

'What makes you think I've been looking for it.'

'Oh, I know you've been looking for it. I know people like you. You won't stop until you've found it.'

'You think?'

'I know.'

Morton smiled easily long enough for Samson to return and rescue him.

'Come on, lad, let's go out the front this time.' He led the way up the street until they came to an alleyway that led to fields behind the buildings. A path ran along the tall wall at the back of the pub garden. The fields were covered by a thin layer of snow. The snow on the path was heavily trampled for a length along the back of the pub wall, and then nothing but more virgin snow.

'Looks like someone got here before us. These footprints are all the same. Maybe this is how he did it. He could have got in over the wall.'

'That's what happens when you have a lie-in, Morton, you miss the important points. These are my footprints. I kept waking up wondering what was behind this wall, so I got up to have a look. Know what I found?'

'No, sir.'

'Nothing. I walked up and down about fifteen times and I found nowt. No footprints. No sign of humans passing through. I guess there's no shortage of litter and Coke cans and fag packets and all the rest beneath the snow or under the hedges, but no-one's been around these parts recently. Goes back to what I said, this was an inside job. Done by more than one of them. I always suspected that. But now that you're awake and here at last, jump up on that wall and tell me what you can see. I couldn't manage it this morning. Not as fit as I was when I was your age.'

Morton jumped up. his hands just claiming the top of the wall. He dragged himself up until his body was half-way over it and his overcoat was being ruined by it.

'Not as stupid, either, mind.'

Morton gritted his teeth.

'Nothing. Just snow. Pub tables. Children's play area. A washing line. A double line.' He leaned over and pulled at it. 'It moves.'

'What do you mean, it moves?'

'It's doubled up. You can pull it so the washing moves along. It's connected to a pulley.'

'Well, the wonders of modern science. What will they think of next?'

'Sir?'

'They had exactly the same sort of thing when I was growing up in the slums of Manchester you idiot. It's hardly rocket science. The other pulley will be just under a window on the first floor. The housewife or maid leans out the window and pegs the first item to the bottom line, pulls the top line towards her, the first bit of washing moves down the line, that leaves a gap for the next pair of bloomers and so on. Means you don't have to go into a courtyard of sludge and dog-shit to put your washing out. How strong is it, could it take the weight of a man?'

'No chance.'

'And no footprints in the garden there, as we saw on the side yesterday.'

'None.'

'Well, then. No footprints this side of the wall, no footprints that side of the wall, ergo nobody got in this way. Come on, Morton. Stop playing with yourself on that wall.'

Morton slipped back down from the wall and followed the old fool.

'I told you, Morton, this is an inside job. The answer is in the pub. I've never seen a case ever so clear as this one.'

Morton decided he'd wait until Samson said 'inside job' ten times before hitting him over the head with something heavy. The thought pleased him so much he almost walked into Samson who had suddenly stopped.

'How close is that line to the top of the wall, son?'

'The washing line?'

'There's another line there?'

'No, I thought –'

'Don't think, lad, you'll do yourself an injury. Come on, get back up there and see if you can reach it.'

'I'm pretty sure I did –'

'Be extra pretty sure. Get back up and measure it.'

Morton trudged back, jumped back up the wall and dragged himself onto the top again.

'Just below the wall, about a foot or two. I can reach it quite easily.'

'Just below the wall? Good thing they didn't do that in Manchester in the old days, washing would have been nicked soon as you put it out. Where does it go to?'

'A window on the first floor.'

'Like I said. It'll be that laundry room.'

'Could be.'

'We'll have to check that. Okay, get down lad.'

Morton glanced at the ground before dropping down. He leaned over and began wiping his overcoat.

'There's a different footprint over there,' he said, nodding at the side of the path. 'It's smaller than the others.'

'Fox,' said Samson.

'Fox? Looks a bit large for a fox.'

'Seen many foxes, have we?'

'Well, not up close, but –'

'I have. Hundreds of the buggers. London's full of them, they're right pests. Feed off any rubbish humans leave out. Grow huge on it. They've got big, padded feet. Wouldn't object if they made fox-hunting legal again, they could do the little buggers around where I live. Were there any skis at the back door?'

'What?'

'The back door of the pub. Were there any skis there?'

'Skis? No. I didn't see any there.'

'Jump back up and have another look.'

Morton was still leaning over from wiping his coat. He closed his eyes and took a breath.

'No, don't worry lad, I'm pretty sure there won't be. Just a thought. Come on, let's go.'

He strode off and Morton hurried behind, still trying to get the dirt off the front of his coat. Samson stopped suddenly again. Morton's bent head almost hit him between the shoulder blades.

'They've been very clever, you know. They could have left footprints and all sorts of false clues for us to chase. Instead we know six or seven of them were involved, if not all of them, or some more, at least. But now we've got to match the would-be murderer to the weapon, and then prove which method was the actual killer. Yes, very sneaky. Say it was the gunshot that killed him. We prove that seven people went into the room, they admit it, but then, and this is the clever bit, each and every one says, Yes, I stabbed him, or I tried to garotte him, or I hit him over the head with a shovel, or I pushed bamboo skewers in one ear and out the other, but I didn't shoot him, so I didn't kill him. Prove that, Inspector Copper. It's your classic; admit something guilty, but not guilty enough. Jury can't decide, so they all get off scot-free with just a smack on the wrist from the judge. Oh, yes, very clever.'

Morton blinked, trying to work out which particular idiocy to address first.

'Um, if it was the gunshot, surely we just need to find the gun. Forensics will match the killer.'

'Nah, son. They'll have washed their hands pretty thoroughly. Probably wore gloves, too. And I bet you we find a haul of all the weapons, all conveniently hidden just out of sight for us to accidentally find after a bit of looking. And all cleaned spotless. Speaking of which, when you get the chance, ask around if anyone was washing their hands more than necessary. In the loo, or, I don't know, maybe in the kitchen.'

'In their bedrooms? In the en suite?'

'Could be. Could be. Somewhere inconspicuous. Ask if there's an outside tap anywhere. Come on, back into the pub. I want a word with Mrs Patsy. And I don't want Mr Constantine around while I do it. I don't trust those two.'

He strode off once more, Morton hurrying up behind. Once more he stopped suddenly and Morton again almost ran into the back of him.

'That washing line.'

'The washing line.'

'It couldn't hold much weight. It couldn't hold a man or woman. What about a child?'

'Very unlikely.'

'No, you're right, very unlikely. What about a dwarf?'

'A dwarf would probably weigh more than a child.'

'True. What about a monkey?'

'A what?'

'A monkey. A trained monkey. Like that one in Indiana Jones that puts the poison over the dates.'

'Poison over the dates?'

'Yes, now there's a thought.'

'Was it carrying a revolver in its holster?'

'Eh?'

'He was shot.'

'Yes, I know, but he was also poisoned.'

'And the monkey took the dates away afterwards? Climbing along the washing line?'

'Don't be sceptical, Morton. It had to happen somehow.'

'I'll make a note.'

'You have to think laterally, Morton. Or in your case, just try to think for starters. We can train you in the difficult bits later.'

Morton's hand closed over his smartphone. While Samson wasn't looking his way he took it out and tapped in

"eez living in iz dreams".

'Okay, so it probably wasn't a monkey. But it could have been a basket.'

'A basket?'

'Travelling along the washing line. One of them is in the laundry room. They put the weapons into a basket. Attach it to the line. Pull it until the basket reaches the wall. There's another one waiting, takes the basket, hurries off to hide it somewhere.'

'Without leaving footprints.'

'Eh?'

'You said there were no footprints here when you checked this morning.'

'Which proves my point. They really are cunning little bastards. Come on Morton, let's have a word with Mrs Constantine.'

'I'll make another note, sir.'

Morton carried on tapping in: "piskies fill an empty space".

They went back to the front entrance to the pub. As they reached the doors Samson held up an arm.

'Just a second, son. That Clarrie reckoned she could get from the front here up the apples without anyone spotting her. What do you think?'

'Up the what?'

'Up the apples.'

'The apples.'

'Yes, that's what I said. What do you reckon?'

'What apples?'

'In the corridor.'

'There are apples in the corridor?'

'Oh, for god's sake, man, what did they teach you at school? Apples and pears, stairs. She said she could get from here up the stairs without anyone spotting her. What do you reckon her chances are?'

'Oh, those apples. Of course. Up the apples. Yes.'

'Well?'

'Well, these doors would have been open, presumably.'

'On a winter's night? Nah, son, this is an old-fashioned pub, not one of your modern wine bars. Built long before central heating and air-conditioning. One huge fireplace in the central bar. Two sets of doors to minimise heat loss when someone comes in or goes out. Both would be closed during winter. Probably both open during summer. And the back door to get a breeze. Remind me to have a look at the back door at some stage. I don't think anyone would have used it, but you never know.'

He opened one of the outer doors and they stepped in.

'Inner doors are glass on top, but patterned. Christmas decorations. Not a lot, but probably enough to hide a man if he stood well back. Or a woman. He – or she – waits for their chance and then quietly opens the internal door and slips in.'

Samson pushed the door softly and silently until there was enough space to slip through. They faced a room full of bar furniture and the bar.

'Well, lad, you reckon you could slip in unnoticed?'

'Difficult to say. It's quiet now. Would have been a lot more noisy on Saturday night.'

'Not that noisy. And there's quite a distance to cover. I reckon not.'

'Maybe as a delivery guy? Carrying boxes that concealed his face?'

'You reckon?'

'Not really. It's unlikely. Someone would have mentioned it.'

'But it's a thought. Maybe whoever it was got here before anyone else and hid somewhere. So instead of looking for someone who was here we should be looking for someone who should have been here but wasn't. That Constable Clueless for a start. Make a note, we need to have a word with him at some stage.'

'But if it was more than one of them –'

'Then we're looking for more than one who should have been here but wasn't unless they were and it's a double bluff.'

'What about the ladies' bar. That has its own entrance.'

'Morton, I don't want to sound sexist, but can you imagine anyone managing to slip in without being noticed by a bar full of women?'

'If the women have been drinking heavily, then yes. My, er – I've had personal experience of that sort of thing.'

'Not the sort of woman who drinks in the Duck. They're more our genteel kind. But we'll have a look later just to be on the safe side. And we've still got a number of people to interview. Later. Come on.'

They crossed the main bar until they came to the passage that led to the other bars and upstairs.

'Hear anything?' Samson whispered.

'Nothing, sir.'

'Right, up the stairs, quick. Let's see if we can get Mrs Patsy on her own.'

Morton followed Samson as he trotted swiftly up the stairs and into the upstairs passage. They had almost reached the door to the upstairs flat when it opened and Patsy came backing out in a hurry.

'Yes, my angel, don't worry, my angel.'

He turned and found the other two in front of him.

'Duck!' he said with a completely deadpan face, before dropping to his knees and then falling flat on the floor.

'What?' asked Morton as Samson almost beat Patsy to the carpet.

'Duck!' said Samson from the floor.

A small frying pan came flying out making a whip-whip-whip noise with its handle. It caught Morton in his forehead just above his nose with a Clonk sound. Then it dropped to the carpet silently. Morton grabbed his face with both hands and fell back against the wall.

'Sure and are you all right, corporal?' asked Patsy, standing up and trying to inspect Morton's head through the other man's fingers. 'Sure and you're fortunate it was the little aluminium one. It's the ideal size when you just want to fry one egg.'

Samson stood up with the frying pan in his hand.

'Dinky little thing. Good thing she hadn't started using it. Otherwise you might have been burnt and well-oiled.'

'That bloody hurt! What the hell did she think she was doing? Assaulting a police officer. It bloody hurt.'

'Oh, come on, Morton, it's just a little light pan. Be grateful it wasn't a fifteen-inch non-stick enamel-coated pre-seasoned square cast-iron griddle pan with fixed handle. You'd be on the way to hospital. Or to heaven.'

'She wasn't aiming it at you, your honour, she was aiming it at me.'

'You sure of that, Mr Constantine?'

'Oh, to be sure, yes, your eminence, she often does that.'

'If I often did that I'd be aiming closer to the floor where your head would be when the flying pan arrived. No good throwing something like that at where the person is when you throw it.'

'Ah, sure sir, please don't go giving her ideas.'

'I don't want to give her ideas, Mr Constantine, I want to ask her some questions. Is she likely to throw anything else if we go in?'

'Ah, well, you can never be sure with her, your honour, she's never been the same since the accident. Her aim's not as good for a start.'

'Lucky for you, you'd be dead otherwise.'

'You mustn't judge her by her ways now. Sure, normally she's an angel. Or was when she was young. She was a nurse, you know, back in the old country.'

'Just what Morton needs, a nurse. In you go, Morton, let her have a look at your noodle. Where you got the dink.'

'Noodle?'

'Nut.'

'Nut?'

'Noggin.'

'Noggin?'

'Bonce. His bloody head you fool.'

'Ah, of course, sor.'

'I'd rather not, sir, I'm fine, really I am.'

'Now might not be the best of times, sor, sure and she'll be fine if you let her calm down for half an hour.'

'Always strike while the frying pan is hot. Come on, Morton, you first, in you go. Here you are, take the frying pan, think of it as a votive offering to restless natives. Pretend you're Captain Cook.'

'He got killed by the natives.'

'Well, pretend you're Captain Cook before he got killed by the bloody natives, get on, lad, chop chop.'

'I'll be downstairs if you need me,' said Patsy from half-way down the stairs.

Morton took the frying pan unwillingly and tried unsuccessfully to resist Samson's chivvying, advancing towards the living quarters with his shoulders hunched, his head almost in his stomach and the frying pan held out in front of him.

'Morning Mrs Constantine, we've brought your flying frying pan back. Could you refrain from chucking anything else at us, we're police officers, on duty police officers. The constable here wants to return your frying pan. It's only slightly dented, like his bonce.'

They stepped into a small lounge in which a woman sat in an old-fashioned bath chair which appeared to have a steering device in front. She was wearing a high-necked red blouse with a frilly white collar, small reflective pebble-glass spectacles, light brown chamois gloves, a tall black Stetson-type hat with a long green feather in it, and a red and blue plaid blanket over her knees. She was waiting for their entrance with hands that clenched and unclenched as her face glared behind the spectacles. Behind her was a fireplace above which hung a portrait of a half-man, half-goat playing a set of flutes, his eyes looking directly at the viewer with the glint of an evil, suggestive smile. There were dozens of different sized and different coloured frying pans hanging from hooks on the walls, black, copper, silver, some with stains burnt into them.

'Detective Inspector Samson, no P. And this is Detective Constable Morton, T but no P.'

'Well?'

'Give the nice lady her frying pan back, Morton. Now, Mrs Constantine, we'd like to ask you a few questions about last night.'

He sat down in an armchair, lay back with his hands over his stomach and his legs outstretched, waiting for her reply. Morton stood holding the pan out towards Mrs Constantine while keeping as far away from her as possible.

'Last night? The night before. Any night. You can see I'm confined to a wheelchair. I'm always here.'

'The incident happened on the same floor. And I presume you have ways of navigating the different floors.'

'So?'

'How?'

'How what?'

'How do you navigate the different floors?'

'With the help of a dumb waiter.'

Her hand shot out suddenly and she grabbed the pan. Morton jumped back two feet just as she brought it down on where his knuckles had been.

'A larger than normal dumb waiter?'

'The larger sort. Big enough to handle my wheelchair.'

'I thought it would be something like that. Lady like you is far too independent not to have ways and means.'

'Get to the point, Inspector.'

'What is your full name, Mrs Constantine? For the record. Do take notes, Morton, make yourself useful.'

'Yes, sir.'

'Elvira Svetlana Magdalen Constantine. Née Doherty, if you need to know.'

'Sorry, Mrs Constantine, how do you spell –'

'With a V, Morton. What were you doing last night, Mrs Constantine?'

'I was doing the factory accounts.'

'The factory accounts. Which factory would that be?'

'The Angel Cake factory. I presume you've heard of the Angel Cake factory. It employs most employed people around here. Most employable employed people around here. Doherty's seeded Angel Cake. You have heard of Doherty's Seeded Angel Cake? The special edition. Or maybe not. It's quite expensive. You won't find it in

Tesco or Sainsburys.'

'I know. Morton here had two helpings for pud last night.'

Mrs Constantine gave Morton a glance which might have been admiration or disbelief.

'You're their accountant?'

'I'm the owner.'

'The owner.'

'Of course. Why do you think we moved here?'

'To run the pub?'

'Don't be a fool.'

'You bought the factory?'

'I inherited it from an alcoholic uncle who had one too many and drove off a cliff. It should have come directly to me after my father died. But he presumably didn't think a woman could do the job. Left it to his brother who started running it into the ground from the first day.'

'In what way?'

'Listened to the accountants. Never listen to accountants. They will always tell you how to save money, never how to make money.'

'And your uncle was trying to save money.'

'He was planning on moving production to Poland because it would be cheaper. Going for mass production. Got in some American consultants who advised him to change the recipe to use palm oil. Awful stuff. Fortunately he died just in time, otherwise I might have had to arrange an accident. I turned it around again, the way my grandfather originally built it.'

'Interesting. Your husband never mentioned that.'

'Would you if you were a man? He likes to think he's the breadwinner with this pub. It's a hobby I permit him. It loses money hand over fist. A bed and breakfast with hardly ever any guests. Underpriced drinks. Half a dozen bars. You can't make a profit out of a pub these days, the supermarkets undercut you way too much. Cheaper for people to sit at home and get drunk than to socialise in a pub.'

'I see.'

'It keeps him happy.'

'While you throw pans at him.'

'That keeps him happy too. It relieves his guilt at putting me in this wheelchair.'

'That was an accident?'

'I wasn't expecting him to get out of the way so fast. He is surprisingly quick at times. The wrong times.'

'Last night, Mrs Constantine. Did you hear anything, see anything that might have a bearing on what happened. A shot, for example.'

'I only heard one shot.'

'You heard a shot?'

'That's what I said.'

'When?'

'When I pulled the trigger.'

'I see. You were firing a firearm.'

'Your deduction is amazing, Inspector.'

'What type of firearm?'

'A point-four-five revolver. A Webley. It belonged to my grandfather. He took it off an English officer during World War Two.'

'He was a soldier?'

'No, he was a thief.'

'I thought he owned the Angel Cake factory.'

'That's obviously the other grandfather, Morton, try to keep up. Were you firing at anything specific?'

'My husband.'

'Do you often shoot at him?'

'Only when there isn't a frying pan nearby.'

'And what time did you hear the shot, Mrs Constantine?'

'About nine o'clock.'

'You were sitting in here?'

'I was sitting over there with the door open. It gives you a clear view of part of the passage.'

'While you did the accounts for the Angel Cake factory?'

'I'd finished those by then.'

'You missed, I presume?'

'Is my husband still alive?'

'I believe so.'

'Then I missed. The Webley is too heavy to aim properly. It wobbles. Too often I hit the floor or ceiling.'

'Did you hear or see anything else?'

'Nothing unusual. A pub is full of noises in the evening, especially on a Saturday.'

'Tell me, Mrs Constantine: every single one of us is concealing a terrible secret. What's yours?'

'What?'

'Every single one of us is concealing a terrible secret. What's yours?'

'You think I'm concealing a terrible secret?'

'Yes.'

'And you want to know what it is?'

'Yes.'

'Very well, Inspector, I'll tell you. You know the recipe for the Angel Cake?'

'I don't know what it is. I presume there is one.'

'Only one person in the entire world has a copy of the recipe.'

'That's like Kentucky Fried Chicken, isn't it? Only there's seven people and they're not allowed to fly together. Or eat fish together. Or any seafood.'

'Shut up Morton. Carry on Mrs Constantine.'

'Where was I?'

'Only one person in the entire world has a copy of the recipe. For the Angel Cake.'

'Ah, yes. And that person is me.'

'You have it securely hidden.'

'It's in a plastic sealed envelope.'

'I see.'

'In my panties.'

'I – I don't think that's relevant to the case.'

'And there's a reason no-one will ever try to take it from me.'

'I can't imagine.'

'Underneath this blanket …'

'Yes?'

'I'm holding the Webley.'

'I think you ought to give that to us, Mrs Constantine.'

'Shut up, Morton.'

'You do believe me, don't you, Inspector.'

'Of course, Mrs Constantine. I think that will be all for now. Come on, Morton.'

'But, sir –'

'Come on, Morton. Try to pretend you aren't as thick as a brick for five seconds. Start with one second and work your way up.'

Morton followed Samson out into the passage. Samson closed the door softly and gently and beckoned Morton to follow him down the stairs. They entered the main bar and Samson led the way to the centre where they were surrounded by empty tables and chairs and no ears.

'Sir, if she's got a Webley revolver, I mean, unlicensed, surely we ought to –'

'We ought to avoid getting ourselves plugged with nasty holes. Do you know how much damage one of those bullets can make? Those things were designed as portable artillery pieces.'

'But –'

'On the other hand, if she isn't packing a piece, if she's just winding us up, what do you think will happen when you try to take it away from her, out of her lap, in fact, very close to where this secret recipe is supposed to be?'

'Ah.'

'Where is the recipe, Morton?'

'In her panties.'

'Precisely. You try explaining that to the Chief Constable. Or in fact anyone. The judge, probably.'

'Ah.'

'Don't get sidetracked, Morton, remember why we're here. Didn't you notice anything about what Mrs Constantine said?'

'She said she fired a shot at Patsy.'

'Precisely. First, why was Patsy upstairs, if he was? Everybody's been trying to convince us that no-one went upstairs the whole of the evening, yet according to Mrs Constantine Patsy was up there long enough to get shot at. Secondly, if she did fire at him, how come no-one has mentioned hearing the shot? Those things don't come with silencers. The entire pub would have heard it, even if they had music playing full blast.'

'Ah.'

'Thirdly, where's the bullet hole? You can't fire one of those things without making an awful mess in something. It would have left a hole in a wall large enough to put your fist through.'

'You don't think she did fire at Patsy?'

'I doubt it. Not a Webley, that's for sure.'

'So why is she feeding us a pack of lies?'

'They're not lies.'

'What?'

'They're not lies to her.'

'I don't understand.'

'See that painting behind her?'

'Yes. It's the only realistic painting in the place. That stuff by Stokes does my head in.'

'Dear god. Think about it, Morton. I'll let you know when you're getting warm. For the moment go find Charity. She promised to make a list of everyone here on Saturday night. I'll be out in the car. Thinking.'

'Carry.'

'That's the one. She's a fit looking little thing isn't she. Needs to wear tighter clothing, mind, that's what all the girls do these days. Nice, tight jeans, showing her bum. Stretch, that's what it's called. And one of those tight tops with cleavage that doesn't leave anything to the imagination.'

Morton watched Samson walk out. Just when you thought the idiot could no longer surprise you he did. Fit looking little thing? Bum? Cleavage? That was downright pervy. The old fool was old enough to be her father.

He looked over the bar counter in case Carry's bum was behind there, packing crisps. There was no-one. He couldn't see a suggestion of a shadow that might indicate she was in one of the other bars. He looked in the snug. There was no sign of Carry or anyone else. One of the horses looked back at him with a sneer on its face. He checked the ladies' bar. It was pristine and human-free. It was so pristine it almost looked at him with the question, 'Yes, young man, and what are you doing here, don't you know where the servants' entrance is?'

A brief movement of light suggested someone was behind the counter in the saloon bar. He hurried on to the saloon bar. That too was spotless and empty, with a residual feeling of a florid-faced lord of the manor wearing a checked waistcoat and a glare. Finally he checked the pool room. Four tables stood heavily and cleanly, as if unpacked the day before and hoovered overnight. The cues stood in their racks at attention. He glanced at the top of them. Not one had any chalk dust on it. They had either never been used or their tips had been recently replaced. He had an urge to take the balls out and have a game, but somehow everything looked too new, as if it was only an image of a pool room, and the tables might collapse into dust if anyone tried to pot a shot.

He wandered back into the passage. It was too early in the morning to be open, but he would have expected some activity. Someone cleaning, or a delivery, or preparations for a Christmas party. He looked down the passage towards the kitchen. There was a bold and very definite notice saying 'STAFF ONLY'. He recalled Carry's warning. He decided to try the office first. After a polite knock and no answer he opened the door. There was no-one in. He double-checked in case someone was hiding behind the door or underneath the desk.

No-one.

He tried the door behind the desk. It was locked. He left the office and walked slowly back to the public bar. Carry sat on her usual stool as if she had been there forever. She was reading a piece of paper. She waited until he was closer before pushing it toward him.

'Your boss's list of suspects.'

'Ah, thanks, I was looking for that.'

'You mean he sent you to collect it. Messenger boy.'

'Why did you agree to write it out for him? That's pretty much aiding and abetting the enemy.'

'You think the inspector's the enemy?'

'Samson's the enemy of pretty much everything. Intelligence. Modern thinking. Good taste. But what I meant is, you hate coppers.'

'Do I?'

'Or is it just me you can't handle.'

'Don't flatter yourself.'

'That's it, isn't it?'

'What makes you think it's accurate?'

'What's accurate?'

'The kama sutra.'

'The list? Is it?'

'What do you think?'

'I don't know. But I wouldn't mind if it wasn't.'

'I thought you knew everything.'

'I know your type likes playing hard to get.'

'How stupid would you say your boss is?'

'He's not my boss.'

'No?'

'Only temporarily. Until he goes back to London.'

'So how stupid would you say he is?'

'On a scale of one to ten? About a fifteen.'

'And yet he's your superior officer.'

'Know what his own people say about him? He couldn't find his own elbow with a Satnav on a sunny day.'

'That's what you call him. Sir.'

'Like I said. Not for long.'

'I think your lord and master is getting impatient. That is the sound that horrible pink thing makes, isn't it?'

'Mauve.'

'What?'

'The Studebaker. It's mauve.'

'It's pink.'

'Who said it's pink?'

'I say it's pink. I say he told you it's mauve. And you believed him. I'm surprised he didn't tell you it was called Cerise.'

'He didn't tell me anything.'

'I don't blame him. He's still hooting.'

'He can hoot. Mrs Patsy says she gets around with the help of a dumb waiter.'

'Must be true, then.'

'So who is this waiter and why is he dumb?'

'Come again.'

'Who is this waiter and why is he dumb?'

'I can't hear you.'

'Who is this waiter and why is he dumb?'

'You're joking.'

'Why should I be joking?'

'Ah, of course. You don't do any cooking.'

'What?'

'Never worked in a kitchen.'

'Certainly not.'

'I should have known. His name's Eric.'

'Eric?'

'The dumb waiter.'

'He helps Mrs Patsy get around.'

'Mmm-hmmm.'

'Can he read and write?'

'What?'

'Can he read and write? We'll have to interview him some time. Will we need someone who can sign?'

'Sign?'

'Someone who knows sign language.'

'You'll need a lot more than that.'

'Where is he?'

'I'll ask Patsy to introduce you later.'

'Okay. Thanks for the list.'

'Do you want to know his surname?'

'Whose?'

'Eric.'

'Go on.'

'Delift.'

'Delift. Dutch?'

'And some. Like you get cream and double cream.'

'Eh?'

'I'll explain it to you sometime.'

'Eric Delift. Right.

Morton went out to the front where Samson was beating a continuous, monotonous rhythm on the hooter. He was only half into the passenger seat when Samson dropped the clutch and the Studebaker spun its wheels before taking off, leaving Morton struggling to close the door.

'How's this for a scenario? Our Vic is walking back from the bathroom with his sponge bag in his hand. Mrs Patsy thinks it's Constantine, takes a pot shot, hits our Vic by accident. He's just about to go into his room, falls inside and pulls the door closed behind him. No-one to blame, pure accident.'

'Apart from the fact that no-one heard the gun go off.'

'Not a Webley. That would have made a much bigger hole. And a hell of a bang. No, she just talks about a Webley because that's the only type of revolver she's heard of. It's like a hoover.'

'What?'

'People talk about using their hoover even when it's not a Hoover. It's a Panasonic or something like that.'

'Panasonic make hoovers?'

'No. That's the whole point. Hoover make Hoovers. Other people make hoovers. It's become a generic term. Same way Mrs Patsy calls a revolver a Webley when it's probably not. That's why no-one heard anything. It was a smaller gun. A pistol. Maybe with a silencer.'

'Why would Mrs Patsy use a silencer? She's quite happy throwing fucking frying pans around with gay abandon. She's hardly likely to worry about a gunshot, is she? Anyway, where would she get a silencer?'

'Where would she get anything? She's a resourceful woman. Think out of the tree for once.'

'But why would he be going to to another bathroom anyway? His was an en-suite. He didn't need to use the bathroom in the passage.'

'Okay, so maybe he wasn't going to the bathroom. Maybe he was standing with the door closed, just in front of the door and the bullet went through and killed him.'

'Without leaving a bullet hole.'

'They changed the door. When they realised what had happened they panicked and put a new door in. While they're doing that – or someone is doing it – the others create a smokescreen with all that other evidence, strangling, stabbing, bludgeoning, all the rest. Then they call us. If we can get them to confess it'll be case closed and we can go home.'

'And Mrs Patsy gets banged up for attempted murder.'

'Nah. It was an accident. They were just playing a game they've played for years. Like bondage. Nothing illegal about tying someone up if it's consensual. Tie a bag around their head, they suffocate, unfortunate accident.'

'I can't see a judge buying that.'

'I can.'

'And how did he get into the cupboard?'

'Maybe he staggered there.'

'And closed it afterwards?'

'I told you. They found the bullet hole. They look inside, find his body, put it into the cupboard and replace the door. Simple. Remember Occam's Shaver. Don't over-complicate things.'

'Should that be Occam's Razor, sir?'

'I told you, it was a sponge bag. Mark my words. Right. Next stop Mrs Sir whatsherface.'

'What?'

'Sir Anthony's missus.'

'Lady Freechin.'

'That's the one. See if we can catch her without her husband.'

'If Mrs Patsy killed him, why are we doing this?'

'I like to be thorough. Don't want any loose ends for people to unravel.'

'So you don't think it was an inside job now?'

'Of course it was an inside job. First the accident of shooting the Polish bloke and then they all tried to hide it.'

'Right. That reminds me, I've got the list.'

'The list? Charity's list? Excellent. Anything interesting?'

'Carry. Well, there are quite a few people we haven't interviewed.'

'I know. There's a time for everything. Keep to the plan, don't let yourself get spooked.'

'Plan?'

'Oh, yes. They might not realise we have a plan, but I do.'

'We have a plan?'

'I told you a thousand times. We follow the plan, lull them into a sense of security, and then, wham! When they least expect it. Watch and learn, my boy.'

'Oh. Of course. I forgot. That plan. Wham. Very well, sir. Wham.'

'Another thing. Mrs Constantine and her wheelchair. When you get a chance, tip her over.'

'What?'

'Tip her over. Make it look like an accident.'

'What?'

'See which way she rolls. Or walks.'

'Rolls.'

'And get a good look at what's in the wheelchair while you're about it. What she's sitting on.'

'I'll make a note of that.'

'Good boy.'

Morton tapped in "ee'z piskie-maized".

Samson rolled his window down, put his elbow on the rest and hand on the roof and tapped as he whistled a tune. Morton put his phone away, pulled his coat in, buttoning it up to his chin. Samson's hair flapped in the wind.

Morton suddenly realised what the tune was.

It was ding, dong, merrily on high.

They drove inland for a while. The countryside changed from beach-type scrub to farm fields lightly covered in snow and bordered with hedges or barbed wire. They passed a golf course and then came to the entrance to a rolling driveway up to a mansion. There was an anonymous silver Volvo parked to one side as if quietly kept out of the way. Samson looked at it as they got out.

'I do not like the look of that,' he murmured.

'Sir?'

'Volvos. In a place like this. Never a good sign. Should be a Jag at least. A Mini for the secretary. Volvos are too sensible, too practical. Like they mean business. You know in the movies, where the baddie says to the hero, I'm going to cut you into a hundred pieces but first I'm going to sing you a song?'

'Er, if you say so, sir.'

'And that gives the hero the time to wriggle out of his bonds and throw the baddie off the cliff before he can get to the second last verse. Well, Volvo drivers don't bother with all that crap. They just pull the trigger and walk away.'

'Shouldn't that be "drive away"?'

'Never mind, Morton, follow my lead, don't get sidetracked. Come on.'

They walked up the steps and Samson rang the door bell.

'Lovely doors, don't you reckon. Lovely knocker, too. I've always liked good knockers. Who do you suppose uses the knocker when there's a perfectly good little bell to press?'

Morton didn't have a chance to answer before the door opened and a man stood back and gestured them in with a fluid movement of his arm.

'Chief Inspector Samson, Constable Morton, my name is Phillip

Codwallader. I'm Sir Anthony's … personal assistant. If you'll follow me.'

He led them to a small huge room off the small huge entrance hall, letting them enter first. He closed the door behind them.

'Now, Inspector, it's my job to protect Sir Anthony and his family from the slings and arrows of an outrageous fortune. I'm afraid he's somewhat of a babe in the woods despite his fearsome reputation in the City.'

'He works in the City?'

'He has a fearsome reputation in the City.'

'And you don't want that fearsome reputation affected in any way.'

'Quite. And he has been of great service to his country as many are aware. Many of us, anyway.'

'Great service to his country?'

'Even if he might not necessarily realise just how much.'

'A Major Martin of his times?'

'I could not possibly comment, Chief Inspector.'

'I see.'

'To put it succinctly, if there's nothing to involve him in this unfortunate incident – and I'm sure you'll confirm that – then it would be most welcome if the press don't become aware of where he was on Saturday evening. Or anyone else.'

'I see.'

'Not that I'm trying to pressure you, or suggesting anything unlawful.'

'I see.'

'Um, is there anything you don't understand, Chief Inspector?'

'No, sir, I understand perfectly.'

'Ah, good.'

'Now, if we could see Lady Freechin?'

'Of course. Follow me. And thank you, Chief Inspector.'

He led them out of the huge reception room, across the huge entrance area, and into a huge lounge that seemed to contain about six couches and fourteen deep armchairs. A woman sat at a table right at the end. They slogged across rugs of varying depth until they reached socially acceptable speaking distance.

'Lady Freechin, Chief Inspector Samson and Detective Constable Morton,' Phillip Codwallader announced. Lady Freechin looked up with bright blue eyes and a welcoming smile.

'Gentlemen, please, take a seat. Would you like something to drink? A tea or coffee? Or something stronger? A brandy or whisky? Or beer? I'm afraid I've never been able to guess gentlemen's preferences. In that department. My husband is very much a brandy man, but my son prefers beer. Though he does play rugby. And squash. And other sports. Perhaps the two are related.'

Samson sat down in the one armchair which didn't look like it might swallow an occupant whole. Morton looked around at the others and chose to stay standing.

'Thank you, Lady Freechin. I'm normally a whisky man, but knowing Sir Anthony's excellent taste, I wouldn't say no to a brandy.'

'On the rocks?'

'No, neat, thank you.'

'And how about you, Detective Constable?'

'Ah, no thank you, ma'am. I'm on ... er ... well, no, thanks, not at the moment.'

'A large brandy for the Chief Inspector, please Phillip. You know, Chief Inspector, I often wished I married someone called Muck. Then everyone would call me Lady Muck. What do you think?'

'That you've also worked out that someone called Muck would never get a knighthood. We won't bother you for long, Lady Freechin. Thank you, Mr Codwallader, very kind. Lady Freechin, could you just confirm that you knew your husband was going to the Duck and Angel on Saturday night?'

'My goodness, Chief Inspector, you don't beat about the bush, do you? Yes, I knew his story about the Fenchincham British Legion memorial dinner was his usual little – well, story. He did used to go to all the legion dinners, he felt it was his duty. But he never enjoyed them. He was never really made for the military life, you know. He hates uniforms, for a start. Then one night he left a dinner early and popped into the Angel and Duck on the way back, and found he rather liked it. And as he neared retirement he began to leave dinners earlier and earlier until he didn't go at all. So now we pretend that he's still going to legion dinners even though he isn't. He feels it's the right thing to do. He's at least appearing to fulfil his duty, which is the important thing, don't you think, Chief Inspector?'

'I fully agree, Lady Freechin, appearances are very important. And there does come a time in life when it's better just to relax and enjoy a brandy in the Angel and Duck if that's what you prefer. '

'You don't think he had anything to do with that terrible business on Saturday, do you?'

'The thought never entered my mind for a second, Lady Freechin. But we had to go through the motions, make sure we'd ticked all the right boxes. It takes time, but there you go.'

'Of course. Would you like another brandy, Inspector?'

'I'd love another brandy, Lady Freechin, It's a very fine brandy. But perhaps better not, I'm driving.'

'You should let Detective Constable Morton drive. I'm sure he'd prefer it, young men do.'

'It's quite a temperamental car. It can get moody if someone else drives it.'

'A Studebaker 1965. A lovely car. But old, like most of us these days. My husband buys a new Jag every year. When we were first married we had the same Jag for ten years. It broke his heart to have to give it up. He wanted to grow old with it. Unfortunately it began to cost too much to keep repairing it. And they do if you keep driving into potholes. He never was a very good driver. So he decided he would never keep another car for long enough to grow attached to it. And of course he now has Huckleberry so ironically the cars last longer.'

'Huckleberry?'

Lady Freechin waved a hand.

'I don't know what you'd call him, really. Driver, caddy, general factotum, bodyguard, gardener. He looks stupid, but he's been trained to do that. He does shopping over the Internet if we run short.

Amazing what they can do these days. I have never had an affinity for machines myself.'

'Bodyguard?'

'Oh, yes, he can kill with one hand, you know. Anthony was very taken with that. Apparently men do.'

'Do what?'

'They're very impressed with someone who can kill with one hand. Aren't you, Chief Inspector?'

'No, Lady Freechin, it's not the most efficient way to kill someone. And I normally end up arresting people like that.'

'Oh. Well, I suppose you would, wouldn't you. What is?'

'What is what?'

'The most efficient way of killing someone?'

'Making sure they're dead.'

'That does seem logical.'

'Well, thanks for the brandy, Lady Freechin, we'll see ourselves out.'

'Oh, don't worry, Mr Codwallader will do that. Be a darling and do, Phillip.'

'Yes, Lady Freechin.'

Codwallader shepherded them politely back to the front door.

'So, Chief Inspector, you won't need to involve Sir Anthony in this business?'

'I can promise you, Mr Codwallader, Sir Anthony's name will not appear in any report I write.'

'Very kind.'

Back in the car Samson reversed out and drove away.

'Don't look back, lad, they're watching us.'

'How do you know?'

'Notice how she mentioned the Studebaker? They were watching us from before we even entered the driveway. I bet you that entrance is covered by cameras long before you get anywhere near it.'

'So why agree to keep him out of it? They sound dodgy as hell.'

'A) Because he's got nothing to do with it. And B), I don't want his associates interfering with my plan. That Phillip Codwallader is a very nice polite man, if he thought it necessary he'd have a very nice polite word with someone more senior, and they'd have a very nice polite word with the Chief Constable, who would give us a very nasty bollocking and probably take us off the case. Morton, in this job you've got to have a one-track mind. Don't let irrelevancies derail you.'

'What if it turns out he has something to do with this whole business.'

'He doesn't.'

'But he could.'

'Morton, if that turns out to be the case we arrest him, lock him up and throw away the key.'

'But you said to Lady Freechin –'

'So I'll have lied. Morton, you have some strange scruples. Phoned your missus yet?'

'I left a message this morning.'

'Let's go into town. We can get some lunch and you can check your fan mail.'

Morton stayed silent as they drove onto a motorway. To his relief Samson kept the window up. It was with mixed feelings that he experienced Samson burp and exhale brandy fumes which made him try to remember how many units were in a double brandy, and how many units were necessary to put someone over the limit. Added to this was the uncertainty as to whether the Studebaker's glory days were over and the sudden small lurches to one side or other were the result of mechanical wear and tear, or whether Samson was more affected by the drink he had taken than would be expected. Fortunately a sign appeared to alert them to the wonders of a retail shopping centre a mile ahead.

'Got a decent signal, son?'

Morton took out his mobile.

'Five bars.'

'Well, we'll pull in to this place. Grace that well-known fast food emporium with our custom. I fancy an egg-cheese burger with chips and all the tomato sauce and mustard in the world. Covered in gherkins. I tell you something, Morton, you have to enjoy it while you can. I'll be going on a diet for the rest of my life after this case. Normally I'd be living off coffee and doughnuts. Not good for anyone, that sort of lifestyle.'

They pulled into a car park outside of a burger bar.

'You make your calls, I'll wait here.'

Morton walked a while away while Samson leaned against the Studebaker's boot and watched the world go by. The retail centre was a huge car park surrounded on three sides by warehouse-type shops, a toyshop, a DIY retailer, a cheap sports shop, a bargain carpet whole-saler, and a branch of an expensive furniture retailer. The fourth side was the entrance and exit roads either side of the huge burger palace. The whole was topped with a frothing movement of humans, cars coming in, adults rushing to shops, others returning with loaded trolleys, people popping into and out of the palace, and cars leaving. There was a frenetic energy without the single sound of a toddler crying or a youngster demanding the need to go. There was something odd about the lack.

Morton dialled a number. He waited until a machine answered, swore, and dialled another.

'Tracey? It's Luke. I've been trying to get hold of Shirley. Is she in today?'

'She called in sick?'

'Yes, I did try the flat, she must be asleep. Probably taken something for whatever she's got.'

'No, no problem, it's just I'm on a case and I've been away over the weekend. I keep missing her.'

'No, I really am on a case, I've been lumbered with this complete idiot of an inspector, you wouldn't believe how thick he is. He's a complete pain in the arse.'

'Okay, I'll call her later. Do me a favour and let her know if she calls in.'

He dialled another number.'

'Dick? Listen I don't have much time. This idiot Samson is waiting for me. Did you get anything on Clarissa Hope?'

'Really?'

'Drugs. Thought so.'

'He what? Forgot to read her her rights? What a complete plonker. Rookie mistake number one.'

'Yeah, well, pity. A bit of jail time would have helped. Listen, can you run some other people through the computer? Here's the names: Sir Anthony Freechin and his wife Lady Freechin; Richard Coombes-Neeston; and someone calling himself Phillip Codwallader. That should do for the moment. I'll have some more names for you later, okay?'

'Excellent, great stuff mate, I owe you a pint.'

He ended the call and walked back to the Studebaker.

'Bought anything for the missus yet, have you, son?'

'Sorry?'

'For Christmas. I was watching these people going shopping and it seemed to me that there were an awful lot of them rushing around without kids, but they looked like the types that are always dragging kids around the shops. Then it struck me: they're hiding something.'

'They're hiding something.'

'From the kids. They don't want them to know what they're getting for Christmas. So they arrange to rush out here at lunch hour or something, some excuse, so they can buy the kids' presents before taking them home to hide, or something like that. And the kids have to pretend that they don't know what's going on. So it's true. Everybody does have something to hide. Come on, let's go fill our arteries to dangerous levels. Tomorrow we die. But it doesn't matter, for life is ultimately meaningless. Know who said that?'

'No, sir.'

'I just did, you idiot. Come on.'

Carry was sitting on a bar stool behind the bar in the public bar, reading a national newspaper. A man in motorcycle leathers wearing a full face motorcycle helmet and reflective dark glasses walked in and placed a shoe-box sized parcel in front of her.

'Parcel for the Angel and Duck,' he said. 'Needs a signature.'

Carry looked at it.

'What is it?'

'Label says serviettes.'

'I know what the label says, I asked what's in it.'

'Don't know what you mean, love.'

Carry turned and picked up the internal phone. She waited a few seconds for someone to answer.

'Patsy, a parcel of serviettes has arrived. It needs a signature.'

'No, I am not going to sign for it. Nor am I going to touch it. If you want your – serviettes – then you will have to come and sign for them and pick them up and take them away. Otherwise I will ask this bloke to take them back where they came from.'

'Yes, I thought you would.'

She put the phone back on its hook, climbed back on the stool and resumed her perusal of the paper.

'He'll be down shortly.'

'Jesus, can't you sign for them? They're only bleeding serviettes.'

'Sounds religious.'

'Wot?'

'Bleeding serviettes. Sounds Catholic. Or that time of the month.'

'What?'

'Oh, dear. Do you need an explanation of that time of the month? Shall I draw you a picture?'

'You're nuts, you are.'

'Not nuts enough to sign for serviettes. When serviettes need signing for that's the time not to sign for them. It doesn't need my signature and it sure as hell isn't getting my fingerprints.'

'Eh?'

'And here's Patsy. Been doing the washing up, Patsy?'

'Eh, yes, that's it, I've been doing the washing up.'

'Which is why you're wearing Marigolds. Handy, that.'

'Where do I sign?'

'Just here, mate.'

'There you are. Thank you, enjoy the rest of the day.'

'You too, mate. Don't use it all at once. I mean them.'

'You see, my little angel, them's just serviettes. For the pub.'

'If you say so, Patsy. Me, I didn't see or hear anything. Three monkeys, I am.'

'Three monkeys?'

'See nothing, hear nothing, say nothing.'

'Ah, them three little monkeys.'

'Brass ones.'

Samson and Morton went into the fast food place. There were two tills open and no queues. Most of the customers were on their own with shopping, hastily consuming fuel, apart from two tables of idle teenagers from some local estate whiling away the hours with orders of fries and Coke.

'Old-fashioned place,' said Samson.

'Old-fashioned?'

'Most of these places are digitised or whatever it's called. You put your order into a machine, pay for it with your credit card, then collect it from the counter.'

'Yes, I've seen that.'

'Oh, well, price of progress I suppose. What do you fancy?' Samson waved a card. 'Perk of the rank, it goes on my official credit card, so don't skimp.'

'Well, I think I might have chicken for a change. Don't want too much red meat. It's not good for you.'

'We come into a burger bar and order chicken?'

'Their chicken is okay. Actually their wings are the best I've had.'

'Okay. I tell you what, we'll have the Family Five,' Samson told the assistant. 'With a two-litre Coke.'

'You do know that that's for a family of five, sir?'

'This lad's young, he needs his calories. Goes all weak if you don't feed him properly. Goes all week if you do.'

'Sorry?'

'Just get us the Family bucket, lass, with all the side bits and bobs plus Coke and don't worry about it. Junior here could have two of those and still have room for more.'

Morton watched as the girl assembled all the requirements needed for a family of five. Fortunately Samson didn't appear in the mood for small talk. Eventually the girl came back with a large tray, a large bucket of chicken, enough fries for a French army, a 2-litre Coke plus glasses, and a stack of little tubs containing five sets of potato salad, five sets of coleslaw and five sets of baked beans.

'Do you want the toys?'

'Toys?'

'Family bucket always comes with toys. Three toys.'

'Three toys, eh?'

'It's a family of five. Mom, dad, and three children. Three toys.'

'Junior here can have the toys. He likes playing with his toys, don't you, son.'

The till assistant dropped three plastic-covered toys on the tray. Samson used the credit card to pay for them and then took them to a table far from the counter and next to the wall.

'Fill your boots. We don't leave until this lot is finished. There are starving children in China, you know.'

Morton shrugged mentally and got stuck in. A full mouth would provide a good excuse not to have to say much. And to his relief Samson didn't appear interested in chit-chat, he was doing his part in demolishing the food. But there were few people to match Morton in that department, and Samson wasn't even close to being one. Samson appeared to acknowledge this by pushing various tubs his way as soon as he had finished something, neatly stacking the empty tubs to one side as if he was suffering some outburst of OCD.

Morton's stomach informed him that it was well and truly above full about thirty seconds after he had gone through every wrapper and tub and bucket to make sure no crumb had escaped. Even the two-litre plastic bottle was empty. He leaned back and burped.

'Victorians used to believe a burp was a sign of enjoyment,' Samson said, idly using a toothpick while looking out the window. 'Old Queen Vic probably did it all the time. You know, they talk about Victorian prudery, but you look at the way she was after Albert died, and they way they banged out brats almost non-stop. At it like rabbits, they were.'

Morton dabbed at his mouth with a serviette so that he didn't have to answer.

'So what sort of toys did they give you. lad?'

Morton picked up the three plastic-wrapped toys as if they were merely of passing interest.

'Oh, wow! It's the duck series. I heard of these.'

'Duck series?'

'They have different collections. Super heroes, Pokemon, Teenage Mutant Ninja Turtles, that sort of thing. Chipmunks. These are from a series of ducks. There's sitting ducks, dead ducks, duck a l'orange. That's a duck with an orange.'

'No? That's cute. What will these advertising people think of next?'

'These are – that's pretty good, really, it's a sitting duck, a dead duck and a spotted duck. When I was a kid you'd get loads of the same thing for ages. Like they did super heroes, and you'd get Batman, and the next meal it would be Batman again, and so on. You'd hear of some kid who had got a Superman, but it was always someone else. And there was supposed to be a Superwoman toy, but nobody ever got that, and if there was one the staff behind the counter kept it for the girls. I mean, how unfair is that?'

'Really unfair.'

'I think I'll keep these,' Morton said, putting the plastic-wrapped toys into his pocket.

'What's spotted duck?'

'It's a play on spotted dick.'

'Spotted duck has a spotted dick?'

'We used to chase the girls with one when we were kids at school. They were terrified of it for some reason. After all it's only a tiny plastic toy.

Samson put his toothpick into one of the empty containers and sighed.

'You know, I think my greatest regret in all my years as a copper has been saying no to drinks.'

Morton patted his pocket to make sure the duck toys were safely in.

'Drinks?'

'I remember my first sergeant when I was a plod on patrol. Lunch time and dinner time we'd do a beat past this pub called, what was it, the Golden Hind or some silly name. East London. Round the back. And there'd always be two pints of ale on this window sill. Nothing said, just a couple of pints of ale for a thirsty copper on his lonely beat, or in our case, two of us. Only I never drank mine. Not on duty, that sort of nonsense. I was young and naive. So he ended up having both pints. Finished the first in one go. Took a bit more time over the second. And, you know, he always chose me for those beats while I was there. Very friendly bloke. Always looked after me, taught me the ropes.'

For a moment Morton felt sympathy for the old fool. Poor old bloke must have realised his career had gone as far as it ever would. And if any proof were required, sending him down to the sticks was as good a way of getting rid of him as any other. Now all he had left were reminiscences. He hoped he'd never land up like that.

'Can't do that these days,' he said in a sympathetic voice he hadn't ever realised he had.

'No, no-one walks a beat any more. All sodding cars and racing around.'

'Well, it is more efficient.'

'It's faster. It ain't more efficient.'

'We couldn't operate without cars around here.'

'We could in London. Need to get somewhere fast, you just hail a cab. That's what they used to do, you know. In the old, old days. Go out with just their uniform, a whistle and their truncheon. Report in from the occasional police box. If they got a call to the next borough or ten streets away or something, they'd just hail a cab and off they'd go. Course these days they carry so much specialist junk in their Butties they need a car for it.'

'Butties?'

'Butty. Jam butty. Don't you know what a jam butty is?'

'A jam sandwich?'

'God, you are new on the block. I don't know, you youngsters.

Listen, twenty, thirty years ago patrol cars used to be mainly white and blue, then they changed them to white with an orange stripe around the middle. Straight off the kids started calling them Jam Butties because they looked kind of like a jam sandwich. Strawberry, you know? Then they dropped the Jam and it became just Butties. Course you know what the new layout is called, don't you?'

'You mean the squares? Yellow and green?'

'That's the badger.'

'Er – no?'

'Battenberg. Cause they look a bit like a cross section of Battenberg cake. Only thing is, that's the official description, the kids never came up with that one. So no-one ever uses it apart from desk jockeys. Know what?'

'No?'

'One of these days they're going to invent a one-man helicopter, maybe a jet-pack. That's how your bobby will get around. Know what?'

'No, what?'

'They'll call it the flying squad, you'll see.' He chuckled. 'Oh, yes, the flying squad.'

Morton was feeling so at one with the world his stomach was even prepared to forgive the old fool that terrible pun.

'D'accord.'

'Duck or what?'

'What?'

'You said, duck or – duck or bloody what?'

'No, I said d'accord. It's French for I agree. There's a D on the end. Only it isn't pronounced.'

'French?' Samson's lip curled. 'Christ, don't we have enough problems without you spouting Frog all of a sudden. I hate frogs. Anything to do with frogs. Frogs and frogs and more frogs. Should send them all home.'

Morton let an inner sigh escape and took out his smartphone.

'Dear god, is that thing glued to your hand?'

'Just making a note before I forget.'

'Good lad.'

Morton took out his smartphone and tapped in, "ee az a piskie face".

Monday afternoon

'Come on, let's take a butcher's at this airfield.'

'What do you expect to find there?'

'Nothing.'

'Nothing?'

'Whatever it is they'll have it well hidden.'

'So why are we going there?'

'I want to see what they aren't going to show us.'

They got into the Studebaker with Morton thinking that his charitable feelings towards the older man we re evaporating quickly.

'Cone on, son, you know what I mean. You're in a suspect's gaff, he's showing you everywhere apart from where he doesn't want you to go, so you wander all over the place, keeping half an eye on him to see when he begins to sweat.'

Personally Morton had a more direct approach when he was allowed, one that involved bouncing the suspect off the walls to see which had a hollow sound, making sure to do it in a way that left no bruises. But he guessed that admitting that would get him a half-hour lecture on procedure. Samson was one of those do-as-I-say-not-as-I-do officers. For a moment the old fool had seemed in a reasonable mood, which was exactly the time not to rely on it lasting.

They drove along the road lined with fields of sparse snow. Samson had his window down again and was tapping away to the radio, occasionally singing along. He or the car had found a country and western station and it was currently playing Rhinestone Cowboy. It reminded Morton that he still hadn't bought Shirley a Christmas present.

They turned left into the entrance to the aerodrome. Samson slowed right down and they coasted slowly along the well-maintained road. The radio had changed to Green, Green Grass Of Home.

'How much do you know about piloting, lad? You know, flying a plane.'

'Not much.'

'Well, that's more than me, I know fuck all about it. Get on the plane, fly to Ibitha, have holiday, fly back. That's about it. I don't ask the driver how he drives the thing. Come to it, I can't remember the last time I looked under a car bonnet. Used to do that a lot back in the day. Car breaks down you try to fix it. Not these days. Why do you suppose this road is so good?'

'What?'

'This road. No potholes. No puddles. Looks like they resurfaced it not so long ago.'

'It's a private road.'

'So? I've seen plenty of private roads gone to pot. Worse than any council.'

'Maybe they do it the same time they do the runway. Can't have a pothole on a runway, you'd kill someone.'

'Suppose. I'd be shitless if I was coming in to land and the runway was full of holes. Mind, things I've heard about in Africa.'

'I was in Cape Town a couple of years back. Airport seemed fine – didn't see any potholes.'

'Not your international airport. I'm talking about the ones carved out in the jungle, or bush, or whatever it's called. You know, when they want to land arms or drugs, or medicine or something.'

'Well, those are technically airfields, not aerodromes. Aerodromes have proper concrete runways.'

'Do they? I shall bow to your superior knowledge then, lad. Told you you'd know more than me about unidentified flying things. Here we go, Let's have a look in this little hangar.'

They pulled up and got out. The hangar doors were slightly open. Samson slipped through sideways and Morton followed suite. There was only space for two average sized single-engined planes, or a medium sized twin-engined aircraft. At the moment it was taken up by what appeared to be a relative giant of a twin-engined winged machine. A man in red overalls was standing on the top of a ladder just managing to peer down into an engine. They walked quietly up behind him. He dropped a spanner onto the concrete and swore. Then he turned slightly, noticed them, let out a yelp and almost fell off the ladder. He grabbed on to the open engine cowling.

'What the fuck are you two doing inside here? Haven't you ever heard of knocking?'

'On a hangar door? Where?'

'Where the inset little door is, of course.'

'Well. The big ones were open, so we thought we'd stroll in.'

'Stroll in? Nearly gave me a heart attack, you did. Who are you? I don't recognise you. Have you got a plane here?'

'We're police. Show him your ID to prove we're kosher, lad.'

Morton held up his warrant card.

'I can't see that from up fucking here.'

'Well, then, you'd better come down fucking here, lad, hadn't you.'

They waited as he came down slowly, trembling and swearing under his breath every step of the way.

'Shouldn't be doing this. All on me own. Using a ladder instead of a proper frame. If I fell and injured myself I could be here for bloody ages before anyone found me.'

'So why do it, lad?'

'Because the bloke who owns it asked me very nicely if I could do a huge favour for him and quickly check the engine out because he was hoping to get across to Paris for Christmas. And like an idiot I said yes, because he's a good bloke. And like an idiot I thought I'd take a chance and have a quick look-over using the ladder instead of doing it proper. You couldn't give me a hand to pull the gantry over, could you? The wheels are a bit stiff, it needs two blokes to do it.'

'Morton over here will give you a hand. He's young, fit, does judo, and loves shoving things around. And pulling.'

'What the fuck is he wearing?'

'It's his dance outfit. Local coppers put a team together to go on that telly show. He was doing the Alabama slow clap when we got called out. His partner's still waiting for him.'

'She is?'

'She's a very patient woman. Face like the back of a bus, too.'

'Well, come on, then.'

Morton reluctantly followed the engineer across the concrete to a tubular construction on wheels. The engineer went around one side to the back and he to the other. Together they pushed the gantry across to the aircraft and into position. The engineer wiped his brow. 'Cheers for that. It's the only bloody plane that docks here that needs a stand to check the engines.'

'Pretty little thing. What is it?'

'Twin Otter.'

'Twin Otter?'

'De Havilland Canada DHC-6 Twin Otter, to give it its full title. It's a real beauty.'

'It is that. What does the DHC stand for?'

'De Havilland Canada. So, what can I help you with, officers of the law?'

'You know that Polish freighter hove to out to sea?'

'No.'

'Don't you ever fly out to sea?'

'I'm a mechanic, not a pilot. I don't fly them. I look after the engines.'

'There's a Polish freighter hove out to sea. Do you reckon it could have some type of aircraft on board?'

'Never heard of a freighter having anything on board apart from freight – those huge containers. I suppose technically it could have a small helicopter folded up somewhere.'

'Not something like this? Maybe something smaller.'

'Can't see it. Maybe in a James Bond movie. Maybe they line all the containers up to make a runway. Not in real life. They'd need a metal grid or something to cover it. Otherwise it would just nose-flip at the first gap. Apart from which there's the sway. Boats are always rolling from side to side, you can't trust them. You'd probably take off straight into the oggin.'

'Oggin?'

'Sea.'

'Ah, that oggin. What sort of range would this thing have? On a full tank?'

'Range? Just shy of fifteen hundred kilometres, according to the manual. Depends on conditions.'

'What's that in English?'

'What?'

'Those kilometre things.'

'Oh, just over nine hundred miles.'

'Enough to get to France.'

'Plenty. I just told you, the boss wants to go to Paris. You know where Paris is, don't you? Paris in France.'

'Not Texas?'

'Eh?'

'Never mind. Okay, Paris, France. I meant in one go. You wouldn't have to pull over and top up anywhere?'

'No, you could do it quite easily.'

'What about Poland?'

'Poland? You'd be pushing your luck there. This is a light aircraft, not a 747.'

'Pretty big light aircraft.'

'Safer than a Cessna. Got two engines.'

'You're right, you know, I've just counted them. What if you had spare fuel on board. In jerrycans or something.'

'Jerrycans? I'd like to see you suggest that to the boss. The interior of this thing is pristine. Catch him taking his latest lady friend up for a spin with jerrycans rolling around.'

'What are those for, then, in the corner? They are jerrycans, aren't they?'

'They're for holding stuff.'

'Stuff?'

'Fuel or oil. Sometimes you have to drain an engine.'

'Not worried about them exploding?'

'Exploding? Pretty unlikely. Catching fire? Yes. That's why I make damn sure they're properly sealed and there's fire extinguishers all over the place, just in case.'

'Anyone else doing any flying recently?'

'Not that I'm aware of. You'd have to ask Jimmy.'

'Jimmy?'

'He runs the place. He should be in later. Maybe.'

'Bit of a late starter, isn't he?'

'Not much going on at the moment. It's Christmas, almost. Most people who are going away have gone away, and those who are staying aren't likely to be flying anywhere in one of these. Weather's too crappy. Permanently low cloud base.'

'But your this other bloke's planning to fly to Paris.'

'He's French. And he wants to see his mistress.'

'His mistress.'

'Yup.'

'Romantic bastard. What sort of security do you have around here?'

'What?'

'Security. Stuff to stop people nicking the planes. Breaking into the buildings. Lifting the silver.'

'Well, the building all have standard locks, mortice, that sort of thing. Keys to the planes are usually left in the main office.'

'Trusting lot. Never had a plane half-inched?'

'Half-whatted?'

'Half-inched. Pinched. Stolen.'

'Never heard of one. Don't you mean hijacked?'

'Nah, that's international. Ever get planes landing at night?'

'What?'

'Ever have planes landing at night? In the dark? Can they?'

'So long as they plan ahead and let the ground staff know to turn the landing lights on. Otherwise they'll just be crashing in the dark.'

'That happened recently?'

'What, crashing in the dark?'

'No. Night landing.'

'Might have done. You can check the log book in the office. But it would be unusual at this time of year.'

'Is it open? The office.'

'Just a sec.' The mechanic felt in his pockets, found a bunch of keys and tossed them over to Samson. 'The one with the strip of black masking tape around the top. Don't forget to bring them back.'

'We won't. Come on, Morton.'

They walked out of the hangar and around to the office block.

'Trusting sort, isn't he?' noted Samson as he unlocked the front door.

'He's a mechanic. He's not worried about an office. But ask to borrow one of his favourite spanners and see how trusting he is.'

'Dare say you're right about that, son. Notice anything strange about those jerrycans?'

'No.'

'Nor did I. They look like they belong there. That worries me. How many fire extinguishers did you count?'

'Eight.'

'Well done, lad, you were paying attention after all. Here we go, a room marked Staff Only, that'll be what we're looking for. I like signs like this. Staff Only. No Entrance. Keep Out. Lovely. I can never resist.'

They entered the room. The opposite wall was an entire window looking out onto the runway. There were two desks, one large, one small, and a smattering of filing cabinets in various stages of disorder, a small fridge next to a sink containing mugs desperately seeking bleach. An old computer sat on a sideboard with the keyboard on top of the screen.

'Interesting,' said Samson. 'The runway is pristine, the road coming up here is pristine, this place is a mess.'

'Priorities. An untidy desk won't kill you, an untidy runway probably would.'

'Mmmm. And sloppy record keeping makes everything deniable. When did Mr X fly in? Let's check the log book. Oh, seems I forgot to enter that flight. Or, my goodness, this handwriting is bad, I don't know if that's a two or a three. That sort of thing. Okay, let's see what we've got on this big desk. I'm presuming that this thing with wires coming out of it is part of an aeroplane they haven't put back.'

'Looks a complete mess.'

'Yes, son, that's what it looks like alright, what it is is another question. You know, I think they'll have all their records computerised and digitised and whatever other ised there is in this modern, wonderful, brand new world. Too easy to hide stuff in those bloody things.'

'Not if the look of that PC is anything to go by. I'd say that was bought brand spanking new about ten years ago, used once and then put to one side. Maybe twenty years ago. I'm sure we had a model like that back in the Dark Ages.'

'If you say so, son. What I know about computers – well, I do know one thing about them.'

'What's that?'

'They have to be plugged in to work. That one isn't. Maybe they've got a more up to date one somewhere.'

'Here's the log book.'

'How do you know it's a log book?'

'It says Log Book on the cover. And it's got a list of flights in it.'

'Okay, clever clogs, check for the past few days. Last night, especially.'

'Last entry is – yes, last night, 18h47. Gives a registration number and a name, Peter K.'

'Eighteen hundred forty seven? What year was that?'

'Thirteen minutes to seven in the evening.'

'That was about the time we saw the lights, wasn't it?'

'Pretty much spot on.'

'Didn't mess around, came straight in. Knew his way around.'

'Peter K – could be an alias.'

'Sounds more like someone this Jimmy bloke knows personally. Doesn't have to write his name out fully. And there's probably another Peter with a different initial.'

'Sounds about right. Just an ordinary aerodrome. So we've drawn a blank.'

'I didn't say that, did I? You've never studied military history, have you, son?'

'Military history?'

'You've got sabre rattling and tub thumping. Make a lot of noise, march your troops and tanks around, make it sound as if you're about to attack. Then you've got your normal. Israelis did it in sixty-seven. Their normal air patrols all appeared on Egyptian radar as they normally did. Their troops and tanks moved around or stood still as they normally did. What the Egyptians didn't realise is that when the Israeli jets dropped off their radar they weren't going home as they normally did, they were flying around at sea level to destroy the Egyptian air force on the ground. Bloody worked, too. Egyptians didn't suspect a thing. Beware the normal, Morton, beware the ordinary. This might be a normal, ordinary aerodrome, but then again it might bloody well not. And if it isn't it's likely to bite us on the bum.'

'If you say so.'

'Morton, think of it as a woman. Just when you think you've got her sussed and she's a perfectly normal person, she suddenly turns around and it's like you're talking to a whole different creature. And it's suddenly got teeth. Big fucking teeth.'

'I know that feeling well.'

'Come on, let's give the keys back to our mechanic friend and head off. Make them think we haven't found anything.'

'We haven't found anything.'

'Yes, but they don't know that, do they, son. Try to keep up.'

They walked back to the hangar and slipped through the open doors after Samson had knocked loudly on them.

'Come to give you your keys back.'

'Ta, leave them on the bench there.'

'Okay. How's the Otter?'

'Engines are ticking over like sewing machines. It really is a beaut.'

'Know who Peter K is?'

'Peter Kay? He's not a rapper, is he?'

'He's a rapper?'

'That's what I was asking you. One of them that's married to one of those celebrities in America. The one with the big arse.'

'No, some bloke who flew in here last night. First name Peter, initial of surname K.'

'Oh. Rings a vague bell. Don't know him myself, but I think Jimmy mentioned him once or twice. Flies a lot.'

'Cause of his job?'

'Nah. Just one of those blokes who loves flying. Every chance he gets. Now you come to mention it, that's the sort of thing he would do, from what Jimmy says.'

'What's that?'

'Take off in the light thinking he can make it before it gets dark. Then end up asking for landing lights cause he can't see the runway.'

'That's normal?'

'For him, from what I hear. Like I said, I never met the bloke myself. He flies late and takes off early.'

'Jimmy doesn't mind?'

'Jimmy doesn't mind what?'

'Having to rush out to put the lights on.'

'Nah, he would have been here anyway. Likes to stay late tinkering with engines and stuff. He often sleeps over and goes home early hours the following morning.'

'Not married, then?'

'He is married. Three kids. That's why he often sleeps over.'

'Takes all kinds. Right, cheers, mate, look after yourself.'

They walked back to the Studebaker. Samson drove off like a normal person not in a hurry. When they came back to the main road he turned left.

'We'll carry on up this way for a couple of miles. As soon as we're out of sight we'll pull over and wait for a few minutes. See if they send up a kite.'

'A plane?'

'Fly a kite. Send a message. Run something up the flagpole and see if anyone salutes. We'll watch and wait for any reaction to our visit.'

'Ah.'

They drove along the road and up a hill until they came to a clump of trees and bushes. Samson pulled over behind the foliage. He got out and looked through the cover at the aerodrome below. Without looking he held out the keys to Morton just behind him.

'There's a pair of binoculars in the boot, lad, get them out for me.'

Morton hesitated. His ego had a brief disagreement with his satisfied stomach as to how irritated he should be with Samson's cavalier treatment of him as a skivvy. In the end his mind mediated a truce until Pay Back Day. Until then he would do as ordered and also keep his own eyes open and be sure to note all the things Samson was missing. He retrieved the binocular bag. Samson took it without looking, took out the binoculars, adjusted them to focus on the aerodrome and swept the horizon.

'Nothing,' he murmured. 'Nothing moving. No-one. No cars. Nothing flying. Quiet as the grave. Very strange.'

Suddenly he stopped and froze.

'Duck!'

Morton hit the dirt before Samson reached the exclamation mark. He lay there completely silent, not even breathing. After a few seconds he raised his sweating forehead very slowly and carefully, his eyes straining upwards to the back of Samson's head.

'What?'

'Well, well, would you Adam it?'

'Adam it? What?'

'Adam. Adam and Eve. Believe. Would you believe it?'

'Believe what?'

'Over there, in the reeds. I think it's a Mallard. Strange. Would have thought they'd all buggered south for the holiday by now.'

Morton stood up, his eyes narrowed, brushing his overcoat with clenched knuckles, glaring at Samson's crown. Samson scanned the area for about thirty more seconds before handing the binoculars over to Morton.

'Your eyes are younger than mine, son. See if you can spot anything.'

Morton took the binoculars with determination. He scanned the area even more slowly than Samson. Then he repeated the exercise. Despite his best efforts he couldn't see anything untoward. But he had to admit that they were bloody good binocs. At one point he spotted a field mouse peeking out from next to a log. A couple of seconds' concentration confirmed that it wasn't doing anything suspicious. High in the sky a kite was treading the thermals, watching, waiting. The field mouse didn't notice.

'Nothing,' he said, lowering them and taking a surreptitious glance at the brand and model. 'If they're concealing anything they're doing a good job of it.'

'Hiding in plain sight, son, that's what's happening. Oldest trick in the book. When you realise how they've done it you want to kick yourself. Come on, let's drive back. Slowly. You never know.'

'So how have they done it? And what is it they've done?'

'Haven't a clue, son. I'll be kicking meself just as much as you when I find out. But find out I am bloody going to do.'

Samson drove the Studebaker back onto the road, switched the engine off and let the car roll down the hill. Despite his scepticism Morton kept his eyes firmly on what they could see of the aerodrome as they approached, forgetting to be afraid at Samson's reckless approach to motoring. The aerodrome did seem abnormally quiet now that he thought about it. It was almost as if there were a hundred hidden eyes watching them, just like the Freechin place. The endless seconds slipped slowly by as they coasted down. And then they were past and Samson switched the engine on again.

'Oh for the wings of a dove.'

'Sir?'

'Felix Mendelssohn. You must have heard it sung at church some time.'

'Not much of a church-goer.'

'In the wilderness build me a nest, and remain there forever at rest.'

'Doesn't ring a bell.'

'Don't worry, son, I won't sing it at you.'

'Strange bird to wish for.'

'What's that?'

'A dove. Why not an eagle?'

'Dunno. Something to do with the church, I suppose. Dove of peace, that sort of thing. Let's have a word with our friend Peter the Pissed.'

'You mean Joe the Drunk.'

'Not him, the other one. The one that drives the boat. The one who found the Pole.'

'Joe the Rescue.'

'That's the one. Could have been worse.'

'What could have been worse?'

'Could have been a pigeon.'

'What could have been a pigeon.'

'In the song. Far away, far away would I roam. Shitting on a statue as I go.'

'Instead of a dove?'

'That's the one. Or a goose. Oh for the wings of a goose. Sounds like someone wishing for Christmas.'

'Thought that was turkeys.'

'What was?'

'Christmas.'

'It was goose. Then it was turkeys. Never read Scrooge?'

'You mean A Christmas Carol?'

'Robins is Christmas. London way, any road. Victorian times.'

'You eat robins?'

'On Christmas cards. Robins and snow. And berries.'

'Ah.'

'Funny thing is.'

'Yes?'

'We hardly ever have snow before Christmas. Or at Christmas. In London, that is. Always January or February. If it does snow, that is. Hardly ever does. People think it does. They remember it snowing when they were kids. But it's all an illusion.'

'Ah.'

'So what bird would you be if you could be a bird?'

'Bird?'

'Flappy thing. Has wings. Flies around. You know.'

'A bird. I'd be a condor. High, high in the sky. Surfing the thermals.'

'Over the Andes mountains.'

'Andes mountains?'

'South America. Condor's South American. Makes you wonder why it didn't fly anywhere else.'

'Maybe it ran out of mountains.'

'Dare say you're right.'

Samson switched off the engine again as they approached the harbour and let the Studebaker glide silently into a parking space, slowly coming to a stop of its own volition.

'That's the only problem with this thing,' he commented. 'It's American. Switch the power off and the brakes don't work.'

He got out, leaving Morton staring at his back in incredulity. It was winter twilight and the lights cut an ethereal glow into the gloom and across the water. Morton got out.

'Looks pretty deserted,' he said, deciding he had misheard something. Hoping desperately he had misheard something.

'Winter. This is retirement country. Old folks like to sail on a summer sea, they're not too hot on freezing in the Atlantic just before Christmas. Come on, let's go have a look in those boat garages or whatever they call them.'

The first set of doors were securely and thoroughly padlocked, including a chain across the handles. Samson gave the chain a tug.

'Interesting. Why do you suppose they locked this up so tight?'

'To deter thieves?'

'More like to prevent petty damage I reckon. What do you suppose is in it?'

'A boat?'

'Yes, but what kind of boat? Speed boat? Motor boat? Sea-going launch? Ocean-going liner? Canoe? Pedalos?'

'Could be pedalos. Locked up for the winter. Bring them out during the spring and summer for the tourist trade.'

'Not much good to us, then.'

The second set of doors were wide open. They stepped inside. A bright yellow inflatable launch sat in its wheeled cradle with a tow-bar in front. In it lay a man in bright yellow oilskins, fast asleep. He was cradling a half-empty bottle of whisky. Every so often he let out a sudden snore. The two policemen walked up to him.

'He's a bit Brahms, I'd say.'

'Brahms?'

'Brahms and Liszt – pissed.'

'Ah.'

'What do you reckon? Joe the Drunk or Joe the Rescue?'

'Sounds like Joe the Drunk. Looks dressed like Joe the Rescue.'

'Wakey, wakey, Joe the Snoozer.'

Samson suddenly slapped the inflatable hard with the flat of his hand. The man sat up in one fluid movement, took a deep pull at the whisky, slipped his legs over the side, stood up and staggered over to the front of the boat. He began tugging at the tow-bar.

'You Joe?'

'What?'

'Are you Joe the Rescue?'

'What?'

'Are you Joe the Rescue?'

'Thas wha I'm doing.'

'What?'

'Rescue. Get boat out.'

'There's no need to get the boat out.'

'What?'

'There's no emergency. We just want a few words with you.'

'No mergency? You sure?'

'No emergency.'

'I thought I heard the siren.'

'In your dreams.'

He sighed.

'One day. One day I will rescue someone in peril on the sea.'

He sighed again and wiped his mouth with the back of his hand.

'Ah, well. In that case.'

He staggered back into the launch and took another glug of whisky.

'Thas better. Keep the cold out. Who you?'

'We're police officers.'

'Ah, About the man in the toilet.'

'No, the man in the room on the first floor.'

'No, don't remember him. Remember the man in the toilet. Saturday night. Remember it like it was yesterday.'

'That's the one. When did you find him?'

'Who?'

'The man in the toilet.'

'Dunno. Sometime. Late. Opened the cubicle, had a wazz, realised he was sitting there on the toilet.'

'After you had a wazz.'

'Sright. Needed it. When you gotta go you gotta go. Feels so good after. You know?'

'He was dead?'

'Dead drunk. Didn't even wake up. Covered in wee and didn't wake up.'

'So what did you do?'

'Finished having a wazz. Pulled the chain. Went to tell Patsy. Funny, that. Found Mrs Patsy. She sent me downstairs. Dunno why I was upstairs. Must have gone up to find Patsy. Went down, told Patsy there was a man in the toilet. Then went home. Tired. Long day.'

'Anything else you remember?'

'Pub was empty. Must have been after closing time.'

'You remember that the pub was empty?'

'Empty. Didn't fall over anyone. Must have been empty. Sometimes I fall over legs. Not often. Never if is empty.'

'What about the man? Remember anything about him?'

'Pissed. Didn't say anything even when I said sorry. Very rude.'

'Have you heard anything since?'

'I've been working the rescue. Waiting. One day I will –'

'Yeah, we know, for those in peril on the sea. Well, if you remember anything else, let us know.'

'Sure there's no rescue?'

'Quite sure. You go back to your bottle.'

'Keep the cold out.'

'Just one more thing.'

'Yeah?'

'Was his mouth open or closed?'

'Who?'

'Never mind. You get some rest.'

'Fell into a lady's lap once. Bloody ear hurt for a week.'

'Don't worry, lad, no ladies around here.'

'Don't think she was much of a lady either.'

'You go back to sleep, son.'

They left him cradling his bottle and falling asleep again.

'Do you believe him?'

'Don't see why not. You heard of a functioning alcoholic? Our friend there is a non-functioning alcoholic.'

'But surely he couldn't have – well, you know. Straight into the Polish bloke's face.'

'Into his shirt more like. His shirt was white. Easy mistake to make. Especially if you're as pissed as a coot.'

Morton rubbed his hands as if trying to dry them.

'Not much use to us then.'

'No, lad. A blind-drunk eye-witness is definitely not much use to us. Still, had to be done. And it does tell us something else.'

'What's that?'

'They haven't had many boating accidents around here. Either that or they get their rescuers from further down the coast. Let's face it, would you want him coming to rescue you?'

'I think I'd rather drown.'

'Likely to end up the same thing. Let's get back to the Duck and Angel and see what's for supper.'

'Angel and Duck.'

'Aye. That's the beaver.'

'Badger.'

'What?'

'The saying is, that's the badger.'

'Is it? All these years I've been doing it wrong. Who knew.'

'Glad to be of help, sir.'

'You'll go far, Morton, I can see.'

'Thank you, sir. Just one thing.'

'Aye?'

'What do you suppose he actually did when he thought he was pulling the chain?'

Monday evening

By the time they parked at the Angel and Duck it was fully dark. The street lights revealed roads and pavements empty of any human trace.

'Be warned, he is pounding out the grapes of wrath,' cried a voice from deep in the shadows.

'Evening, Molly, bit cold to be outside. Why don't you get back into the warmth.'

'The wages of drunken sin is death.'

'Who's she?'

'Molly? You've met Molly. She pokes her head into the pub every so often and goes on about the wages of sin.'

'Does she?'

'Oh, wait a minute, you were looking for Clarry last time our Molly turned up, that's right. Don't worry about her, she's harmless.'

'Carry's harmless?'

'No, Molly. Bonkers, but harmless.'

'She could have seen something.'

'Clarry?'

'Carry. No, this Molly woman.'

'Morton, if you want to ask her some questions, be my guest. Just don't lean on her, she's already cuckoo.'

Morton stepped over to the shadows that almost hid a Molly dressed in faded black.

'Your name is Molly, is it?'

'Ah, bless you, Miss, it is. Do you have any spare change?'

'What?'

'For a cup of wholesome tea. I never drink the devil's brew. Just some spare change, Miss, if you could.'

'What do you mean, Miss?'

'Sorry, is you a missus?'

'Do I look like a woman?'

'Sorry, Miss, my eyes ain't what they used to be. Any spare change?'

'I'm a police officer. '

'Sorry, Miss Police Officer.'

'I'm telling you, I'm a mister police officer.'

'Lawks, ee ba gum, I ain't done anything wrong, mister police officer. I'm just trying to spread the good word. Got any spare change?'

'Here you go, Molly, here's a fiver,' said Samson coming up beside him, 'go get yourself a couple of cups of tea.'

'God bless you, Inspector. Glory, glory, hallelujah, glory, glory, hallelujah.'

'Come on, Morton, I can't spend the entire day standing her watching you have the piss taken out of you by an old woman. Not sure I'd hang around even if it was a young woman. Speaking of which, let's see if Charity is at home.'

'Who the hell is she?'

'Charity? Don't tell me you've already forgotten such a beautiful young woman. Wouldn't have expected that from you.'

'I meant Molly.'

'Molly? Oh, Molly. She's a woman who saw the light once and couldn't take it. Shined too bright. Fried her brain, what there was of it. Happens to people who ask why once too often. Stick to the whos and whens, leave the whys for politicians and priests. And liars and fakers.'

'Whos and whens?'

'Who did what and when. Facts. Never ask why someone does something, even worse, why something happened. Never look for the truth. You'll go nuts. Stick to the facts, they can't harm you. Well, not always.'

Morton followed him into the pub. The public bar was empty apart from an old couple in the corner, and Patsy behind the counter, with Richard Coombes-Neeston and Sir Anthony Freechin standing in front of it.

'Good evening Sir Anthony, Mr Constantine,' Samson said. He turned to Richard Coombes-Neeston. 'GOOD EVENING GENERAL.'

Richard Coombes-Neeston jumped back a bit, holding his ears.

'There's no need to shout, Inspector.'

'JUST TRYING TO BE POLITE, GENERAL. HOW'S THE HEARING TONIGHT.'

'Hearing? Oh, the hearing. Ah, the hearing.'

'YES, THE HEARING, HOW IS THE HEARING TONIGHT?'

'No need to shout, inspector, I, er, I, well, yes, I picked up my latest hearing aid this morning. So I can hear perfectly.'

'AMAZING WHAT THEY CAN DO TODAY, I CAN'T SEE A THING.'

'Inspector, there really is no need to shout.'

'WAS I SHOUTING? I mean, was I shouting? It must be a very small hearing aid. I can't see a thing.'

'It's – it's an implant. They use a syringe. A bit like a little chip.'

'Amazing. So how are the peonies, general?'

'Peonies?'

'For the spring parade. Penelope's peonies.'

'Ah, those peonies. Yes, the peonies are fine. Now, if you'll excuse me, the ladies are playing bridge in the ladies' bar and I'm dummy. I think they must have just finished a round.'

'The ladies normally play bridge on a Monday evening?' Samson asked once Coombes-Neeston had disappeared to the ladies' bar.

'Not as a habit, sor. I think maybe they wanted a bit of company, what with events and the season and all.'

'The season?'

'Ah, Christmas and winter and all that. It's cold and it's dark and there's nothing on the television and a murderer running around. Speaking of which, what can I get you, Inspector? On the house.'

'I think there's time for a quick one before getting ready for dinner. I'll have a pint of that Bishop's Drain. Put it on my tab. The taxpayer will pick that one up. Spread the cost.'

'One pint coming up. And yourself, corporal?'

'Detective constable. I'll have a pint of Stella.'

'So, Inspector, how's this investigation of yours coming along? Found any clues?'

'Oh, plenty of clues, Sir Anthony, a veritable treasure trove of clues, you could say. Quite a few of them red herrings.'

'Herrings? Must say, it's been ages since I had herring. That was in – where was it? Denmark? Pickled, I think I was. They eat it on toast, you know? Or was it that diet biscuit with seeds in? Strange chaps. But it tasted all right with vodka. Not a fan of vodka, normally, but it tastes good with the pickled stuff.'

'Sure, now there's an idea. Herrings on toast for Sunday. Rather than roast spuds and drumsticks.'

'Don't think that would go down too well, Patsy. So, Inspector, where are these herrings leading you to? Are we going to have that – that French thing, the denoo-thingy sometime soon? Just before Christmas?'

'Denouement. Yes, Sir Anthony, I think I can say with confidence that I will be able to reveal all within twenty-four hours.'

'I say. Twenty-four hours. That's impressive.'

'Your Drain, Inspector. Are you sure of that? You know who done it, as they say?'

'I've known right from the start. All very obvious when you've been in the job as long as I have. There's just one piece of the jigsaw missing, though.'

'Is it a piece of the sky? I always find those impossible to do. Unless there's something in the sky, a bird or plane or skyscraper or something. Clouds. Clouds are nice. The puffy little ones.'

'Your Stella, constable. Will you be needing the saloon, Inspector?'

'The saloon? What for?'

'To reveal everything. Shall I tell everybody they should be here?'

'No, that's not necessary. You'll know when I've got all my ducks in a row. You know, I'm going to miss this Bishop's Drain. I was just getting a taste for it.'

'Well, your honour, if you ever want a holiday hereabouts, I'm sure we could arrange a special rate. Bring the missus.'

'What sort of a rate do I get if I leave her at home?'

'Eh? Oh, I see, a joke, very funny, Inspector.'

'Right, time for a shower, another pint and then dinner. I'll see you back down here then, Morton.'

Morton blinked at Samson's empty glass. He took a quick breath and then downed half of his pint.

'Your Inspector seems confident.'

'Yes, he does.'

'I say, he knows how to finish a pint off.'

'It's a copper thing. You learn to drink fast on the job or lose it.'

'On the job, eh?'

'He shares everything with you, no doubt, constable.'

'Naturally. I think I'll go have a shower too.'

'I say, you don't share showers too, do you? Is that also a bobby thing?'

'No, Sir Anthony, we definitely do not share showers. Excuse me.'

Richard Coombes-Neeston materialised again once Morton had gone.

'Dummy again? I say, hard luck, old boy. Still, maybe you could do it professionally one day. With all the experience you're getting.'

'Huh? I dare say you're right, Sir Anthony. So, Patsy, what did our friend Inspector Plod have to say?'

'He needs another little piece of the jigsaw and he'll know everything. He'll let us know when he's got all his ducks in a row, but I'm not sure how, he didn't want the saloon bar for a denouement.'

'I don't think it's a cloud though.'

'He thinks he's got it all sown up?'

'Tighter than a tailor.'

'Sorry, Sir Anthony?'

'He's got it sown up tighter than a tailor, as we used to say. Good chap, that Samson, one of the old school. Head down and batter away until you win through. Like rugger, you know.'

'Well, that is a relief.'

'It certainly is.'

'He'll be gone by the end of tomorrow and we can look forward to a quiet Christmas.'

'I'll tell the others. We can have a little celebration tomorrow night.

You don't have any more foreigners staying overnight, do you, Patsy?'

'I think that's the last time we ever have any foreigners staying overnight. They're just too much trouble.'

When a freshly-showered Samson returned to the public bar it was empty apart from Carry behind the counter. He slid onto a stool.

'Quiet night. Pour us a Drain, love.'

'Monday normally is.'

'That poker game still going on in the ladies bar?'

'Bridge. The snug's where they play poker. When they play poker. Which they don't.'

'Of course, I should have realised.'

'You aren't interested in their poker games, are you?'

'As a rule I'm interested in everything. I'm interested in their playing poker. In terms of their playing poker illegally, that's something I'll leave to the local constabulary. Thanks, love.'

Carry sat on her stool, put her chin in her hands and looked at him.

'What are you going to do for Christmas?'

'I was going to buy a bottle of whisky and play Russian roulette like I did last year. Trouble is, last year I kept losing. But I think I've figured out where I was going wrong. You have to use a pistol rather than a revolver. It's cheating, but only a little bit.'

'Seriously.'

'Seriously? If I can arrange it I'll be spending Christmas somewhere sunny and far from any other coppers. The job's bad enough, I have no urge to socialise with the buggers as well.'

'Where?'

'That's the big question. Somewhere sunny where they don't practise Christianity so I don't have Christmas shoved down my throat, but not one of those Mormon places where they don't allow alcohol.'

'Mormon? Or Muslim?'

'That's the badger. Though I don't think the Mormons allow drinking either. Interesting, that. They both believe in having many young wives as young as possible, but not in booze. Why do you suppose that is?'

'You tell me, you're the detective.'

'Do you want the psychological explanation or the straightforward one?'

'Try the straightforward one.'

'They're fucking nuts. What are you doing for Christmas?'

'Working.'

'Here?'

'Yes.'

'You planning on staying here for the rest of your life?'

'Maybe.'

'Might as well shack up with that artist then.'

'Maybe I will.'

'Sacrifice yourself for the greater good.'

'The greater good?'

'Art. Some people think it's important.'

'Do you?'

'Do I what?'

'Think art is important.'

'Wrong question.'

'I should have known. What's the right one.'

'Is it art?'

'Is it?'

'Some of it is. Some of it's just crap.'

'What about Nigel's?'

'What about Nigel's what?'

'Art.'

'Oh, that stuff.'

'Do you think it's art?'

'Some of it is. Some of it's just crap.'

'Which?'

'Haven't worked that one out.'

'Tell me something.'

'The square route of the hypotheses is equal to the sum of all the

triangles on a sunny day.'
'Why haven't you ever tried to get off with me?'
'Come fly, come fly with me.'
'What?'
'It's an old song. Bloke trying to get a girl to run away with him. As far as the local knocking spot, I would imagine.'
'So what's the answer?'
'What was the question?'
'You know what the question is.'
'Wouldn't work. I'm too old and you're too young.'
'That's never stopped most men. Most coppers, either.'
'Don't have the money. Need a bit of brass. Both ways.'
'Aren't you supposed to say, I'm not most men?'
'Dunno. Are you most women?'
'I expect so.'
'Doubt it. Certainly not in London you weren't.'
'Why not?'
'You're special. Tell you what, even down here you're special.'
'Here comes your faithful bloodhound.'
'Chance would be a fine thing. The only thing he's faithful to is himself, and I'm not even sure he gets that right. Hello, Morton, that's another thing they have in common. They don't play cricket.'
'What? Who doesn't? Pint of Stella, Carry.'
'I hear and obey.'
'The Muslims and the Mormons. Neither of them play cricket.'
'That'll be news to the Pakistanis.'
'I mean the serious ones. The orthodox lot. The ones who ban dancing and smoking and mixtures of the sexes.'
'Pretty sure the Pakistani Muslims are reasonably orthodox. Don't they go around stoning adulterers? Thanks, love.'
'There's something in your pint.'
'Where?'
'At the bottom.'
'So there is. Give me a straw, Carry. Ta. Now, out you come – it's ...'

'Something you dropped in your room.'

'My wedding ring.'

'You're married? I'm shocked. And you trying to chat up all the local virgins.'

'Anyone wants me I'll be in the ladies' bar.'

'Carry, wait, I can explain –'

'Come on, lad, let's go into the snug for supper. Just pray it's Anne-Marie doing the cooking tonight. Otherwise your first course might be toasted testicles. Yours.'

Morton followed Samson to the snug, throwing a backward glance at the bar in case Carry had come back.

'The path of true love never runs smooth, son. More like a perpetual train wreck, as it happens.'

'I never said anything about love.'

'With women you never need to. It's all they think about. When's my prince charming going to come and sweep me off my feet? They get married to the first bloke who's got a steady job and a retirement plan. But they're still waiting for Mr Right. Mr Rich and Right, with a big fat wallet in his trousers. And a house in the country. They all dream of Mr Darcy. What was that acronym? OCOH. Own Car, Own Home. Should be OROM. Own Rolls Own Mansion.'

'Carry's not like that.'

'You reckon?'

'I know.'

'Ever heard of Pemberley?'

'Pemberley? That's in Wales, isn't it?'

'It's Darcy's gaff.'

'Darcy?'

'In Pride and Prejudice. It's what every girl wants, a tall, dark, handsome man with a huge fortune. What they get is a one-bed flat in Slough with three kids. If they're lucky.'

'That's a bit – well, what's the word, stereotyped?'

'Suit yourself, son. Ah, Anne-Marie, que est-ce pour notre dejeuner?'

'Your traditional English dish. Sausage, eggs, chips, and peas. With that gravy you English love. Onion gravy.'

'You say the nicest things, Annie. That looks gorgeous.'

'Enjoy.'

'Merci, love, we will. Tuck in, son, try not to drown everything in tomato sauce before you try it.'

'At least Anne-Marie knows how to do chips properly. Nice and thick, and not out of a bag from the freezer.'

'There you go, forgotten about Charity already. Easiest way to get a man to forget his heartbreak. Chuck a plateful of food in front of him.'

'I'm not – better get on with it before it gets cold.'

'That's what you want, some tubby little thing who loves you dearly, is a brilliant cook, and just wants to make you fat.'

'I'm married already, thanks all the same.'

'Could have fooled me.'

'I just don't go shouting it from the houses.'

'But she doesn't cook for you.'

'Sometimes. She's got her own job. She doesn't always have the time.'

'And she's on a permanent diet.'

'How did you know?'

'That type always are, my son. Now, be silent like a good trencherman.'

Morton's mouth was too full to reply to that.

They sat in silence, steadily ploughing through the mass of food before them. Samson finished slightly ahead of Morton, who had been slowed down by the extra six slices of thick white bread and butter he had added to the meal. Anne-Marie appeared with their dessert as Morton finished wiping his plate with the last slice.

'Angel cake with cooked apples avec cinnamon and custard,' she announced, placing a soup plate of the dessert in front of each of them.'

'Thanks, Anne-Marie, Danger Mouse here can have mine. I'm full and I don't do dessert. Never could abide sweet things. Food, anyhows.'

'You should try some. I don't normally do dessert either, but this Angel cake is something else.'

'I'll take your word for it, son.'

'I see what you mean about making them look like angels on the plate. It is very pretty. Seems a shame to eat them. Ah, well.'

Samson sat picking his teeth with a toothpick, looking into the distance as Morton devoured first his own plate and then Samson's. He was almost finished when Anne-Marie re-appeared.

'Enfin, monsieurs, cheese, coffee and biscuits.'

'Anne-Marie, you're spoiling us.'

'You are the only guests here at the moment. It is something to do. Otherwise I get rasty.'

'Rusty. And I thought we were special to you. Instead we're just practice. Mademoiselle, je suis desolee.'

'I too am gutted, monsieur. Have you tried the Angel cake with the Edam?'

'Cake with Edam?'

'It is a favourite around here. And at Christmas we have Christmas pudding with cheddar. That is good. I like it.'

'Some weird tastes around here.'

'I've heard of that. Yorkshire thing, isn't it?'

'I think it is perhaps so. Would you like anything else?'

'Is, er, Carry –'

'I'll have a large scotch, thanks, Anne-Marie.'

'Oh, okay, large scotch for me too then.'

'Bon. Back in a tick.'

'Back in a tick? She's picking up the lingo alright, not sure it's the right kind.'

'Sweet kid.'

'Over Carry already? Have a slice of Edam and a water biscuit. Actually, try some with that bit of dessert you've still got left.'

'There's nothing between Carry and me. I don't get involved with potential witnesses. Or potential suspects.'

'How did you meet your wife?'

Morton wiped the dessert bowls clean with a slice of bread and ate it.

'Were you serious about twenty four hours?'

'Twenty-four hours?'

'You said you'd reveal all within twenty-four hours. Who killed the Polish bloke. That sort of thing.'

'Course I was serious.'

'You know who done it?'

'I have a feeling in my water.'

'That's it? What about proof?'

'If everything goes as I planned it, that too.'

'You can't be serious.'

'Son, this will go down in the annals of crime history, trust me. It'll be up there with Sherlock Holmes and The Count of Monty Christo.'

'What?'

'That Anne-Marie's amazing, isn't she?'

'What?'

'The way she put the dessert together.'

'What?'

'Not only did it look like angels, but they were nude angels. Incredible what some people can do. Never seen a nude angel before.'

'What?'

'You learn something new everyday as they say. But it's getting late and I'll need my beauty sleep. It's going to be a long day tomorrow. I'll see you at sparrow's.'

'Sparrow's?'

'Sparrow's fart. Break of dawn. That sort of time.'

'Sparrow's fart.'

'Yeah. See you tomorrow.'

'I'll make a note.'

'That's the spirit.'

Morton watched Samson disappear and then looked at the empty dessert bowls.

They weren't nude, he told himself.

He turned one empty bowl towards the light.

Then the other.

He shook his head.

'Nah.'

He took out his smartphone and typed:

"little grockle's piskie crazed"

Tuesday morning

Morton was flying again. He was flying between huge clouds way above the earth. The clouds turned into chicken-fillet cheeseburgers with mayonnaise and it began to rain chips. He dived towards the mauve-pink Studebaker for cover. He flew into the engine through the grill and began buzzing around in the bonnet. Thuthan was sitting on the rocker cover sharpening her knives and looking at him with a vague carnivore interest. Someone opened the bonnet and Carry stared down at him with the face of the psychopathic doll. It opened her mouth which turned into a writhing wedding ring. He fled to the recesses of the engine to escape the shiny, golden, twisted metal. The head shrank and followed him, wedding ring, making a low gargling noise. He flew back up, out of the bonnet and into the bright open air. Up and up towards the safety of the clouds, huge, towering clouds, white and grey and immense and safe with their peaks and valleys and softness and angels. Angels, nude angels, made of nude angel cake came flying towards him to devour him, revenge for their sisters, they clung to him and around him smothering him stopping him from flying dragging him down and he plummeted to the earth and bashed his head against the headboard of the single bed. Everything had turned dark. He could feel that he was tangled up in the sheet, he'd thrown the duvet off and was covered in sweat.

He lay breathing heavily for a minute, looking into the blackness and trying not to think of what he had just dreamt.

He reached out a hand and toggled the switch on the bedside lamp. Nothing happened. He tried again. Still nothing. He climbed warily out of bed, feeling the wall with his left hand, feeling for the stool with his toes. He found the stool and pushed it gingerly to one side. He found the light switch and switched it on. As his eyes cleared and became accustomed to the bright light he noticed that he lamp was plugged into a power socket which wasn't switched on. He swore, stepped towards it and fell over the stool, banging his head against the wall. He swore again, dragged himself up, picked up his watch and opened the cover. It was 04h15.

Again. Too soon to get up. Too late to get back into bed. Too scary to fall asleep. Too early to have a shower and get dressed.

Coffee. What he needed was coffee. His throat was dry as the desert. He needed something hot, sweet, liquid and caffeine-based. His entire being shrieked rage at the little room which didn't have space for a little kettle. He remembered a Teasmade he had once broken in a fit of anger and regretted it.

But there had to be somewhere in this hotel, this pub, this hostelry, where he could find the ingredients for a cup of tea or coffee. Perhaps not as good as his espresso maker, but something warm and liquid and caffeine.

He put the judo uniform on, wrapped the black belt around his waist, switched off the light, gave it a count of ten thousand in thousands to let his eyes acclimatise, and opened the door a centimetre. He crouched down and his eye peeked briefly out where a waiting assassin wouldn't expect it. The passage was dim and empty and funereal. And deathly quiet. Too quiet. He remembered what Samson had said about the aerodrome.

He gave it a count of twenty thousand in thousands, opened the door, slipped out and closed it behind him. He padded softly towards the office, keeping close to the wall. He stood outside the door and listened.

Nothing.

He kneeled down and put his eye to the keyhole. There was a key in it but he could see that a light was on inside. He stood up and held his hand on the door knob for a few seconds. Then he knocked softly and opened the door. Carry was sitting behind the desk, looking at him, a book in her hands.

He closed the door behind him and sat in the chair facing the desk, crossing his leg over his knee. They looked at each other for about ten seconds.

'Would you like to be an angel?'

'Not particularly.'

'Be an angel and tell me where I can find a cup of coffee. I'm dying for a cup of coffee.'

'I'll watch that.'

'What?'

'You dying.'

'You're not going to tell me.'

'When you said, Tell me where I can find a cup of coffee, you meant, Please make me a cup of coffee, didn't you. Or did you forget the Please?'

'I'm not that bad. I can make my own coffee. I make pretty good coffee as it happens.'

She jerked a thumb towards the sideboard. On top of it sat a coffee-maker with the jug half-full, and four or five upturned mugs.

'Was that there yesterday?'

'Of course. How do you think I get through the night?'

He stood up and went to the sideboard. There was even a large jug of milk. He poured himself a coffee, added milk, three sugars, and sat back down in the chair. He took a sip and closed his eyes

'God that's good. '

He took a deeper sip.

'Is there something weird about this place?'

'Run that one by me slowly again. You're a police officer, dressed as the Karate Kid, it's not even five o'clock on a winter's morning just before Christmas, it's a pub, and you're asking me if there's anything weird.' She paused. 'You don't suppose some people think there's something weird about coppers full stop?'

'I don't normally have nightmares two nights on the trot. There's definitely something not quite right here. My brain's trying to tell me something.'

'I am surprised.'

'About what?'

'That you have a brain.'

'Very funny. You wouldn't be laughing if you'd had the sort of night I've had. Twice in a row.'

'Nightmares. About what. Do tell. Do they involve wedding dresses by any chance?'

'Oh, you know. You're rushing somewhere, or flying, or something impossible. It all seems life-threatening. Rush, rush, rush. Running. Sprinting. Flying. Then suddenly you wake up covered in sweat wondering what the hell it was all about.'

'Are you sure it's sweat?'

'What?'

'Did you have cheese before going to bed?'

'Cheese?'

'They say it causes nightmares.'

'Well, I had some Edam with dessert. It seemed an odd combination, but Anne-Marie said it was quite popular around here. I wasn't sure if she was joking or not. Actually it didn't taste too bad.'

'Anne-Marie never jokes.'

'Do you?'

'Do I what.'

'Do you like jokes?'

'Only if they're funny.'

'Okay. Have you heard of the dyslexic man who walked into a bra?'

'No.'

'Well?'

'Well what.'

'It's a joke.'

'Is it.'

'Don't you get it?'

'No.'

'Comedians normally start a joke off with This man walked into a bar. Only he's dyslexic, you see, so he walked into a bra.'

'Oh, I get it now.'

'Yes?'

'Yes. You're a comedian.'

'Okay, how about something a little less funny. A little birdie told me about a girl in London who got caught carrying drugs for her boyfriend. She only got off because the idiot investigating officer forgot to read her her rights. Ring a bell?'

'Not a tinkle.'

'Strange. She had the same name as you.'

'Must have been my twin.'

'You don't have a twin. Anyway, even if you did she wouldn't have the same name as you. You're getting confused.'

'Am I.'

'Does Patsy know you have a record?'

'I have a record. Was it in the top ten.'

'Okay, maybe not a record, but you only got off because of a technicality.'

'You mean that technicality called the law.'

'So what would Patsy say if he came to find out?'

'Nothing. Do you like frying pans.'

'Frying pans?'

'If Patsy came to know anything that wasn't true Mrs Patsy would also come to know. She's very protective of her girls.'

'Her girls?'

'Anne-Marie and me at the moment. Thuthan. She loves Thuthan. Others during summer.'

'You're threatening me with Mrs Patsy? In a wheelchair?'

'And I could tell Thuthan you want to play hide and seek. She likes that. She plays it with knives. She likes pretending to be a Red Indian stalking her prey. Have you been scalped before.'

'You have a strange sense of humour.'

'Strange to you. Do you know what Anne-Marie's real job is?'

'She works a guillotine in Paris.'

'She's a drummer in a Heavy Metal band. Goes touring during the summer.'

Not my thing. Heavy Metal.'

'Do you know how her ex-boyfriend died.'

'Her ex-boyfriend died.'

'Drumstick up his arse. Perforated something.'

'Definitely something weird about this place.'

'You call it weird. Some people call it normal.'

'No, I know the difference between weird and normal, and this isn't normal.'

'Did you know, children born in prison never acclimatise to freedom.'

'Bollocks. You can get used to anything.'

'Why are you here?'

'To investigate this murder.'

'Not doing too well, are you.'

'You ask too many questions.'

'Do you believe in love.'

'Of course.'

'So why hide your wedding ring.'

'I wasn't hiding it. It's a bit tight. I need to get it fixed.'

'Have you thought about taking an enema.'

'An enema?'

'Because you're full of shit.'

She stood up, picked up her book and disappeared through the staff door into the internal recesses. There was the sound of a key turning in a lock. It seemed to echo down through a dozen frozen corridors.

Morton finished his coffee and went for a shower. It washed away the screaming heebie-jeebies of the night. His confidence began to return.

'Likes playing hard to get,' he decided as he dried himself off. 'Standard practice. All girls do it. At first.'

'Oh, is there not a maiden breast,' he sang to himself.

He washed his teeth and combed his hair. He remembered the previous morning and bent over to inspect the top of his head for any excessive thinning. But he couldn't see it. Each time he bent down he lost sight of the mirror at the exact time the top of his head began to come into view. He looked around for a second mirror. There wasn't one. Finally he gave up and turned his attention to shaving. Then he remembered that he had completely forgotten to pick up a razor and shower gel the previous day.

'You had one job to do,' he told himself.

Having returned to his room his spirits dropped a bit more at the sight of his suit. It was an expensive one made more expensive by having to be dry-cleaned. Normally he could keep it going for six months between dry-cleans by using it sparingly and getting Shirley to press it once a week. It was now definitely getting the look of something that had been slept in. He should have asked Carry if she could iron it for him. Or maybe Anne-Marie.

The shirt. It looked like a black and white prison with gold burning bars ready to lock him in.

It was Shirley who had insisted that he buy it.

"It suits you."

For a very brief moment he wondered if anyone would notice if he went out in the judo suit.

He concluded that he must be suffering some form of mental breakdown just by contemplating that option.

He would get home eventually. When he did the suit and coat were going straight to the dry-cleaner. And probably then into the cupboard never to be taken out again. Maybe he'd just throw them out and save the money. The shirt was … He'd put the shirt into a dustbin, pour some petrol on it and set it on fire.

The thought of the clothes' future made it somehow easier to get moving.

He dressed, trying to ignore the feel of the shirt and trousers against his skin. Then he took out his smartphone despite knowing there wouldn't be any messages. No signal, no messages, no contact. He noticed his reflection in the screen. He looked like a tired old man, eyes blood-shot and puffy. Not "Rambo coming out the jungle bloody but unbowed" tired, more "too much drink and too much food and too little exercise and too little sleep and you're getting a little old and flabby to be doing these silly things aren't you" tired.

On the plus side, he wasn't Samson. He wasn't tired and bitter and finished like Samson. There was that. He wasn't beaten yet. A voice at the back of his mind told him to buck up and march straight. He was feeling sorry for himself. Idiot. Idiot. Idiot.

He looked at the painting above the bed, the two golden wings coming out of a blade, backed by a red and blackened boiling sky, signed NAR stokes.

He smiled. Nigel Stokes could never have realised the similarity of what he had painted to the men who dared and won, but he did.

Before putting his smartphone back into his pocket he typed in a message to himself:

"wakey, wakey, cakey, cakey".

Ten minutes later he was on his way to Cemetery Ridge. As he walked swiftly he kept glancing back to check for speeding artics or other homicidal drivers. When he got to the top of Cemetery Ridge he gave one final glance backwards before looking down into the valley, just as a bright pink-magenta-purple-in-the-half-light 1965 Studebaker came flying over the hill. He dived for the cover of the rocks, landed on Snuffles' grave, tearing his coat.

'What the fuck?'

'Fucking hell.'

'Where the fuck?'

He stood up, brushing the gravel from his chest and suit.

'What the fuck is that stupid old fart up to now? Bastard could have killed me.'

'He could have said he was coming this way and saved me the walk.'

'You stupid fucking old bastard! I hope you crash that stupid fucking thing! Jesus!'

He stood watching the road for a few seconds where the Studebaker had disappeared, breathing hard, his heart pumping. Then he took out his mobile phone and switched it on. He noticed that the battery was rapidly reaching empty. He checked his voicemail. There was one message, from Dick.

'Hiya Luke. I called around for missing persons for you. No Poles. Three or four men believed to have run away from their wives with their young totty, lucky bastards. All older than your vic. As usual the wives all insist that their hubbies would never leave them. Other than that, nothing. Guess this time of the year is a bad time to run away from home, never know what you're going to get in your stocking, eh? Speaking of which, that new young thing was asking where you were, reckon you might be in with a chance there. If I don't get in first. You know, distance makes the heart grow fonder.

Of someone closer.'

He scratched his nose before giving Shirley a call. It went straight to voice mail. He switched the phone off and looked down into the valley. The sky was almost pitch black, a sliver of an ice-cold moon shining, the valley a mixture of white where the snow had set, black where it had melted. It was all shadows apart from the occasional light from a house, presumably farm houses. The aerodrome runway again seemed to stand out in its own blackness, an unnatural straight line in a world of camouflaged curves. It was almost as if it was trying to disguise itself, pretending not to be there.

Eventually he realised that he was getting cold. The wind was far more brisk than the previous day. His head was colder. But there was something else. He checked the damage to his clothes. The buttons on his camel-hair coat had torn open. Those on the jacket and waistcoat of his suit had also pulled loose. It was as if his stomach had made a sudden lunge for freedom.

He rubbed his arms and pulled the camel-hair overcoat together. At least he would be back in his own bed that evening. He could be certain of that. Samson wasn't the type of man to ever admit that he'd got anything wrong. He had said they would be leaving that day and leave they would come what may.

Though he was certainly also bloody-minded enough to change his mind and decide to stay on for another night just to spite the world.

Samson – Bloody Samson.

Morton made a mental note to ask Carry how to get out of this miserable place without a car. Maybe he could get Joe the Rescue to take him somewhere with a train station attached. He would even risk a boat journey with the bastard.

He'd take his bottle away first, though.

Probably drink half of it himself before they left.

He looked at Snuffles' grave. The wooden cross had been knocked over by his fall. He pushed it upright and made sure it was firmly seated in the soil. He stood for a while before saying, 'So long, Snuffles. Rest in peace, little fella' Then he began trudging his last walk back down Saxon Way.

Back in the Angel and Duck Morton left his overcoat in his room and went in search of Samson. He found him in the snug reading his paperback. Samson held a hand up to indicate silence while he read. Morton sat down and watched as Samson slowly and laboriously read each word, turning a page occasionally with reverence, as if a monk reading the Holy Scriptures, his mouth opening occasionally as his tongue silently spoke a word. Eventually he reached some cut-off point. He carefully folded a corner of a page, closed the book, put it down and looked at Morton.

'Do you know, they never have sex in these stories.'

'Sex?'

'No. It's an American thing. If it were French they'd be at it like rabbits from page one. If it were British they would be discreet, but you'd know they were at it. But then the French and British wouldn't have the kid.'

'The kid?'

'The little boy. The one who hero-worships the hero. The one the mother doesn't want hero-worshipping the hero. Cause he's one of the bad guys. Only we know he's really one of the good guys. But the thing about the kid –'

'Yes?'

'Well, main place you find kids in English books is in children's books. English as in British. You don't get them in the classics, like James Bond.'

'James Bond.'

'No. Ever see a Bond movie with a kid in a main role? No, it would get in the way of his totty. But you look at Indiana Jones. There's that one where it's all about saving kids in a mine. Arnie Swarzenegger. He did kindergarten cop. Thing is, where do kids come from?'

'Where do kids come from?'

'Yeah. You know, sex.'

'Sex?'

'They did teach you about the birds and bees at school, didn't they.

Or do I have to draw you a picture?'

'No, I mean, where does sex come into it?'

'That's the point. So the Yanks have lots of kids without sex, the French have lots of sex without kids, and we Brits don't have neither. Morning Carry, what's for breakfast?'

'Usual. Cereal if you want. Fruit. Full English or scrambled eggs. Or as you like.'

'Poached?'

'If you want.'

'I do, thanks. I'll have poached eggs, sausages and toast. With fried tomatoes, if you have.'

'I'll have the full English.'

'I see your waistcoat has already made space.'

'Blimey. What on earth happened to your buttons, lad?'

'I think the waistcoat must have shrunk in the last dry-clean.'

'Your jacket too, and all. You want to be careful, lad. That's what comes of too many Masonic dinners. You can always tell which coppers are Masons. They keep having to buy larger suits.'

'Poached eggs and full English coming up.'

'That girl could go far. Why do so many girls like that end up waitressing in places like this?'

'Not a bad place. Must be pretty good in summer if you like solitude and long walks. And no mobile connection.'

'Suppose so. Must admit I prefer to find solitude in big towns. London. So many other buggers floating around you can virtually disappear. Places like this every bugger knows who you are and what you're doing.'

'Except for the Polish bloke.'

'Yeah, but he was an outsider. And he'd only just arrived. If he'd been here for a week they would have known his birthday and shoe size.'

'What makes you think he would have stayed?'

'He wouldn't have. According to Constantine he only had a little bag. He wasn't planning on staying more than a night or two.'

'Eastern Europeans are different. They don't feel they have to change clothes so often.'

'If you say so, son. Thank you, Carry, those look delicious. Do you normally serve four poached eggs at a time? In butter? With four slices of toast?'

'It saves on having to go back to the kitchen again. I've never known anyone fail to finish them. They're fresh from the farm, not from the supermarket. Your full English, constable. Oh, and the poached eggs aren't done in butter, that's a drizzle.'

'A drizzle, eh? Looks more like a downpour to me, but I'm not complaining.'

Samson watched Morton drown his full English in tomato sauce as Carry left. Then he added salt. Samson winced and picked up his knife and fork.

'I went for a drive up to that airfield earlier this morning. Couldn't sleep. I know there's something about that airfield. And I was right. It was as quiet as the grave. Dead quiet. Too quiet. There's something going on there, my lad.'

'What time was that?'

'Time? About five o'clock, I suppose.'

'Wouldn't you expect an aerodrome to be quiet at that time?'

'Precisely. A normal airfield should be quiet at that time. But not this one. This one isn't normal. That's exactly why you'd expect something to be going on. But it wasn't. And that's why it's so odd. It's what I always say. Beware the normal. Now eat your breakfast before it gets cold.'

The two men ate in silence. It was the normal thing to do. But it also allowed Morton to avoid asking the other man what made an aerodrome abnormally quiet because it was as normally quiet as you would expect it to be at five in the morning. It also meant he could ignore things like wedding rings and why Shirley wasn't answering her mobile. Above all he could stop trying to work out what on earth made Samson think he had everything sown up bar the last point. If he had missed something that Samson had spotted he might as well resign there and then and become a street-sweeper or a teacher or something.

Samson finished before Morton who had added four thick slices of white bread to his full English. He sat staring blankly into space as Morton ploughed on with the occasional burp. Finally Morton finished everything including the last tea in the pot.

'Had enough, son?'

'Keep me going until elevenses.'

'Right, time to get moving. I'm going to get my coat. Meet you in the main bar.'

Morton strolled back to his little room, got his coat and went back to the main bar. Samson was already coated up and sitting on a bar stool.

'Could I ask one thing, sir?'

'What's that, son?'

'Couldn't we pop back to town for half an hour? I could really do with some fresh clothes, sir.'

'I know, son. Not to worry, you'll be back soon enough.'

He looked around at the empty pub.

'We're alone here, aren't we?'

'It is well before opening time.'

'I meant including bar staff, cleaners and any other passing nosey-bodies.'

'No, we are alone.'

'Have a look over the counter and make sure there's no-one busy washing the floor on their knees.'

Morton gave him a look before leaning over and taking as much of a look as the depth of the counter and his stomach would allow.

'No, no-one washing the floor. Or doing anything else on the floor.'

'Never do it on the floor, son, it ruins your knees. And her back.'

'What?'

'Never mind. Listen now, I can let you into a little secret, my lad.'

'Yes?'

'Luke, I reckon you'll be home by this evening, my son. Probably long before that. We're going to close this up at twelve o'clock. Twelve o'clock this afternoon. That's when I reveal who done it. At the altar in the priest's church.'

'The altar.'

'That's the one.'

'At the church.'

'Where you normally find altars.'

'Why there?'

'Why there? Why not.'

'Why not indeed, I suppose.'

'I hate churches.'

'You do? So why –?'

'People get married in them.'

'So why –?'

'I hate priests. They marry people.'

'He's a vicar, not a priest.'

'I hate vicars. They marry people.'

'Why then?'

'Why then? Trust me Morton, I have my methods. Come on, let's take a drive up Saxon Way.'

Morton didn't trust him. He didn't believe that Samson was about to reveal the truth, either from the high altar or Mount Ararat. But he'd be going home that evening. That was all he cared about. Going home to Shirley. He had some making up to do. But at least now he was going to get a chance to do it. After a long, hot bath and some fresh clothes. And a shave.

Standing in the saloon bar bar Patsy raised his eyebrows and polished a glass a lot faster and a lot harder. After about five seconds he held it up to the light, whistling softly and silently. Then he polished it some more. Held it to the light. Cocked his head. Listened.

He put the glass and cloth down and slipped back to the main bar. He picked up the phone and dialled a number.

'Mrs Coombes-Neeston? It's Patsy here, from the Angel and Duck. I think Mr Coombes-Neeston might have left something here last night. Could you ask him to pop in and pick it up when he gets a moment? It's rather urgent.'

'No, that's awful kind of you to offer, Mrs Coombes-Neeston, but it's personal like. Better he calls in himself.'

'Oh, no, Mrs Coombes-Neeston, nothing like that at all. I'm sure the general – I mean Mr Coombes-Neeston – doesn't indulge in that sort of thing. No, shall we just say – "Christmas"? You know, the season of giving, only keeping it secret until the big day. That's why it's quite urgent.'

'Well, yes, Mrs Coombes-Neeston, presence is the word. Can't say any more, of course.'

In the ladies' bar Carry closed her eyes.

'Never heard that,' she murmured. 'Heard nothing, saw nothing, said nothing. I am just a little girl who doesn't know a thing. I am five going on four.'

'Where are we going, sir?' asked Morton as Samson drove idly along Saxon Way, window open, hand tapping on the roof.

'Up the hill, son. As in all good fairy tales.'

'And then?'

'And then we wait.'

'And then we wait,' echoed Morton.

On top of Cemetery Ridge Samson pulled over and parked the car. They got out and Samson gestured to the grave of Snuffles.

'Ever wonder why someone chose this place to bury a cat?'

'Do we know it's a cat?'

'Good point, Morton, good point. You're learning. We'll make a half-decent copper out of you yet. For all we know it could be an elephant under there.'

'An elephant named Snuffles.'

'Or even someone's nan.'

'A nan named Snuffles.'

'Maybe she had a cold. Maybe that's what killed her. Probably not. But you never know. Point is, normal people look at it and presume it's a pet, and probably a cat. We, as coppers, have to think differently. ABC.'

'ABC?'

'Assume nothing. Believe nobody. Check everything.'

'Ah, yes. Of course.'

'Get me the binocs, Morton, I want to have a closer look at something. Here's the keys.'

Morton took the keys, went back to the car, opened the boot and brought back the binoculars. Samson took them and scanned the area in the direction of the aerodrome. He repeated this several times, eventually checking his watch.

'Just as I thought. Let's have a look out to sea.'

He wandered over to the other side of the hill and swept the horizon. The freighter was still hove to.

'Clever buggers,' he murmured. He kept the glasses to his eyes for a while more before handing them to Morton.

'Have a look and tell me what you see, son.'

Morton took the binoculars and slowly scanned from left to right. Then back again. Then left to right again. Then back again.

'Freighter's still there.'

'Anything else?'

'No. Not that I can see.'

'Try the aerodrome.'

Richard Coombes-Neeston walked up to the doors of the Angel and Duck.

''Ere, you can't go in there, ain't opening time yet. I'm not ready. I ain't got me teeth in yet.'

'I'm just collecting something, Molly.'

'Drink is the wages of sin. And stuff.'

'Too early to collect my wages yet, Molly.'

'What the lord giveth the lord altho taketh away.'

'Hiccups to the lord, Molly.'

He slipped into the pub. Patsy was standing at the main bar polishing a glass.

'You left something behind last night.'

'So Marge said. What was it?'

'I don't know. You'll have to buy something for her that you can forget and give her for Christmas. What's more important right now is that that inspector is on to something.'

'Samson? On to something? That moron?'

'No, not the constable, the inspector. Samson.'

'Samson? Without a pee or a clue?'

'That's the one I meant. He's found something out.'

'Found something out? He couldn't find his backside with a Satnav on a sunny day.'

'Well, whatever it is he's going to be discussing it with Vicar Brayley at twelve at the altar in the church.'

'What?'

'That's what he said.'

'Why Brayley?'

'Why the altar?'

'I think we'd better get the others in. Just to be on the safe side.'

'They've gone up Saxon Way.'

'Who? The others?'

'No, Samson and the Moron. Maybe one of us should follow them.'

'No need. If the stupid fool let slip he's meeting the vicar in the church at twelve o'clock we don't need to follow them. We can be ready and listening somewhere discreet.'

'At the church.'

'I don't think I've been in that church before.'

'Nothing,' said Morton.

'That's what I thought. Oh, well, might as well have some coffee while we're waiting. I had them make a flask up. It's in the boot. Do the honours, Morton, one more time.'

Morton trudged back to the Studebaker. He opened the boot. The contents looked exactly the same as two days before. An old car jack with associated long-handled iron lever alongside; a dark green Wellington boot; an old tartan blanket; a bright green coiled mountain rope; a baby doll which looked at him with wide open psychopathic eyes and looked as if it were about to suddenly cry, "Mummy! Mummy!" before pulling a knife out and running amok. For a brief moment he imagined it had come alive and turned into

Thuthan holding her swords and staring curiously up at him.

'The dark red one,' called Samson.

Morton snapped himself out of it. There was the hamper containing two vacuum flasks labelled 'Thermos', one dark blue, one dark red; two insulated plastic mugs with lids, one luminous yellow with a picture of a smiling Mickey Mouse, the other luminous pink with a smiling Minnie Mouse. The mugs and red Thermos looked as if they had recently been cleaned. He picked them up, took them around to the front of the Studebaker and poured coffee for them.

'Lovely and peaceful, isn't it?' said Samson, looking through the binoculars. 'Just right for Christmas. Nothing was staring through the house, not even a mouse.'

Morton sipped his coffee and looked around Cemetery Ridge. It looked like the sort of place boys with new cars brought their girlfriend to watch the sun set, before breaking up because she wasn't that kind of a girl. Or perhaps breaking up because she was too much that kind of girl.

The coffee didn't taste the same as the one he had had on the beach on that distant Sunday. Whoever had made it obviously lacked Samson's special blend.

'Hello, hello, hello,' said Samson. 'Thought so.' He tossed his untasted coffee away and dropped the mug and binoculars in Morton's arms. 'Come on, lad, action stations. Put that lot away and let's get moving.'

'What –'

'No time for chit chat, let's go.'

Morton rushed to the boot and threw the mugs and flask in. He just had time to slam it shut and scramble into the passenger seat before Samson floored the accelerator and the Studebaker shot off back down Saxon Way towards the harbour.

'Tis far too early in the morning for orgies.'

'Oh be quiet, Molly. We're far too old to indulge in orgies.'

'The demon drink gives you youth and takes your soul.'

'If we ever find that drink we'll share some with you. For the moment it's not even opening time. We're just here for a meeting of concerned citizens. Come on Bertie.'

'Well, we could have just one,' said Bertie as she followed Phillipa Mountjohn into the Angel and Duck.

'No we can't. Well, Richard, what's going on?'

'Probably nothing. But Patsy here says that that idiot of an inspector thinks he's found something. He's going to reveal all to the vicar at the altar in the church at twelve o'clock.'

'What?'

'You heard, Philly.'

'I heard, Richard. I heard total and utter gibberish. It's not like you. You're a lying, back-stabbing, wife-cheating, mistress-cheating son of a bitch, but you normally make sense.'

'Am I missing something?'

'It's old history, Patsy. Before you came down here.'

'Yes, he's moved on a few mistresses since then.'

'Shut up, Philly. Tell them, Patsy.'

'It's like he says. I overheard Samson saying to his sidekick that he'll be speaking to the vicar at the altar at twelve and all will be revealed. He told the constable he'd be able to go home this afternoon.'

'So? If it's about the Polish man it's got nothing to do with us.'

'Let's hope so. But just in case there's any overlap I think one of us should be at the altar when he makes his announcement.'

'Can't be you, Richard. You've led enough women up the garden path, not so many up to the altar. Only one, in fact. Though how she nailed you I don't know, she's got a head full of cotton wool.'

'Oh do shut up, Philly. That was years ago.'

'I have a long memory, Richard.'

Morton thought he had known what fear was. As Samson raced toward the beach he discovered that he had been wrong. Fear was being in the passenger seat of a 1965 bright purple Studebaker while Chief Inspector Samson threw it around corners like a ten year-old with a scalextric set. Every time he tried to start saying something like 'Don't you think –?' another corner would appear and he would be tossed in a different direction. He could have sworn they were on two wheels as the car screeched into the parking lot next to the beach and came to a halt that would have thrown him through the windscreen had it not been for his seat belt. Samson had switched the engine off, got out of the car and was striding towards the beach bench before Morton had his breath back. He managed to get out and stumble toward the bench as Samson stood there hands on hips, staring at the freighter like Cortez infuriated by some indigenous peasant in a canoe

'You must have said something that let it slip, Richard, you always did have a bad habit of boasting.'
'Look, he does not know about the parcel, okay.'
'Then why are we all standing here?'
'As a precaution. We have to know what he tells the preacher boy. One of us has to be in that church.'
'I'll go.'
'We'll all go.'
'With respect, Elvira, we can hardly all traipse down to the church with you in your bath chair. We'll stick out a mile.'
'I said we'll all go. Do you wish to argue, Richard.'
'Okay, Elvira, we'll all go.'
'Carry? Carry? Where's Carry? Ah, there you are. We have to go out. Will you be okay on your own for a while?'
'I'll be fine. Thuthan will be here shortly. And Anne-Marie's starting early.'
'Good girl, we won't be long.'
Carry sat down on the stool behind the counter and watched as Patsy's platoon marched and waddled and wheeled out of the Angel and Duck. She shook her head slowly.

'I've got them exactly where I want them. Morton, I want you to get in this rowing boat and row out to that freighter. Tell the captain I want to see him. As in now.'

'What?'

'Come on, no time to waste, I'll give you a hand getting it into the sea.'

'Chief Inspector, that freighter is beyond the 12 mile zone. It's in international waters.'

'Nonsense. It's no more than three miles out, four at the most.'

'I can't –'

'Come on, grab that end. Stop dilly-dallying, Morton.'

'Inspector, why don't you row out there?'

'Can't, I suffer from claustrophobia.'

'Claustrophobia is an irrational fear of enclosed spaces.'

'Angoraphobia or something.'

'A fear of mountain goats?'

'I don't like to talk about it too much. If they knew I had it I'd lose my job. You take the front end. Come on, heave.'

'It's bloody heavy.'

'Positive thinking, Morton, remember, if you don't have a can-do attitude you'll never get promotion.'

'Anyway, I told you I get –'

'Move the bloody thing, Morton, I can't do it all on my own.'

Morton looked at the rope that tied it down to put another argument forward, only to discover that it was undone. He picked it up and began feebly pulling. To his surprise it was easier than he expected to slide the ugly boat along the damp gravelly beach, almost as if it was seeking its natural element. Within a short time he felt the cold sea swirl around his ankles as he pulled the front of the rowing boat and Samson pushed from the other end. He almost gave himself a hernia as he tried to keep his shoes out of the salt water while his feet were in them. Finally the boat was just floating and he clambered in to get out of the freezing water.

'Good lad, put the oars in the rowlocks.'

Morton stumbled to one side and grabbed the oar. It felt like it weighed a ton. He shoved it into the rowlock and held onto it with one hand while grabbing the other oar. The boat swayed and slopped from side to side. Morton managed to get the second oar in the oarlock, slipped and sat down on the rowing bench suddenly. He felt a bolt of pain shoot up his spine.

'Good lad,' said Samson. 'Now, row! Row! While you've got the current with you, row! Row like the devil!'

Morton gritted his teeth and pulled at the oars. Slowly, slowly he began to make headway, inching past the surf on onto the sea proper. Each time he bent in to pull he could see the old fool standing on the beach watching him, hands on hips.

He had already got about fifty yards out before the thought crossed his mind, 'What the fuck am I doing this for?'

'I have seen the coming of the angel of the lord.'

'Found your teeth have you, Molly?'

'He hath loosed the fateful lightning of his terrible swift sword.'

'Molly, do you mind? We're just going for a quiet walk.'

'You're going to another den of iniquity.'

'We're going down to the church.'

'So I was right. Priests. Priests and nuns. Priests and nuns and sex.'

'Molly you've got a one-track mind.'

'And I don't like the track.'

'Shut up and push faster, Patrick.'

'Yes my angel.'

'Bloody old fool,' Morton said to himself, 'and puulll.' And then 'Up ... and back ... and .... puuulll .... Take a note ... '

He risked a look behind him.

'Bloody freighter is miles away ... and ... puuulll .... and .... up... and back and ... puuulll ....

'Count to a thousand ... and puuulll .... and ...... up .... and start with .... and one .... and puuulll ....'

Water slopped into the boat from the oars.

'Count the objects in the old fool's boot .... and puuulll .... and up and one length of plastic rope and up and back and .... puuulll ....

The bottom had a lot more water in it than he expected. It did not look the way he expected the bottom of a boat to look. Not a healthy boat.

'One iron lever for use with a jack and puuulll ... and up and one jack and puuulll ...

A lot more water than had come in via the oars.

'One mad dolly and puuulll .... and up and ...

In fact, it was almost as if there was some sort of hole in the bottom.

He paused to focus on the distant beach. The old fool was now so distant he was too small to be seen.

It was so far he couldn't even see the old fool's car.

Correction.

He couldn't see the old fool's car because it wasn't there.

He couldn't see the old fool because he wasn't there.

The rowing boat was in its element. It bobbed easily on the flow and swell of the sea, moving out toward the open Atlantic. It seemed happy enough to tolerate its passenger for a few moments.

'Okay, hold it, keep out of sight.'

'Aren't we going in there?'

'We don't want Brayley to see us.'

'I'm not going in there. Disgusting. Priests and nuns and sex.'

'In that case the sooner we get in the better.'

'Tell me about the priests and nuns and sex, Molly.'

'Dear god, Bertie, this isn't the time nor the place.'

'Okay, listen up, we're all going to slip across one at a time. Go fast, go low.'

'Swing low, sweet chariot, coming for to take me home.'

'Apart from you, Molly.'

'This will be your military training, will it, Richard?'

'Yes, Philly, trust me, I know what I'm doing.'

'I wish I'd known what you were doing thirty years ago.'

'Jesus will you give it a rest, woman.'

'Thou shalt not use the lord's name in vain.'

'Oh fuck it. Run for it.'

'Last one in is a sloppy meringue.'

'Thank you for that, Bertie, your contribution is gratefully

acknowledged. Now fucking run.'
'This is fun, isn't it.'

Morton heard the ring tone of a mobile phone. He looked around. Who the hell had a mobile going off around here? He looked over the side in case there was a periscope there. Then he recognised the ring tone. It was his mobile.

You can get a signal out to sea, they had said.

He clutched one oar in his left hand, the other under his right arm and pulled his mobile out. He pressed the answer button.

'Hello, Inspector? What?'

'What? Who?'

'Shirley?'

'Shirley, why the hell are you calling me now? I'm halfway out to sea in a rowing boat on my way to a Polish freighter.'

'What?'

'Did you hear what I said?'

'Shirley, this is not the time for that sort of thing, I'm in the middle of a murder case.'

'Shirley we'll talk about this later. I don't have the time now.'

'Gareth? No, I don't remember Gareth. Shirley –'

'Fine, you're leaving me. Running away with Gareth. Gareth the hairdresser. Okay. Fine. I'll speak to you later. Make sure he gives you a discount in future.'

He killed the call and put the mobile back into his jacket pocket.

'Calls to tell me she's leaving me in the middle of the fucking ocean. With a hairdresser. Christ. Like I want to discuss marriage now. Hasn't she heard of a post-it fucking note on the fridge. Send me an email for Christ's sake.'

He paused to get his breath back.

'Why the fuck do women always say no and then yes when you don't want them to?'

The party slipped into the church quietly and quickly, bent over double. They crept up behind the back pew.

'Sure and it's quiet in here.'

'It's a church. They don't often hold parties here, you know.'

'Ah, but it's a heathen church. I'm used to Catholic churches.'

'And they have shout-alongs in Catholic churches?'

'Well, no, but I've heard things about Anglican churches. Happy clappies and that sort of thing.'

'Well, this isn't one of those churches. Now we've got to find somewhere to hide within ear-shot of the altar.'

'Where? That looks like a Catholic altar. The priest always stays the other side, keeps well away from the parishioners in case he catches something. Like the plague.'

'There's probably a side door just behind that pulpit on the left hand side.'

'How do you know?'

'I was an altar boy many years ago.'

'Then you'll know, if it's the same as the Catholic version, that door leads to where the priest gets dressed.'

'Gets dressed?'

'Puts his robes on. For mass and such. That's a thought. If it is like a Catholic church there'll be surplices and stuff for altar boys.'

'And?'

'We could disguise ourselves.'

'What as?'

'Altar boys.'

'Yeah, like there's probably only one altar boy in the entire village and Brayley wouldn't recognise us. Give me a break.'

'Just thinking aloud.'

'Let's have a look around the altar.'

'Looks like it's ready for mass.'

'How do you know?'

'The candlesticks. With candles. They'd normally be locked away. I remember me grandad telling as how they'd nick the candles if they got a chance.'

'Just the candles?'

'Well, you wouldn't want to get caught with the candlesticks, it'd be

a great shame on the family.'
'What about the candles?'
'They burn.'
'Let's see what's under the tablecloth.'
'This altar's hollow. There's nothing underneath apart from an electric fan.'
'Quick, get underneath and pull the tablecloth back into place.'
'Elvira, you can wait in the confessional. There should be enough space there. Philly, Bertie, hide behind some pillars somewhere.'

'And puuulll … Ninety-two green bottles … and puulll … hanging on the wall … and puulll … Ninety- … where the fuck was I … and puulll … Ninety … three … and puulll … Ninety-three green bottles … and puulll … I just hope to hell that stupid old git knows what he's doing … '

The side door behind the pulpit opened and Vicar Brayley entered wearing a heavy winter jacket. He looked around as if expecting to find someone, took a second look, shrugged, and took off the jacket, placing it neatly on a chair. He walked up to a plug-point to the left of the altar. He switched it on and moved towards the altar. There was a whirring noise as the fan heater started. An outbreak of muted voices came from the altar.
'Jesus Mary and Joseph what's that?'
'It's the bloody fan heater.'
'It's bloody blowing hot air right up my –'
'Look out, your jacket –'
Vicar Brayley looked down in astonishment as the fan switched from a whirring sound to a cluck-clucking noise and someone or something yelped. Richard Coombes-Neeston and Patsy rolled out, dragging the altar-cloth and candles down over them. They carried on rolling around until they had disentangled themselves from the cloth. Richard Coombes-Neeston stood holding onto the altar for support while Patsy danced around trying to hit the fan heater gripping the back of his jacket.

'Turn it off, for God's sake, turn it off, it's trying to eat me.'

Vicar Brayley stepped across to the plug switch and switched it off. Patsy shrugged his coat off and the fan heater clanged onto the floor with it.

'Bloody Anglican churches.'

'It's a Catholic heater.'

'What?'

'It's made in Italy.'

'What on earth were you two doing beneath the altar, if you don't mind me asking?'

'Saying our prayers, vicar, what do you think?'

'I must say it's a strange place to be saying prayers. Most people use the pews.'

'What the hell are you doing in that getup anyway? You look like you're about to conduct a funeral.'

'Well, now you mention it –'

'Where's that idiot Samson? Has he arrived yet?'

'Chief Inspector Samson? Was he supposed to be here? Only –'

'What's the time? Five past twelve. He was supposed to be here at twelve.'

'Was he? That's strange because –'

'He's probably been delayed. Vicar, we're going to get under the altar again. Patsy, drag that tablecloth back into position.'

'I'm not going down there again.'

'Vicar, put the candlesticks back when we're in.'

'I don't quite understand –'

'Shut up and get down, Patsy. Give the vicar back his candles.'

'I'm too old for this.'

'Are you sure –'

'Now, vicar, not a word to Samson, understand? You haven't seen us, we're not here, okay?'

'But –'

'We aren't here and you haven't seen us. Got that?'

'But –'

'Vicar, stop blathering, he mustn't know we're here.'

'But I think he already knows you're here.'

'What? Where?'

The two men looked up from underneath the altar as Vicar Brayley took an envelope from his pocket.

'He asked me to read this to you. Then he said you'd be needing the last rites.'

'The last rights?'

'Extreme unction.'

'Extreme unction?'

'Anointing of the sick.'

Samson strode through the doors of the Angel and Duck. Thuthan sat cross-legged on the bar counter with a sword, watching Carry behind the counter playing cards with Anne-Marie sitting in front of it.

'Hello, Carry, bon jour Anne-Marie, hello Thuthan, don't mind me, I'm just passing through. I need to interrogate that genetically modified dumb waiter of yours, Eric Delift.'

They watched him walk straight past the Staff Only sign and on towards the kitchen. There was a good deal of humming and then sounds of something being enthusiastically broken into. Samson came out of the kitchen carrying the parcel the motorcyclist had delivered.

'I don't know anything about that.'

'I know you don't, love. Otherwise I might have asked you to come fly with me. Can't have a good-looking, law-abiding young woman like you aiding and abetting a naughty copper like me.'

'Naughty.'

'You look after yourself now.'

'I will.'

'Maybe I'll come back one summer wearing a moustache.'

'I doubt it.'

'You'll probably have gone by then, anyway, I suspect.'

'Probably.'

'Must fly.'

'Good luck.'

'Thanks. You too. Goodbye.'

'Goodbye.'

'Au revoir, monsieur.'

'I don't think we'll be revoiring, but adieu and best of luck.'

'Bye-bye, inthpector.'

'Bye-bye, Thuthan, happy dancing. Bon chance, everyone. By the way, you might want to get some blankets out, someone is likely to need them. I think a space blanket would be appropriate.'

Morton's phone rang. It sounded tired. He looked at the caller number before answering it.

'Dick? Be quick, I'm in a rowing boat in the sea.'

'Don't ask. What news?'

'Samson wasn't sent from London? What do you mean?'

'He was supposed to be on a mountaineering holiday? Samson? You've got the wrong man. He can't even get over a six-foot wall.'

'Look, Dick, I've got to go. But have another word with London, they've got their wires twisted somewhere.'

He ended the call and looked at the freighter. Then he looked at the water gathering in the boat.

He didn't want to take his shoes off.

He couldn't swim with them on.

He didn't want to drown.

He was going to have to row a lot faster.

'"Dear Patsy, Elvira, Richard and Philly

I would include Bertie, but I don't think she really understands what's going on, poor duck. The rest of you listen carefully, it's what they call your denouement. And I have a little secret to share with you. I trust you to keep it our little secret. And I will tell you why.'

'Jesus, will you get on with it, vicar.'

'I'm only reading what the chief inspector has written, Mr Coombes-Neeston, really. Would you like me to skip some of it?'

'Skip the unimportant bits.'

'No, don't skip anything, sure and how would we know if something was unimportant?'

'Thank you, Patsy. I must say, some people lose all their manners sometimes.'

'Just fucking get on with it, vicar.'

'Including the fucking unimportant bits, Mr Coombes-Neeston?'

'What? Yes, yes, including the fucking unimportant bits. Just read them faster.'

'Where was I? Shall I start from the beginning?'

'No! Start from – start from "I have a little secret".'

'Let me see. Ah, okay.

"And I have a little secret to share with you. I trust you to keep it our little secret. And I will tell you why."

And he goes on to say:

"When you enlarged the dumb waiter to take Elvira's chair you had to move the wall of room number fourteen. It wasn't a load-bearing wall. I know this because whoever did it replaced it with a plasterboard wall. Normally that wouldn't have made a difference to anything if they'd done the job properly. But they didn't bother padding it for noise. And did you know that, when the dumb waiter is on the ground floor, and the door to your kitchen on the first floor is open someone in number fourteen can hear every word from your kitchen? Like, say, Saturday night when the dear deaf general and Patsy slipped into the kitchen and took the dumb waiter up to have a discussion about highly secret deliveries with Elvira."'

'The parcel! He knows about the parcel!'

'I say, what parcel?'

'Never mind, we need to get out of here.'

'I haven't finished yet.'

'How on earth can he know about the parcel?'

'He overheard us, you idiot.'

'Do you want to hear the rest?'

'How could he have overheard us?'

'Because he was in room number fourteen killing that Pole.'

'How could he overhear us if he was killing the Pole?'

'After he'd killed that Pole, you moron.'

'I thought he wasn't a Pole.'

'What else is there, Vicar?'

'Why would he want to kill a Pole?'

'Are you saying Chief Inspector Samson – No, that would be ridiculous.'

'Read the rest, Vicar.'

'Let's see. He says, You do know what you're doing is illegal, don't you?'

'Do you know what the street value of that stuff is? Half a million pounds.'

'Call it a million for insurance purposes.'

'Illegal? That – working class wanker – just killed someone. What the fuck is he talking about, illegal?'

'I say, Miss Mountjohn, that's a bit – a bit – a bit'

'Insurance? How the fuck are you going to insure that shit?

'Call it something else. Something for the kitchen.'

'What, fucking garlic?'

'We have to have it or the recipe won't work.'

'What, fucking garlic?'

'No, what was in the package, you dumb cluck.'

'Cluck? I'm afraid I'm rather lost.'

'The special edition Angel cake.'

'It has garlic in it? I'm most surprised. I couldn't taste it.'

'Jesus give me strength.'

'Well, you're in the right place for that. I don't understand anything else, but of that I'm quite sure.'

Morton looked at the freighter. It looked miles away. He looked back at the beach. That seemed as far. His mobile rang again. He swore and took it out.

'Look, Shirley, I told you, I –'

'Doctor Shepstone.'

'Where am I? Well, Doctor, since you ask, I'm in the middle of the ocean rowing towards a Polish freighter.'

'No, I don't know why. Inspector Samson told me to. But I still don't know why.'

'Preliminary results. That's wonderful, Doctor, but now is not really the time or the place –'

'He was poisoned. Not shot then.'

'Oh, poisoned and shot. But pretty much dead already when shot. So that was a red herring then. Well, well. What about bludgeoned?'

'That too, eh? But it didn't kill him. Because, again, he was already dead. What about drowning? He was wet, wasn't he?'

'Traces of urine. Ah, so that was piss. Lovely.'

'The poison was in his coffee.'

'A special blend of Kenyan and Ethiopian roast beans. Well, well. You do know your coffees, don't you, doctor. Most impressive. Now I really must –'

'They took his fingerprints. Amazing. Well done, now if you don't mind –'

'Jason Frogmore. No, I'll remember that, I'm not in a position to write it down right now. But as soon as I –'

'A second-hand car salesman. History of petty crime. Well, well. Fascinating. Doctor, I do need to get along now –'

'A bit of a Lothario. Yes, Doctor, I'm sure that information will come in handy at some point, however there's not much I can do about it now. Now, if you don't mind, I must go and catch a freighter –'

'Likes wearing golfing clothing. Bright yellow shirts and two-toned golf shoes, braces, that sort of thing. Marvellous. Now if you don't mind –'

'Last seen driving a bright mauve-pink 1965 Studebaker. Well, that should be easy to find oh fucking no are you sure?'

'That's fucking impossible. That is seriously fucking impossible. Are you sure it was a special blend of Kenyan and Ethiopian?'

'Yes, it is important.'

'It was. So how the fuck did he get in without being seen then?'

'Sorry, Doctor, talking to myself. I know who done it and why. Just not how. Do you know if Inspector Samson was ever into any kind of sport?'

'A pilot's license. Of course it had to be fucking flying. A mountaineering holiday. A pilot's license Couldn't climb the wall. Knew diddly squat about aeroplanes. The bloody fucking little liar.'

'Never mind, Doctor. I'll tell you later.'

'Oh, and doctor? Just one more thing.'

'You're an arsehole.'

'Thank you.'

He killed that call and began the process of turning the rowing boat about. The boat rolled back. It had got quite used to the idea of going out to the freighter. It seemed almost sociable.

'Bloody fucking little liar? Bloody fucking big liar. Bloody fucking two-toned shoes. Got the car in part exchange for his wife.'

'I need to take a note.'

'He's got our package! The bastard's got our package'

'Well, can't you just ask him for it? I'm sure he'll give it back. He is a police officer, after all.'

'I don't fucking believe it.'

'Shut up, Vicar, he's not keeping it for us.'

'He knew all along.'

'Not keeping it for you? How do you mean?'

'I do not fucking believe it.'

'He's fucking stolen it.'

'I'm afraid it's true.'

'But he's a police officer. They don't go around stealing parcels, do they? I thought that was the delivery companies.'

'The mother-fucking son of a bitch knew I wasn't deaf all along.'

'You don't know the half of it.'

'Never mind that. We'd better get back to the Duck before he gets there.'

'He's been and gone. Trust me.'

'We can still try. You push Elvira.'

'Mrs Constantine. I'm terribly sorry, I didn't notice you there. Have you come for confession?'

Morton looked back towards the land. There was a pink Studebaker. It was climbing the hill up to Cemetery Ridge.

He carried on turning the boat around. It took ages and all his remaining strength. He wasn't feeling too good.

Two Thermos flasks. One had a coffee stain running down it. The blood-red one. The old fool had told him to get the dark blue one.

Two insulated mugs. He had chosen Minnie Mouse. Or had he?

Had he chosen what the old fool had wanted him to choose each time?

One of the oars slipped and shot a gallon of ice-cold seawater straight into his face.

He spat out a mouthful of salt with water in it.

His mouth felt bitter.

He sensed an ache in his stomach

The rope. Plastic rope. Useless plastic rope. Only not if it were top-grade mountaineering rope that looked exactly like the cheap useless stuff sold in hardware stores. A proper mountain rope. He could have tied it to the washing line, pulled it through the opposite pulley and back again. The pulleys were large and strong enough to take it. And voila, one not so easy way of getting into the pub via the first floor. But that didn't matter, he was a fucking mountaineer, wasn't he. Or had been. Was. He was supposed to be on a mountaineering holiday.

His colour was supposed to be puce for fuck's sake.

He had asked whether the washing line was strong enough to take the weight of a man. He didn't ask whether the pulleys were strong enough to do that. Because he didn't want idiots like Morton thinking about that.

Except there had been no footprints on the other side of the wall.

None apart from Inspector Samson's from when he had been out earlier.

And what looked like part of a much smaller foot.

Like that of a madwoman. Molly in fact. Molly who had known he was an inspector. How had she known that? She was mad. She wouldn't understand. Didn't mean she wouldn't remember.

He felt a different sort of emptiness in his stomach.

But Samson was a flabby old fool who never did any exercise if he could avoid it.

Except he danced over those swords like old twinkle toes.

And when Patsy shouted Duck he almost beat Patsy to the floor he was that fast. Faster than the bloody frying pan, at any rate.

And all that food. Every meal time Samson treated him like the fattened calf. And there had been something in those dinners, it wasn't the sea air sending him to sleep. Sea air didn't give him weird dreams. Samson must have slipped something into his food.

It must have been in the dessert. Samson was careful about not eating dessert.

He heard a noise coming from the freighter. He looked up. Some sort of low, small motor launch was coming his way at high speed, bouncing over the waves. There was a noise from landward. He turned that way. Joe the Rescue's launch was headed towards him, also bouncing on the waves, but appearing to try to corkscrew at the same time. He could swear it bounced out of the water before doing a three-sixty degree turn and landing back in the water going the same way.

The cold, cold, grey water.

The cold, cold, icy, salty, grey water.

'Are you okay?' called a man from the freighter's launch.

'I'm fine. Just heading back to the beach.'

'What, and I hope you don't take this personally, what the fuck are you doing in the middle of the Atlantic ocean in a rowing boat in the middle of winter?'

'I'm a police officer.'

'That might be a statement of fact, it doesn't really answer my question.'

'It's a long story. Are you a Polish freighter?'

'Do I look like a Polish freighter?'

'Not you, the boat. Is it Polish-registered?'

'No, we're registered in Panama like ninety nine percent of other freighters. What makes you think we're Polish?'

'I think someone wanted us to think that.'

'Why? Why Polish?'

'I think any reasonably strange foreign nation would have done. Any one where murdering people isn't unusual.'

'I know plenty of Polish seamen and hardly any of them go around murdering people. Not more than once, anyway. It's illegal, you know.'

'Yes, I know. I am a police officer, you know.'

'So you said.'

'I don't suppose you could give me a tow to the harbour by any chance.'

'What's that bloody idiot doing?'

Morton looked around. The rescue launch had corrected itself again and was heading straight towards them in circles.

'I think the driver might be drunk.'

'It's a rescue launch. How the hell can the pilot be drunk?'

'He drinks a lot. That's how. It's not too difficult once you get the hang of it.'

'He's likely to crash into us if he's not careful.'

'Oh, Christ, I think I know why he's coming.'

'Why is that?'

'He's coming for me.'

'To rescue you?'

'He's coming for those in peril on the sea.'

'Looks like he's going to be the peril on the sea. Is he sane?'

'Maybe. Maybe not. I'm sure he thinks so. But I'm not sure that matters right now.'

'No time to throw you a tow. Jump for it.'

'Jump for it?'

'It's either that or take your chances with that maniac. Come on, this is the closest I can get to you, jump for it.'

Morton dropped the oars, stood up, stepped on the side of the boat and dived, hands outstretched to grab the gunwale of the motor launch, forgetting that he was in a boat. The rowing boat tipped over, he missed the other boat and plunged into the water. He almost gasped as the ice-cold water hit him, remembering just in time not to breathe. He shot up again and managed to get a hold of the motor launch. The pilot leaned over at full stretch, held out a hand and grabbed him while keeping hold of the wheel with the other hand.

'In you come.'

The pilot hauled him over the gunwale and let him fall into the bottom of the launch, before turning back to the controls and opening up the engine. They just managed to get away from the rowing boat before Joe the Rescue's rescue launch came bouncing over the waves and hit it a glancing blow. The rowing boat sauntered off sideways while the rescue launch shot off towards the freighter with Joe the Rescue's legs waving back at them.

'Have some of this,' the pilot said, handing Morton a bottle of rum without looking back.

'Thanks.'

'Keep it. Drink it. You'll need something to keep you going until you can have a hot bath and get some dry clothes on. Try to keep moving. People don't realise what the cold's done to them until the shock hits them, then it's too late.'

'Keep moving? In this boat?'

'Windmill your arms. Do the squats. Anything. It doesn't have to look pretty. Just keep moving. Keep your blood moving.'

Morton took a sip of the rum and almost choked as it sandpapered his throat. Within a few seconds it had anaesthetised his throat and set his stomach on fire. He windmilled his arms and then tried a squat. He had once been very good at squats. He repeated the exercise. He took another shot of the rum. And again. Another another squat. He was becoming quite proficient at it as he watched the harbour come closer. He did another and split his trousers. He didn't mind. He was trying to think, but it felt as if his brain had gone on holiday.

If this had been America it would mean him having to mount up and go after his former boss and take him in, dead or alive. His gun against Samson's. A chance to prove beyond doubt who was the better man, the faster shot.

That image just wasn't working.

He took another slug of the rum. He felt better. His brain was still vacant. But he felt better. He took another slug and wondered if his watch was as waterproof as the salesman had claimed. Waterproof down to ten metres. Did that include the temperature?

'Here, you go, grab the ladder,' the other man said as he brought the boat up to the harbour. Morton put the bottle in his coat pocket, grabbed the ladder and stepped onto it. He hauled himself up step by step.

'You'll be okay?'

'I'll be okay. I just have to keep going until the denouement.'

'The denoo-whatty?'

'You know when the master detective finally reveals everything, who did what, the guilty party, that sort of thing?'

'Yeah. I think so.'

Morton turned to look at him.

'Well, I'm pretty certain the master detective is the one who did it, and he's fucked off, so it looks like I'll be the one trying to work out what the fuck happened.'

'Could you try not swearing like that?'

'What?'

'The captain's a born-again Christian. He doesn't like swearing.'

'Well, you must give him my apologies then.'

'Thank you. Mind if I ask you something.'

'Go ahead. Make my day.'

'Where did you get the shirt?'

'Sorry?'

'The shirt. Black and white with that gold embroidery. It looks pretty good.'

'You think so?'

'Suits you. Probably looks even better when it's dry. And when your suits been dry-cleaned. And the buttons sown back on.'

'Thanks. I got it through the Internet.'

'Pity. They don't deliver at sea.'

'No? Sounds like a gap in the market. I'll consider it when I've finished this job.'

'Good luck with that. I'm getting out of here before that lunatic comes home. I just hope he hasn't torpedoed the freighter.'

'Yeah, good luck to you too. And thanks for all the fish.'

'That was rum.'

'That too.'

The pilot turned the boat back out to sea and roared off. Then there was the sound of wet clothes slapping together as Morton slowly and purposefully marched off in the direction of the Angel and Duck. His shoes had lost their shape. It felt as if the heels were trying to climb up his ankles. His socks were drooping just above.

He took the bottle of rum out and swallowed a mouthful before putting it into his jacket pocket. The he took his overcoat off and threw it over his shoulder. His suit wasn't quite as wet as the overcoat. But it had shrunk.

'London calling. Fucking London calling. And I'm fucking Father Christmas.'

'Or the angel with the tree shoved up its arse.'

'Every single one of us is concealing a terrible secret. And now I know what his is. Can't you wheel that bloody thing faster?'

'It's not designed for a race track.'

'You certainly weren't designed for a race track.'

'I used to be the one hundred metres champion at university, I'll have you know.'

'Richard used to be the five times a night champion. Five different girls, that is.'

'Ooh, isn't this exciting, Philly. What's that about Richard?'

'You went to university?'

'Push faster, Patrick, push faster.'

'Trinity College, Dublin. Got honours, First.'

'Wasted it a bit, haven't you?'

'No, Bertie, it isn't. It was a long time ago, they speak a different language. Like lying.'

'I had great plans.'

'Wasted that too.'

'So why are we hurrying then?'

'Elvira and I were going to go places.'

'She's not going very far very fast now, is she.'

'Stop talking about me as if I wasn't here. And push faster.'

'We want to see just how much Richard has fucked this one up.'

'You could try pushing her yourself if you're so impatient.'

'Not bloody likely.'

'Oooh, Philly, you are swearing.'

'I'm not as fit as I was once.'

'So you just said. Your memory's going as well. Can you hear a noise?'

'Right, revolver time. Maybe you'll go faster with a bullet up your backside.'

'There's going to be a lot more swearing before the day's over.'

'I can hear lots of noise. Mostly my blood pounding through my head. I'm not sure this is good for me.'

'What on earth are you doing here anyway, vicar?'

'You can't get a bullet up my backside from there, my angel.'

'No, it sounds like an aircraft. Low flying. Where the hell is it coming from?'

'I can if I put it through your dick first.'

'I don't know. I saw all of you run out of the church and felt that, well, maybe I should be running with you. As pastor of the flock, as it were.'

'Vicar, where we're going I don't think you want to go too.'

'Well, I certainly don't want to get a bullet where Patsy's going to get one. I'm not even married.'

'Where I am going you cannot follow.'

'You don't think I let her have bullets too, do you? I'm not that stupid.'

'For your sake, I bloody hope not.'

Morton slopped his way up the street towards the Angel and Duck.

He pushed through the doors and into the main bar. Thuthan, Anne-Marie and Carry looked up. Morton took the bottle of rum from his coat pocket, put it on the counter and dumped his overcoat on a bar stool. Carry picked up a blanket from behind her and handed it over to him.

'He said you might need this.'

'Thanks. Fucking thoughtful of him.'

'Do you want a glass for that?'

'For what?'

'That triple strength rum. That bottle wasn't full when you started, was it?'

'Yes. No, I don't want a glass. It's already in a glass.'

'It's rough stuff. They use to kick-start tractors.'

'You haven't shaved this morning.'

'Very observant, Anne-Marie. In fact I haven't shaved for three days.'

'Where did you get it?'

'Very French. I cannot stand a cheek not shaved. French men are not nice.'

'Get what?'

'The rum.'

'I won it in an Atlantic swimming competition. Where is he?'

'Who?'

'You know who. No, Thuthan, I am not going to play dances with swords right now. Where is he? What's that noise?'

'Sounds like an aircraft.'

'Fuck that was low. Who the hell?'

Morton picked up the bottle of rum, slopped back to the doors with the blanket around his shoulders and went outside. Carry slipped from her stool, came around to the front of the counter and held her hand out to Thuthan. Thuthan put the sword back in its box and jumped down. Carry took her right hand and Anne-Marie the left. The three of them followed Morton out to the front. He was standing outside arms-akimbo with his legs splayed and the neck of the bottle of rum in his hand, watching a twin-engined plane wheeling around in the distance.

'It'th a plane.'

'It's a Twin Otter.'

'A twin otter?'

'De Havilland Canada DHC-6 Twin Otter, to give it its full title. It's a real beauty. So I'm told.'

'What's the DHC stand for?'

'De Havilland Canada.'

'You know a lot about planes?'

'Bugger all. But I'll bet Samson does. That's who's flying that thing. Fucking – fucking – fucking –'

'The inspector?'

'Fucking – fucking – fucking – inthpector?'

'Now, now, Thuthan.'

'Thorry.'

'Full of surprises, isn't he, the son of a bitch.'

'No, Thuthan.'

'Mon dieu.'

'You can say that again.'

'Mon dieu.'

'He didn't mean it literally, Thuthan.'

'Thorry.'

'That's okay, thweetie.'

'Thank-oo.'

The Twin Otter completed its turn and came back towards them, flying up the street at roof-top level. Richard Coombes-Neeston, Phillipa Mountjohn, Bertie Berenson and Vicar Brayley came around the corner, running at different speeds and gaits towards the Angel and Duck. A few seconds later Patsy appeared, pushing Elvira in her bath-chair. The Twin Otter flew low over them, causing them to dive for cover, sending Patsy dropping to the left and knocking Elvira over to the right. It flew over Morton and Carry and Thuthan, waggled its wings and then swung out to sea.

'A fucking B fucking C.'

'Sorry?'

' A fucking B fucking Thee.'

'Thank you, Thuthan, there's no need to repeat it. I meant, what does it stand for?'

'Thoorryy.'

Elvira righted the bath chair, pulled herself into it, and fell over the other side.

'It's an acronym Samson reminded me of. They use it in forensic work. Assume nothing. Believe nobody. Check everything. Fucking bastard.'

'Ah.'

'Fucking bathtard.'

'Thuthan.'

'Thoorryy.'

'It's the excitement.'

'Yeth. Fucking ekthitement. Fucking yeth.'

Elvira managed to right her bath chair again. She dragged herself onto it without falling over, and began searching for something in her lap.

'Where do you reckon he's going?'

'The Bay of Biscay. Metaphorically speaking.'

'Why? Why the Bay of Biscay?'

'There are no storms that way. In the Bay of Biscay.'

'There are no storms in the Bay of Biscay. Makes sense. Why metaphorically?'

'He'd like us to think that. He's not that stupid. He's probably headed for Ireland or Morocco or somewhere. Somewhere no-one would think of looking for him.'

'Somewhere within a nine-hundred mile limit.'

'Why nine-hundred?'

'That's the range of the Otter.'

'He can probably get further. But he won't. Or he might. Or maybe not.'

'You know him that well?'

'You know the incompetent officer who forgot to warn me of my rights?'

'Yeah?'

'It was him.'

'It was him. I should have known. I should have fucking known.'

'He wasn't being incompetent. He was being sympathetic. I thought I loved him.'

'Samson?'

'No. My boyfriend. The one who asked me to carry his drugs. Only I didn't know they were drugs.'

'He arranged to meet you here?'

'My boyfriend?'

'Samson.'

'No. That was just coincidence. I think it annoyed him slightly. He didn't want anyone to know we knew each other.'

'He didn't want anyone to know anything. Except what he wanted us to know. Or wanted us to believe. Smoke and bloody mirrors.'

'Can you have a boyfriend you don't love?'

'You can have a wife you don't love.'

'Yes, but a boyfriend is voluntary. A wife is a prison sentence.'

'You English are charming.'

A silver Volvo drew up next to Patsy as he was on all fours clambering to get up. The driver's window wound down and a young blonde-haired woman with bright blue eyes and a huge lip-sticked smile with sparkling teeth looked down at him.

'Excuse me, do you know where the Angel and Duck pub is?'

'Do I know where the Angel and Duck is?'

'Yes. I'm in a bit of a hurry. I have an appointment there. Or had. I'm a bit late, I was supposed to be here on Sunday. I thought my boyfriend had left his car for me but I couldn't find it.'

'You have a reservation at the Angel and Duck hostelry?'

'No. He did. We were planning on driving on straight-away. We're kind of eloping. Don't tell my husband. It's all very romantic. He has this lovely old car. It's a Studebaker, you know, with those flared wings and lights and engine and everything. I really could have sworn he said he'd leave it for me to drive down, just outside the garage. But I keep getting these things wrong. I thought Tesco was on the left last week but when I went by it on the bus it was on the right. Only I was going the wrong way. And their sale had ended anyway. I thought it was on until the Saturday.'

'This car of your man's. Would it be bright pinky-mauve by any chance?'

'No, it's a silver Volvo. Fortunately I had the spare keys.'

'Sorry?'

'My husband's car. It's this one.'

'Ah. No, I meant your man's car. Your boyfriend's car. Is it bright pinky-mauve?'

'Yes. Yes, exactly. Sort of. Well, mauve-pink. Plum. More kind of plum. I like plums. Tesco ran out so I had to try Sainsbury's. You've seen it?'

'Sainsbury's?'

'The Studebaker.'

'This man of yours. He wouldn't be a second-hand car dealer, would he?'

'My boyfriend?'

'Yes, that's the badger.'

'Badger?'

'Your man the boyfriend.'

'Oh. Oh, yes. Yes, exactly. That's it. Sort of. Only he's not a badger. He's a pre-loved car salesman. You've met him then?'

'Possibly post-loved, too.'

'Sorry?'

'Ah, to be sure, just meandering. You wouldn't be Mrs Samson, by any chance?'

'Well, yes. Call me Delilah.'

'Why?'

'Because that's my name.'

'Oh.'

'Did he tell you?'

'The badger?'

'My boyfriend. We weren't going to tell anyone until we got to Los Angeles. It's in America, you see. You can get a licence quite easily.

They don't ask questions. I've seen it on television.'

'I see. I see. Now are you sure you don't mean Las Vegas.'

'Do I?'

'Los Angeles is the city of the angels. Las Vegas is where they do the gambling thing and have all-night wedding churches. With men wearing moustaches.'

'Oh, of course, you're right, it's the Elvis one, isn't it? Have you been there?'

'Ah, no, I'm just beginning to put two and two together. I've got to twelve so far. To be sure.'

'So where is the Duck and Angel? According to my Satnav it's quite close.'

'The Angel and Duck hostelry?'

'It's hostile? I thought it was a pub.'

'You know, I think you want the Angel in Three Oaks.'

'Do I? Oh, I'm such a ditz. First I get it wrong about his car, then it's Los Vegas instead of the Las Angeles one, now I've got the pub name wrong. I'd forget my head if my name wasn't screwed on, as mummy used to say.'

'Yes. It's three villages away. But lovely people, very friendly, service with a smile and very reasonable rates. And if they don't get it right the first time they use dynamite for no extra charge.'

'Dynamite?'

'It's a word the kids use these days. Like wicked.'

'Oh. I see. I'm not quite with it these days. What do they call it? Down with the children?'

'Nor are we all. Down, that is. Fortunately.'

'Will it take me long? I'm in a bit of a hurry. I'm terribly late as it is.'

'You aren't the only one.'

'Sorry?'

'Of the late variety. But I don't think you need to worry about that. If you do a U-turn and drive for about five miles you'll come across the signs. You'll have plenty of time.'

'Oh, thank you, it's very kind of you.'

'My pleasure, Mrs Samson. Ask for Doctor Shepstone, he has all the details.'

The Twin Otter was becoming a speck in the sky just above the sea.

'Found it!' declared Mrs Patsy. She lifted a revolver. 'He's not going to get away!'

There was a click as she waved it in the air and pulled the trigger.

'What's wrong with the thing?' she asking, looking down the barrel.

'No bullets.'

'Sure, of course there's no bullets. I told you. Do you never listen? What sort of eejit do you take me for?'

'A fucking stupid one.'

'There's one, I can see it.' Mrs Patsy pointed the revolver heavenwards again and pulled the trigger. There was an almighty bang as it fired. A burst of flame spewed from behind the Twin Otter and a ball of dirty smoke rose from the water. The recoil from the revolver caused Mrs Patsy's chair to begin to roll backwards down the hill as Patsy, Richard Coombes-Neeston and Phillipa Mountjohn dived for cover again while Bertie clapped her hands in delight.

Morton chuckled and clapped, the bottle getting in the way. He took a slug from it and clapped some more.

'Very good, Inspector Samson without a P, very good.'

'What do you mean? His airplane's just blown up.'

'Yes, Mrs Patsy fired vaguely in the direction of up and somehow immediately hit the Otter ten or fifteen or twenty miles away with a revolver she can't control. I don't think so. No, I would say a jerrycan of fuel just exploded on the sea. He added something to make it smoke like all hell. Talk about a fine touch. I wonder how he did that. Must have strapped it on somehow. Or maybe he had it on auto-pilot while he did it. Pushed it out the door or something.'

'Are you sure?'

'Look closely.'

'Ah. Yes, I can just see the plane still flying. It's almost on the sea.'

'No, you can't.'

'What?'

'When the nice police officers come calling, the last thing you saw was the plane exploding. Far out to sea where they probably won't be able to recover anything. In the deep, deep, deep, cold waters of the nasty Atlantic ocean.'

'I see.'

'I've been seeing what he wanted me to see. Might as well carry on that way.'

'I'll give you a blue straw.'

'Sorry?'

'Never mind.'

'I preferred him when he was stupid. He was easier to understand then.'

'I would imagine so.'

'You know, London called in the middle of Saturday night to tell us he was coming down to take over. Never crossed my mind to wonder why. Why would London call? Why would they send someone down? London who? Of course they wouldn't. I asked the bloke I spoke to what Samson was like.'

'And?'

'He said, you don't think we send our good detectives down to you yokels, do you?'

'Yokels.' –

'And then he said he couldn't find his own elbow with a SatNav on a sunny day. Samson, that is.'

'Hith elbow. Not hith –'

'No. What else did he call him? Obtuse, irascible and unpredictable. Yes, that's what he said.'

'That's not the way I remember him.'

'So, I was all prepared to meet a complete moron. And guess what I got? A complete moron. Talk about swallowing it hook line and sinker.'

'He wath clever. He could danthe.'

'Oh, yeth, yes, Thuthan, he was clever. I'm damn sure it wasn't some DC in Scotland Yard I was speaking to. It was Samson all the way, probably sitting in the Studebaker on Cemetery Ridge with his mobile. Oh, yes, yokels is the word. For the rest of my life I will eat straw.'

'Cemetery Ridge?'

'Up Saxon Way.'

'You call it Cemetery Ridge?'

'Don't you?'

'We call it Snuffles' Store.'

'Snuffles' Tor. Well, that makes sense.'

'Did the inspector call it Cemetery Ridge?'

'No, I think I made that one up all by myself.'

'It happens.'

'It doesn't bloody happen to me. Or it shouldn't do. It never used to.'

'You were younger then.'

'Oh, thank you very fucking much.'

'It wouldn't have been the Studebaker.'

'What?'

'Someone would have noticed the Studebaker. He only turned up in it this morning.'

'So he came here in a Volvo or something. Our Polish friend told him about the Studebaker, he thought, that'll do me as a good disguise, I'll leave the Volvo in its place. The Studebaker's like a clown's big boots or something. It's there to distract you from the whoopie cushion you're about to get hit with. I can't believe I fell for that.'

'You shouldn't blame yourself.'

'Ducks.'

'Don't call me Ducks.'

'You can call me thweetie.'

'No, not Ducks. The ducks. Have you ever heard of the ducks? The ducks? Heard of the ducks?'

'Herd of ducks? Ducks don't go around in herds. They flock together.'

'That'th what the mummy duck and the daddy duck do to –'

'No, heard. H-E-A-R-D.'

'Ducks? That go quack?'

'Ducks that go quack. Ducks and geese. Ducks and geese. According to him it's Cockney rhyming slang for police.'

'Never heard of that before.'

'He pulled me up for using – yokel talk, I think he called it. Then he dropped Cockney rhyming slang all over the place. Left, right, centre and bloody backwards.'

'To wind you up.'

'Precisely. And it worked. I could have bloody killed him.'

'Duckth and geethe. Purleethe.'

'They don't do that in London, not really, do they?'

'Wind you up? They do that all the time. Only way to get through the day. Most days.'

'Use Cockney rhyming slang, I meant.'

'Not really, no. Only for the grockles.'

'Grockles. I forgot you were bi-lingual.'

'They put it on the tea-towels and things.'

'Bugger was even slipping something into my food.'

'He was?'

'That's why I kept having those nightmares.'

'I don't think that was the inspector. You're beginning to shake.'

'No?'

'You aren't beginning to shake?'

'No, what you said about it not being Samson.'

'You didn't hear this from me, but the special editions of the Angel cake contain a bit of extra flavouring.'

'They do?'

'The sort that people normally take for recreational purposes. That's why they sell so well. Especially in foreign countries. Where they don't do much food testing.'

'Recreational purposes.'

'Mmm-hmm. So they say. I wouldn't know myself. I'm three brass monkeys, I am.'

'Class A or Class B recreational purposes?'

'I don't know. I think they called it popping candy, if that helps.'

'Otherwise known as space dust.'

'I think it's a code word.'

'And I had a double helping every night.'

'I'm afraid so.'

'You gave me a double helping, knowing what was in it.'

'We gave you a single helping. You helped yourself to a double helping.'

'But even so, do you normally feed that stuff to your guests?'

'Oh, yes. It's why they come here in the summer. To remember the summer of their youth. They talk about Woodstock a lot in the evenings. Then they go sleep in other peoples' beds. Sometimes in the garden. The summer of love. Free love.'

'And Samson didn't touch the stuff. But how did he know?'

'I don't know. I suspect he overheard something about a parcel. Which I know nothing about.'

'I too know nothing.'

'I know thjack –'

'And when did this parcel arrive?'

'I know nothing about it yesterday morning.'

'Can I get my thwords?'

'No, Thuthan, not now.'

'Yesterday morning. Of course. Of fucking course.'

'Sorry?'

'Of fucking courthe.'

'You can get your swords just now, Thuthan.'

'I think I know what happened. He came down to sort this frog out –
'

'He was French?'

'French? No, his name was Frogmore. Anyway, I reckon Samson conned him into letting down his guard first. That was the phone call. Told him, I don't know, look, no grudges, you can keep the wife, I didn't like her that much in the first place, I'll pop in, we'll have a coffee together to bury the hatchet, then we go our separate ways. He uses the washing line at the back to thread a mountain rope between the two pulleys and pulls himself across, into the laundry room next to room fourteen. Knocks on room fourteen, the vic – Jason Frogmore – opens the door, lets him in. In the room Samson feeds him the special blend of Kenyan and Ethiopian roast beans which kills him, throws in lots of smoke to confuse us, shoots him with a silencer, stabs him, garottes him, smacks him over the head and so forth.'

'Kicked him in the ballth.'

'Probably, Thuthan, thank you. I know I would.'

'My pleathure.'

'Then I reckon he planned to disappear leaving an unsolvable crime. Nobody has seen him, he's away on a mountaineering holiday, probably has a cast-iron alibi. Only he overhears Patsy and co discussing the parcel and thinks, what the hell, I'm up to my neck in it, I can't stand the day job, my wife is leaving me, why don't I go the extra mile and pick up a pension pot while I'm about it. Exits the same way, goes up Saxon Way to get a signal, calls us and leaves a lovely trail of complete bullshit.'

'Leaving no trace.'

'He couldn't avoid leaving a trace after the wall. If he'd disappeared after sorting lover-boy out it wouldn't matter, it would just have been someone's footprints. But when he decided to stick around he couldn't take the chance of someone noticing they came from his shoes. So first thing Monday morning, while it's still dark, he goes out to investigate. Only he wasn't investigating so much as jumping all over his own footprints from Saturday night.'

'He'th a good danther.'

'Yes. It wouldn't surprise me if his Ghillie Callum wasn't a dress rehearsal. Carry, are there foxes in London?'

'Loads.'

'Big buggers?'

'Big buggers? No, they're mostly scrawny and have mange. They live off rubbish from dustbins. The remains of fast food take-aways, that sort of thing. Not a good diet.'

'He got me there, too. Told me a footprint was from a fox. Bloody obvious it wasn't. But I believed him because he was the big-town Chief Inspector.'

'He left his book behind for you.'

'Sunday morning. He made me get the coffee out of the boot. Christ, the one flask must have been the stuff he gave to the frog. Jesus, I could have drunk that shit by mistake.'

'I don't think he would have made a mistake.'

'He left his book behind for you.'

'What?'

'He left his book behind for you.'

'Did he?'

'It's called Lucky Luke.'

'Lucky. I suppose I am lucky. For a moment there I thought he'd fed me some of his special mixture this morning.'

'Did he?'

'I think it was probably just sea-water in the end. But I'm pretty sure he sent Joe the Rescue out to get me when I was out in that rowing boat in the Atlantic.'

'To rescue you or to sink you?'

'I don't think he knew that himself. With Joe the Rescue it's toss the coin time.'

'Oh, and his credit card is behind the bar. You might as well have that.'

'I shall treasure it.'

'You aren't going to use it?'

'I don't fancy going to jail. Did he pay the bill before leaving?'

'He did that just after breakfast.'

'Considerate son of a bitch. That makes me wonder.'

'Makes a change.'

'It makes me wonder when he realised you were here.'

'Me? Why?'

'Because maybe it wasn't just the parcel that made him change his mind. Maybe he was all set to leave his false trail behind when he discovered that you were here. Maybe he realised that you'd be a prime suspect once they found out who you were. Maybe he decided he didn't want to leave you at the mercy of the local plods. Taking the parcel was an added bonus.'

'Why would I be a prime suspect?'

'Your name is on file. I know how coppers' minds work. They would have found the dope sooner or later, and put you and it and the vic together.'

'You reckon.'

'Somewhere along the line he appears to have appointed himself your guardian angel.'

'I think he wath in love with you, Carry.'

'You're an incurable romantic, Thuthan.'

'Thankth.'

'I like that ending. I too am an uncurable romantic.'

'I used to be. Then I got married. Never get married.'

'So, what are you going to do about the parcel?'

'What parcel?'

'I see.'

'Anyway, I forgot to read him his rights, in a manner of speaking. And it's too late now.'

'Careless.'

'It happens.'

'I know.'

'Do you know, I think I might spend Christmas here.'

'You reckon?'

'Shirley's left me.'

'Shirley?'

'My wife.'

'Sorry.'

'Don't be. Better now than later. Besides, I wouldn't want to end up driving a bright pinky-mauve 1965 Studebaker. metaphorically speaking.'

'Mauvy pink.'

'Magnolia.'

'Thrawberry mauve.'

'And probably Polish.

'You haven't thought of killing her?'

'Who?'

'Your wife.'

'Sheryl? She's not worth it.'

'That's a bit harsh.'

'You English! A Frenchman would always kill his wife.'

'Theryl?'

'Under such circumstances, I mean. Frenchmen do not normally kill their wives for no reason.'

'French women, on the other hand –'

'Tholly, Thuthan? I mean, sorry, Susan? I mean, sorry, Thuthan?'

'That was the accident. I was doing a drum solo and then I find it is a duet up his arse.'

'You thed Theryl.'

'I thed what? Said what?'

'Theryl.You thed Theryl. Not Thirley.'

'Did I? I meant Thirley. Shirley. I think the cold is making me stutter.'

'I had a thtutter onethe.'

'You'd better come inside. You'll need a hot bath and some dry clothes.'

'D'accord.'

'Duck or – duck or what?'

'Don't you bloody start, Anne-Marie.'

'Is a joke.'

'I know. Samson beat you to it.'

'His French is very good. He does not have the accent most English have. He is very handsome, you know?'

'Quelle surprise.'

'Pardon?'

'He said he hated Frogs. Anything French. Like everything else that wasn't quite true. A complete load of bollocks, in fact.'

'Everything else?'

'I think I know where he's gone.'

'What? Where?'

'Paris.'

'Paris?'

'He said he preferred to be alone in big cities. He speaks French very well. He's got a lot of dope to flog. Paris. It has to be Paris.'

'In which case it's probably London.'

'Probably. You've just reminded me. I need to make a note.'

Morton took out his notebook and pen. He wrote:

"who the piskied fule, he or me?".

'And after a long hot bath –'

'Yes?'

'I'm going to go looking for that nude. Everybody should have a hobby.'

'That nude?'

'The one that's busy rising.'

'And some coffee.'

'No thanks. In future I'm going to stick to tea.'

'Good old Rosie.'

'Rothie? Not Theryl or Thirley?'

'Rosie Lee, Thuthan. It's Cockney rhyming slang for tea.'

'And maybe I'll start learning French.'

'Whatth Cockney rhyming thlang for Thuthan?'

'Hello? Angel and Duck? It's Jimmy from the aerodrome. Listen, some bastard has left a bright raspberry 1965 Studebaker parked in front of the hangar doors. Bloke here says it belongs to one of your people. We can't get into the hangar. Tell him to get it out the way sharpish or we'll have to shift it ourselves. Oh, and it's got a parking ticket on the windscreen.'

Other novels by Bill Dughaille:

The Window

Little does Jim Allbright realise just how much paperwork his letter containing a simple enquiry to his local council is about to produce, nor the strange events he will experience as a result of the 'system'. But if the system cannot be beaten the interchange of letters can be used to have a little fun and get to know some of the people struggling behind it, especially the woman who signs herself as 'Sandi (pp the Administrator)', and perhaps, one day, even meet her.

Diary of a Sane Man

In a cross between 'Last Of The Summer Wine' and 'One Flew Over The Cuckoo's Nest', set against a backdrop of the brave new world of New Labour's end of honeymoon, Fred is the Last Cynical Optimistic Realist.
Believing that he's found the perfect niche – three square meals a day plus all the newspapers he can read just for occasionally pretending to be mad – he's not going to be the one to rock the apple cart. Oh, no.
Safe from the wiles of women and the woes of the world, he's not going to rock the boat. Oh, no.
No, he's just going to sit and observe, and comment quietly on the insanity of life outside.
Well, maybe just little one tug of the loose strand of wool on life's jersey ...
Did you know they elected a monkey as mayor in Hartlepool?

The Weekend At Longwood

A whodunnit in the classic sense, set against the backdrop of World War II and the trials, tribulations and romances of nine suspects.
A group of friends get together during the last weekend of August

1939 at the rural retreat named Longwood, just a few miles from Portsmouth. They are there to celebrate the last time they will see Georgina Riley, famed American novelist and socialite, for some time, as she is scheduled to leave for her native New York in order to marry her childhood sweetheart. During the afternoon they good-humouredly assign to each other the most suitable names of the nine muses, the daughters of Zeus and Mnemosyne:

Calliope: the muse of epic poetry and rhetoric

Clio: history

Erato: love poems and mimicry

Euterpe: lyric poetry

Melpomene: tragedy

Polymnia: hymns to the gods and heroes

Terpsichore: dance

Thalia: comedy

Urania: astronomy, astrology and prophecy

The following morning Georgina is discovered in her bedroom covered in blood, her throat slit, barely alive. Her American maid is dead. A tiara Georgina had been flaunting the day before has disappeared.

Detective Inspector Rudman arrives to investigate. But with Georgina in a coma and no solid evidence there is little he can do apart from haunt their lives. With Germany's invasion of Poland a week later they disperse across the land, some to the air-force, some to the army, others to reserved civilian jobs.

But Rudman does not give up. Wherever they are he can be found. Whatever other duties he is tasked to, he will find time to keep tabs on them. Whatever the defeats and victories of the Allied cause, he has only one aim: to find the person responsible for the murder done that weekend in Longwood.

The war ends; some of the Muses have survived, some not. Some have prospered, some married, some matured, others have found despair. And then comes invitation to spend another weekend at Longwood. The message is that Rudman has found the evidence he has been looking for.

And so one of the surviving couples motor slowly down to Portsmouth, remembering the original weekend, the trials and the tribulations of the past years, and wonder: what will be revealed during the coming weekend at Longwood?

Firelight

A modern-day tale of an ordinary family gathering at Christmas; the good, the bad, the dysfunctional and the forgotten.

George Browne and his wife Winifred have retired to a large, run-down pile in the country. Rumour has it that it was once the abode of a mad aristocratic family with a penchant for Satanism, and that both they and their victims still haunt the corridors. Other rumours are that it was a lunatic asylum for much of the nineteenth and twentieth century, and bodies of the inhabitants are buried around the large gardens in unmarked graves.

The Brownes are an unremarkable retired couple who, depending on who you might ask, have bought it as an investment, or alternatively as somewhere with enough bedrooms to accommodate their children, grand-children, and the little baby great-grandchildren. Too often in the past excuses have been made at special times, the most common of which has been of the 'I don't want to put you to any trouble' variety. That excuse can no longer hold water.

Now it is approaching Christmas. Winter has set in, but the house is snug with oil heaters and real fires. As the various relations arrive, or don't arrive, it becomes clearer why invitations might have been refused in the past. The men of the family believe in having their way. The women of the family are strong-willed and have various means of getting what they want.

The guests of the family – friends, boyfriends, girlfriends, wives and husbands – discover that their partners have a totally different side to them as the explosive hatreds of long-nurtured fights and feuds simmer to the surface before quickly boiling over.

One evening Winifred Browne encourages them to each tell a story as they sit in the lounge with the large fire warming them, the television off, no access to broadband, computers or mobile connections. Reluctantly at first they begin. As each evening passes: with different members taking turns, they announce in stories the feelings and hopes they cannot voice in public.

Finally it's the turn of Winifred Browne. Her story will be the one that tells them who they are, where they come from, and maybe why they have turned out the way they have.

... 13 ...

This is a story about a trial that never took place. The prosecuting counsel wasn't a nine-foot high vulture wearing what looked like a budgie as a wig; the defence counsel wasn't short and roly-poly and didn't wear a huge bright-blue-rinse wig. The defendant wasn't called Norah the Nose, the litigant wasn't known as Edgar The Ears. The judge wasn't called Judge Beak. The jury did not include a Quiet American, Miss Strawberry Mousse, The Major, Hugo The Accountant, Miss F, Miss F's Mother, Mr Sleepy, Vicar Preachy, Mrs Baggs, Mrs Plum, a Prim Maiden Aunt, Clowns named Clyde and Bonnie, or a Nun With Guitar who didn't speak in a deep Russian accent and didn't wear Goth make-up and tight-fitting sequinned habits which didn't shimmer with thousands of blinking, winking dots. The narrator did not fall in love with the Nun With Guitar who wasn't and hadn't. And it's only ever ... 11 ... 12 ... ... 14 ... 15 ... There never is a ... 13 ...

81 minutes to Maddening

With one arm in a brace, stitches in his forehead, and having just lost his job as a teacher, Mark wakes up on Friday morning to discover a message from his girlfriend Madeleine informing him that she is now his ex, pregnant, and leaving him to return to Australia. As his car is in for a service and no taxis are immediately available, he catches the Underground Piccadilly Line to Heathrow, believing that the five hours before her flight departs will give him time for the 33 stations and 81 minutes between him and reconciliation with she who he calls Maddening. But the Piccadilly Line is in meltdown and each passing minute sees his hopes of keeping the woman he has determined to marry recede. As he battles signal failures, security alerts and broken wipers he writes notes for his unborn child to read in twenty-one years' time, the story of how he and YBM (your bloody mother) met, fell in love, and why it wasn't quite his fault when it went wrong.

The FFSG series (aka the Wellbury Chronics)

Summers

The first in the FFSG series.
Detective Sergeant Frank Summers is a man on a mission: to keep his head down, stay out of trouble and enjoy the relaxed atmosphere of the easy-going, genteel town of Wellbury, his new posting. It's a town just made for him, where, he believes, even the criminals take bank holidays off. But, while perceptive in his professional life, he tends to miss the subtleties in his private life. In this case he fails to realise that his own tranquillity is being threatened by three women and a philanderer. The fact that the women in question are his boss, his constable and the local pathologist adds just the touch of danger to his life that he had hoped to avoid. The philanderer has been dead several decades. The women are very much alive.

The Eighty-five-percenters

The second in the FFSG series.
Detective Sergeant Frank Summers is faced with an unexpected crisis as the staid citizens of the genteel town of Wellbury rapidly descend into disorganised anarchy after a sociology professor announces on radio that eighty-five percent of the population will die

in a coming cull. The prediction appears to be coming true as apparently total strangers are felled one by one according to a list of the ten-most-disliked Wellburians, from nagging neighbours to estate agents ... and the police, at a poorly performing number ten. But Frank fails to realise that there is a graver danger closer to home. Three women have decided that he is their responsibility: his boss, his constable and the local pathologist have agreed to become best of enemies. Now they intend to re-arrange his fate the way it should be. And they aren't asking anyone's permission.

Fakes, Fraud and Deception

The third in the FFSG series.
Detective Sergeant Frank Summers is in the doghouse, despite having recently arrested an internationally sought con-artist. And since he is in the doghouse he has no intention of pointing out that there is something very strange about the attractive French police woman who has come to interview the arrested man, not to mention the two detectives claiming to be from Scotland Yard. Oh, no, he is going to stay well out of the way this time. Definitely.

Jokers

The fourth in the FFSG series.
The doctors have pronounced Detective Sergeant Frank Summers physically fit following recovery after his shooting, but his colleagues fear that his sense of humour was extracted along with the bullet. They are, as always, more than willing to interfere in his life in the pursuit of a good cause. If that wasn't enough, a bunch of criminals calling themselves the Joker Gang are laughing at him, the university students are creating mayhem during their rag week, and someone called The Shocker is trying to kill him. The only advantage is that it take his mind off of the ultimatum the three women in his life have given him, one that he has only until the Sunday to resolve. Or leave town.

Prophecies

The fifth in the FFSG series.

Detective Sergeant Summers is under a hex, otherwise known as his colleagues. First they don't want him to get married, then it is imperative it must happen. Then they decide that a prophecy has been made which threatens the wedding. They don't believe in prophecies, but aren't sure that prophecies understand that. So they'll have to Do Something About It. And if their bumbling efforts aren't enough to ensure he never makes it to the altar, he has to cope with visiting aliens and resident ghosts. He does have tiny Squishy to protect him, but what match can even this plucky little kitten be against a prospective mother-in-law?

Loonymoon

The sixth in the FFSG series.

The Inspectors Summers have tied the knot and embarked on their honeymoon in a small family-run hotel in Normandy. She has very definite ideas of what she wants out of a honeymoon: to set a seal on their love, and to form a foundation for life-long devotion. He just wants to nick a French police officer's kepi. He had a Bobby's helmet nicked from him once by a French girl while he was on crowd duty one New Year's Eve in London, and now he intends to return the favour. Neither is about to achieve their aim unless they can solve the mystery of the woman in the bath and the missing heroin. Which means pitting their minds against the French Inspectors Simenon. That's Mr and Mrs Simenon, whose marriage has gone beyond the rocks and is now beating itself to death against humdrum reality. One or either or both or neither could be the guilty crumpet. More importantly, is their marriage a portent of what could become of the Loonymooners? Ultimately the decisive question could well be: on which side do the peas go?

Hordes

The seventh in the FFSG series.

Detective Inspector Frank Summers has been booked off work following a near fatal anaphylactic shock. His wife is determined that he should obey his doctor's orders. As she is also his boss that should be simple. But he is determined to identify the perpetrator or perpetrators behind a series of attacks on little old ladies. Both their efforts are impeded by various movements becoming increasingly militant. The police station appears to have gone feminist. The Old Birds army (TOBs, Women Only) is planning a pre-emptive defence of helpless little old ladies. The Cult of The Clueless (TCoTC, Men Only) are demanding their right to ignorance. The Religious Once are threatening outright violence if their tolerant beliefs are not respected. Various New Age and Old Hippy believers, followers and troublemakers are descending on Wellbury in search of ley lines. Frank is embroiled in an e-mail game of double-chess with an anonymous person calling himself A Mason who sends messages which might make some sense if anybody could work out what they meant, but whatever they are they sound distinctly threatening. Frank and Frieda are running out of time as they approach Demonstration Day, when TOBs and TCoTC plan on settling the Religious Once's hash.

And, being off work, it's Frank's turn to cook dinner.

Painter 8

The eighth in the FFSG series.

A new sergeant arrives at Wellbury police station, the emotionless but paranoid Sergeant Gote, a man with a phobia of eggs. Detective Inspectors Summers are enjoying the renovation of their new home in preparation for the birth of Baby, their first child, when Frank stumbles on a hidden alcove which contains what could be the original world-famous Fountain created by Marcel Duchamp in 1917. Their attempts to conceal the discovery go wrong, and suddenly it appears that every art fanatic and conspiracy theorist is on their way to Wellbury to view the miracle, along with several unknown parties ready to use illegal means to get their hands on something priceless. Added to this is the anonymous person threatening to poison jars of Binkertys Baby Food unless a ransom is paid, a far closer and real danger, as that is planned to be Baby's food of choice. Frank and Frieda are forced to juggle hiding places for the Fountain while the officers at the station polish their truncheons in preparation for welcoming the extortionist when he or she is run to ground. For them, nobody threatens Baby and survives. In the end it is a wounded Sergeant Gote who is celebrated hero, though quite how that happened he will never be sure. Left unresolved is the crucial question of whether or not Binkertys should have an apostrophe.

For further details on these, visit:

www. dughaille. info

www.ingramcontent.com/pod-product-compliance
Lightning Source LLC
Chambersburg PA
CBHW070542260626
47161CB00002B/484